Praise for the
Morganville Vampires Novels

Ghost Town

"Fast-paced adventure. . . . Claire's tough-girl attitude may remind adult readers of Rachel Morgan and her world of human-vampire interactions. A tremendously popular series." —*Booklist*

Fade Out

"Book seven of the Morganville Vampires series won't disappoint readers, as Claire and her friends find themselves in the middle of a potential catastrophe wrought by a publicity-seeking filmmaker." —Monsters and Critics

"Full of drama, pathos, and a touch of romance with characters larger than life, especially the teens trying to survive in a town run by vampires. . . . This is a must read for teens and adults." —The Best Reviews

Carpe Corpus

"Ms. Caine offers readers an intriguing world where vampires rule, only the strongest survive, and romance offers hope in the darkest of hours. Each character is brought to life in superb detail, with unique personality quirks and a full spectrum of emotions. *Carpe Corpus* is well described, packed with action, and impossible to set down." —Darque Reviews

"Rachel Caine has carved out a unique niche in the urban fantasy subgenre with her super young adult Morganville Vampires. The latest thriller contains plenty of action, but as always in this saga, *Carpe Corpus* is character driven by the good, the bad, and the evil." —*Midwest Book Reviews*

"The pace is brisk and a number of loose ends are tied up as one chapter on the town of Morganville closes and a new one begins." —Monsters and Critics

continued . . .

Lord of Misrule

"We'd suggest dumping Stephenie Meyer's vapid Twilight books and replacing them with these." —*SFX Magazine*

"Ms. Caine uses her dazzling storytelling skills to share the darkest chapter yet . . . an engrossing read that once begun is impossible to set down." —Darque Reviews

"Filled with delicious twists that the audience will appreciatively sink their teeth into." —Genre Go Round Reviews

Feast of Fools

"Fast-paced and filled with action. . . . Fans of the series will appreciate *Feast of Fools*." —Genre Go Round Reviews

"Thrilling . . . a fast-moving series where there's always a surprise just around every dark corner." —Darque Reviews

"Very entertaining . . . I could not put *Feast of Fools* down. . . . There is a level of tension in the Morganville books that keeps you on the edge of your seat; even in the background scenes, you're waiting for the other shoe to drop. And it always does." —Flames Rising

"Fantastic . . . the excitement and suspense in *Feast of Fools* is thrilling, and I was fascinated reading about the town of Morganville. I greatly look forward to reading the next book." —Fresh Fiction

Midnight Alley

"A fast-paced, page-turning read packed with wonderful characters and surprising plot twists. Rachel Caine is an engaging writer; readers will be completely absorbed in this chilling story, unable to put it down until the last page." —Flamingnet

THE MORGANVILLE VAMPIRES NOVELS

Glass Houses

The Dead Girls' Dance

Midnight Alley

Feast of Fools

Lord of Misrule

Carpe Corpus

Fade Out

Kiss of Death

Ghost Town

Bite Club

THE
MORGANVILLE
VAMPIRES

Bite Club

Rachel Caine

 NEW AMERICAN LIBRARY

NEW AMERICAN LIBRARY
Published by New American Library, a division of
Penguin Group (USA) Inc., 375 Hudson Street,
New York, New York 10014, USA
Penguin Group (Canada), 90 Eglinton Avenue East, Suite 700, Toronto,
Ontario M4P 2Y3, Canada (a division of Pearson Penguin Canada Inc.)
Penguin Books Ltd., 80 Strand, London WC2R 0RL, England
Penguin Ireland, 25 St. Stephen's Green, Dublin 2,
Ireland (a division of Penguin Books Ltd.)
Penguin Group (Australia), 250 Camberwell Road, Camberwell, Victoria 3124,
Australia (a division of Pearson Australia Group Pty. Ltd.)
Penguin Books India Pvt. Ltd., 11 Community Centre, Panchsheel Park,
New Delhi - 110 017, India
Penguin Group (NZ), 67 Apollo Drive, Rosedale, Auckland 0632,
New Zealand (a division of Pearson New Zealand Ltd.)
Penguin Books (South Africa) (Pty.) Ltd., 24 Sturdee Avenue,
Rosebank, Johannesburg 2196, South Africa

Penguin Books Ltd., Registered Offices:
80 Strand, London WC2R 0RL, England

Published by New American Library, a division of Penguin Group (USA) Inc. Previously published in a New
American Library hardcover edition.

First New American Library Trade Paperback Printing, October 2011
10 9 8 7 6 5 4 3 2 1

 REGISTERED TRADEMARK—MARCA REGISTRADA

New American Library Trade Paperback ISBN: 978-0-451-23468-1

The Library of Congress has cataloged the hardcover edition of this title as follows:

Caine, Rachel.
    Bite club/Rachel Caine.
        p. cm.—(The Morganville vampires)
    ISBN 978-0-451-23318-9
    [1. Supernatural—Fiction. 2. Vampires—Fiction. 3. Colleges and universities—Fiction. 4. Texas—
Fiction.] I. Title.
    PZ7.C1198Bi 2011
    [Fic]—dc22   2010052168

Set in Centaur MT
Designed by Patrice Sheridan

Printed in the United States of America

To Bizzie O'Meara.
Congratulations on your new job as Amelie's assistant.

To Sarah Weiss, for the unenviable job
of trying to help keep me out of the paper jungle.

And to you, dear reader,
because only you have made *Bite Club* possible.
Bless you.

ACKNOWLEDGMENTS

R. Cat Conrad
J. T. Entzminger
Heidi Berthiaume
P. N. Elrod
Jackie Leaf
Bill Leaf
Joanne Madge
Amanda Hughes
Jamie Bartholomew
Janet Cadsawan
Shannon Aviles
NiNi Burkart
Charles Armitage
David Simon
Joe Bonamassa
    and
Borders Express, Exton, PA
All of whom deserve more praise
    than I can possibly give.

Bite Club

INTRODUCTION

WELCOME TO MORGANVILLE. YOU'LL NEVER WANT TO LEAVE.

So, you're new to Morganville. Welcome, new resident! There are only a few important rules you need to know to feel comfortable in our quiet little town:

- Obey the speed limits.
- Don't litter.
- Whatever you do, don't get on the bad side of the vampires.

Yeah, we said vampires. Deal with it.

As a human newcomer, you'll need to find yourself a vampire Protector—someone willing to sign a contract to keep you and yours from harm (especially from the other vampires). In return, you'll pay taxes . . . just like in any other town. Of course, in most other towns, those taxes don't get collected by the Bloodmobile.

Oh, and if you decide *not* to get a Protector, you can do that, too . . . but you'd better learn how to run fast, stay out of the shadows, and build a network of friends who can help you. Try contacting the residents of the Glass House—Michael, Eve, Shane, and Claire. They know their way around, even if they always end up in the middle of the trouble somehow.

Welcome to Morganville. You'll never want to leave.

And even if you do . . . well, you can't.

Sorry about that.

ONE

Looking back on it later, Claire thought she should have known trouble was coming. But in Morganville, *anything* could be trouble. Your college professor doesn't show for class? Probably got fanged by vampires. Takeout forgets to put onions on your hamburger? The regular onion-delivery guy disappeared—again, probably due to vampires. And so on. For a college town, Morganville had a remarkable lot of vampires.

Claire was an authority on those subjects: Texas Prairie University and, of course, the vampires. And mysterious disappearances. She'd almost been one of those, more often than she wanted to admit.

But this problem wasn't a disappearance at all. It was an appearance—of something new, something different, and something cool, at least in her boyfriend, Shane's, opinion, because as Claire was sorting through the mail for their weird little fraternity of four into the "junk" and "keep" piles, Shane grabbed the flyer she'd put in "junk" and read it with the most elated expression she'd ever seen on his face. Scary. Shane didn't get excited about much; he was guarded about his feelings, mostly, except with her.

Now he looked as delighted as a little kid at Christmas.

"Mike!" he bellowed, and Claire winced and put her hands over her ears. When Shane yelled, he belted it out. "Yo, Dead Man, get your ass down here!"

Michael, their third housemate at the Glass House, must have assumed there was an emergency under way—not an unreasonable assumption, because, hey, Morganville. So he arrived at a run, pushing the door back and looking paler than usual, and more dangerous than usual, too. When he acted like a regular guy, he seemed quiet and sweet, maybe a little *too* practical sometimes, but vampire Michael was a whole different, spicy deal.

Yeah, she was living in a house with a vampire. And, strangely, that was not the weirdest part of her life.

Michael blinked the tinges of red away from his blue eyes, ran both hands through his wavy blond hair, and frowned at Shane. "What the hell is your problem?" He didn't wait to hear, though; he walked over to the counter and got down one of their mismatched, battered coffee mugs. This one was black with purple Gothic lettering that read POISON. The cup belonged to their fourth housemate, Eve, but she still hadn't made an appearance this morning.

When you sleep later than a vampire, Claire thought, *that's probably taking it a little too far.*

As he filled the mug with coffee, Michael waited for Shane to make some sense. Which Shane finally did, holding up the cheaply printed white flyer. It curled at the edges from having been rolled up to fit in the mailbox. "What have I always wanted in this town?" he asked.

"A strip club that would let in fifteen-year-olds?" Michael said.

"When I was *fifteen*. No, seriously. What?"

"Guns 'R' Us?"

Shane made a harsh buzzer sound. "Okay, to be fair, yeah, that's a good alternate answer. But no. I always wanted a place to seriously train to fight, right? Someplace that didn't think aerobics was a martial art. And look!"

Claire took the paper from Shane's hand and smoothed it out on the table. She'd only glanced at it when sorting mail; she'd thought it was some kind of gym. Which it was, in a way, but it wasn't teaching spin and yoga and all that stuff.

This one was a gym and martial arts studio, and it was teaching self-defense. Or at least that was what Claire took from the graphic of some guy in a white jacket and pants kicking the crap out of the air, and the words DEFEND YOURSELF in big, bold letters at the bottom.

Slurping coffee, Michael leaned over her shoulder. "Huh," he said. "Weird."

"Nothing weird about people wanting to learn a few life-preserving skills, man. Especially around here. Not like we're all looking forward to our peaceful old age," Shane said.

"I mean, it's weird who's teaching," Michael said. "Being that this guy"—he tapped the name at the bottom of the page—"is a vampire."

Vassily was the name, which Claire made out only when she squinted at it. Small type. "A vampire's teaching self-defense," she said. "To us. Humans."

Shane was thrown for just about a minute, and then he said,

"Well, who better? Amelie put out a decree that humans were free to learn this stuff, right? Sooner or later, some vamp was bound to make some cash off it."

"You mean *off us*," Claire said. But she could see his point. A vampire martial arts instructor? That would have to be all kinds of scary or awesome, or both. She wouldn't have gone for it, personally; she doubted she had half as much muscle or body mass as it was going to require. But Shane . . . Well, it would be natural for Shane. He was competitive, and he didn't mind taking some punishment as long as he enjoyed the fight. He'd been complaining about the lack of a real gym for a while now.

Claire handed the flyer back to him, and Shane carefully folded it up and put it in his pocket. "Watch yourself," she said. "Get out of there if anything's weird." Although in Morganville, Texas, home of everything weird, that wasn't an entirely reasonable request. After all, there was a vampire teaching self-defense. That in itself was the strangest thing she'd heard of in a while.

"Yes, Mom," Shane said, but he whispered it, intimately, close to her ear, and then kissed that spot on her neck that always made her blush and shiver. "Eat your breakfast."

She turned and kissed him full on, just a sweet, swift brush of lips, because he was already moving . . . and then he did a double take and came back to kiss her again, slower, hotter, *better*.

Michael, sliding into a seat at the kitchen table with his coffee cup, flipped open the thin four-page Morganville newspaper and said, "One of you is supposed to be somewhere right about now. I'm just saying that, not in a dad kind of way."

He was right, and Claire broke off the kiss with a frustrated growl low in her throat. Shane grinned. "You're so cute when you do that," he said. "You sound like a really fierce kitten."

"Bite me, Collins."

"Whoops, wrong housemate. I think you meant that for the one who drinks plasma."

Michael gave him a one-fingered salute without looking up from his study of the latest Morganville high school sports disaster. Claire doubted he was actually interested in it, but Michael had to have reading material around; she didn't think he slept much these days, and reading was how he passed the time. And he probably got something out of it, even if it was just knowledge of local football to impress his girlfriend, Eve, with.

Claire grabbed her breakfast—a Pop-Tart just ringing up out of the toaster—and wrapped it in a napkin so she could take it with her. Book bag acquired, she blew Shane and Michael an air kiss as she hit the back door, heading out into a cold Morganville fall.

Fall in other parts of the world was a beautiful season filled with leaves in brown, orange, yellow. . . . Here, the leaves had been brown for a day and then dropped off the trees to rattle around the streets and yards like bones. Another depressing season to add to all the others that were depressing in this town. But at least it was cooler than the blazing summer; that was something. Claire had actually dug out a long-sleeve tee and layered another shirt over it because the wind gusts carried the sharp whip of approaching winter. Pretty soon she'd need a coat and gloves and a hat, and maybe boots if the snow fell hard enough.

Morganville in summer was dull green at best, but all the grass had burned dry, and most of the bushes had lost their leaves. Now they were black skeletons shivering in the cold. Not a pretty place, not at all, although a few house-proud people had tried some landscaping, and Mrs. Hennessey on the corner had put out weird concrete animals. This year, she had a fake gray deer sipping from an empty stone fountain, and a couple of concrete squirrels that looked more menacing than cute.

Claire checked her watch, took a bite of her Pop-Tart, and almost choked as she realized how little time she had. She broke into a jog, which was tough considering the weight of the bag on her shoulder, and then kicked it to a full run as she passed the big iron gates of Texas Prairie University. Fall semester was a busy time; lots of new, stupid freshmen wandering around confusedly with maps, or still unpacking the boxes from their cars. She had two or three near collisions, but reached the steps of the Science Building without much incident, and with two whole minutes to spare. Good—she needed them to get her breath back.

As she munched the rest of her breakfast, wishing she had a bottle of water, others she knew by sight filtered past her: Bruce from Computational Physics, who was almost as out of place here as she felt; Ilaara from one of the math classes she was in, but Claire couldn't sort out which one. She didn't make close friends at TPU, which was a shame, but it wasn't that sort of school— especially if you were in the know about the inner workings of Morganville. Most of the just-passing-through students spent the year or two they were here with the usual on-campus partying; except for specific college-friendly stores that were located within a couple of blocks, most students never bothered to leave the gates of the university. And that was probably for the best.

It was dangerous out there, after all.

Claire found her classroom—a small one; nothing at her level of study had big groups—and took her usual seat in the middle of the room, next to a smelly grad student named Doug, who apparently hated personal hygiene. She thought about moving, but the fact was there weren't many other places, and Doug's aura was tangible at ten feet away, anyway. Better to get an intense dose close-up so your nose could adjust quickly.

Doug smiled at her. He seemed to like her, which was scary, but at least he wasn't a big chatterbox or one of those guys who came on with the cheesy innuendos—at least, not usually. She'd certainly sat next to worse. Well, maybe not in terms of body odor. "Hey," he said, bending closer. Claire resisted the urge to bend the other way. "I hear he's springing a new lab experiment on us today. Something mind-blowing."

Given that she worked for the smartest guy in Morganville, maybe the entire world, and given that he was at least a few hundred years old and drank blood, Claire suspected her scale of mind-blowing might be a little bigger than Doug's. It wasn't unusual to go to Myrnin's secret lair/underground lab (yes, he actually had one) and find he'd invented edible hats or an iPod that ran on sweat. And considering that her boss built blood-drinking computers that controlled dimensional portals, Claire didn't anticipate any problems understanding a mere university professor's assignments. Half of what Myrnin gave her to read wasn't even in a living language. It was amazing what she'd learned—whether she wanted to or not.

"Good luck," she said to Stinky Doug, trying not to breathe too deeply. She glanced over at him, and was startled to see that he was sporting two spectacular black eyes—healing up, she realized after the first shock, but he'd gotten smacked pretty badly. "Wow. Nice bruises. What happened?"

Doug shrugged. "Got in a fight. No big deal."

Someone, Claire thought, *disliked his body odor a whole lot more than usual.* "Did you win?"

He smiled, but it was a private, almost cynical kind of smile—a joke she couldn't share. "Oh, I will," he said. "Big-time."

The door banged open at the far end of the room, and the prof stalked in. He was a short, round man with mean, close-set eyes, and he liked Hawaiian shirts in obnoxiously loud colors—in fact, she was relatively sure that he and Myrnin shopped at the same store. The Obnoxious Store.

"Settle down!" he said, even though they weren't exactly the rowdiest class at TPU. In fact, they were perfectly quiet. But Professor Larkin always said that; Claire suspected he was actually deaf, so he just said it to be on the safe side. "Right. I hope you've all done your reading, because today you get to do some applications of principles you should already know. Everybody stand up, shake it off, and follow me. Bring your stuff."

Claire hadn't bothered to unpack anything yet, so she just swung her backpack onto her shoulder and headed out in Professor Larkin's wake, happy to be temporarily out of the Doug fug. Not that Larkin was any treat, either—he smelled like old sweat and bacon—but at least he'd bathed recently.

She glanced down at the professor's wrist. On it was a braided leather band with a metal plate incised with a symbol—not the Founder symbol Claire wore as a pin on the collar of her jacket, but another vampire's symbol. Oliver's, apparently. That was a little unusual; Oliver didn't personally oversee a lot of humans. He was above all that. He was the don in the local Morganville Mafia.

Larkin saw her looking and sent her a stern frown. "Something to say, Miss Danvers?"

"Nice bracelet," she said. "I've seen only one other like it." The one she'd seen had been around the wrist of her own personal nemesis, Monica Morrell, crown princess (she wished!) of Morganville. Once the daughter of the mayor, now the sister of the *new* mayor, she thought she could do whatever she wanted ... and with Oliver's Protection, she probably could, even if her brother, Richard, wasn't quite as indulgent as Daddy had been.

Larkin just ... didn't seem the type Oliver would bother with, unless he wasn't what he seemed.

Larkin clasped his hands behind his back as they walked down the wide, almost empty hallway, the rest of the class trailing behind. "I ought to give you a pass from today's experiment," he said. "Confidentially, I'm pretty sure it's child's play for you, given your ... part-time occupation."

He knew about Myrnin, or at least he'd been told *something.* There weren't many people who actually knew Myrnin, and fewer still who'd been to the lab and had any understanding of what went on in there. She'd never seen Larkin there or heard his name mentioned by anybody with clout.

So she was careful with her reply.

"I don't mind. I like experiments," she said. "Providing they're not the kind that try to eat me or blow me up." Both of which, unfortunately, she'd come across in her job at the lab.

"Oh, nothing that dramatic," Larkin said. "But I think you might enjoy it."

That scared her a bit.

As she arrived at the lab room, though, there didn't seem to be anything worth breaking a sweat over. Some full-spectrum incandescent lights like you'd use to keep reptiles warm; on each table, some small, ranked vials of what looked like ...

Blood.

Oh, crap. That was never a good sign in Morganville (or, Claire thought, anywhere else, either). She came to a sudden stop and sent Larkin a wide-eyed look. The rest of the class was piling in behind her, talking in low tones; she knew Doug had arrived because of the blanket of body smog that settled in around her. Of course, Doug took the lab stool beside her. *Dammit.* That blew, as Shane would have said; Claire covered her discomfort by sending him a small, not very enthusiastic smile as she dropped her backpack to the ground, careful of the laptop inside. She hated sitting on lab stools; they only emphasized how short she was. She felt like she was back in second grade again, unable to touch the floor from her chair.

Larkin assumed his position in the center of the lab tables and grabbed a small stack of paper from his black bag. He passed out the instructions, and Claire read them, frowning. They were simple enough—place a sample of the "fluid" on a slide, turn on the full-spectrum lighting, observe, and record results. Once a reaction was observed, mix the identified reactive blood with control blood until a nonreaction was achieved. Then work out the equations explaining the initial reaction and the nonreaction, to chart the energy release.

No doubt at all what this is about, Claire thought. The vamps were using students to do their research for them. Free worker bees. But why?

Larkin had a smooth patter, she had to admit; he joked around, said that with the popularity of vampires in entertainment it might be fun to apply some physics to the problem. Part of the blood had been "altered" to allow for a reaction, and part had not. He made it all seem very scientific and logical, for the benefit of the eight out of ten non-Morganville residents in the room.

Claire caught the eye of Malinda, the other one in the room who was wearing a vampire symbol. Malinda's pretty face was set in a worried, haunted expression. She opened her eyes wide and held up her hands silently as if to say, *What do we do?*

It'll be okay, Claire mouthed. She hoped she wasn't lying.

"Cool," said Stinky Doug, leaning over to look at the paper. Claire's eyes watered a little, and she felt an urge to sneeze. "Vampires. *I vant to drink your bloot!*" He made a mock bite at her neck, which creeped her out so much, she nearly fell off the stool.

"Don't *ever* do that again," she said. Doug looked a little surprised at her reaction. "And by the way, showers. Look into them, Doug!"

That was a little too much snark for Claire's usual style, but he'd scared her, and it just came out. Doug looked wounded, and Claire immediately felt bad. "I'm sorry," she said very sincerely. "It's just . . . you don't smell so great."

It was his turn now to look ashamed. "Yeah," he said, looking down at the paper. "I know. Sorry." He got that look again, that secret, smug look. "Guess I need to get rich enough nobody cares what I smell like."

"That, or, you know, showering. That works better."

"Fine. Next time I'll smell just like a birthday bouquet."

"No fair just throwing on deodorant and aftershave or something. Real washing. It's a must."

"You're a tough sell." He flashed her a movie-star grin that looked truly strange with the discoloration around his eyes. "Speaking of that, once I take that shower, you interested in going out for dinner?"

"I'm spoken for," she said. "And we have work to do."

She prepped the slide, and Doug fired up the lamp. The instant the full-spectrum lighting hit the fluid, there was a noticeable reaction—bubbling under the glass, as if the blood were carbonated. It took about thirty seconds for the reaction to run its course; once it had, all that was left was an ashy black residue.

"So freaking cool," Doug said. "Seriously. Where do you think they get this stuff? Squeeze real vampires?" There was something odd about the way he said it—as if he actually knew something. Which he shouldn't, Claire knew. He definitely shouldn't.

"It's probably just a light-sensitive chemical additive," Claire said. "Not sure how it works, though." That was true. As much as she'd studied it, she didn't understand the nature of the vampire transformation. It wasn't a virus—exactly. And it wasn't a contaminant, either, although it had elements of that. There were things about it that, she suspected, all their scientific approaches couldn't capture, try as they might. Maybe they were just measuring the wrong things.

Doug dropped the uncomfortable speculation. He wasn't so bad as a lab partner, if you forgot the stinky part; he was a good observer, and not half bad with calculations. She let him do most of the work, because she'd already done much of this with Myrnin. It was interesting that Doug came up with a slightly different formula in the end than she had on her own, and, she thought, his was a little more elegant. They were the first to come up with a stable mixture of the blood, and the second to come up with calculations—but Doug's, Claire was confident, were better than the other team's. You didn't have to finish first to win, not in science. You just had to be more right than the other guys.

All was going okay until she caught Doug trying to pocket a sample of the blood. "Hey," she said, and caught his wrist. "Don't do that."

"Why not? It would be awesome at parties."

Again, there was that unsettling tone, a little too smug, a little too *knowing*. Whatever it was he intended to do with it, she doubted he was going to show off at parties with it.

"Just don't." Claire met his eyes. "I mean it. Leave it alone; he might be checking. It might be . . . toxic." *Fatal*, she meant, because if the vamps discovered that Doug was sneaking out samples . . . Well, accidents happened, even on the TPU campus. Stupidity wasn't covered by the general Protection agreement, and Doug seemed to have caught a little bit too much of a clue.

Doug grudgingly dropped it back to the table. Professor Larkin came around, checked out the sample bottles, and recorded them against a master sheet. As he walked away and she and Doug packed their bags, Claire said, "See? I told you he'd be checking."

"Yeah," Doug whispered back. "But he already checked us out."

And before she could stop him, he grabbed a couple of the vials, stuck them in his bag, and took off.

Claire swallowed the impulse to yell, and a second one, to kick the table in frustration. She didn't dare tell Larkin; he was Protected, and Doug had no idea what he was getting into. She had to get him to give the vial back. Dumb-ass wouldn't have any idea what to do with it, anyway.

She hoped.

TWO

Unfortunately, Stinky Doug wasn't that easy to find. For one thing, she'd never learned his last name. Hacking into Professor Larkin's class records would be easy enough, but Claire had other classes, one after another, right up through midafternoon. Then she was scheduled for the lab—the real one. And an evening of weird science with the weirdest boss ever.

Myrnin, she hoped, wouldn't notice if she was a little late. He had a pretty flexible concept of time.

Claire stopped off in the University Center, which had Wi-Fi, and claimed a table in the coffee bar area. Her housemate Eve must have finally dragged herself out of bed, because she was behind the counter, yawning and sipping a massively large cup of what, knowing Eve, must have been pure espresso.

"Hiya, cutie," Eve said, and leaned on the bar to smile at Claire. "Mornings are hard."

"It isn't morning," Claire said, straight-faced.

Eve made a tragic face. "I stand corrected. Afternoons are hard. Mornings are pure evil from the pits of hell, which is why I don't do them anymore." She took a gulp from her cup, shuddered, and said, "Oh, yeah, that's the stuff. Caffeinate me. So, Beautiful Brainiac, what can I do for you?"

"The usual, I guess."

"One piping-hot mocha, extra large, coming up!" Eve rang it up and took Claire's money. As she counted out change, she shook her newly shag-cut black hair back from her pale face and grinned. The grinning didn't really go with the whole Goth thing, but that was Eve. She didn't do labels. "Hey, did you get how excited Shane was about that martial arts thingy? He almost ran me over when I came downstairs. I never saw somebody so thrilled to be invited to an ass kicking."

"He was pretty stoked," Claire agreed. "How about you? Are you going?"

"Take *classes*? That I actually *pay for*? What do you think I am—a college girl or something? Besides, I defend myself just fine." She did, actually. Eve not only made her own stakes, but she also blinged them out with crystal designs. The wooden ones were sort of like stun guns for vamps; wood couldn't kill most of them, just immobilize them, unless the vamps were very young, like Michael.

But Eve also made silver ones, and those were deadly. Claire felt a shiver along her spine as she remembered just *how* deadly they could be. She hadn't meant to, but she'd destroyed one vampire that way. Nasty. And even though she'd done it in self-defense, she hadn't felt good about it.

"Hmmm," Eve was saying now, in a contemplative kind of way. She tapped her lip with one black fingernail and smiled. "There *could* be a use for that gym after all, now that I think about it. You know, there is one martial art I like."

"Which is?"

"A surprise, Claire Bear. Yeah, that might definitely be some fun. You might even enjoy it, too." A cute, tiny frown line slowly appeared between her eyebrows. "You okay? You look kind of spooked."

"Yeah, coming from someone who looks like an actual *ghost* . . ."

"Respect the awesome look, girlfriend. Okay, if you don't want to talk, don't. One mocha, coming up! Sit down; I'll bring it over. It's slow, anyway."

It wasn't just slow; this hour of the day, it was deserted. Claire left Eve to the espresso construction (something Eve was amazingly good at, actually) and flipped open her laptop. It took her exactly seven minutes to hack into Larkin's class roster and discover that Stinky Doug's full name was Doug Legrande. Larkin, creepily enough, even had all their addresses, phone numbers, and e-mails, although Claire was pretty sure she'd never provided him with any of that intel. Either the university was really free with their personal details, or Larkin had connections.

Duh, she already knew that. He had a bracelet from Oliver. *Connections* didn't quite cover it.

"You gonna drink that?"

Claire looked up. Eve was sitting across from her, slumped in the rickety plastic chair, sipping her massive cup of whatever—it was Eve's own cup, with a cartoony GOT BLOOD? on the side. On campus, it was funny. Off campus . . . not so much.

As Claire stared blankly at her, Eve nodded to the mocha that had magically appeared next to her laptop. "The whipped cream is getting all melty," Eve said. "Whipped cream is a terrible thing to waste. Oh, except it's not real whipped cream—it's that canned stuff, which is kind of nasty, so there's that. Maybe a good choice after all, letting it melt. Whatcha doing?"

That was Eve, through and through, even when she was sleepy. Keeping up with her required a healthy gulp of the mocha and a very active brain. "I'm trying to find Stinky Doug," Claire said. "He lives on campus, in Lansdale House, I guess."

"Stinky Doug? Oh, God. Please tell me you're going to do everyone a public service and deliver him some shower gel. The last time he came in here, I thought I was going to have to call those biohazard guys. Although if this is some weird and inconceivable college-crush thing, I don't want to know. Let me have my fragile illusions."

Claire rolled her eyes. "Trust me, I wouldn't kiss Doug even *after* the shower gel and decontamination. No, he did something stupid, and I need to convince him not to make it worse—that's all." She explained about the experiment, the blood, and Doug's boneheaded move. Eve kept steadily drinking her coffee, eyes half closed.

"You considered snitching on him?" she asked. "Because, honestly, wouldn't be the worst idea ever. Just make sure Larkin knows you didn't take it. Let him draw his own conclusions."

"That's the same thing as throwing Doug under the bus," Claire said. "Look, he's just dumb, that's all. And he doesn't know about"—Claire waved vaguely around, indicating Morganville—"all this." Well, she wasn't one hundred percent sure of that, actually, but he *shouldn't* know. That counted.

"If he had any kind of a clue, he wouldn't be caught dead with that stuff. See what I did there? *Caught dead?* I crack myself up." Eve sipped more coffee she probably, at this point, didn't need.

"So you're visiting Stinky Doug and warning him off, without explaining why. Is that your whole plan?"

"Kinda."

"Awesome. Let me know how it goes, Plan Girl."

"You have any better ideas?"

Eve took another delicate swallow of coffee. "Well," she said, "Stinky Doug has a lot of classes. If you've got his dorm room address, how difficult would it be to toss the place, find the stuff, and get rid of it? Nobody has to know."

"Great. And do you actually *know* a ninja?"

"Yep," Eve said, and gave her a sleepy, luminous smile. "He's my boyfriend."

Hmmm. Claire had to mull that over for a few seconds, because technically vampires *were* like ninjas—quiet, sneaky, fast, and deadly. And when they wanted to be, they could be disturbingly invisible. "Would he do it?" she asked. That wasn't what she wanted to ask, actually; she wanted to ask, *Will he tell Oliver?*

Because, like it or not, Michael was a vampire in equal measure to being her friend, and even though he tried to stay on the human side, sometimes he had to be a vamp first. Maybe this was one of those times.

Eve jacked up her black eyebrows another half inch in answer.

"Okay," Claire finally said. "I admit, he has significant ninja qualities."

"Booyah. I will summon the ninja. Oh, and take a lunch break while we burgle."

"You're going, too?"

"Am I not ninja enough? Are you saying that I lack ninja?"

"No, I was just thinking you're a little, uh, recognizable, maybe?"

Eve batted her thick eyelashes. "Why, thank you, sweetie. That's the nicest insult I've had today, not counting the jock who said he'd date me but he had a restraining order out for necrophilia. I promise, I'll dowdy up for the occasion. It'll take me five minutes." She took her cell out of her pocket and texted as she spoke. "Promise me you won't leave without me."

"I promise."

"Want me to organize Shane into this posse, too?"

"He's at work." Claire sighed. She would have gladly had Shane added to the mix at this point, but he was already on fragile ground at work, considering he'd ditched twice this month— once for a legitimate sick day, but the other had been just plain boredom. "Next time we commit crime, we'll make sure to include him."

Eve held up one fist while she kept typing with one thumb, and Claire tapped it. Eve finished with a flurry of keystrokes, snapped the phone shut, and drained her coffee. "Right. Mikey's on the way. I'll be anti-Eve in five. Enjoy your mocha."

Claire did, drinking fast. It was a good thing she did, because in just about five minutes, Michael was walking through the big UC open hall outside the coffee area, a guitar case slung over his back. He should have drawn attention—Michael was just plain gorgeous, and girls *looked*—but he was walking with his shoulders slumped, hands in his pants pockets, looking down, and the whole aura just projected *Don't look at me* so strongly that Claire couldn't see a single person other than herself actually taking notice of him.

He slid onto a seat next to her, leaning the guitar case against the table. "So, now we're going to be actual criminals," he said.

"And, see, you brought a guitar."

He gave her a *look*. "I was on my way to practice."

"Oh. Well, thanks."

"Sounds like I didn't have much of a choice. This guy has vampire blood?"

"I guess so. Larkin was using it for some experiment. I suppose it was authorized."

"Larkin? Had to be. He wouldn't dare do it on the side." Michael nudged her empty mocha cup with a fingertip. "Where's Eve?"

"Right here, Ninja with Fangs." Eve leaned over behind him, put her arms around his neck, and kissed him right over the cool blue veins. "Claire said I had to go in disguise as a regular person."

And she had. Eve had scrubbed off every trace of her Goth persona and tied her black hair back in a tight ponytail. She'd changed into a plain black hoodie—one without skulls or symbols, so Claire could only figure she'd raided someone else's locker for it. The only thing left to indicate she wasn't like every other college-age girl on campus were the thick-soled boots she was wearing. Still, those weren't all that noticeable. She'd even thrown on an old pair of blue jeans.

"Wow. We really are stealthy now," Claire said, and shut her computer. "Can we store stuff in the back?"

"Sure, my locker has an actual lock."

Claire raised her eyebrows and tugged the cord of the black hoodie. "And you keep this in it?"

"I didn't say that the locks couldn't be picked. But actually my good buddy Edie never locks hers, anyway. Come on, let's get the storage taken care of."

In the end, they left Michael's guitar, Claire's backpack (with laptop), and pretty much everything else behind, as Eve set up the LUNCH BREAK sign on the counter and locked up the register. In a surprisingly short time, they were headed out again. Michael had brought a leather hat, which looked kind of sloppy-cool and shaded his face and neck. He kept his hands in his pockets.

"You're not as sensitive anymore," Claire said. "To the sun, I mean." Because when Michael had first been venturing out, he'd had to drape himself in a blanket to keep from burning.

"Well, it's cloudy," he pointed out. It was; there were ominous dark masses in the sky, and the sun had disappeared behind the curtain. "And I've got on two layers. But, yeah, it's better now than it was." He said it as if he wasn't sure how he felt about it, which was strange. Claire supposed that becoming more stable meant he also felt more like a vampire. "I'll be okay unless the sun comes out full strength again."

Which, Claire could tell, it wouldn't. Rain was coming, the kind of torrential desert rain that would drown the streets and create flash floods out in the arroyos outside of town, and would be completely gone tomorrow. There were already flashes of hidden lightning inside the clouds.

Luckily, they weren't far from Stinky Doug's dorm. It housed both male and female students, which was lucky, because it meant the three of them were even less noticeable, and there weren't any sign-ins required. Once they'd made it to the stairwell, Michael took off the hat, stuffed it in his jacket, and ran up the steps with so much ease that Claire, puffing a little in his wake, wondered if maybe this vampire thing might not be okay after all. Eight flights of stairs wasn't her thing.

At the top, she and Eve caught their breath and joined up with Michael as he stepped out to check the hallway. He motioned for them to follow, so it must have been clear. Claire was surprised to see that this dorm hall was pretty much like her old one, the one she'd first lived in when she'd moved to Morganville—dingy, battered, smelling like old beer and desperation. Doors were closed all along the hall, except for a couple at the end that blasted music she didn't recognize at top volume in some kind of stereo war.

Stinky Doug's room was the third on the left. Michael paused in front of it, leaned forward and listened, then nodded. He jiggled the knob. Locked.

That was why it was good to have a vampire along, because a simple twist of his wrist, and that lock problem? Solved. Michael pushed open the door and disappeared inside, and Eve and Claire followed, shutting the door behind them.

And Claire choked, because Stinky Doug's personal aroma was *nothing* compared to the state of his dorm room. Her eyes watered. She couldn't stand to take a full breath, because she was deeply afraid she was going to vomit. Not that it would make the stench any worse.

"Eww," Eve said, pitifully, holding her nose shut. "Oh, my God! What died?"

Michael turned on the lights. For a couple of seconds, they stared in silence, and then Eve said, in a very small, muffled voice, "It was supposed to be a rhetorical question."

Because Doug was lying on the bed, eyes open and staring, and he was definitely, completely dead. Not for long, Claire guessed, because blood still dripped from the wound in his neck.

It wasn't a vampire bite. There was a huge pool of blood soaked into the mattress beneath Doug, staining his T-shirt crimson.

Michael had gone very, very pale—marble white, in fact. He leaned over the body, maybe checking for signs of life, and shook his head. As Claire and Eve stood rooted to the spot in shock, he ransacked Doug's backpack, then patted down the dead man's pockets, pulling out keys, a cell phone, breath mints (it made Claire suddenly sad that he carried those when he was so generally unpleasant to the senses), a wallet, some change.

No vials of blood.

"We have to go," Michael said. "Now. Right now."

"Was it— Was it the vamps?" Eve asked. "Can you tell?"

"I don't think so."

"But—"

"The ones I know wouldn't be that bloody," Michael said. "We have to go."

They were heading for the stairs, and Claire was still feeling a strange, distant sense of disconnection, when the reality of what she'd seen actually hit her, like color and sound and smell all snapping into focus at the same instant.

Doug was *dead.* He'd been *murdered.*

She stopped, put her back against the hallway wall, and slid down to a crouch. She couldn't breathe. Her whole body was shaking. She'd seen a lot of unpleasant things since moving to Morganville, but this . . . this was worse. This seemed so . . . cold.

And the worst part of it was, Michael thought that the monsters hadn't done it. Not the side of town she usually thought of as monsters, anyway.

Eve was bending over her, pulling on her arm. Having lost the Goth makeup, she looked stark right now, washed pale. "Come on, Claire, we need to get the hell out of here. Too many questions."

"But we can't . . . just leave him—"

"We won't," Michael said, and took her other arm. He pulled her to her feet and held her there until her knees stopped shaking. "But we're not staying. Eve's right."

Claire clung to the handrail on the way down. She couldn't get the image out of her mind, the way Doug's face had seemed so slack and empty, the way his eyes stared, all pupils. The way the blood had soaked his bed beneath him.

She stopped on the third-floor landing and put her head down, breathing fast. Eve and Michael were already halfway down to the next level, but they turned and came back. They were talking, but she couldn't hear them.

It took forever to get moving again and, once they were out in the dorm lobby, to try to act normal. She held on to Michael's arm, mostly for support. Outside, he put his hat on again and led her to the shade of a tree, where she collapsed in a pathetic heap on the dying grass. Overhead, the dry leaves rattled and hissed. A few broke loose in the freshening breeze.

Michael crouched down beside her, and Eve knelt on the other side. "Claire?" he asked. His eyes were very blue, very clear, and very worried. "Claire, talk to me. You okay?"

"No," she said. Her voice sounded small and fragile and very far away. "He's dead. Someone killed him."

Eve and Michael exchanged worried looks. Michael shook his head. "I'll get hold of Richard and Hannah," he said. "This needs to be handled quietly. They need to know what happened before it gets out of hand."

And right on cue, the thundering music from the top floor of the dorm cut out, and from an open window came the sound of a girl's scream, long and loud, with razor-edged horror in it. That was the scream Claire hadn't voiced, the one that still bubbled inside her. Somehow, hearing someone else do it helped ease the pressure. She didn't feel quite as faint and sick.

"I think that ship's sailed, Michael," Eve said, staring toward the dorm. Without the makeup, she looked so young—and so determined. "Better make the call quick. This is going to get crazy fast."

Michael nodded, stood up, and used his cell phone. It wasn't a long conversation, but then he dialed another number, and that was a lot longer. Oliver, Claire figured, from the general tone and Michael's body language. Only Oliver could make him that tense.

He came back as he was ending the call, and looked down at her. "You going to be okay?" he asked.

"You mean now or generally?"

That made him smile a little. "Now."

"I can deal," Claire said. "Generally, that's going to be a little bit tougher. I wasn't born in Morganville. Still getting used to all the . . ."

"Mayhem," Eve said, for once not laughing or making a joke. "Blood. Death. Yeah, sadly, it *is* something you get used to. But still, this one caught me off guard, too. I'll call Shane, okay?"

"No, no, don't. He'll take off from work, and I'm all right. I'll be fine." She was lying through her teeth. She felt cold and shaky and she wished—oh, God, more than anything—that Shane were here right now. Or her parents. She'd never missed her mom and dad more than she did right at this moment, which was dumb, because what were they going to do?

Hug her. Make her feel safe again, just for a little while. Because that was what parents did, or at least what they were supposed to do. Eve hadn't had that privilege, because her home life had been crap, and neither had Shane, who'd had the worst dad in the world. But Claire's family had been great, and she hadn't even known how much she missed it until . . . well, now.

While they waited for the sirens to arrive, Claire pulled out her phone and dialed her dad's cell phone number. He answered on the third ring.

"Hey, sweetheart," he said. He sounded better than he had before, almost normal. Strong. Considering that he'd left Morganville in an ambulance and had almost died—not from the vampires, but from his own bad heart—it was so good to hear him be more like himself. The connection crackled and hissed. "Sorry for the noise. I'm out walking. It's getting windy."

"Here, too. Looks like it might rain."

"We had some rain earlier this morning. Cooled things down quite a bit. How are you, Claire?"

"Good," Claire said, and swallowed. "I . . . just wanted to see how you were doing, Dad."

"Doing great. They've got me walking a lot, trying to build up the old cardiovascular health again. I have to say, I'm glad I finally got that surgery. I didn't realize how bad I'd been feeling until I felt better." He paused, and, with that Dad radar she'd always both loved and dreaded, said, "You didn't just call to say hello, honey. What's wrong?"

"Nothing." The concern in his voice turned her all trembly again, and made her want to cry, but she couldn't do that. Wouldn't. "It's pretty much the same here; you know how it is. How's Mom?"

"She's joined some kind of scrapbooking club. I never knew you could spend so much time and money on sticking photos in albums, but that's your mom. Once she gets excited about something . . ."

"I know, she's a madwoman," Claire finished, and smiled a little. She could just see her mother coming home with bags and bags of stuff to hot-glue into memories. "How's the new house?"

"Embarrassingly large. With a yard, too. I may have to learn how to garden."

"Grow me something. Irises. I like irises."

"Purple ones, right?"

"Yeah, purple's good."

"Honey, are you sure you're all right? You sound odd."

"Just . . . allergies," she said, and wiped her leaking eyes. "You take care, Daddy. I'll see you soon, okay?"

"Okay," he said, doubtfully. "Call tomorrow. Your mother will hate me if she doesn't get her turn."

"I will. Bye."

Eve had turned away, watching the dorm, but she'd been paying attention. As Claire finished her call, she said, "Feel better?"

"Yeah," Claire said. She did. Still shaky, but steadier inside, where it counted.

"I wish I could do that," Eve said. "Call my mom. But no. Whiny, self-absorbed bitching from her probably wouldn't have the same effect, although it definitely *would* make me forget about Doug for a second."

Michael held out his hand, and Eve took it, and their eyes met for a second before Eve looked away. "Yeah," she said. "Life sucks, we die, or not. Mom is the least of my problems, right?"

"Right at the moment? Yeah," Michael said. "And now I want to call *my* parents."

Claire thought he might be joking, but with Michael, you never could tell. His parents were cool; she'd met them once, but they didn't live in Morganville anymore, and they weren't even nearby. Like Claire's parents, they'd been given permission to move because of medical problems. Michael didn't say much about them, but then, Michael was the quiet type.

In any case, he didn't have time to do anything, because a police car, siren blasting and lights flaring, pulled up in front of the dorm in the parking lot, where a crowd of students was gathering. Almost all the students promptly pulled their cell phones out and began busily clicking pictures and taking videos of the police presence. Next stop: the Internet. "Worst invention *ever*," Claire muttered. Myrnin was already talking about how to disable the features on all cell phones inside of Morganville. At times such as this, she kind of saw his point.

Hannah Moses was second to arrive on the scene, looking crisp and starched in her police uniform; she'd tucked her cornrowed hair up under her cap, and apart from the gold bar on the lapel of her blue shirt, she looked exactly like the other police, who got busy cordoning off the scene. Two other men got out of a plain gray car that pulled up behind hers. Claire recognized the men with a little start, because she hadn't seen them in a while.

"Hey," said Detective Travis Lowe, nodding to her. He'd lost weight, she thought, and he looked a little bit grayer than before. Detective Joe Hess hadn't changed at all, except that his smile was more guarded as he nodded, too. "I heard you found yourself a genuine dead person."

"Travis," Hannah said, frowning at him. "Go easy on the kid."

"Her? Listen, I know her. She's tough. She can take it. Right, Claire?"

She nodded, because what else did you do when someone said something like that? But she didn't feel tough. Not right at this moment. As if he sensed that, Detective Hess cut in front of his partner and came to talk to her. He had a soothing sort of manner, and the gentle tone of voice he used made her feel a little less . . . lost.

"Someone you knew, right?" Hess said. "Can you tell me what happened?"

"I—" Claire suddenly realized that she had a decision to make: tell about the whole reason she and Eve and Michael had come over, or lie and pretend like it was just another of those wacky Morganville coincidences. She didn't feel like lying, though. Not to Detective Hess. "It's Doug—Doug Legrande. He was my lab partner in Professor Larkin's class. He took something he shouldn't have, and I came to ask him to give it back."

Detective Hess was a hell of a lot sharper than most people in Morganville, and he gave her a sideways look as he said very casually, "Would that thing be something that some people in town wouldn't want to get out?"

"Blood," she said, keeping her voice in a whisper. "You know what kind of blood."

"I do. So, tell me what happened when you got here." And he slowly walked her through it, step by step, from the beginning. He'd also walked her off a little from her friends, and Claire saw that Detective Lowe was talking to Eve, while Michael had Hannah as a conversational partner. Double-checking facts, Claire guessed. The low-key way it was done made her feel a lot less nervous. By the time she was finished, Detective Lowe had finished up with Eve and was sitting on the back bumper of the gray car, making notes with a pad and pen as he talked to Chief Moses. Hannah had notes, too.

"Did we do anything wrong?" Claire finally asked, as Hess jotted down something, as well. "I mean, we tried to do the right thing. For Doug."

"You probably would have been better off reporting it immediately," Hess said. That was one thing she liked a lot about him:

he was kind about it, but he told her the truth, no matter how difficult it was to hear it. "I can't say this wouldn't have still happened, because we can't jump to the conclusion that his theft had anything to do with his murder, but you need to understand that if it did, Doug didn't have to die. He might have been in jail, but he would have been safer. Understand?"

She did, and she felt miserable . . . but, oddly, also more centered. It was what she'd been thinking, anyway. Hearing him say it didn't make her feel any worse; it made it real enough that she could move on, accept it as a mistake, and plan to never let it happen again.

"I'm sorry," she said. She wasn't sure if Hess understood, but she thought he probably did.

"You're learning," he said. "Sometimes those lessons come harder than others. I'm glad you're all right."

"Thank you." She cleared her throat. "Um, how have you been? I haven't seen you since, you know . . ." She didn't know how to put it. They all avoided talking about Mr. Bishop, definitely the coldest vampire she'd ever met; he'd been cruel, calculating, and way too powerful. The fact that they'd survived his attempt to take over Morganville had been amazing . . . but nobody wanted to risk going through that again.

"Yeah, since that," Hess said. "We've been working. Travis took a vacation for six months, out of town. Other than that, the usual. This is the first outright murder we've had in a while, though."

He didn't sound either bothered or excited about it. Just businesslike. Claire didn't know what to say to that, but it didn't seem to matter. He walked her back over to the police cars and went to consult with Hannah and his partner.

"You take me the most interesting places," Eve was saying to Michael when she rejoined them. "Murder scenes, interrogations . . ."

He hugged her silently. Overhead, thunder boomed and the first drops of rain began to fall.

A police officer brought them a collapsible umbrella from his squad car, and the three of them stood in its shelter as the rain poured down and the police started their investigation. By the time it let up, Hannah said they could leave.

Claire said good-bye to her friends, picked up her backpack from the coffee shop, and then went straight to Myrnin.

"It's possible," Myrnin was muttering to himself as he paced the floor of the lab. "Entirely possible. Likely, even."

Claire, coming down the steps from the entrance, dumped her book bag at the usual strategic location—meaning it was equally accessible whether she needed to defend herself or make a quick exit. She was used to coming into the middle of Myrnin's conversations with himself. "What's possible?" she asked.

"Anything," he said absently. "But that's not what I was talking about. Oh, hello, Claire. You're in good time. I need an extra pair of hands."

"As long as I keep them attached," she said, which earned her a startled stare.

"The things you say to me, you'd think I was some sort of monster. Oh, here, help me with this." He gestured to one of the lab tables, which held some gleaming new device with brass fittings and—as always with Myrnin—pipes, wires, and some kind of strange-looking vacuum tubes. "I need it over there." He pointed to an empty table across the room. And then he kept on pacing, his white lab coat (a recent discovery of his; he thought it made him look more official) flaring around him. It was somewhat spoiled by the flopping bunny slippers, their fangs showing with every step.

Oh. He wasn't going to *help* her move it. Well, of course he wasn't. Myrnin could have picked it up with one hand and carried it easily from one spot to another, but he was busy thinking. Carrying things was her job. Today, anyway.

Claire picked up the engine—if that was what it was—and staggered with it over to the other table. It felt as if he'd packed it with lead, and knowing Myrnin, that wasn't much of a stretch. It smelled like blood and flowers, and she hesitated to even guess what its purpose might have been.

"What's possible?" she asked again, leaning against the table and trying to work the kinks out of her arms after stretching them about six inches with the weight of that stupid *thing*, whatever it was.

Myrnin was muttering under his breath, but he paused and glanced at her, even though he kept pacing. "That your friend was murdered by someone who believed he had a drug. Perhaps he was trying to sell the blood."

"How did you hear about that already?" She was surprised, because she'd meant to tell him all about it. Myrnin waved that away.

"Interesting news travels quickly in a town as boring as this," he said. "Also, I tend to monitor police broadcasts. Your name was mentioned in connection with the investigation. I made a few calls to find out the rest. So, do you think he was trying to develop some sort of drug?"

"Myrnin, Doug was stinky, but he wasn't crazy. There may be people in Morganville who will just take any old thing to see if it gets them high, but he just saw that blood *boil* under the lights. He wasn't not going to try to sell it as a drug."

"You'd be very surprised what people get up to. But, in any case, it's possible someone else understood the potential of it, and Doug was simply collateral damage." Myrnin sighed. "I understand it was quite bloody. What a terrible waste."

He didn't mean of Doug, of course. He didn't know Doug, and Claire doubted he would have really cared. No, Myrnin was talking about the waste of *plasma*. Which made Claire shiver, and reminded her again that no matter how cute and cuddly Myrnin could sometimes be, there was something about him that just . . . wasn't quite right.

Not for a human, anyway.

"Frank!" Myrnin yelled, making her jump. "Do you have any insights to share? At all?"

Frank Collins's voice came out of every speaker in the room— the old radio set in the corner, the newer TV mounted on the wall, the computer on the antique desk, and Claire's own cell phone in her pocket. "You don't have to yell. Believe me, I can hear you. Wish to hell I could shut you off."

"Well, you can't, and I need your particular expertise," Myrnin said. He sounded smug and a little bit vindictive; Myrnin didn't like Frank, Frank didn't like anybody who drank plasma, and the whole thing was just plain *weird*.

Because Frank Collins, Shane's dad, had once been a badass vampire-hunting criminal, and then Mr. Bishop had made him a self-loathing vampire, and now he was . . . dead. She was listening to a dead man speaking over the radio.

Well, not *dead*, exactly. After Frank had died saving Claire and Shane, Myrnin had scooped out his still-sort-of-living brain, stuck it in a plasma bath, and hooked it up to a computer. Frank Collins was now the brain that ran Morganville, and, thankfully, Shane didn't know.

Claire could honestly not imagine how *that* conversation was going to go when he found out. It made her ill to even try to imagine it.

"This would go easier if you'd show your face," Myrnin said. "Please. You may be assured that by *please*, I mean *do it*, or I'll put an injection of something nasty in your plasma."

"Myrnin!" Claire blurted, wide-eyed. He shrugged.

"You have no idea how difficult he's been lately. I thought *Ada* was a problem, but she was positively the model of decorum next to this one," he said. "Well? I'm waiting, Frank."

In the corner, a faint shadow appeared, a blur of static that resolved into a flat image on the three-dimensional background. He wasn't bothering with a color image; maybe Frank thought shades of gray made him look more badass.

If so, he was right.

His computer image looked years younger than Claire had last seen him. He had grungy good looks, though his hair was long and messy, and he still had a wicked bad scar on his face. He was dressed in black leather, including a jacket with lots of silver buckles, and big, stomping boots. "Better?" his voice asked. The image's mouth moved, but his voice still came in surround sound from the speakers. "And if you mess with me, I'll hit you back, you bloodsucking geek. Don't think I can't."

Myrnin smiled, fangs down. "Well, you can *try*," he almost purred. "Now. Let's have a chat about the criminal elements of

Morganville, since you have such a fine and intimate acquaintance with them."

Frank's 2-D avatar didn't have much in the way of facial expression, but, then, Frank in 3-D form hadn't been big on emoting, either. His voice, however, was full of sarcasm. "Always glad to be of help to the vampire community," he said. "We all know there is no crime in Morganville. And the humans are all just happy to be here. It's paradise on earth. Ain't that what it says in the brochure?"

Myrnin lost his smile, and his dark eyes got that dangerously hot look that made Claire nervous. "I suppose you think you're irreplaceable in your current position," he said. "You're a brain in a jar, Frank. By definition, you are eminently replaceable."

Now Frank's avatar smiled. It seemed just as artificial as the rest of him. "Then pull the plug, if you think you can do better."

Myrnin's gaze slid to Claire, and she felt that chill again, the one that rushed from the bottom of her spine right up to the top of her head. He didn't say anything. He didn't have to. She knew he'd always thought she was a better candidate for the brain-in-a-jar thing—which meant he thought she'd be easier to control. Frank had just been at the right, or wrong, place at the right time to take her place.

That could always change.

Frank must have figured that out, too, because he said, "You touch my kid's girl, and I'll end this miserable town. You know I can."

"Ada couldn't pull that off, and she had much longer to think about it than you have," Myrnin said, suddenly back to his old self. "So let's abandon the empty threats, shall we? And get back to the subject. I need to understand who in this town might be willing to kill for a sample of vampire blood."

Frank's laugh was dry and scratchy and full of contempt. "You want me to print out a phone directory? Between the people who want to figure out how to kill you faster, the ones who want to protect you because they have money riding on it, and the ones who just dig the whole undead look, it could be anybody."

"A list of anyone who is known to be making antivampire weapons, then," Myrnin said with icy precision. "And anyone who might possibly be researching how to use vampire blood as a drug."

"That ship sailed last century," Frank said. "Everybody knows it makes a crap drug. No real high to it. Makes you stronger for a while, but it's got no bump, and the fall's worse than steroids. They tried combining it with other stuff, but there's nothing you can add it to that vampire blood won't break down in a hurry."

Silence. Myrnin was surprised, Claire realized; he hadn't known humans had even thought about any of this. And it bothered him. If it bothered *Myrnin*, it would make the other vampires crazy. "How far back does this go?"

"It was already old news when I was in high school." Frank shrugged. "People kept on trying, but nothing ever worked. So I think you can write off the drug angle. Now, the killing-your-kind-better motive . . . that I can believe. It would have been at the top of my Christmas list."

Frank was still identifying vampires as *you*, not *us*, which was interesting. He'd been a vampire a relatively short time, and Claire knew he'd been forced into it; it wasn't something he would ever have chosen for himself. He took a special delight in seeing the vamps one-upped.

"Then I'll need a list of those people," Myrnin said. "We'll need to interview them."

"No."

The word came out flat and final. And it rang on the cold stone of the lab's walls and floors, until Myrnin repeated it very softly. "No?"

"No. I was one of them, and I'm not going to put their names on a piece of paper for you and yours to go out and hunt down."

"Maybe your son knows," Myrnin said. He said it in a very offhand way, and without looking at Claire. He was staring at Frank's flickering image. "Maybe I should ask him instead. Forcefully."

Frank's image shifted, and Claire could actually *feel* the menace coming off it now, like an icy wind. "Maybe you shouldn't even think about going there."

"Oh, I do," Myrnin said, and raised his eyebrows. "I think about it quite a lot." There was something fey coming out in him in response to Frank's defiance; it was something Claire hardly ever saw. Maybe it was a guy thing.

She picked up the first pointy thing that came to hand—a pair of scissors—and jammed them against Myrnin's back, not *into* his back, stabby-wise, but enough to make an impression.

"Ow," he said absently, and looked over his shoulder at her. "What?"

"Leave Shane out of it," she said very quietly. That was all. No explanations, no threats.

Myrnin turned very slowly to face her. That strange, uncomfortable light in his eyes was still glittering, but as he stared at her, it faded, like someone turned down a dimmer switch. "All right," he said. "Since you ask so nicely."

"I wasn't asking."

"I'm aware of that. The sharp point in my back did make it

clear." He caught her wrist in one of those lightning-quick vampire motions and took the scissors away from her. He put them in the pocket of his lab coat. "Wouldn't want you hurting yourself."

"No," Claire said. "You think that's your job."

A quick flash of a smile, not a very nice one, and Myrnin turned back to Frank. "All right, my unpleasant friend, we'll have done with threats, both yours and mine. Please, for the sake of young Claire here, will you be so kind as to provide me with a few places where I might look for a murderer?"

"The mirror's a great place to start," Frank said. "But if you're talking humans, I can give you maybe two names. We'd be better off if they were off the streets, anyway."

"Détente," Myrnin said. "How lovely."

THREE

Claire wasn't needed for the actual investigation. Myrnin wanted to do it himself . . . a fact that left her a little bit worried, not so much for him as for the people he was out to question (not very nice people, granted, if Frank Collins had decided they were worth losing). She left a message for Oliver, figuring that it was his problem now, and headed for home.

She expected to find everyone there, but when she unlocked the front door of the house on Lot Street, it sounded quiet. Way too quiet. They weren't a studious bunch, her housemates. If Shane was home, there should have been game noise; if Eve, loud music. If both, shouting plus *both* those things.

Michael wasn't home, either, because she didn't hear guitar.

"Helllooooooooo," she called, as she locked the door behind her in standard Morganville precautionary measure. "House ghost? Anybody?" Not that they had a house ghost anymore, but it always seemed polite to ask. Weirder things had happened.

Silence. Claire dumped her book bag on the couch, on top of

a sweatshirt someone (Shane) had left balled up there, flopped down, and stretched out. She rarely had the house to herself; it felt nice. Strange, but nice. When nobody was moving around, she could hear something like a low, electric vibration from all over— walls, floors, ceiling. The life of the house.

Claire reached down and patted the wooden floor. "Good house. Nice house. We should do a repaint or something. Make you pretty again."

She could have sworn that the house's low hum cycled, like a very faint, approving purr.

After half an hour, she got up and checked the table and other likely spots for any sign of notes left behind, but there weren't any hints about when she might expect anybody to show up. She was about to go upstairs to study when the flyer caught her eye. It had slipped off the kitchen table and was lying curled against the wall. She picked it up and smoothed it out.

The new martial arts gym. Not likely Eve was there, but for Shane, it was definitely a safe bet that was where he'd gone off to. Claire tapped the paper thoughtfully, then smiled.

"Why not?" she asked. The house didn't answer or have any opinion one way or another. "I could use the exercise. And I've *got* to see this place."

She raced upstairs, changed into a pair of low-riding sweat-pants and a faded T-shirt that advertised The Killers, and at the last second, added the gold Founder's pin to her collar. It scratched, but better that than getting caught outside without Protection. After all, she hadn't gotten martially arted *yet.*

It was still light out, but fading fast toward twilight. Cold wind twirled the leaves in the gutters, and as she walked, Claire wished she'd thought to bring a sweater. A few cars passed her, some with blacked-out, vampire-friendly windows, but nobody paid her more than a glance that she could tell. The new gym was located in one of the less-trafficked parts of town, near a bunch of warehouses that had seen better days and businesses with long-ago-faded CLOSED PERMANENTLY signs in the windows. In all that industrial devastation, one neon sign still glowed, with a red-and-green dragon swishing its tail.

The storefront looked newly renovated, and Claire could swear she still smelled fresh paint. There were a lot of cars in the parking lot and lining the street. With surprise, Claire recognized Eve's black hearse; she didn't expect Eve to be a fan of sparring. Well, people probably wouldn't have bet on her showing up, either.

There were no windows to look in through, so Claire pulled open the heavy metal door and walked into a large tiled area with a wooden counter. A buffed-up guy of postcollege age sat on a stool behind it, reading a magazine. He had a lot of tattoos, and a particularly sharp buzz cut. When he glanced up and saw her, his sandy eyebrows went up.

"Here for class?" he asked.

"Uh, maybe. I just want to check it out."

"All right. You can do a pay-as-you-go for the first couple of visits, but after that, it's a monthly fee, no refunds." He shoved a clipboard at her, along with a pen. "Fill out the forms. It's ten dollars."

Ten was a lot for just checking it out, but Claire put her name on the papers, along with her address, phone number, medical history, and all the other stuff that was asked about exercise and mobility. Some of it seemed pretty intrusive. She handed it back, along with her faded ten-dollar bill, and got a sticky name tag to slap on her T-shirt. Then the bouncer—she couldn't think of him as a receptionist—hit a hidden button, and a sharp, electronic buzz sounded.

"Push the wall, right there," he said, pointing. She pushed, and it opened, cutting off the buzz. It swung shut behind her as she stepped through, and if it locked, she couldn't hear it over the noise.

Amazing that she'd missed it on the other side of the barrier, because this gym was *working*. The clang of free weights hitting supports. Solid, heavy clunks from the weight machines as men and women sweat, grunted, and worked at the stations. Whirring wheels on exercise bikes. And in the center of the room, a large open space with mats in the middle, and about thirty people dressed in white martial arts clothes, kneeling with their hands on their thighs, all facing in toward the middle.

Claire looked quickly around, and although she recognized some of those doing the straight exercise stuff, she didn't see Shane or Eve among them. She edged around toward a stair-climber not in use and stepped on so she could get a better vantage point of the class in progress. Whoever had used it before her had set it to murderous levels; she had to back off on the resistance almost immediately, and so she almost missed Shane, who was sitting facing the mat at an angle.

She spotted him only because he got up and walked to the center of the mats. He wore his uniform well, she realized, like he'd done this before. Maybe he had. He had that look, the one she recognized from watching him fight, though those had been more down-and-dirty street things than martial arts bouts. He wasn't looking at anything but the man facing him.

Shane was a pretty big guy for his age—broad shouldered, kind of tall. And he had at least a foot on the man facing him, who looked frozen at the age of about thirty. *The vampire instructor*, Claire thought. He had long hair he'd tied back in a ponytail.

They bowed to each other formally and settled back into some kind of stance, almost mirroring each other.

Shane kicked, high and fast. The vampire ducked and let Shane's momentum spin him out of position, and with one economically placed, almost gentle push, sent him tumbling to the mats. Shane rolled and came up with his hands out, ready to defend, but the vampire was just standing there, watching him.

"Nice attack," he said. "But I can move out of the way of a kick. You'd do much better to move in close, reduce my reaction time. It's the only real chance you have, you see. You need to remember how much faster we can move, and how much more observant we are of things like shifts of weight and eye movements."

Shane nodded, shaggy hair rippling around his hard, intent face, and took two quick, light steps in to close the distance. He struck as he did it, and even though he didn't land the punch, he came closer. The vampire's open hand stopped it less than an inch from his face.

He hadn't flinched.

"You're quick," he said. "Very quick, and unless I miss my guess, very well accustomed to fighting all sorts of enemies. You're young to be so angry, by the way. That can be either an advantage or a disadvantage, depending on who you're fighting. And why."

Shane fell back into a waiting stance and didn't answer. The vampire gave him a little one-more-time signal, and Shane went for a punch . . . but it was a distraction, and this time, his kick actually hit the vampire in the side of his knee, forcing a shift in balance.

The vampire, without seeming to even think about it, spun

and kicked Shane right off the mat. He tumbled across the wood floor and into the kneeling students like a ball into bowling pins. They scattered.

Claire gasped and gripped the stair-climber handles more tightly, resisting the urge to jump off and run to him. He was already rolling up to his feet—slower than last time, granted—and walked back to the mats. He put his right fist against his left palm, put feet together, and bowed.

The vampire bowed back. "Again," he said. "I congratulate you on being the first to actually touch me. Now see if you can hurt me." He bared his teeth in a savage little smile. "Come on, boy. Try."

Shane settled into attack stance again, and then, very suddenly, it wasn't all about the polite martial arts form at all. He went all street fighter, and the vampire wasn't prepared for it. In fact, despite the vampire's being faster and deadlier, Shane got him off balance in two quick, well-placed punches, swept his legs out from under him, and sent him on his back to the mat.

And he didn't stop there. Claire gasped and stopped climbing, frozen, as he dropped down on the vamp, slamming both knees into the man's chest, and pantomimed ramming a stake into his heart. There was something savage on Shane's face, something she remembered seeing before, but only when he was fighting for their lives. A real, deep, burning hatred.

Shane didn't move. He was staring down at the fallen vamp, and the vamp was locking eyes with him. Then, slowly, he stood up, hand with the invisible stake falling back to his side.

The vampire rolled up to his feet in one fast, fluid movement, keeping a healthy distance between them. He stared at Shane for a beat too long, then did the formal bow. Shane echoed him.

"You have a gift," the vampire said. It didn't sound like a compliment, exactly. "I think you're too advanced for this entry-level class. See me later. I think you may be suitable for some advanced placement."

Shane bowed again, stepped back, and took his place at the edge of the floor, kneeling down.

A thin blond girl got up to take his place, looking terrified. Claire didn't blame her. Shane had brought a sense of real violence into the room, and that had gotten everyone's attention; the sound of weights clanging and people talking had hushed and slowed, if not stopped.

Claire realized she was standing still on the stair-climber, and began pumping her legs again, mind not on the exercise at all, even though her calf muscles were already burning. She couldn't stop looking at Shane now. She could see only a thin slice of his face between the others, but from that she knew that he wasn't paying attention to the blond girl getting her ass kicked—gently—in the middle of the floor. He was staring straight ahead, face set and still, and if the victory had given him any kind of peace or triumph, she couldn't see it.

SHANE
)

I wasn't always like this. I know people think I like to fight, and, yeah, maybe they're right—I do—but I didn't when I was little. I just wanted to fit in and get along. The usual crap in a town where not fitting in got you a whole lot of trouble.

I guess the first time I hit somebody was in elementary school, which is pretty standard for guys, but it wasn't because I was person-ally getting attacked. No, I threw the first punch.

I hit a guy named Terrence James because he was shoving around my best friend, who was littler and couldn't stand up to save his life. I was about Terrence's size, and there was something about seeing a big guy pick on a little one that made me see red.

Yeah, I'm not that complicated. I know why I felt like that. My dad. My dad, the guy who was okay when he was sober, but was a mean drunk. He didn't hit me much, not then, but he was scary, and he'd always liked to push people around.

Felt good to push somebody like him around for a change. Punch-ing Terrence didn't feel nearly as good, though. My knuckles felt like I'd broken them into little pieces, but after the first horrific shock the pain was a good kind of pain, and it all fed into a red haze of euphoria as I looked at Terrence lying on his back, tears streaming down his face, tell-ing me he was sorry and that he'd never do it again, ever.

And that's how I discovered that I liked that feeling, that righteous, hot feeling of winning for what I thought was the right cause. I wasn't afraid of a little pain to get there, either, which is a huge advantage in a fight. Let's face it: most people don't like to get hurt, so if you show you're okay with it, they're going to get a little bit weird. And maybe walk away. I don't mind a win by default, as long as I win.

When I got older, people pretty much left me alone. I had that pit-bull mentality and a useful amount of height and muscle, both of which I probably owed to my father. Girls liked it, too, but not the right kind of girls, generally. I won most fights, lost a few, but I never quit. I took boxing and wrestling in high school and did okay, but I didn't like the rules that much. I was a street brawler.

I guess I was on track to being my dad—maybe not as bad, but let's face it, it wasn't easy to resist the black hole that was Frank Collins, and I'd always done what he said. He liked that I could hold my own in a fight. After my sister and mother died, well, it got worse—a whole lot worse. Sending me back to Morganville to scout out the weaknesses had been a real show of faith from my dad, but the farther I got away from him, the more I realized that I didn't want to be him anymore. He'd taken it too far.

Meeting Claire made me realize that I could be something different. Something better. The first time I saw her, black-and-blue but with this strange little core of strength . . . I recognized something we had in common. We didn't quit. And we suffered for it.

I started out wanting to protect her, and the more I was around her, the more I realized that she was one girl who could take care of herself. I wasn't used to chicks being equals—and Claire was, and is. She's not that physically strong, but she's quick and smart and fearless, and if sometimes I get overprotective about her, she's the first one to remind me of that.

But I want to be ready, if it comes to a fight again—which it will. Not just against the normal human bullies and criminals; those were a piece of cake. No, I want to be able to defend her against the vampires, and that is a whole lot harder. Weapons are good, and I never turn those down, but the reality is I can't count on always having one. I worry. There have been a couple of times—more than a couple—when only the fact that Michael had vampire strength he could throw in with mine had saved us.

And that really bothered me. I couldn't depend on Michael, either. Or anybody else.

Mixed martial arts—that was the ticket. Hit your guy however you can, and put him down fast. My kind of fighting, and something that could work on vampires, if you knew what you were doing. I'd been itching to try it, and when the flyer came in the mail, it seemed like somebody up there liked me after all.

Michael had pulled me off to the side after Claire left to say he didn't think it was a good idea. I told him to stuff it, but in a nice way, because even though he's got fangs and a thirst, he's still my bro. Most times. Took me a while to accept that, but I'm almost okay with his whole night-stalking lifestyle now.

Doesn't mean I don't want to be able to kick his ass if I have to, though. The chance to learn martial arts from a vampire . . . that was way too good to pass up.

I know how to do the real kind of martial arts. I mean, I had karate until I was thirteen and decided I was too cool for it. So I know how to put on a gi and tie a belt and be formal on the mats. Turned out that was good, because the instructor—some dude named Vassily, with an Eastern European accent straight out of an old movie—wanted to start out that way.

I was okay the first couple of passes, when he got me up to spar. It was like fighting anybody else, no big thing, until he started using vampire speed and strength on me. I couldn't help it; that made me angry, and anger kind of makes me forget the rules. I went for his knee. He hit me like a wrecking ball smashing a wall, and next thing I knew, I was shaking it off with a giant ache in my chest. I'd been lucky. He could have caved in my ribs and Swiss-cheesed my heart if he'd hit full strength.

Then don't let him hit you again, loser. *I could almost hear my dad's voice, dry and mocking. He was dead now, but in my mind he was always there, always watching, and always judging. He'd hated vampires. I didn't much like 'em, either. We'd always had that in common.*

I didn't think about walking away. I went back to the mat and bowed, and the second I got a chance, I attacked with everything I had. Full-on blitz. I knew I was going to get hurt, maybe badly, maybe killed, but I wasn't going to be humiliated. Not by a vampire. No way in hell.

I got him. Hard. I could see the shock in his face, and the rush of rage, and as I stood there with the bloody taste of victory in my mouth, I actually wanted him to go for it, come get me, because, damn, I felt alive, actually alive. . . .

But he shut me down, said something I didn't register, and bowed me off the mat. I don't remember leaving or kneeling down. I just remember thinking, Next time, next time, next time, regular as a bell ringing in my head and drowning out every other thought.

I watched him go through the rest of the class. He didn't hurt anybody else, but he could have. He wanted to; I could see it in flashes in his eyes. They're all alike, you know. Hunters. Even Michael's got it, though he hides it, and sometimes I pretend like I don't see it, either. You have to be ready for them to turn on you.

Because if you're not ready . . . somebody you love could get hurt.

I closed my eyes and imagined Claire. She always made me feel better. But although I could see her face, her smile, almost feel her presence, all I could think about was how easy it would be for them to take her away from me.

I couldn't let that happen.

It occurred to me that what the vamp had said to me was that he'd see me later. Some kind of special class? Hell, yeah. I could do that. I needed to do that.

I needed to understand how to fight them, one on one, without help or weapons or hope.

Only the vampires could show me that.

Still . . . sitting there, hands on my knees, breathing fast, I couldn't *help but feel that even though I'd won, even though I'd done the impossible . . . somehow, I'd lost.*

And it was first of a whole lot of losses.

Watching Shane kneeling there, so closed-in and so . . . cold, Claire felt a little sick. She didn't like it. She didn't like how he'd just fought, and she didn't like how he looked afterward. Shane was usually *happy* after a fight, not . . . angry.

This whole thing is a bad idea, she thought. She didn't know why, but she knew it was true.

"Hey," said a low voice at her back, and Claire looked back to see Eve standing there. For the gym, she'd dispensed with the Goth makeup, but her tight T-shirt had a pink skull with a bow on it, and there were a skull and crossbones in rhinestones down the sides of her workout pants, too. She'd tied her straight black hair back in a shining ponytail. It was about as unadorned as Eve ever got, unless she was in disguise. "Did you see that? What the hell was *that*? Did Shane just go all Wolfman, or what?"

"I don't know," Claire said, and jumped down from the exercise machine. "But—"

"Boyfriend's got issues," Eve finished. "Yeah, no kidding. So, you came to spy, too?"

"Too?"

"Really, come on. Do you see me as the heavy-sweating type? So very not." Eve looked her over critically. "And you aren't, either, but you can pass for it, probably. Did they make you pay the ten bucks to get in?"

"Yeah."

"This is so much less fun than I'd hoped. For one thing, nobody here is worthy of being ogled, and if they are, they're way too sweaty. Or scary. Or both." Eve gave a theatrical little shudder. "What do you say we do something else?"

"Like what?" Claire was still distracted by the sight of Shane, kneeling like a statue at the edge of the sparring space. He was still in that other world, looking off into the distance. Scary.

Eve gave her a slow, wicked smile. "Let me ask you this. Have you ever fenced?"

For a second, Claire thought she meant the traditional kind of thing, like hammering pickets onto rails in front of a house, but then she figured it out. "Oh. You mean with swords?"

"Exactly. If I'm going to sweat, I'm going to sweat in a cooler way. Follow me."

"Wait. You *fence?*"

"I took it up in high school," Eve said. "Come on, walk and talk, walk and talk. That's a girl. Yeah, I had to have a sport, but I don't like those icky team things. Fencing seemed retro cool, and plus, there were pointy things you try to stick into your opponent. It seemed like a good idea."

Eve had clearly spent her time in the gym checking out every corner of it, because Claire had no idea there was another part to it, behind a door near the restrooms. Behind it lay a couple of racquetball courts (safely caged up behind clear plastic), and even an indoor tennis court; maybe the vampires had been craving it and couldn't get out in the sun. But at the very back was a wood-floored room with racks on the walls that held swords, as well as neat stacks of white uniforms and those funky mesh helmets.

"Right. I wouldn't start you out with a saber," Eve said, moving Claire from contemplation of one particular row of choices. "Too whippy for a beginner. How about a plain old foil? You can only target from the neck to the waist; no double touches. Easy peasy."

She grabbed a couple of the long, slender weapons and tossed one to Claire, who caught it. It felt strange in her hand, but not at all heavy. The blade was kind of square, and there was a round tip on the end. She made a tentative slashing motion with it, and Eve laughed.

"It's a lunging weapon," she said. "Hang on, let's get you suited up before you start attacking anything."

Suiting up sounded much less complicated than it actually was; by the time Eve had finished dressing her like a sword-bearing doll, Claire felt clumsy, hot, and claustrophobic. Between the thick padding and the tight mesh helmet, she had no idea how she was supposed to move, much less fight.

Eve had her own fencing suit, which she took out of a cheerful, skull-featuring bag of her own. Her outfit was black, with a pirate skull and crossbones where the heart would be. She looked *dangerous*. And a little bit crazy, even without the beekeeper helmet.

"Okay," she said. "First fighting lesson is, we don't fight, so stop pointing that foil at me. It's not going to go off."

Claire blushed and dropped the point down toward her toes. "Sorry."

"No worries. You couldn't hit me, anyway," Eve said, and smiled. "I'm going to line up next to you. Just do what I do, okay?"

The first thing, apparently, was how to grip the sword properly. That took a while. Then there was lunging, which involved stabbing the sword out in a smooth, straight line while stepping out on her right leg in a deep crouch.

It hurt. A lot. In fact, after about ten of those, Claire was gasping for breath and sweating; in about fifteen, she was ready to cry.

Eve stopped after twenty, but it seemed like she could have gone all day.

"I had to put all this on for *that?*" Claire muttered, as she pulled off her helmet. Her hair was soaked with sweat and sticking to her face. "Seriously? Nobody even waved a sword at me!"

"You have to get used to the weight and moving in it," Eve said. "Suck it up, newbie."

"You're enjoying this."

"Yeah, well, a lot. I had to do it. You should, too." Eve winked. She moved off to a padded pole that had a red circle marked on it, and practiced some lunges on her own. Her sword point landed in the circle every time.

Claire spun around at the dry sound of hands clapping. She hadn't heard anybody come into the room, but there he was, dressed in white fencing gear, with a sword in one hand and his helmet tucked under his arm. *Oliver.* He looked leaner and harder in the uniform.

Next to him, also dressed in white, was another figure. *Amelie.* The Founder of Morganville had never seemed so small before; the clothes she wore tended to enhance her height, as did the high heels. But like this, Claire realized that Amelie wasn't much taller than she was, and was very slender. In the fencing clothes, she could have passed for a boy, except for the feminine curves of her face.

"You're coming along, Eve," Amelie said. Eve broke off her lunges and stood very straight, sword point down. "I remember when you first began your lessons. I had to give personal approval for anyone who practiced those types of martial arts."

"Yeah, well, it's been a while since I was competitive," Eve said. "Hey, Ollie."

"For that," Oliver said, "you may step onto the piste."

"I didn't come to fight."

"You're dressed for it. What is that—a foil? Nonsense. You're more suited to an épée." Oliver snorted and took another weapon from the wall, which he threw in Eve's direction. She grabbed it out of the air with her left hand. It had a deadlier look to it, Claire realized; more like a triangular blade than the square base of the foil. Still had a tip on it, but it looked like a tougher thing to master.

Eve shrugged and tossed the foil back to Oliver, who put it on the rack. "All right," she said, and cut the weapon—the épée—through the air with a hissing sound. "Your funeral, dude."

Oliver bared his teeth in a grim smile and put on his helmet. "I doubt it," he said.

Eve put on her helmet, too, and stepped into the narrow path marked on the floor. Claire moved back to stand by Amelie, who watched with an intense, focused expression on her pale face. As Eve and Oliver raised their swords in salute, she nodded and said, "Go."

It was literally over in seconds. Claire was used to the kind of fighting from the movies—long, clanging duels with lots of moving around and occasional cape swirling. This was fast and incredibly deadly. She didn't even see what happened, only that there was a blur of motion, some metallic clangs that came too fast to register, and suddenly Eve was standing there with Oliver's sword tip tenting the fabric of her pirate-skull emblem, right over her heart. "Well, crap," Eve said, and took a step back. "No fair using vampy speed."

"I'm not," he said. "I don't need to. Fencing was a survival skill in my day. Again?"

"Sure." Eve backed up to the far end of the marked-off strip—the piste?—and settled into a low crouch that somehow didn't look at all awkward.

"Go," Amelie said, and there was another blur of motion. This time, Claire made out a couple of things—one, that Eve seemed to lunge for Oliver's chest and then dropped way down, and her point took him in the lunging leg. His slid over her shoulder. Eve hit the ground and rolled up to her feet, raising her épée in triumph.

"Dude, *gotcha!*" she said. "Mortal wound, right there. Femoral artery. You are so *dead.*"

He didn't respond at all, just walked back to his spot on the other side of the strip.

"Seriously? You can't walk away with a tie?" Eve asked. She'd pulled off her helmet, and her black eyes were wicked bright. "Can't we all just get along?"

"Fence," he barked. "Don't talk."

Eve popped her helmet back on and took her place on the strip. Amelie drew in a breath, and instead of giving the signal, said, "Oliver, perhaps you should let it go."

His helmeted face turned toward her, as if he couldn't believe she'd said it, and then focused back on Eve, who was taking the en garde stance. "Start us," he said. "Two out of three."

"He doesn't like to lose," Amelie said to Claire, and shrugged. "Very well. Go!"

Claire focused, and managed to see exactly what happened this time. Oliver lunged. Eve parried, but he was ready for it, and got his blade back in line by knocking hers out of line. She tried for another thigh wound, but that didn't work this time.

Oliver slammed the point of his épée into her chest so power-fully, it drove her back a step and made her drop her sword.

"Oliver!" Amelie snapped, and he backed off. Eve staggered backward, lost her footing, and fell on her butt. Her épée clat-tered away across the floor as she put both hands to her chest, then reached up to rip her helmet off. Her face had gone chalk white, and her eyes were huge.

"Ow," she said. "Damn. That's going to leave a mark."

Oliver walked away, circling restlessly, turning his épée around and around in his gloved hand. "You asked for it," he said. "Now get off the piste if you're going to complain about a bruise."

Eve slowly rolled up to her knees, collected her helmet and sword, and stood up. She didn't seem too steady.

"Help her out," Amelie said. "Make sure she's not broken a rib. Oliver, that was unnecessary."

"What was *unnecessary* was her gloating," he replied. "I didn't come here to fight children, and she needs to learn the same harsh lesson I did: taunting those who are stronger has consequences."

"The stronger have a responsibility to the weaker," Amelie said. "As you very well know."

"I've had quite enough responsibility. And I thought we came here to fight, woman. If all you want is to hold philosophi-cal discussions while attractively dressed, surely we can do that elsewhere."

Eve looked better now, with the color coming back to her face—coming back too fast for Claire's comfort, because there was an angry, frightened glitter in her eyes. "Bully," she muttered.

Oliver took off his helmet and stared at her. He looked as solid as bone, and like someone nobody wanted to mess with. "I don't al-low people to mock me," he said. "And the next time you presume to call me by a pet name, I'll do worse than crack a rib for you on the piste. Now get out of the way. The adults require space."

Amelie cocked her head to one side, studying him, and said, "I'm bored with all these rules. Shall we dispense with the conventions, then?"

"By all means," Oliver said, and tossed his helmet into the corner. She put hers safely out of the way. "Weapons?"

"I prefer the épée," she said. "Two of them."

"Ah. Florentine. That suits me well enough."

They each took two swords, and as Claire and Eve retreated back to a bench in the rear of the room, Amelie and Oliver faced off. Amelie crossed her two swords in front of her face, and Oliver followed suit; the sound of four blades cutting the air in salute made Claire shiver. "What are they doing?" she whispered.

"Free fighting," Eve answered, keeping it quiet. "No rules. More like the old-style duels."

"Not quite," Amelie said. She was almost *smiling*. "This likely won't end in death."

"But no guarantees," Oliver said. He *was* smiling, and not his usual eviler-than-you sort of twisted lips, either. He almost looked *happy*. "Ready?"

"Of course." Amelie didn't seem to be; she was holding her swords down, almost not seeming to know what to do with them.

Oliver took one step toward her, and the weapons snapped up and targeted him so fast, Claire blinked. Oliver raised one over his head in a pose that made her think of a scorpion's stinger, and circled to the right. Amelie circled, too, keeping the distance between them ... until suddenly she was moving, two light, quick steps, a sudden jump that ended in a sliding lunge, and *both* her épées hit targets, one slicing across Oliver's leg, the other under his arm. He whirled and hit her in the back with an underhand stroke—or tried to. She must have known it was coming, because she bent forward, graceful as a willow, and rolled up on her knee to parry the next lunge.

And that was just the *start.*

"You know," Eve said distantly, about five minutes later, as the two vampires were still circling, slashing, hacking, and scoring points on each other, "I'm thinking that maybe I shouldn't ever piss him off. Or her. Again."

"You think?" Claire whispered back. "Jeez. It's like *The Terminator* meets *Buffy.*"

"How do they decide who wins? I mean, clearly, they're hitting each other, but they don't even pretend those are going to hurt...."

"I don't think it matters," Claire said.

She was proven right just thirty seconds later, when Amelie reached down and tapped the point of one épée three times on the floor. Oliver, moving in for a lunge, veered off at the last second and went to a neutral position.

"Done?" he asked.

"Most enjoyable," she said. "Thirty-two mortal touches for you; thirty-one for me. But I don't mind losing to a master, Oliver." She bowed slightly, swords down.

He bowed back, a little more deeply. "Nor do I," he said. "But winning is always better. You're favoring your right again, you know."

"I noticed. We can't all overcome nature's disadvantages so easily."

They exchanged a smile, a real one, and Claire exchanged a look with Eve. Eve cleared her throat.

"Are you still here?" Oliver asked without changing his expression. He didn't look away from Amelie. "Leave."

"Right," Claire said. "Going."

She picked up Eve's stuff and walked with her to one of the small changing rooms to strip off the sweat-damp uniforms. Eve stuffed hers into the bag and stripped off her pink shirt. Claire gasped at the forming bruise, which was at least three inches across and looked very painful.

"Dammit," Eve said. "That's going to show over my bra. Got to rethink the wardrobe for the next few days." She probed at the bruise with a fingertip and winced. "Nothing broken, just a nice reminder not to screw around with Ollie on the pointy-object dance floor."

"I can't believe you fought him."

"Fought him? Damn, girlfriend, I got a *touch* on him. You know how difficult that is? I've been a serious fencer for years, but I never even got close to a touch on anybody without a pulse. He used to duel for real, you know. Without the safety tips on the blades."

Claire could believe it. What she couldn't get her head around was that Eve thought that was cool.

Maybe, she thought, *fencing isn't my sport after all.*

FOUR

ichael was home when they arrived, and surprisingly, he wasn't playing guitar. He was sitting on the couch in Shane's customary spot, playing a game. "Hey," he said as Claire and Eve entered. "Nobody made dinner."

"Nobody but you was home to eat it," Eve said. "And I'm taking a wild guess that you didn't make it, either."

"Nope." He killed a zombie with a chainsaw, and ducked instinctively as another one lunged at him out of the shadows on the screen. "Guess we're all going to bed hungry, like the bad children we are."

"Guess not." Eve winked at Claire, who held up a grease-stained bag. "Seriously, you couldn't smell the burgers? Is your vampire nose on the fritz, Michael?"

"I was hoping I was imagining the burgers."

"Shut up. I got you one made extra rare. With pickles. I know you like pickles."

Michael paused the game and put the controller aside, and as he stood up, the door opened and Shane came in. He nodded to Michael as he dropped his canvas bag in the hallway, next to Eve's. "Who got burgers?"

"See, *he* can smell the burgers!" Eve yelled from the kitchen.

Michael ignored that. "You guys go to the gym?"

"Yeah," Shane said. "The martial arts guy is pretty hard-core."

"I got a bruise!" Eve shouted. "Big one! Right over my heart! Guess who put it there?"

Michael raised his eyebrows at Shane, who held up his hands. "Not me, man. I never touched her."

"Oliver!" Eve backed out of the kitchen door, holding plates, balancing them like a pro. "Michael, here's your almost-cooked one. Shane, got you the jalapeño burger. Me and Claire have plain old boring ones."

"We're branching out into different forms of junk food," Michael said. "Exciting."

"Shut up. Do you want your juice warmed up?" *Juice*, Claire figured, was Eve's new code for *blood*. Well, technically, it was juice, Claire supposed. People juice.

"I'll get it," Michael said. "Thanks. Shane, Claire—Cokes?"

"Yes!" Claire yelled, at the same time Shane did. He walked over to put his arm around her and bent to kiss her.

"Jinx," he whispered.

"I like this version of jinxies better than the one I did in grade school," she said. He tasted like salt and metal, but it still seemed sexy—and so did the way his damp T-shirt clung to his shoulders and chest. She'd never thought sweaty was all that sexy before, but Shane . . . well. Shane rocked it.

"So, what did you do at the gym?" he asked. "I thought I saw you on the stair machine."

Oops. Busted. "I was on it for a while," she said. "Then Eve took me to teach me how to fence."

"Not so much how to fence as how to hold a sword and not drop it," Eve said. "And then I fought Oliver to a draw."

Shane fluttered his hands. "Oh, and then we were all elected as ice princesses and asked to go to Disneyland!" He rolled his eyes.

"Laugh all you want. I'm going to look *way* better in full skirts than you," Eve said. "And besides, I'm not lying. I got a mortal touch on Oliver. Ask your girlfriend."

"She hit him with her sword," Claire said, when both Michael and Shane looked at her. "I saw it."

"And then, to make sure I knew my place, he practically rammed his épée through my heart, but, you know, details. Hence the bruise." She dragged down the neckline of her shirt to show off the top of it. Shane whistled appreciatively—not at her assets, Claire felt sure. The bruise. That was Shane, through and through.

"I didn't know fencing was a contact sport," he said. "I thought it was more, you know, a pretend sport. Like golf. Or competitive eating."

"Hey, golf is hard." Eve shrugged. "Anytime you want me to whip your lame ass on eighteen holes, let me know."

"I got whipped enough, thanks." Shane flopped down in his chair and pulled the plate toward him. "I could eat roadkill, I'm so hungry. Without hot sauce."

"Well, you're in luck, because I have no idea what's really in these burgers," Eve said. Michael came out of the kitchen and put three cold cans of Coke on the table, and one sports bottle that *might* have possibly held juice. Warm juice. Claire was glad it was opaque. "Dinner together. Wow. This is an event."

It was, recently. They'd all been doing their own thing so much, it had been more like two of them eating together, or maybe three. Having all four at the table was great for a change. Eve chattered on about work, and how awesome the fencing room (the salle?) was at the new gym. Michael put in a few tidbits about what was happening with his music, which was still up in the air after their road trip to Dallas to get his demo recorded. It was sounding positive, but Michael was all about the caution and pessimism.

Claire almost blurted out the whole Myrnin/Frank face-off, but realized that she couldn't, because Shane was there, and Shane still didn't know his father had survived . . . at least, in the form of a brain in a jar, hooked up to a computer. Shane thought Frank was dead, and he was at peace with that, kind of. Claire didn't know how he was going to feel about the rest of it, and she couldn't stand to hurt him. There was no reason he had to know.

Or so she kept telling herself, anyway.

It was a nice time together, and it felt like home. The laughter made her warm, and the occasional glances and smiles from Shane made her tingle all over. After dinner, she and Eve did the dishes (but only because it was their turn) while Michael and Shane claimed the couch and loaded up the new game. Turned out it was—no surprise—another zombie game. Blood and guts ensued. Claire curled up between them on the couch with a textbook, while Eve stretched out on the floor and flipped through a magazine.

A normal night. Very, very normal.

Until Shane lost the game.

"Damn it!" he yelled, and threw the controller at the screen. Like, really *threw* it. It hit the edge of the frame, instead of the softer LCD part, and pieces of the controller broke off and went everywhere. Eve yelped and rolled over, brushing off pieces of plastic. Claire flinched.

"Jesus, Shane, get a grip," Michael said. "You lost. BFD, man. It's not the first time."

"Shut up," Shane said. He stood up, grabbed the controller, and glared at it. "Piece of crap."

"Don't blame the equipment. It *was* working fine before you scrapped it."

"How the hell do you know? Were you playing it?"

"I know you owe me for a new controller."

"Screw you, bro." Shane threw the broken controller at *Michael* this time. Not that it was a risk; Michael calmly reached up and caught it, so smoothly it might have been some kind of special effect.

"Maybe you should chill out."

"Maybe you should stop with the vampire reflexes in game!"

Michael frowned. He didn't usually let Shane get to him, but Claire could see the anger forming. "I played you fair."

"Fair?" Shane barked out a laugh. "Man, you have no idea what you're talking about anymore, do you? You don't even know when you're screwing us."

"Hey!" Claire said, and stood up between them, as Michael got to his feet. The air felt thick and ominous now, the house's reflection of the feelings of its owners. "You guys, stop! It's just a *game!*"

"No, it's *not* just a game. Get the hell out of the way!"

"Stop!" she said sharply, and punched Shane in the shoulder. "Jeez. Didn't you get enough fighting in for the day? What *is* this? Michael's right. You don't get to destroy stuff just because you lost a game. You're not three years old, Shane!"

His dark eyes focused on her, and she felt a very real, very cold chill go through her. That was *not* the Shane she knew. That was the *other* Shane. "Don't hit me," he said. "I don't like it."

Claire let her hands drop to her sides and took a deep breath. "Sorry. I shouldn't have done that. I just wanted to get your attention."

Well, she'd gotten it, all right. She wished she hadn't. But at least it had broken the momentum of whatever was going on between Shane and Michael.

Now it was just between her and Shane.

"Claire," Michael said. She held out a hand without looking at him, and he fell silent.

And she waited for Shane to say something.

SHANE
☽

I hate losing. I mean, really, a lot. I usually try to cover it up and pretend like I don't, but there's something inside me that gets twisted up and desperate. Because losing means that you're at someone else's mercy, even if it's just a game. Even if it's not supposed to mean anything.

I'd had too much of that in my life, being in someone else's power. First my dad's. Then the vampires'. There was always somebody looming, somebody faster and stronger and crueler than me, and it made me feel like a scared kid inside all the time.

I wasn't lying. The game controller had flaked out on me. The buttons stuck. It wasn't my fault that I lost; it was the tool's. I wasn't going to lose, not to Michael. Not anymore. Yeah, losing my temper was stupid—I mean, it was my favorite game controller I'd busted—but thinking that it wasn't fair, that he'd cheated, that he'd used those vampire reflexes to win and didn't deserve it . . . It burned me, okay? Burned me bad.

And I wanted to kick his ass.

Maybe it was just that something had gotten loose in the gym, something I usually kept locked down inside some dark cave. I mean, it was Michael. But just now, staring him down, I was reminded that he wasn't actually my friend. Not the one I'd grown up with, the one who'd had my back, anyway. This was Michael's body, but he wasn't the same person inside of that shell. Not at all.

The girls were upset. Claire was trying to talk to me, but I wasn't hearing her, not until she smacked me in the shoulder. It felt like a sharp, stabbing blow, although I knew it wasn't; it was just that all my nerves were on fire because I was so hyped, and I probably had a bruise there on top of everything. I said something to her, something that probably wasn't very nice, and I felt a particularly nasty impulse race red from my brain to my hand.

My fingers clenched into a solid ball of muscle, bone, and power.

Claire looked up at me, worry and anger on her face, and for the first time, I saw myself reflected in her eyes. I saw what I was doing.

I knew that look. That face. I'd seen it throughout my childhood, when Dad came stumbling home from the bar. I'd seen it heavy-duty industrial strength after Alyssa died, twenty-four/seven.

Oh, God. God.

It was like some curtain got snapped back, flooding my insides with light, and I didn't like what I was seeing in myself, not at all. Fighting was one thing. But this . . . this was something else. It was me becoming what I never wanted to be.

. . . But deep down . . . way deep down, I realized why my dad had been the way he was. It was easy to let go of all those demons, let them roar.

And it felt good.
That was more frightening than anything else I'd ever known.

Claire actually saw something happen inside him, some kind of snap. Shane blinked, and then he was totally *Shane*—warm, real, and contrite. "Oh, God, I'm sorry," he said, and put his arms around her. "I didn't mean that. I'm so sorry." She felt his body language shift, and guessed he was looking at Michael, even while he was holding her. "Sorry, bro."

"Yeah," Michael said. He didn't sound convinced. "Okay. Just don't take it so seriously next time. It's just a game, man."

"I'll pick up a new controller tomorrow," Shane said. "Really. Sorry." Claire could tell from his tone that he meant it; he wasn't just saying it. And she guessed Michael could tell that, too. "I guess I just got too much adrenaline going."

Eve, who'd been lying on the floor, staring up at them, finally got to her feet. "Men," she said, and shook her head. "I am not picking up plastic shards. Collins, that's your job. Enjoy. I'm bouncing."

"Yeah, but are you *leaving*?" Shane asked. It was a weak effort at insult from him, but at least he'd tried. She gave him a quick smile and flipped him off—first time that evening—and headed upstairs. Claire caught herself yawning and checked her watch. Wow, it *was* late. And she had an early start in the morning.

She kissed Shane's cheek, and he turned his head and it turned into a much longer, sweeter kiss. Which she broke, regretfully, and said, "I have to get to bed, too."

He made a low, questioning sound in his throat. She blushed, because Michael was *right there*. Michael pretended to be doing something else, which didn't mean anything. Vampire senses. He could probably feel how fast her heart was racing. "No," she whispered, in Shane's ear. "I've got to rest."

"Okay," he whispered back, and kissed her neck, just where it made her shiver. He knew it was her favorite spot, and it made her weak in the knees. "I'll be good. Oh, wait, I'm always good. . . ."

"Stop it." Her voice didn't sound so sure now. "I need to *rest.*"

He let go of her and stepped back, hands up. "Cool," he said. "Go."

She did, reluctantly—and when she looked back, Shane was picking up shards of broken controller from the carpet, and Michael was watching him with a small frown still grooved between his eyebrows, as if he couldn't quite figure out what he was seeing.

Michael looked up at her as she paused on the steps. "Good night," he said.

She waved. "No fighting between the two of you," she said. "Promise?"

He crossed his heart and pretended to drive a stake into it, which made her smile and wince at the same time. "We'll be okay," he said. "Right, Shane?"

Shane looked up. "Right," he said. But there was something odd in his face when he looked at Michael, a kind of wariness that reminded Claire of the old days, when Michael had first turned vamp. Shane hadn't trusted him then, not at all.

And she wasn't sure why he'd suddenly decide not to trust Michael again . . . but she was almost sure that's what she was seeing.

It was all very confusing, and she was too tired to process it. But once she got in bed, with the moonlight falling cool over the sheets, she couldn't sleep after all. She tossed and turned, watching the black branches scratch at the windows like skeletal hands, and wondered what Shane was doing. She'd half expected him to come knock on her door, but he hadn't.

Finally, she started getting drowsy, and was almost asleep when she had the unmistakable impression that someone was in the room with her, *right there*, standing beside the bed.

She turned over, heart pounding. The moonlight didn't reach that side of the bed, and the room was dark, but she could make out something . . . a shadow . . .

And then the shadow stepped forward, into the light, and it was Myrnin. *Not* Shane.

He looked . . . dangerous. His dark hair curled black around his pale face, and his eyes were very wide, very dark. Claire opened her mouth to demand to know what the hell he was doing *here*, in her *bedroom*, but she didn't get the chance. His hand flashed out and covered her mouth with cold flesh.

She tried to scream, but it came out a muffled buzz, not nearly loud enough to alert anybody. Myrnin held a long, slender finger to his lips and bent close.

"So sorry to do this," he whispered. "I realize it's not appropriate. That's right, isn't it? Coming to a lady's boudoir without an invitation is still inappropriate, even in these lax social circles?"

She nodded emphatically. He didn't let go, probably because he could tell she was going to yell the house down if he did.

"Well, so sorry, but this is a bit of an emergency. Get dressed. Amelie wants to see us."

Oh. Well, vampires didn't keep regular people hours, but still. *Not cool.*

"Please don't scream," he said. "It would look so very bad for me, all things considered."

That, more than anything, made her nod. Myrnin's cold hand moved away, and she pulled in a deep, convulsive breath . . . but didn't yell. She *did* scoot all the way over in the bed, preparing to eject at a second's notice.

"You could have called," Claire said. Her voice sounded a little higher than usual. "I have a phone."

"I lost mine," he said. Claire could *so* believe that. "Stupid things. So small. So easy to put in a pocket and forget them when you wash your clothes . . . Well. It just seemed easier to come over. Are you dressed?"

"I can't *believe* you're asking me that. Standing in my bedroom in the middle of the night. Don't you think that's a little creepy? Maybe even perverted?"

"Ah, excellent point. I'll just . . . wait outside. But hurry. And tell no one."

Claire expected Myrnin to head for the bedroom door, but no, of course, that was too *normal*, wasn't it? Instead, he opened the window, the one that overlooked the backyard, and climbed through. He dropped down with all the ease of someone stepping off a curb, only it was twenty feet down, if not more.

Claire didn't even bother to look. Of course he was okay, and she didn't care if he wasn't. How *could* he just show up like this while she was *sleeping* . . .

She was fumbling in the dresser for clean underwear when there was a soft knock at the door. "Claire? You awake?"

Shane. She froze and held her breath. She wanted to open it, fall into his arms, and forget all about Myrnin and his weird behavior, but the truth was that Myrnin didn't show up for nothing. Something was wrong, and he'd said, *Tell no one.* That included Shane, unfortunately. She watched the doorknob, but it didn't turn, and after another quiet knock, she heard his footsteps moving away, toward his room.

Claire let out her breath, shook her head, and muttered, "And again, I hate you, Myrnin."

Dressed, if not exactly stylish, Claire stuck her head out of her bedroom window. As expected, Myrnin was pacing there, hands behind his back, head down. He was wearing some kind of neon-bright shirt that was probably a holdover from the eighties, and was back to his shorts and comfortable sandals. These were leather, at least, and looked kind of like something a guy would wear. If pushed.

Not exactly vampire chic, as pop culture defined it, but Myrnin wasn't one for fitting in. Ever.

He looked up at her, black hair falling back from his moon-pale face, and said, "Well? Jump!"

It was one thing for a vampire. Quite another for a breakable, not-too-athletic human. Claire shook her head. Myrnin sighed, tugged at his hair with both hands as if wanting to pull out his brain by the roots, and then seemed to have a bright idea. He dashed off into the darkness.

A moment later, he was back, carrying a ladder—and not their ladder. He'd ripped it off from a neighbor, Claire guessed. Well, it was better than jumping.

The climb down was chilly and scary, because Myrnin didn't think about bracing the ladder, which bounced and shifted uneasily with every step she took. Claire jumped the last couple of rungs, landing flat-footed, and whispered, "Where did this thing come from?"

"Oh, out there," Myrnin said, and waved vaguely at the darkness. "We don't have time for niceties. Keep up, please."

Oh, right. Myrnin didn't drive, so there was no car; that meant walking. In the dark. In Vampire City. Well, at least she had an escort, although he had longer legs and didn't bother to slow down for her, so she had to almost jog to stay with him.

"What's going on?" she asked, by the time they'd reached the corner of Lot Street. The streetlight was out. Most of the streetlights in Morganville stayed off when you needed them most. "What's the emergency?"

"I found out who killed your friend."

"Oh." She sucked in a deep breath as they crossed the street and took a right, heading for Founder's Square in the center of town. "Who?"

It was a simple question, but she didn't expect a simple answer. Myrnin was always being vague when she most needed clarity.

So it surprised her when he said, "Do you actually want to know?"

"Of course I do!"

"Think carefully before you answer. Do you want to know, Claire?"

That sounded . . . ominous. And Myrnin sounded very, very serious and in control, which was odd, to say the least.

"Is there some reason I shouldn't?" she asked. He glanced over at her, and she was unsettled again by the concern in his expression.

"Yes," he said. "Several that I can think of."

"Then why drag me out of bed about it?"

"Not my choice. Amelie's orders. Trust me, I objected. I was overruled."

Claire concentrated on walking for a few moments, until the

pale glow of the lights from Founder's Square warmed the night ahead of them. The houses they passed were silent and dark. Apart from a few barking dogs, nobody seemed to notice them.

"Tell me," she said. "Tell me before we get there. It's better if I know what I'm walking into."

"I knew you'd say that." She couldn't decide whether Myrnin approved or sounded resigned about it. "Very well. It's Eve's brother. Jason."

Jason. Well . . . that didn't shock her quite as much as it probably should have. Jason had sat with them at their dinner table. He'd even kind of saved her life once. But on the other hand, he'd terrorized her, threatened her, and he'd actually *hurt* Shane. With glee. Jason was not a good person, deep down.

"Eve's going to be so upset," Claire said. She couldn't imagine how bad her friend would feel; Eve had been so excited about Jason's supposed turnaround, so supportive of his attempts to make himself better. And now this. It would knock her flat.

"You're not surprised."

"Not . . . really. I mean, I'm disappointed more than surprised. I wanted him to be . . . better."

"Ah, Claire." Myrnin shook his head and reached out to give her a quick, fierce, one-armed hug. "You want us all to be better than we are. That's charming, and alarming. I've disappointed you many times."

"Not like this."

"Very much like this," he said. "But perhaps not so bloodily."

"What's going to happen to him?"

Myrnin gave her a long, sideways look. She realized that it maybe wasn't the most perceptive question she'd ever asked. "No," she said. "*No*, Myrnin. He didn't kill a vampire, no matter how it turns out. Human violence gets judged and punished by humans. That's the rule."

"Amelie makes the rules, dear child."

They were in a relatively deserted part of town now, heading for Founder's Square. Normally, Claire wouldn't have liked walking out here in blazing noon sun, not even with an escort, but having a vampire at her side had made her careless.

She never saw it coming, not until Myrnin suddenly stopped and raised his head, face gone still and unnaturally pale in the silvery moonlight. He usually had a kind of awkwardly angled grace that was almost human, but now he took on that weird vampire stillness that made Claire feel so . . . clumsy. So vulnerable.

Except Myrnin hadn't abruptly gone all fangy on her; he was focusing on something out in the dark.

"Claire," he said, in a low, soothing, carefully controlled voice. "I would like you to take out your mobile phone and call the police, please. Do that now. Perhaps that emergency number."

It was so utterly un-Myrnin that it scared her into fumbling her phone out of her pocket. "Why?" she whispered, as she started punching the three numbers in.

"Because it's an emergency," he said, and then something *hit him*, something faster than Claire could actually see, and she'd only just gotten the 911 entered and hadn't pressed CALL, and before Myrnin fell, something had her wrist in a crushing grip. She had a confused impression of a stench like the worst body odor in the world, like poor Stinky Doug times a thousand, and a feverish glitter of eyes, and a face that looked like a skeleton with skin stretched over it. . . .

With sharp, sharp, *sharp* fangs that glittered like knives and were heading straight for her throat.

Myrnin hit him—it?—with so much force that the two vampires skidded at least fifty feet, rolling and punching and fighting, and Claire realized that just standing there like a total idiot might not be the best survival strategy. She felt numb and stupid with shock, but she saw the glowing blue screen of her phone in the grass, scrambled for it, and hit the CALL button. She looked around wildly, trying to get her bearings; it all seemed dark and murky and strange, but she saw the street sign in the faint gleam of the underpowered streetlight at the corner.

She was only two blocks from Founder's Square.

Claire ran, holding the phone to her ear. Her heart was beating so fast it felt like a sledgehammer hitting her chest. The sidewalk was dark, very dark, but she didn't worry about cracks or uneven pavement or anything else but running as fast as she possibly could, heading for the somewhat questionable safety of even more vampires, and, *God*, she couldn't believe she was running *to* the vampires, but that thing, that thing wasn't—

"Nine-one-one. What is your emergency?"

She didn't have any breath, she realized. Claire gasped out something about where she was and was about to try to explain what the hell had just happened, when she tripped and the phone went flying as she lost her balance and momentum carried her forward into what was going to be a bone-snapping impact with the pavement.

She got her hands in front of her, but it wasn't the pavement she hit.

It was Myrnin, who caught her, gave her a look she couldn't read at all, and grabbed her fallen phone when she pointed numbly at it. He had blood on his face and long, animal scratches that were healing slowly. His clothes were ripped and shredded, too.

Without another word, he scooped her up in his arms and ran for Founder's Square. It didn't take long—thirty seconds, maybe—but Claire used the time to get her head back together and try to slow down her flailing heartbeat. *You're not going to die. Calm down.*

She ran it through her head again. Myrnin's alarm. The glimpse of that skeletonized face. The smell of death.

That had been a starving, savage vampire, and in Morganville, that shouldn't be happening. Vampires had ready access to the blood bank, if nothing else. If they were lawbreakers, they had plenty of easy targets. How did one get that skeletal, that savage? And why attack *Myrnin* first, before going for her? She'd had the feeling it had come for her only because she was calling for help.

It didn't make sense.

"Something's going on," she said as they turned the corner and she saw Founder's Square dead ahead. "Put me down."

"I'm fine," Myrnin said, and stopped to let her slip down to a standing position. "Thanks for asking, Claire. Considering I subjected myself to unimaginable danger to protect the contents of your veins and your immortal soul, one might imagine you to be able to ask." He was trying to be the old, casual Myrnin, but he was rattled, badly rattled. Claire found herself clutching her phone like a life preserver as she stepped away from him, and also realized that the police were still on the other end of the line, asking questions.

"Hello?" she said. "Police? You need to send a patrol car to—"

Myrnin took the phone away from her with a casual swipe of his hand and said, "Never mind. Everything's fine now, no problem at all. Thank you for protecting and serving. Please don't mind her at all." And hung up.

"Hey!" Claire lunged for the phone. He held it up out of her reach.

"If you send human police after him, they'll be handy snacks," he said. "And they will also die, if they're lucky. Come on." He grabbed her wrist and dragged her along at a quick-march pace. He was using a little bit more force than he should have, and Claire tried not to wince. She'd already been grabbed way too much at that particular collection of bones.

"What just happened?" she asked. "And don't tell me it was just a random vamp attack."

"It wasn't," he said. "And we'll talk when we're there. Not before."

They were coming up on the guard checkpoint now, and the uniformed policeman stepped out to give them a once-over. He nodded and waved them on. Myrnin didn't even slow down, so neither did Claire.

"Where are we going?"

"To talk to Jason, obviously."

"What? But—"

"I believe it's connected. Jason is a pawn on the board, and we need to confirm just whose pawn he is. It's thought that you might be able to extract that information from him."

"Wait—you . . . you want me to *interrogate* him?"

"Talk to him. You established a rapport with him before; he may say things to you he would not to vampires. As a fellow human, you're already advantaged."

"Advantaged?"

"Let's just say that he's developed a deep distrust of vampire kind."

"What the hell did you do to him?"

Myrnin didn't look at her. Now they were walking down a wide sidewalk, spacious, framed by tall dark trees on both sides. Pretty in daylight. A prime ambush place in the dark. But there were vampires out strolling in the moonlight, living their lives in an entirely weird and alien sort of way from what she knew. Here, that awful skeletal thing wouldn't attack. It wouldn't dare.

She suddenly, badly, wanted to be back home.

"Myrnin? What *was* that?"

He didn't say another word, all the way to the building where Jason was being held.

FIVE

Being in a vampire stronghold, essentially alone, was horribly unnerving . . . especially since Claire realized that she'd sneaked out a window, and nobody, not even Shane, knew where she was. That hadn't been the best plan ever, probably. *Note to self: in the future, leave an I-know-who-killed-me message.* Morbid, but practical, at least in her social circles.

This wasn't the clean, sterile confines of the building where Amelie had her offices—although that was funeral-home creepy—but a different building, a windowless structure that didn't have the chilly elegance of marble and thick carpeting. It was more . . . functional. Bare walls. Harsh lights. Plain floors.

And it smelled like disinfectant, which was very frightening.

There was a plain wooden desk in the entry hall, and a vampire Claire recognized—one who'd originally had dark skin, but vampire life had lightened it to an unsettling ashen gray. He was blind in one eye, and when he saw her, he smiled, all teeth.

She'd first met him in the library at Texas Prairie University, and he'd tried to kill her. Not a very nice vampire at all, in her experience.

"It's the apprentice vampire hunter," he said. "Good. I was getting hungry. Thanks for bringing me lunch."

"She's with me, John," Myrnin said, and waggled his finger. "No snacking. And, besides, you'd have to ask Amelie's permission first. Which you wouldn't get, you know. You're on probation for your last, ah, incident concerning a Morganville resident with a pulse."

The vampire shrugged and looked disappointed. "Fine. What do you want?"

"None of your business, John. Just do your job and be quiet," Myrnin said, and pulled her along. "This way."

They passed through a *very* thick steel door, one that slammed shut with a finality that made Claire shiver, and then through a series of barred gates that looked thick enough to discourage even vampires. Some were warped. Some even had fingerprints pressed into the metal where vamps had tried to bend it. Unsuccessfully, it looked like.

They all locked behind her, cutting off any possibility of retreat. Yeah, that note she didn't leave was looking more important all the time. Claire furtively eased her cell phone from her pants pocket and checked the reception.

Zero bars. Of course. She couldn't even text for help.

Myrnin glanced back at her as they walked down the long, featureless hallway. Well, *featureless* was wrong—it was meant to be featureless, but, in fact, it had all kinds of scratches, gouges, and chunks torn out of it. Probably by people and vampires struggling to get free. Definitely not design features, because one of the gouges held a spark of red that, as Claire looked closer, became a torn-off, red-painted fingernail tip.

"Are you all right?" he asked her. She nodded, determined not to show him how unnerved she felt. "It's just down here."

He paused in front of just another doorway, one without a knob. It had a keypad next to it, and Myrnin entered some numbers and pressed his thumb to a glass plate. The door popped open with a hiss of air, as if it had been pressurized inside.

No sound at all, other than that.

Myrnin swung it open and stepped inside first—in case, Claire guessed, Jason was waiting with some blunt object, or, knowing Jason, a sharp one. But he needn't have bothered, because Jason was sitting braced against the wall, knees up, on the small, narrow prison bed. He was dressed in glaring white hospital scrubs, stenciled with the word PRISONER on the front and, she supposed, the back.

He looked up at them, expressionless. Beneath the tangled mop of dark hair, his face was still and set, his eyes as blank as stones.

"Hey, Jason," Claire said. She sounded nervous. Well, she was. "Is it okay if I sit down?" The only place to sit was on the bed. Jason didn't say yes, but he didn't say no, either, so she sank down on the end farthest from him. "Are you okay?"

He shrugged. It was just a very, very small movement of his shoulders, hardly anything at all. His dead-looking eyes moved quickly toward Myrnin, then back to her.

Jason was dangerous; she knew that. She's seen him hurt Shane; she'd seen him do worse than that, too. *If I get up and leave, nobody would blame me,* she thought. *Not even Eve.*

But the thought of Eve, crying and miserable, made Claire find the last, fraying threads of resolve and hang on tight. She looked at Myrnin, who was standing in the corner, near the door. "Would you mind waiting out there?" she asked him.

"Outside of this room."

"Yes."

"You're quite certain."

She wasn't, but she nodded, anyway. *It's a sad day when Myrnin is the safe choice*, she thought. Apparently, he thought so, too, because he gave her a long, troubled look before pressing his thumb to a glass plate inside the room and opening the door.

After it had closed behind him, Claire looked back at Jason. "Better?"

For a second, she thought she saw a ghost of a bitter little smile, but it was gone before she could be sure. "You think they're not watching?" he asked.

"I'm pretty sure they are. Sorry."

He shrugged again. "Doesn't matter. Why are you here?"

"Myrnin brought me."

"He thought I'd talk to you."

"Yeah, I guess."

Jason slowly shook his head. "Got nothing to say."

"Jason—this is serious. This isn't just something that's going to land you in jail for a while. This is *murder*. In *Texas*. They don't fool around in this state, never mind in this town."

This time, she didn't even get a shrug. Just a blank stare.

"They want to know who put you up to it. Who hired you to steal the blood back from Doug?"

"Who's Doug?"

"The guy you killed," she said, staring him straight in the eyes. "My friend."

That made him flinch, just a little. Barely a shiver, but there. "Sorry," he said. He didn't sound particularly sorry, though. "You've got the wrong guy. Didn't do it."

"They're pretty sure you did."

"They're always sure, but that doesn't mean they know. You think they care who actually did it? Their idea of justice is to haul in the usual dickheads and throw somebody to the wolves. Doesn't matter who it is."

"You're saying you're not guilty."

"I'm the usual dickhead. Claire, you don't understand. *It doesn't matter.* I'm the one who's going down for it." He shrugged again. "Whatever."

"*Whatever?* Jason, it's *murder!* I know you're . . . not perfect—"

He laughed. It was a dry, papery sound, no amusement behind it at all.

"—but I know you've never killed anyone."

"Oh yeah? You know that. You're sure."

Well . . . maybe *sure* wasn't the right word. "I'm sure you'd tell me if you did it."

"Why?"

"Because you're not afraid," she said. "You're not afraid to freak me out. You'd *rather* freak me out. But you won't lie about it."

"Oh, I lie."

"I know. But you don't lie to me. Not anymore." She leaned forward. The smell of the cell—industrial cleaners, sweat, fear—made her throat ache, or maybe that was just her general tension. "Not since you tried to save my life."

He looked away, and that was a victory, Claire thought. They'd never talked about it, never had the chance, but here, he was a captive audience.

"You knew I was going to die down there in the tunnels. And you went to get the cops, even though you knew it would get you arrested. You tried to save my life when you could have just run."

"I *didn't* save your life, though. They didn't believe me. So all I got for it was jail. No good deed goes unpunished, right?"

"It still means something to me that you tried. That's why you'll tell me the truth, Jason. You care enough about what I think that you'll try again."

He gave her a look, one she couldn't interpret. "You think a lot of yourself."

"No," Claire said softly. "Not really. I think you know that, too."

Silence. She thought that it was going to go on forever, that she'd have to get up and leave him here to whatever would happen next, but then Jason said, "I didn't kill him. But I know what happened."

Progress. "Okay. So, what happened?"

"All I did was get the killer into the dorm and show him where to find the guy. Your friend. Doug."

"Get *who* into the dorm?"

His answer caught her by surprise, but suddenly, the overwhelming vampire response in the middle of the night all made sense, because he said, "I didn't know who he was at first. I mean, he was filthy and skinny and all kinds of crazy."

"Who?"

"That old guy, the one who gave Amelie so much trouble. Mr. Bishop."

Bishop is out. And he was starving. And he was massively pissed off.

And, Claire realized with an icy, horrible, sickening shock, she had just seen him out on the street, going after Myrnin. *That* was why he'd seemed familiar. The terrifying night stalker out there *was* the boogeyman.

No wonder the vampires were panicking.

*   *   *

Once he started talking, Jason had a lot to say. He'd been approached by a guy he knew, somebody on the not-so-legal side of Morganville society, who paid him cash to find out details about a TPU student . . . Doug. Jason delivered the info, but then was told that to get the rest of his money, he'd have to escort a visitor to Doug's dorm room. That sounded simple enough, until Jason arrived at the tunnel where he'd been told to meet his contact, and discovered that it wasn't just any old vamp waiting for him—it was Bishop. Amelie's vampire father. And the meanest, coldest vampire Claire had ever met. He made that creepy bald guy from the old movie *Nosferatu* look sweet—and a little handsome, even. There was something so icy and wrong about Bishop that it made her shiver to remember him . . . and she'd thought, honestly, that he'd been executed.

Turns out that if he had, *that* hadn't gone as planned, either.

"I didn't know it would happen," Jason said, looking down. He'd put his arms around his knees and drew them in, and he looked thinner and younger than Claire in that moment. A scared little boy. "I was standing there when Doug opened the door, and Bishop just   waved his hand. Or that's what it looked like. Next thing I know, Doug is on his back, on the bed, throat cut, and he's bleeding out. Bishop takes something out of his backpack and he says, *Did you think you could threaten me?* And I book the hell out of there. I didn't care who saw me. I just cared about getting away before he decided to get rid of the loose ends. The look on his face—I thought he might kill everybody in the whole dorm." Jason swallowed. "He was having fun. And he was starving."

Claire thought about the two students on the floor conducting their stereo wars, not even aware of death passing by. Lucky. So lucky. "What did he take?"

"Search me. Looked like a vial of something, and some papers. But it's not like I *wanted* to know. I was mostly just getting the hell out. Believe me, I wished I hadn't seen anything and didn't know anything." Jason rested his forehead against his knees. "I don't know where Bishop is. I don't know what he's doing. And, trust me, I don't work for him. It was just supposed to be an introduction, a friend-of-a-friend kind of a thing. I figured he was scoring drugs or something. Once I realized who he was, I should have just gotten the hell out, but I was too scared to run. I knew if I didn't get him where he wanted to go, he'd—"

Claire could only imagine what Bishop would have done if disappointed, and it wasn't good, that was certain. "It's not your fault," she said. "You didn't have a choice." Jason was lucky to be alive at all.

"And I don't have a choice *now*, either," he said. "Claire, if they think they can torture some info out of me about where Bishop's new hideout is, they can't. I'd give it up if I had it, in a heartbeat, because, damn, does that thing scare me. But I just don't *know* anything."

She believed him. She glanced up, looking for the cameras, and found a tiny glass eye in the far corner of the ceiling. She stared up at it for a few seconds, wondering who was watching this. Amelie, almost certainly. And probably Myrnin, if he wasn't still lurking on the other side of the door.

"I'm going to try to get you out of here, Jason," she said. "I don't know if I can do anything for you with the police, though."

He shrugged, falling into that silence again. His eyes still looked dead, but now she realized that it wasn't indifference.

It was fear.

She got up and walked toward the door, waiting. The lock disengaged and the door popped open.

"Claire?" Jason said suddenly. She looked back. "If I don't see you again, thanks for trying. Nobody ever tried before. Not even Eve. I mean, she's my sister and I love her, but . . . I think she always knew I was a lost cause."

That was the saddest thing she'd ever heard. Claire tried for a smile, but she didn't think it was authentic. And Jason didn't smile back.

"You'll see me again," she said. "I promise."

She hoped she wasn't lying, as the door clicked shut behind her and locked with a thick, chunky sound of metal. The hallway was deserted, both directions, just straight lines and scratches on the walls and a sense of despair as thick as the white paint.

And then the vampire from the front desk—John, the one who'd called her the apprentice vampire hunter—appeared in the corridor. Claire stopped dead in her tracks, tense and ready for anything. He stared at her for a second, then beckoned.

She stayed where she was.

"Suit yourself," he said. "I was told to get you out. You want to stay, I can make that happen, girl. I got plenty of open cells."

"I'm waiting for Myrnin."

"You'll be waiting a while," he said. "He's up with the boss lady. You come with me or get in a cell. Your choice."

If Amelie was watching the closed-circuit feeds, she'd see Claire in the hallway and witness whatever might happen. Hopefully John knew that, too. That, and only that, made Claire nod and move toward the other vampire.

He didn't touch her. He opened and closed gates, and finally they were in the last section, barred at one end, thick steel door at the other.

And, Claire realized, there were no cameras right in this particular section.

Oh, God.

John stopped and turned toward her. "I don't forget what you did," he said. He tapped the skin below his clouded, blind eye, eerily silver. "This is on you. You hurt me so bad, it's never going to heal."

Well, she'd done this to herself, trapped with a vamp who *really* didn't like her, knowing she was responsible for his current not-so-great looks. "You were trying to kill me when I did that," she said. "So it's on you. If it helps, it makes you look way scarier than before."

He bared fangs, and the look on his face made her feel painfully aware of the blood running under her skin and the terror that seemed to be growing spikes in her stomach. "You want to say that again?" he said. "How it was my fault you threw liquid nitrogen in my face?"

"Maybe it's shared responsibility," she said. "But that's as far as I'm willing to go. Now open the door."

"Once I'm done," he said. "Eye for an eye. That's what the Bible says."

"I'm thinking you don't live by the commandments too much."

"Oh, I do. I pay special attention to the parts I agree with, same as everybody else. Now, if you stand still, it won't take long." He grinned evilly. "Not saying it won't hurt, of course. What'd be the point if it didn't hurt?"

She took a giant step back. Useless. Close quarters, no place to run, no weapons. Hand to hand with a much bigger, stronger, vampire-type dude, she had zero chance, and she knew it.

But she wasn't going to beg. Even if the screaming voice in her head wanted her to.

Should have left that I-know-who-killed-me note.

And then the door next to her popped open with a harsh buzzing sound. She didn't hesitate. As the vampire lunged for her, she shoved the door open and ran out into the lobby, dodging the wooden desk.

The angry vamp came after her and skidded to a fast stop when he saw who was standing there in his path.

Amelie.

She wasn't a tall woman, but she *looked* tall in her carefully tailored silk jacket and skirt and heels, with her pale hair piled on top of her head in a crown. The silk clothes were one shade paler than her skin, giving her a sleek, marble look that was enhanced by the stillness of her body.

"I also believe in an eye for an eye, John," she said. "Quite strongly, in fact. It's one of my founding principles. You'd do well to remember that."

John gave Claire a fast, furious look, and bowed his head. "Yes, ma'am. I will."

"I believe I employ you for a specific job, John. Guarding a very valuable, and possibly very dangerous, prisoner."

"You do, ma'am."

"Then perhaps it might be good for you to return to it and stop indulging your own petty little grudges."

He silently crossed to the desk and sat down behind it. Claire let out a trembling breath. She would have said *thank you*, but she didn't think Amelie wanted to hear that, not now.

"You did me good service, Claire," Amelie said, turning to face her. "And now I need your word that you will forget what you heard here tonight."

"You mean about—"

"I mean *forget*," the vampire queen of Morganville said, and the force of her personality hit Claire like a wall of cold water. "I can't compel you, but I *can* assure you that if you share the information you heard here, I will know. And we've already established how I view betrayals, I believe."

This wasn't Amelie, the one who'd sometimes unbent enough to *smile* . . . no, this was Queen Amelie, the Founder of Morganville, who never smiled. The daughter of Bishop. The one who'd survived ages and every enemy thrown at her through all those dangerous years.

And Claire never doubted for a second that she meant what she said.

"I won't say anything," she said. "But I need help getting home."

"You'll have it. Myrnin!" Amelie's voice was sharp, brittle, and impatient. "Out here. Now."

A section of the wall opened—one that Claire would never have guessed for a door—and Myrnin leaned out, eyebrows raised. "Then we're finished here?"

"For now," Amelie said. "Take her home. And—"

"Say nothing—yes, yes, I heard you the first seven hundred times," Myrnin said, much too sharply. "I'm ancient. I'm not *deaf.*"

Amelie's cold expression deepened, and her gray eyes took on an unpleasant reddish glitter. "Do you think I find this a joking matter?"

"Maybe you should," he said. "And maybe you should have cut

off the old man's head when you had the chance. Absolutely no one would have argued with that choice. Merely walling him up, to increase his suffering and create an example—that was unmerciful, and, worse, it was sloppy. I believe that flapping sound you hear is pigeons, coming home to roost."

If Amelie had looked any colder, Claire would have expected frost to form on the floor around her. "Really? Because I believe it's the sound of my patience with your nonsense running out. *Old friend.* Do remember your limits."

He crossed the room in a flash, standing toe-to-toe with her. He was taller than she was, and gangly, and raggedly just the opposite of her elegance . . . but there was something about him, something that made Claire catch her breath and hold it. "I am your friend," he said quietly. "I've always been your friend, dear one. But on the subject of your father, you've never been very rational. Don't let him drive you. Don't play with him; he'll always be crueler than you. *Kill him when you find him.* I'd have killed him for you just now, if I'd been able. But he's fast and strong, and I couldn't afford to let him bite me. He can assemble an army frighteningly fast. You have to find him, and when you do, you must execute him. Immediately."

For a second, Claire thought that he'd reached her—that she was listening to the quiet pain in his voice. But then her pale, strong hand closed around Myrnin's throat and *squeezed.* Spots of blood formed where her fingernails dug in. With a single jerk, she pulled him off balance and sent him crashing to his knees and held him there.

He didn't try to struggle. Claire wasn't sure he could; there was a thick, cold wave of menace coming from Amelie that froze Claire where she stood.

Amelie bent toward him very slowly and said, "My hateful father never had a better student than me, Myrnin. And I *will* kill him, but I'll do it in my own time. Don't tell me what to do, or I might find it necessary to remind you that *I* am the Founder of Morganville. Not *you*."

"I never forget," Myrnin said in a choked whisper. "Certainly not with your nails in my throat. They're quite an excellent mnemonic device."

She blinked and let him go. As she stepped away, she frowned down at her bloodstained fingernails.

Myrnin rose to his feet in a smooth, effortless motion, and whipped a black handkerchief out of the pocket of his shorts. She took it without a word, wiped away the blood, and gave it back. He cleaned the red from his neck. The wounds had already closed.

"That's the second time I've spilled my blood for you tonight," he said. "I believe I've made my point, and you've made yours, most graphically. So I'll be taking my leave. Oh, and Claire. I'll be taking Claire."

Amelie nodded. There was a slight groove between her eyebrows—the ghost of a frown. As Myrnin and Claire—who'd finally dared to breathe again—headed for the outer door, Amelie said, "You're right. My father's escape has . . . unsettled me."

"Couldn't tell," Myrnin said. "My advice is sound. Don't punish him. Don't make an example of him. When you find him, kill him quickly and quietly. It's the only peace you can hope for. You can't afford to allow him to become a power in this town again. Someone is working with him, helping him, or you'd have him by now. He wouldn't dare to be out there, hunting. This is going to go bad, quickly. *Act.*"

She nodded slightly, still frowning.

And Myrnin grabbed Claire's arm and propelled her fast, outside, down the steps, and into the dark. This time, he ordered one of Amelie's cars.

Armored.

The fact that Myrnin had actually been scared enough to be careful with her . . . that said more about the danger than anything else.

SIX

The ladder was still in place when she got home. Myrnin, in typical Myrnin fashion, delivered her to the base of the ladder, and by the time she'd climbed three steps and looked back, he was gone. Of course. She pulled herself up the rest of the way, *carefully*, trying not to notice how the ladder shivered and rocked around as she shifted her weight.

Achieving the open window was a massive relief, and she wriggled through and landed with an unbalanced *thump* on the floor. It was still dark outside, but not for too much longer—another hour and a half, max, from her glance at the glowing digital clock on the bedside table.

God, this was *terrible*. Just when she'd thought things in Morganville might be stabilizing, just a little bit . . . now Bishop was on the loose again. He'd come so frighteningly close to bringing it all down once; he considered Amelie and everyone in town his rightful property. His playthings.

What he'd do this time now that he was actually *angry* . . .

Myrnin was right. Claire wasn't one to yell for anybody to die, but for Bishop, she'd make an exception. He needed killing, quickly.

Why was he still here? Why hadn't he blown out of Morganville first thing?

Revenge. He was the kind who lived for it. And what had Jason said that Bishop had said to Stinky Doug? *Did you think you could threaten me?*

How could a mere human ever hope to threaten Bishop enough to draw his full, personal attention, in broad daylight, in a public place?

Doug had something. The blood—sure, that was bad enough, but he'd had other things. Papers. Bishop had taken them.

Doug had been blackmailing *Bishop*. Not only Bishop, though—because Bishop couldn't be out on his own. He'd have been caught already.

Claire sank down on the bed, rested her head in her hands for a moment, and then began to untie her shoes.

Then she heard something.

Voices. Low voices, coming from down the hall. Michael, probably, talking to Shane or Eve . . . but it didn't sound right, somehow.

She took off her shoes and walked to the door in her socks. It wasn't locked; she hardly ever locked it. The knob was cold in her hand but turned easily, and she pulled back until there was a narrow crack of light coming through from the hallway, and she could see . . .

Nothing. No sign of anybody in the hallway. She opened the door wider, slowly, and edged out. *This is stupid. It's my own house. I should be able to just walk right down there. . . .*

Except it didn't feel that way. It was, she realized, the house itself. The Glass House had always been a little bit alive, and just now it felt . . . anxious. Worried, maybe. And that was making her move quietly and cautiously.

The voices were muffled, but they were coming from down the hall.

From Shane's room.

Maybe he's watching TV. But he didn't usually watch TV. She supposed he could have turned it on and fallen asleep, but . . . no, she was almost sure that one of those voices was Shane's.

And the other one was a girl's.

And then the girl *laughed.* And it wasn't a friendly laugh; it was a low-in-the-throat, teasing laugh, a flirting laugh.

Oh, *hell*, no, that wasn't going to happen.

Seeing red, Claire gritted her teeth and grabbed the handle of the door, staring at the rusted metal of the TRESPASSERS WILL BE SHOT sign that Shane had nailed up on his door.

She was not going to take this lying down. Or at all.

SHANE
☽

I couldn't sleep after Michael and the broken controller and Claire. I felt restless and weird and wired, like I'd drunk about fifteen cups of coffee and chased it with Red Bull. Not a good feeling. I tried the headphones, but blasting speed metal through my skull didn't help, either. I had a heavy bag in the basement, and I could have gone down there to work off some frustration, but it seemed like the wrong thing. Just . . . wrong.

Finally, I got up and prowled the house. Michael was still up, strumming his guitar downstairs. That was usually cool—I liked his music, always had—but tonight I just wanted him to shut up. I didn't want to be reminded of him, of having a vampire living a few feet away and pretending to pass for human. It hadn't bothered me so much recently, but now all that discomfort was back with a vengeance.

I thought I heard whispers coming from Claire's room, but they were faint and my ears were still buzzing from the headphones. I thought about her, and the next thing I knew I wanted . . . Well, I'm a guy. You know what I wanted. If she was awake, maybe she felt the same way.

Maybe being so close together would make both of us feel less . . . trapped.

I knocked, the quiet way I always had, and maybe I had imagined it, because there wasn't any sound at all, nothing. She's asleep, I told myself. Chill out. Go take a cold shower. Or I could work my sore fists against the heavy bag; that would do the same thing—wear me out, drain the adrenaline out of my overactive body.

Instead, I went back to roaming the house.

I don't know when exactly I noticed the ladder; about two hours later, probably. I had wandered down to the kitchen to fix myself a sandwich. Michael had bagged his rehearsal and gone upstairs to bed, so I had the darkness and shadows to myself. I thought about practicing for the rematch on Dead Rising, but even that didn't have any appeal.

As I passed the window at the back, I saw a glint of silver outside where it shouldn't have been. I backed up, and, dammit, there was a ladder leaning up against the side of the house. A big silver ladder that didn't belong to us.

I stared at it for a few seconds, then realized that it was leading up to Claire's window, and my stomach went cold and twisted and I ran up the stairs, three at a time, down the hall, and threw open her *door, ready to attack whatever was in the room with her, ready to kill or die, and . . .*

. . . and she wasn't there. Nobody was there. Her bed was rumpled, but when I touched the mattress it was cold. She'd been gone a while.

Ladder. Open window. I tried to imagine Claire being abducted without making a sound, and I just couldn't. She'd have found a way to fall off the ladder, if nothing else, or bang it against the house.

It had all happened so quietly that she had to have done it herself, on purpose.

She'd left, and she'd gone without even telling me. Probably with some vamp, I thought; she trusted them way too much. She just didn't have that instinct that Morganville natives had growing up, to mistrust everybody, always.

If it was that ass hat Myrnin who'd lured her away in the middle of the night, I was going to have to hurt him. Bad enough he acted like he owned her when she was at his lab, but hell if he got to come here, to our house, and haul my girl away in the thick of darkness, for who knew what insane reason.

She didn't see him that way, but Myrnin was still a guy. An old, lonely guy. I'd seen him looking at her, and maybe it was just fondness, and maybe it was something else—truthfully, from time to time I've wondered about that, and him and her. It sometimes made me want to wrap my hands around his neck, but I hadn't. Yet. I didn't believe Claire had any idea Myrnin felt anything for her at all.

For Claire's sake, I'd hidden a lot of what I felt about her boss, but lately it had come leaking out a little. And Myrnin didn't like me much, either—I'd seen it in his eyes, especially when he'd found us together in his lab. Myrnin was territorial; so was I. Claire wouldn't like that, but it was a cold fact.

And if Myrnin had taken her somewhere, from my territory . . . if he did anything to her . . . Well. I was going to spill some crazy vamp blood. Maybe a lot of it.

I sat in the dark and stared at that ladder for a long, long time before I went back to my room, stuck the headphones back on, turned on the TV to some brainless flickering channel, and zoned out, because there was nothing else to do right now.

When I opened my eyes again, there was a dream girl sitting on my bed.

I knew it was a dream because I felt no sense of alarm at seeing her; it was like she was supposed to be there, so there was no reason to get scared or think it was weird. She was beautiful, too, in a whole different way from Claire: long blond hair that rippled in thick waves around her heart-shaped face, all the way down her back. Small, but with a lot of personality; her smile was like morning sunrise, and she had eyes the color of summer skies. And, yeah, okay, I checked her out. She was worth checking—curves, nice ones, in all the right places. Not fashion-model skinny, but real-girl sexy.

It occurred to me after a few seconds of admiring all that lushness that I shouldn't be feeling quite this attracted to a vampire. Because she was a vamp, of course. One hundred percent. You'd think that if I'd wanted to put a couple of vamps through the wall earlier, including my own best friend, I'd have felt the same way about her, but . . . I didn't. I liked her.

Just like that.

And I kind of recognized her in a distant way. Like I'd seen her before or known her before. But I didn't feel compelled to reason it out, either.

"You were impressive today," she said. Even her voice sounded like a dream, like one of those voices you hear in whispers that leaves you feeling warm and sweaty when you wake up. "Vassily was surprised,

you know. He's never had a human touch him in a fight, let alone put him on the mat. I think he was impressed as well as annoyed."

"Thanks," I said. I was smiling at her, and it felt good. "It felt good, taking him down a peg."

"It was enjoyable to watch. You're so very . . . solid." She looked at me through lowered eyelashes, and my heart almost stopped. She just had that kind of presence and power. Like a dream. She was a dream, of course. She had to be. Every few minutes, one of those sex-line commercials was coming on TV. She was probably put together in my brain out of that, and the vampire obsession I seemed to be developing. Even the voice sounded like something you'd pay money to hear murmur your name. "Vassily said it earlier, but he wanted me to extend a personal invitation to you to join his exclusive sparring group. But you can't tell anyone, whether you decide to join or not. It's more fun that way. Our secret, you see."

"Fun," I echoed. "Are you in it?"

"Only as a spectator," she said, and smiled again, a slow, wicked stretch of those wet, full lips. "I'm a lover, not a fighter, Shane. Although I'm quite sure you're both."

I felt hot all over, and, yeah, again, I'm a guy—don't judge. I love Claire, I do, but this was a dream. And besides, Claire had just ditched me to run off on her own when I needed her.

I tried to think about Claire, but the perfume in the air was so strong, so sweet, and I could almost feel how good it would be to sink into this dream, let it take me away. . . .

"I think it's time for me to go," Dream Girl said, and I felt a cool brush of lips on my cheek. It made me shiver all over. She laughed, low in her throat. "Do think about my proposition, sweet boy. I'll talk to you soon."

"When?"

"When you come to the new group," she whispered, and put her fingertips against my lips. *"Quiet now. Someone's here."*

Best dream ever.

Right up until the door flew open.

Inside the room, Shane said, "When?" and Claire just couldn't stand it, not at all.

She threw open the door so forcefully it banged into the wall and almost hit her on the backswing.

There was a blur of motion, too fast for her eyes to track, and a flutter of curtains at the window, and when she blinked, Shane was sitting alone on his bed, headphones on, looking dazed. He picked up the remote, flipping channels on the TV, moving like a sleepwalker.

"Shane?"

He looked up at her, face bathed in that pale blue light, and for a second, he didn't look anything like the Shane she knew.

Then he looked straight at the screen again as he shoved his headphones back.

"Hey. I thought you were sleeping," he said. "Then I checked again, and you were gone."

All her righteous indignation fell into confusion. She'd been going to accuse *him*, not the other way around . . . but now, she wasn't sure anymore what she'd actually seen. A blur. It could have been the flickering TV light combined with the wind blowing the curtains on the window. And the voices . . . the voices could have been the TV, too.

But she, on the other hand, had undeniably sneaked away, in the middle of the night, without telling him.

"There was a ladder under your window," he continued. "And unless you were planning to do late-night house painting, I don't know why you'd be out there climbing on a ladder. Front door's perfectly good if you want to leave, far as I know."

"I had to . . . It was—" This was ridiculous. She hadn't come in here to *be* confronted. "Who was in here with you? I heard her talking to you."

Shane raised his eyebrows and looked back at the TV, where a woman was lying around in skimpy lingerie, talking on the phone and winking at the camera. Some kind of phone sex ad. "You mean her? She's been on five times an hour. Sometimes they even run the ads back-to-back."

"No, I mean—" What *did* she mean? How had this gone so wrong, so fast? "I mean, there was a girl in here. A vampire." It had to be a vampire, to move so fast.

Shane shook his head. "You're kidding, right? You know how I feel about them. And I'm not a fang-banger."

"You said you'd stop saying that." Because of Eve, of course. And Michael.

"Yeah, well, nobody here but us breathers. Or is that something I can't say, either?"

She was losing the thread of all this. It was all slipping away, like a dream at dawn. "Shane, I *saw* her. I thought—"

"Yeah," he said. "I thought the same thing when you were gone without saying a word to me. Just be straight with me, okay? Was it Myrnin?"

She was speechless, absolutely speechless. For one thing, she couldn't lie about it—it *had* been Myrnin who'd shown up in her room in the middle of the night. And she *had* run off with him. And now, inexplicably, she felt guilty about it, too. She could feel a traitorous burn in her cheeks, but the words just wouldn't come to save her.

Shane's face went still and cold. "Yeah. That's what I thought."

"Shane, I—"

"Morganville's changing you," he said. "You used to be scared of them, but the more you're around *him*, the more you think the vamps can be your friends. They aren't. They can't be. They're ranchers. We're cattle."

Where the hell was all this coming from? She knew how he felt about the vampires, about Morganville, but this seemed—so edgy. So bitter. "We're here," she said. "We have to make the best of it until we can leave. You've said so yourself."

Shane shook his head, still not looking at her. He looked drawn now, and a little bit haunted. "I need to get you out of this place before it's too late. I should have done it before the barriers went back up around town, but now . . . now it's going to be more difficult. Got to do it, though. You can't be here anymore."

"Shane, what are you talking about? What makes you think I want to go right now?"

Suddenly, his focus shifted, and she felt hot and cold all over at the passion and intensity in his eyes. "Why wouldn't you want to go? Because of him? Myrnin?"

"No!" She felt appalled now, entirely out of control. This had *not* gone anything like she'd thought. "God, Shane, are you *jealous*?"

"Do I need to be? 'Cause you're running away in the middle of the night with him, Claire."

"I— But it was—"

He turned away. "Just go, Claire. I can't talk right now."

She felt tears well up in her eyes, tears of anger and sheer, maddening frustration. It didn't matter what she said now. Shane had just shut her out, as effectively as if he'd slammed the door between them.

As she watched, he turned off the TV, pulled up the blanket, and rolled over on his side.

Away from her.

"Shane," she whispered.

No response.

She couldn't take it—she *couldn't*. Maybe it would have been better to stay there, tell him everything, but she felt trapped. She felt like she couldn't breathe, and she just wanted . . . wanted . . .

She wanted out.

Claire didn't even make the conscious decision to run, but she did—out the door, into her own room, slamming and locking it behind her.

And then she sank down to a crouch against the door, wrapped her arms around herself, and cried like her heart was broken.

Which, in fact, it was.

SEVEN

Morning felt like the end of the world. Claire didn't remember sleeping, but she supposed she must have a little. Outside her window the sun was shining, and when she pulled the sash up a warming breeze fluttered the white curtains. It was going to be a nice day.

For the end of the world, anyway.

She rolled over in bed and found herself facing a lot of empty space—space that Shane had occupied sometimes, whether they were just lying together talking or watching TV or . . . doing other things. But no Shane. Not today. That side of the bed was smooth.

Claire rolled back over to face the other side, which was just a view of the blank wall and a dresser. On the dresser was a picture of her and Shane, arms around each other, laughing.

She squeezed her eyes shut. They felt raw and red, swollen from crying, and she knew she looked as miserable as she felt.

Get up, she told herself. *You can't just lie around here all day, feeling sorry for yourself.*

But if she got up, she might run into Shane in the hall or down-stairs in the kitchen or . . .

Get up. You live here, too.

She didn't want to, but the idea of wallowing around in her misery didn't sound so great, either. She was tired of crying, and her head hurt. She needed something to drink, something to eat, and to tell Eve all about it.

Crawling out from under the covers, Claire realized that she was still wearing the clothes she'd thrown on to follow Myrnin; she hadn't bothered, in her generally awful mood, to undress. She took a fresh set with her to the bathroom (she noted that Shane's door was closed as she passed) and showered and dressed and fixed her hair. When she realized that she was actually taking lon-ger than Eve generally did, mainly to avoid any possibility of com-ing into contact with *him*, she sucked in a deep breath, dumped the old clothes in the laundry basket, and reached for the bathroom doorknob.

Her cell phone went off, scaring her so badly, she banged her elbow into the sink while reaching into her pants pocket. *Ow.* That hurt, hurt bad enough to make her take an extra second of deep breaths to stare down at the lit-up screen. She didn't recog-nize the number, not even the area code. *Probably a wrong number.*

She answered, and a voice on the other end, sounding brisk and businesslike, said, "May I speak with Claire Danvers, please?"

"I'm Claire." She swallowed a bubble of anxiety. Could it be about her dad? No, he was doing better—he'd said so himself. Everything was all right.

Then why was some stranger calling her? *Now?*

"My name is Mr. Radamon, and I am in charge of the Atomic, Biophysics, Condensed Matter, and Plasma Physics program at

the Massachusetts Institute of Technology. Did you receive our
letter?"

Claire went entirely blank. "Your . . . letter?"

"You applied for admission into our program last year," Mr.
Radamon said. He sounded so . . . *normal*. So *human*. Somehow,
she'd expected an MIT honcho to sound more godlike, with
thunder rolling in the background. "We replied about six months
ago with an acceptance letter to your home address. I just wanted
to be sure you got it."

"Oh. *Oh*, no, I didn't. My parents—my parents had to move.
My dad is sick." MIT. MIT was on her phone. She took it away
from her ear and started at it in dreamlike disbelief. "You said . . .
I was accepted?"

"Yes," he said. "We do have an opening. But, of course, we
need to confirm that you'll be able to attend at the beginning of
next year. If you can't, we'll have to give the opportunity to another applicant. You understand?"

"Of course," Claire said, and felt a wave of hot excitement roll
over her, followed by an ice-cold wave of realization. "You said . . .
next year? As in January?"

"Yes, January," he said. "I hope that gives you enough time
to make your arrangements. I'm sorry to hear your father is ill. I
hope it's nothing serious."

Claire honestly didn't know what to say, and wasn't sure she
could say *anything*. She'd been dreaming of this moment for years,
thinking about how cool and perfect she was going to sound, how
she'd impress them with her adult attitude and control.

All she wanted to do was cry. *I can't. I can't go. They won't let me,
and this is my chance, my only chance. . . .* MIT had been her dream ever
since she'd been able to understand what they did there, what

they taught, what they achieved. There, she'd learn things that even Myrnin couldn't fathom. She'd discover the secrets of the universe.

All she had to do was get the hell out of Morganville. Which she couldn't do.

"Miss Danvers?" said the voice of the future on the other end of a very long line. "Are you there?"

"Yes," she said. "I'm here." *All the way* here. "Mr. Radamon, I'm sorry. I'll need to get back to you a little later. I need to, uh, talk to my parents before I tell you for sure. Would that be okay?"

"Oh yes, absolutely. I'm sorry to spring this on you without any warning." He chuckled. "I know how exciting it can be to get this kind of news. I think I yelled my parents' house down when I got my acceptance letter. Most exciting moment of my life. Well, congratulations, Ms. Danvers. Please call me back when you have all your arrangements in hand. I'll need to hear from you within the week, of course."

"Of course," she repeated numbly. "Thank you, sir. Thank you very much."

"No thanks necessary; you were a brilliant candidate, and your scores are extremely impressive. We look forward to having you on the team here."

She must have said something else, something nice and appreciative, but honestly, Claire couldn't think of anything except the giant letters flashing in front of her eyes . . . one set was MIT, and the other was OMG. She'd expected to feel a tremendous rush, but all she felt was . . . conflicted. And deeply, deeply scared.

The world had just opened up for her. Doves and angels and choirs singing. And all she could feel about it was . . . dread. Dread because she didn't think Amelie would release her in the first place, but even if she did . . . even if she did, what about Shane? If Shane was even talking to her ever again.

God, it was such a *mess.*

She took another five minutes, sitting in silence, staring at her turned-off phone. Wondering who she should call. Her parents would support her no matter what; no help there. She wanted to talk to Shane, suddenly, but . . . but after last night . . .

She had nobody she *could* talk to.

Well, she would have said something to Michael, who was in the living room, getting his stuff, but by the time she got her courage together, he was on his way. He just waved as he put on a sun-blocking black coat and hat and headed out the back door.

She shut her mouth, still trying to figure out how she felt. Mostly she just seemed . . . confused.

Eve was in the kitchen making pancakes. Alone.

"Morning, girlfriend," Eve said, and dumped some lumpy batter into a hot pan, where it immediately started to sizzle. "You look like you need carbs."

"Totally," Claire said, and sat down to rest her forehead in both hands. "Thanks."

"Yeah, no problem. Here." Eve grabbed a mug, filled it with coffee, and slid it to her on the table. "Caffeine. Makes the world all bright and sparkly, or maybe that's just me. Look, I gave you the fun mug."

In Eve's world, it was. It was a coffee mug with a dead-guy chalk outline on it, and it said HE HAD DECAF.

Claire mixed the coffee with all the things that made coffee drinking possible for her—milk, sugar, a little cinnamon—and sat nursing it, staring into the light brown surface but not seeing anything. She couldn't think. All she could do was . . . feel awful.

She needed to tell Eve, but saying it out loud would make it all real. *MIT wants me to go there.* Because part of her was so excited it was vibrating apart, and the other part, the practical part . . . that was crying. Did she *want* to go . . . leave behind Morganville? Well, yes, obviously. But that meant leaving the people, too. Eve. Michael. Myrnin. *Shane.*

She wanted to talk about that, badly, but she just . . . couldn't. Not yet.

"Incoming!" Eve said, and as Claire looked up, slid a plate in front of her with two thick, steaming pancakes. A pat of butter melted like lava on top, and Eve thumped down a bottle of syrup. "Everything gets better with pancakes. It's a law of the universe. Bonus for bacon, but we're out."

Eve had a plate, too, and sat down opposite her. Claire hadn't noticed, but Eve was makeup-free this morning, and her Goth-black hair was tied back in a simple ponytail. Even her clothes were subdued, or as much as Eve ever got—a form-hugging tee with a black-on-black skull design and a pair of black jeans. She picked up her fork and dug into her own plate.

Claire just watched the butter melt and poked at the pancakes a little. She dragged her fork through the syrup and spelled out *MIT.* Finally, she took a bite. They were good, really good, but as soon as she started to chew, tears came to her eyes and she could hardly swallow. She coughed to cover it, but Eve was watching her with a steady kind of focus that made it unnecessary.

"Hey," Eve said. "You know you can talk to me, right? About anything?"

Not about that. Not yet. But the other thing, yes. "Shane hates me," Claire said in a very small voice, and dragged her fork through the moat of syrup around the fortress of pancakes.

"Seriously?" Eve waited for Claire's nod before eating a bite of pancakes. She chewed and swallowed before she said, "Sorry, Claire Bear. He doesn't."

"You didn't hear what he said to me last night." That did it— the tears came now, for real, and she picked up her napkin and tried to wipe them away with shaking hands. God, what a mess she was.

"I heard what he said this morning before he blew out of here. He was angry at himself, not you—or, at least, more than at you. He said you'd gotten dragged away by Myrnin last night and he'd acted like a dick about it. Isn't that what happened?"

"Well, sort of. He was right—I *did* go off with Myrnin."

"On a job."

"Yeah."

"Not on a date."

"Oh, God, no!"

"Then Shane acted like an ass, and he's got nothing to be jealous about, and he knows it. I saw him, Claire. Believe me, he knows he was wrong. He feels bad."

"Then why—?" *Why didn't he come talk to me? Why didn't he try? Why did he just . . . leave?*

"He's cooling down. It's a guy thing," Eve said. "He'll be okay when he gets back. And you? He said you were all angry about him watching sexy commercials on TV, which, frankly, is weird—you being mad about it, not him watching them, because I'm pretty sure teen boys get a pass on that. They can't help hitting the PAUSE button when the half-naked girls show up."

"No, that wasn't it. It was—" She replayed it in her mind. A blur, a flutter of curtains. Whispers and laughter in the dark.

In the end, nothing she could truly say wasn't just a product of her tired mind and of jealousy.

"I thought he was with somebody," she finally said, miserably. "In his room. Some girl."

Eve ate a bite of pancakes, thinking about it, and then said, "And you honestly think he's that big a jerk, that not only does he cheat on you, he brings her back here, to our house? Where, I might add, I would personally open up a ten-gallon drum of whup-ass on him and any skank he dragged in here. Not to mention what Michael would do."

"No, I—I don't honestly think that. And, uh, thanks?"

"It's what friends do," Eve said graciously. "He didn't bring anybody back here—you know that. Besides, you were with us last night when he came home. What'd he do, smuggle her in under his coat?"

"I think she was a vampire," Claire said in a rush, without looking at Eve. In her blurry peripheral vision, she could see that Eve had stopped in the act of raising her fork to her mouth. Syrup dripped off, but the plate caught the damage.

Eve slowly put her fork back down.

"You think Shane's getting it from some vampire girl?"

Claire's frustration burned up suddenly, like flash paper. "I don't *know*! I'm just telling you what it *felt like*, Eve! There was a woman talking and laughing, and I went in his room, and there was a blur and wind and then he was alone. *You* fill in the blanks!"

"Oh, sweetie," Eve said. "You know that's totally frickin' insane, right? Because for one thing, Shane hates the hell right out of vampires. For another, he loves you."

"Maybe she's—I don't know—making him do it. They can do that, right? Yvette did."

"The last one who tried it didn't get very far, if you remember," Eve said. "And I heard on good authority that Yvette's ashes got sprinkled on the Founder's rose garden, so there's that. Shane's strong, and I don't just mean the muscles. I've never seen any bite marks on him. Have you?"

Claire had to shake her head reluctantly. She definitely hadn't seen any bites. *She*, on the other hand, had a collection of them, the worst from Myrnin. So maybe she was still, and badly, overreacting. Shane was acting jealous, but maybe he had reason, considering everything that had gone on with Myrnin.

Maybe that was why he was turning antivamp again.

"You're kind of freaking me out, you two," Eve said. "I mean, you're the *stable* one. And Shane, he's loyal to the point of stupid. If you two can't keep it together . . ." She didn't say it, but Claire knew she was thinking, *What chance do Michael and I have?* Claire had heard gossip when Eve wasn't around. Nobody was giving their vampire-and-human Romeo-and-Juliet act anything like good odds to go the distance.

And what *was* the distance, for a relationship where the vampire wasn't going to get any older, while Eve would? She knew, without even thinking about it, that Eve had spent long nights considering all this, going over and over it. So had Michael, probably.

Maybe love would conquer all. That was a nice thought, even if it wasn't realistic.

God, she wanted to blurt it all out to Eve—about Jason being held in that room at Founder's Square. About Bishop out stalking the streets. But she knew that would be a very bad idea. Amelie had been clear enough, and she wasn't in any mood to be forgiving.

She could tell her about MIT, but . . . no. That was private. She didn't want Eve to think she didn't care about her, because she did. She loved her.

But it was *MIT.*

Eve ate a couple of bites of pancake, and so did Claire, even though she couldn't taste it at all.

"CB," Eve said, and made her look up. "It's okay. Whatever it was, Shane's not that guy you're thinking about. He's *your* guy, and he's always going to be. Trust me. I know Shane, and he can be a jerk, but he can also be the best man I've ever met. And you, you make him better every day he's with you. Okay?"

"Okay," Claire said. She felt a little better, and also a lot worse, because that made leaving for Boston much harder. Maybe she *had* been tired and made a lot out of nothing. "I should get going. I'm going to be late for class."

"Whatcha learning?"

"Probably nothing, considering how sleepy I am. But in theory, it's about multidimensional analysis and waveforms." Like she'd be studying at MIT. Only that would be a thousand times better, somehow.

"I have no idea what that is, but yawn, anyway, just on principle. Eat up. Pancakes is brain food."

"Apparently not grammar food."

"Wow. You college girls are *mean*."

Claire had a pleasant enough morning. . . . The class ended up short one professor, so after ten minutes, they were free to wander off. Her next class was a lab, which she loved (and always aced). Then lunch, and a free afternoon to think things over.

As she sat outside under a tree, listening as the cool wind rustled the leaves overhead, she kept pulling out her phone. Kept pulling up the caller list and looking at the number. Finally, she typed in the contact info. *Mr. Radamon, MIT.*

Her finger kept hovering over the CALL button, but she didn't push it.

Yet.

It scared her when her cell phone vibrated. The picture that came up was a close-up of Myrnin's vampire bunny slippers. She sighed and answered, a little too sharply. "What?"

His voice sounded metallic and impatient over the tiny speaker. "Is that any way to speak to someone who employs you? And, I might add, could kill you at any time?"

"But won't," she said. "Has something happened? You know, with *him*? The old guy?"

"Him," Myrnin repeated. "No, *he* is still safely obscure at the moment, although there is an unprecedented effort to locate him going on, of course. But I need you for something else. Here, in the lab. Now."

"I thought you didn't need me today."

"In fact, I didn't. And now I do. Please."

"Thanks for saying *please*."

"I do try to be polite. Now, do get a move on."

She hung up and, just for the sake of being stubborn, finished her Coke before getting up, dusting off, and grabbing her book bag.

She got a text message before she could take more than a few steps, and stopped in the shade of a tree to read it from the tiny screen. It was from Shane, and it said, *Sry abt last night luv u.*

She smiled in relief, and texted back, *OMG luv u 2 so sry.* She almost added *I need to talk*, but that might make things worse. She'd talk later. Tell him. Ask him what to do about . . . about everything.

Claire closed the phone and held it to her heart for a few seconds, then slipped it back into her pocket. She felt about a thousand times better, no matter what was waiting for her at the lab; in fact, she hadn't realized how down she was until suddenly she was up again.

She was humming her new favorite song when she walked around the corner, heading for a shortcut to the lab, and ran into a crying girl who was running blindly for the shelter of the trees.

The girl went down. She looked terrified. It took Claire a second to recognize her, because she was expecting a student . . . but Miranda was far too young to be a student, maybe fifteen years old, and also Miranda was way, way too crazy.

Miranda was—or had been, anyway—Eve's friend, mostly because Eve took up strays and the vulnerable, and Miranda was both. Eve had also believed the girl was psychic, and Claire was inclined to believe it, too, because Miranda's guesses on things she shouldn't have known had always been too close for comfort. She was certainly weird enough, too.

Miranda had come into Claire's life early on in her Morganville experience, and she'd been vague and dreamy and sported vampire bites from her so-called Protector, whom Claire had considered a lot more predator than anything else. Since his death, Miranda had improved, but she'd stayed vague. Her clothes looked completely random and mismatched. Same for her makeup; she had some on, but it looked more like she'd forgotten to wipe off what she'd put on yesterday and just added to it. It was smudged and smeared, and not at all attractive.

She looked like a thin, starving rabbit of a girl.

And she was terrified.

"Hey," Claire said, and offered her a hand up. "Sorry about that. Miranda, what are you doing here on campus? You never

come here. Do you?" The girl stared up at her in frozen dread, and
Claire frowned a little. "What's wrong with you?"

"I came to warn you," Miranda said in a breathless rush. Her
eyes were very wide and more than half crazy. "But it's all gone
wrong." She took Claire's hand and pulled herself up, but she
didn't let go. Her skin felt icy, and her eyes darted around in a
paranoia Claire knew all too well. "They're coming!"

"No, they're not," said Monica Morrell, stepping around the
corner of the concrete building where the groundskeepers kept
their tools and mowers. "They're here, you crazy bitch. Oh, look,
you found a little friend. A little friend who's completely stupid if
she doesn't start walking away right now." Monica was pretty, perfectly made up, and wearing designer jeans and a spangled top, but
she had an expression that made Claire's stomach twist. "Danvers.
Don't you have to go save a puppy or the whales or something?"

Claire said nothing. Now it wasn't just Monica, but both her
Lipstick Mafia girls, who came a few seconds late to the party.
Gina was wearing a denim skirt and ass-kicking shoes, and Jennifer was basically a duplicate of Monica, only with knockoffs instead of designer originals.

That they'd target Miranda wasn't unusual; it was their standard operating procedure to pick out the weak and (presumably)
helpless. It had been Claire's introduction to the warm, welcoming
community of Morganville, running into these three in her dorm.
She'd gotten beaten up and tossed down stairs, and, frankly, she
knew she'd been lucky to get off that lightly.

Even so, even as bold as Monica was in her bullying, it was unusual that the Evil Trio was chasing Miranda around outdoors, in
full view of the campus. Granted, they were herding her into the
trees, where whatever unpleasant thing that was going to happen

would happen in relative privacy, but still . . . this was bold, even for Monica.

Even when Miranda was easy, friendless prey.

"I said get lost, Claire," Monica said as Gina and Jennifer spread out to cut off easy retreat. "You've got about five seconds before I forget you're wearing that Founder's Pet pin and start kicking your skinny ass, just like old times."

"You're forgetting? I didn't know you were old enough to get Alzheimer's," Claire said. She tugged on Miranda's cold, trembling hand. "Just that you looked it. Come on, Mir. Let's go."

"Wait." That was Jennifer, stepping up to block their escape. "Not her. She stays."

"Why?"

"None of your business, bitch. You can go. She can't."

Claire glanced over at Miranda. "You said you came to warn me? About what?"

She looked miserable and defeated. "About them," she said. "I woke up and my head was hurting and all I could think about was that I had to tell you, had to warn you before it was too late. But I think I did the wrong thing. Sometimes it all gets mixed up in my head, what's coming, and what I should do about it. Sometimes it seems like I actually cause it. But this is definitely wrong now."

Gina said flatly, "No shit. I was just walking along and that crazy bitch came right up to me, babbled at me, and *hit me*. Look, I'm going to have a bruise." She pointed at her chin, which did look red on the side. "So I'm going to hit her back. That's all. You just stay out of it and we'll all be fine."

Claire looked at Monica and Jennifer. "Are *your* friends staying out of it?"

"You really want to go there?" Gina's flat, dark stare was unsettling. "This isn't your business, Danvers. Walk away, go do whatever it is that smart freaks do when they're not being completely annoying."

She should have. That would have been the smart thing, the easy thing. But instead, something flared up inside her, something stubborn and bright and obstinate, and Claire said, "I'm not leaving anybody for you to pound on, especially not some helpless fifteen-year-old kid. You know that, right? That's what you're afraid of, that I'm going to stick around. Because now you've got *two* of us who aren't afraid to hit back. And *one* of us has people on speed dial that you don't want to mess with."

"Are you threatening me?" Gina asked softly.

"Crap," Monica sighed. "Danvers, you've stepped in it now. It's all on you."

Gina's eyes were like a shark's, Claire realized; just blind menace, no thinking behind them at all.

When she smiled, that made it all the more eerie. Especially when she unfolded the pocketknife with the long, sharp blade she had hidden at her side. It made a soft, metallic clicking sound as it locked into place.

Miranda took in a sharp, shaking breath. "Oh no. It's all going wrong, so wrong. . . . This isn't what I meant to do. . . ."

Claire shifted her attention to Monica, who was standing very still, face closed into a pretty, shallow mask. "You're going to let your psycho friend come after me. Even knowing what will happen when Amelie finds out."

Monica smiled, just a little. "What makes you think I can't make you disappear? Lots of places in this town to hide a body, especially if it's in little pieces. And you're just a little bitty thing, anyway."

Claire shook her head and looked at Miranda. "Why did you hit her?" she asked. "Gina. You came on campus, looked for her, and hit her. Why?"

"Because it had to happen that way." Miranda sometimes didn't make a whole lot of sense, and this was definitely one of those times.

Monica wasn't going to back down, not in front of her friends. Something had to change first. The balance had to shift, and fast, because Gina was working herself up to some genuine psycho-quality violence. As Gina was wont to do, actually.

Claire looked at Jennifer.

Jennifer seemed scared. This had clearly gone further than she'd thought or was comfortable with; Jen had always been the softest of the three of them, and this was especially true now. She'd been hurt recently, when a rave in town had turned into an all-out humans-versus-vamps brawl. When Shane and Claire had finally found her, she'd been balled up in a corner, thin party dress torn and stained with blood. She'd been cut with broken glass, and had a couple of cracked ribs.

But from the haunted look in her eyes, Claire had to wonder if maybe, just maybe, she'd learned how it felt to be on the receiving end.

"Jen," she said, very quietly. "You don't have to be here. You know what it's like to be hurt, and you don't want to make some-one else go through that. Just walk away."

Jen flinched and took a small step backward. She looked over at Monica, then at Gina.

"We were there for you, Jen," Monica said. "We've always been there for you. Don't you turn your back on us now. We know where you live, bitch."

"Yeah, she knows where I live, too," Claire said. "But she knows better than to show up there." She turned her attention back to Monica. "It's not just about scaring people out of their lunch money anymore, Monica. You're not the school bully. You're talking about real trouble, *jail* trouble, and you know how this is going to end. You need to stop this before you all get hurt, lots worse than anything you'd do to Miranda. Or to me."

Monica was staring back at her, and Claire had the oddest feeling that for the first time, Monica was *seeing* her. After all this time, all this anger, she was actually *communicating*.

"Think," Claire said very softly. "Just *think*. You don't have to make this happen. You don't *need* it, Monica. Everybody knows who you are. You don't have to keep on proving it to yourself and to everybody else."

That rocked Monica's head back, as if Claire had actually punched her in a vulnerable spot. Her lips parted, but whatever she was going to say . . . she didn't have time.

"You know what? I'm tired of the blah, blah, blah. Screw all this talking," Gina said, and came at Claire with the knife.

"Gina, *no!*" Monica yelled. She sounded shocked, as if she hadn't actually thought Gina would do it. As if Gina was all threat, no action.

But Claire had always known better.

That didn't make it feel any better as she watched Gina and the knife lunge straight for her.

EIGHT

Claire's world got suddenly very clear—high-definition clear. She could see the light glittering along the blade of Gina's knife. The sweat on Gina's forehead. The way she balanced her weight as she attacked.

Claire shoved Miranda out of the way, and in the same motion, slammed her forearm at a right angle to Gina's as the hand holding the knife came at her. She remembered Eve's fencing poses. Seemed like the right thing to do.

Gina's knife missed. Claire watched the edge glide past her, an inch from her left elbow, and knew she ought to be afraid, because, my *God*, she was in a knife fight with *Gina*, and nobody was coming to help her. Nobody even knew what was going on. Not Shane or Michael or Eve, not Amelie, not even Myrnin.

But, weirdly, right now it didn't matter. Everything was still and quiet inside, and she supposed she should have felt scared, but she didn't. She didn't feel anything.

Shane had given her lessons in how to trip people up—it had

been a game, one that had ended up with her on her back more than him on his, and she'd loved the laughter and the feel of his weight pinning her down. But now she walled all that away and stripped it down to its purest parts.

She could do this. She had to do it.

She stepped forward into Gina's body, and got her left foot behind and between Gina's. That put her lower leg at an angle, below Gina's knee.

As Gina stabbed at her with the knife, Claire grabbed her wrist, forced it up and in, and overbalanced her. Gina started to step backward, then yelped as Claire's braced leg took the strength out of her knee.

She went down on her back. Claire twisted the knife out of Gina's hand and dropped down with one knee on her chest, holding her down. She froze, looking down at her, breathing hard. She felt hot and shivery now, and the impulse to take that knife and do something terrible with it boiled up inside. It tasted like rage and fear and all the terrible things she'd ever felt, and for a second, just a second, she thought about what it would be like to make Gina feel that, to make Gina *hurt*.

Gina's eyes went wide, watching her. She knew. She could see it, too, and for the first time ever, Claire saw that Gina was actually afraid.

"This is what I saw," Miranda said, a quiet little voice at Claire's elbow. "But you're not going to do it. You're a good person."

Claire didn't feel like a good person, not at the moment. She felt sick and a little bit faint, and she didn't resist when Miranda took the knife out of her hand.

"But I'm not that good," Miranda said, and stabbed the knife down at Gina's chest.

Claire screamed and knocked Miranda out of the way, a firm body check that sent Mir stumbling, then rolling. The knife fell to the grass. Gina scrambled for it, but Claire got there first, picked it up, and held it at her side. Gina slowly climbed to her feet, breathing fast, chin down. The fear was gone now, replaced with an insane amount of rage.

"Monica," Claire said. "Call off the pit bull. Now, before this gets worse."

A few torturous seconds of silence passed before Monica said, "Gina. Yo, bitch, chill. We'll finish this some other time."

"Give me back my knife," Gina said.

"Um . . . no." Claire folded it up and slipped it into her jeans pocket. "The last thing you need is a weapon."

"I'll buy you another one. Come on, Gina. We're going." Jennifer took Gina's arm and tugged on it, glancing at Claire with a mixture of fear and respect. "Like Monica said. We'll get this later."

Gina pointed at Claire. "You. I'll get *you* later."

Claire shrugged. "Go for it."

Jennifer pulled her friend away. Monica had already turned her back and was walking away. She paused right before she turned the corner to glance back and nod slightly to Claire.

Odd. It almost looked like respect, too.

Silence. Claire listened to the breeze, the distant laughter of students coming from beyond the trees, and all of a sudden she couldn't stay on her feet. She sat down—sprawled—and rested her forehead in her hands.

Miranda crawled over to sit next to her. "Thank you," she said.

"For what?"

"Stopping me. But you don't know. You don't know what it's like."

"Getting bullied? Kind of do."

Miranda was looking at her with sadness and a strange kind of pity. "No, you don't," she said. "It's been happening since I was in kindergarten. Not them all the time, but other kids, you know. Every day. It never stops, and it never goes away, thanks to the Internet—it just keeps happening every minute, every day. And I just want it to stop. I think about how to do it, you know. How to kill them. All kinds of elaborate things, like trapping them in pits and burying them alive, or covering them with concrete."

It was the most sensible thing Claire had ever heard her say—and the most painful, too. She put her arm around Miranda. Close up, she expected Mir to smell bad, but she didn't; she smelled like lemon shampoo and soap. With a little clothing upgrade and better makeup and hair, she'd be pretty.

Oh, God, she thought, amused. *Eve's rubbed off on me.* Because the old Claire, the one she'd been before the Glass House, would have never even thought about Miranda's appearance.

"Explain to me why you came to find me," she said. "Was it just that you saw the knife fight?"

"Yes," Miranda said. And then, immediately, "No. There's something else."

"What?"

Miranda looked up at her with those odd, unsettling, luminous eyes. "It's about Shane. I think he's in trouble. There's something wrong in his head. I can almost see it."

Claire's phone beeped for attention—a text. She checked it. It was, shockingly, from Myrnin; she didn't think he even knew *how* to text. Evidently, he'd found his cell phone again.

It said, *Where are you, stupid girl? Run faster!*

Claire sighed. "Dammit! Can you tell me about it while we walk?"

Miranda didn't, of course, have many details. Psychic impressions were the most useless things *ever*, as far as Claire could tell . . . it was always feelings and impressions and vague warnings, and half the time it seemed like Miranda made things worse by trying to prevent something bad. Like today. The whole thing with Gina wouldn't have happened if Miranda hadn't come along trying to stop it. Well, probably.

Miranda's cold-blooded violent streak worried Claire almost as much as Gina's psycho tendencies. She thought about revenge in dangerously graphic terms.

"Let's try this again," she said as they walked down the mostly deserted street that led to the cul-de-sac where Myrnin's lab entrance was located. "So what you see is that Shane's in trouble because he gets in a fight."

Miranda nodded, so vigorously her tangled hair bounced. "A bad one," she said. "And gets hurt. I can't tell how much, but he gets hurt a lot, I think."

"Is it day or night?"

Miranda thought about it, frowning. She kicked an empty plastic bottle and flinched when a dog barked in one of the yards they were passing. The houses on this street were run-down, with bars on the windows. Only the Day house at the end of the street—a mirror for the house where Claire lived, the one owned by Michael Glass—looked nicely kept up, and even it needed a new coat of paint. "I can't tell," she finally said. "It happens inside. In a room. People are watching. There are bars."

"Like, with drinks?"

"No, like a cage."

That was sickly likely, because Shane seemed to end up behind *those* kinds of bars way too often. "How many people?"

She shrugged. "It's dark; I can't tell. Maybe a lot? No—more. More than a lot. From a long ways off. There but not there."

That was definitely vague and not at all helpful. The fighting— well, that was something that honestly wasn't all that unusual. Shane was a born fighter. But the getting badly hurt—that was unsettling, all right.

"Is there any way to tell when it's going to happen?"

Miranda shook her head. "It's pretty clear, so maybe a few days? A week? But I don't know. Sometimes it's tricky. And some- times it goes away, too. Things aren't always obvious."

"Okay, well, thanks. I'll try to look out for him." That wasn't much, because Claire knew she couldn't spend all her time watch- ing out for him. Warning him would help, but knowing Shane, it wouldn't solve the problem, either. If he felt like he needed to be in the fight, he'd be in it—whether he got hurt or not.

"You should get home," Claire said. "I have to go to work. Mir?"

Miranda stopped, looking at her. She was getting taller, Claire realized; still growing. She was taller than Claire was now, and would probably be Eve's height or better before she was done.

"Tomorrow, meet me at the house," Claire said. "If Myrnin doesn't need me, we'll go shopping. Okay?"

Miranda smiled at her—a sweet, delighted, heartfelt expres- sion that lit up her whole face. No, her whole *body*. It was like no- body had ever offered before. "Okay!" she said. "I've never been shopping."

Claire blinked. "Never?"

"No. My parents used to buy me things before they died. And now people sometimes bring me things, but I've never gone myself. Is it fun? It looks fun."

"It's fun," Claire said. She had a sudden impulse to hug the girl, so she did. Miranda felt all bones and awkward angles, but she hugged back enthusiastically. "You go straight home and stay there. Monica may back off, but Gina's kind of nuts. I think she's after me, though."

"She is," Miranda said, in that distant, weird kind of voice Claire dreaded. "She'll be coming. Soon." She blinked and smiled. "See you tomorrow!"

She practically skipped away. Claire watched her go, shook her head, and headed into the monster's lair.

The monster himself was standing in the middle of the lab, pacing and shaking his cell phone as if he was trying to get it to work by sheer force. He'd changed clothes again—this time, to a Victorian long-tailed coat in black, a purple vest, no shirt, and black pants. He'd ditched the bunny slippers this time, in favor of real shoes. When she came jogging down the steps, he looked so relieved she almost backed up a step or two.

"There you are!" he cried, and held his phone out to her. "This thing doesn't work."

"It does. I got your text."

"But I've been sending it over and over, and then it just stopped working."

It had stopped working because, evidently, he'd been pushing buttons so hard he'd broken them. Claire shook her head, took the phone, and tossed it in the garbage can in the corner. "I'll get you another one," she said. "Well? I'm here. What's the crisis?"

He stopped and stared at her. "Bishop is on the loose, and you're asking me what the crisis might be? Really?"

"I . . . thought the vampires would be taking care of that."

"Indeed. Oliver's got half the vampires in Morganville making inquiries of the other half."

"Only half?"

"The half we can trust interrogating the half we can't," Myrnin said. "A sad truth, but there are more than a few who preferred Bishop's open tyranny to Amelie's more reasonable approach. There are always a few, Claire, who like being told what to do instead of being required to think. And those are the ones you should fear. That goes equally for humans, I'm afraid. Critical thinking has become a sadly rare skill these days."

She nodded, because she already knew that. "So what do you want me to do?"

"I want you to speak with Frank. We need him to be on the alert for any sign of Bishop. He has control of the monitoring systems, and he should be able to provide us solid leads."

"Wait, you want *me* to do it? Why didn't you?"

Myrnin drew himself up to his full height, hands clasped behind his back. "I have things to do," he said. "And . . . Frank and I *may* have had a little disagreement. He isn't speaking to me anymore."

"He— Wait, can he do that?"

"Damn straight I can." Frank's gravelly voice came from her cell phone speaker, muffled by her pocket, but still clearly audible. "I can do what I want, and I don't want to hear anything from that jackass anymore."

"Frank—" Claire sighed. "Fine. I hate this, you know. I hate that you're all fangs-out at each other when one of you doesn't even have any fangs anymore. But we don't have time for your girl fight, okay? Will you please look for Bishop, so he doesn't get us all killed horribly?"

"Well," Frank said, "you've got a point about that."

Claire turned to Myrnin. "Anybody else you want monitored?"

"Well, there's Gloriana," Myrnin said. "I would definitely look out for Gloriana, since she's the newest in town, and, well, you've met her, haven't you?"

Claire frowned. Gloriana . . . *oh*. She'd met her once, briefly, at a party about a month ago. Gloriana—or Glory, for cutesy-short—was beautiful, in an antique kind of way; she had waves of long blond hair and bright blue eyes and a smile that made men melt like ice cream in the sun. Vampire, of course. Charming. But she'd taken a special interest in Michael, and that hadn't sat very well with Eve at all. "Glory's a Bishop girl?"

"I wouldn't put it like that," Myrnin said, "but Gloriana has a history of betting with the winners, and she was Bishop's pet for a short time, about three hundred years ago, I believe. She may still have some fond memories of him, as difficult as that is to understand. Old loyalties die hard among our kind. So do old enemies, and she never was Amelie's friend, though they're polite enough in public."

"Is she *your* friend?" Claire hesitated, then said, "Or, you know, *friend*?"

He raised his eyebrows and air quoted. "Friend?"

"You know what I mean. Oliver practically admitted he'd had a fling with her once."

"I don't have *flings*." Again with the air quotes. "And, no, Gloriana is not my friend. Nor my enemy, particularly; I rarely had anything to do with her at all. She's agreed to abide by the laws of Morganville, but if a situation arises where she might sidestep them . . . well. I would not like to stand between her and her desires. She can be quite cold-blooded."

Claire felt a stab of dread. "Uh, she could be after Shane, then?"

"Shane?" Myrnin rolled his eyes. "Why in the world would you leap to such a conclusion? Definitely not. She doesn't do humans. She finds them commonplace. And, strangely enough, not everyone is as fascinated by your beau as you are."

"Well, then, would she be after *you*?"

That made him stop for a second, as if the idea had never occurred to him. "No," he finally said. "No, I don't believe she would be at all interested. I'm not . . . suitable. By which I mean, sane. She can't show me off in public, which is very important to her; she likes to be seen with her conquests. Also, I'm not sure that she could affect me in any significant way. My patterns of thought are quite . . . different, you know."

"Oh, I know. Frank, are you getting this?"

"Bishop, check. It's not like I'm going to forget that the bastard who ripped out my throat and made me the walking dead is out there. Gloriana, yeah, I know her. Gloriana's on my radar. She just left the gym about ten minutes ago, and she's arriving at Common Grounds right now."

Myrnin nodded. "She does like it there. Claire, perhaps you should make friends. You're quite a friendly person."

"Be your spy, you mean."

"Inelegantly put, but accurate. I have things to do. Frank, please stay in touch with Claire via her communicator."

"Cell phone," she said. "*Star Trek* had communicators."

He flapped a hand. "I hardly see the difference."

"I'm still not listening to him," Frank said. "But, yeah. I'll stay in touch, kid. You got some kind of headphones? Bluetooth?"

"Earbuds," she said. "Why?"

"So I don't broadcast all over the place when I talk to you, kid. I thought you were smart."

"It's been a bad day," she said. "I almost got stabbed."

Myrnin stopped pacing, looked at her for a moment as if trying to see any possible wounds, and then said, "*Almost* doesn't count, now, does it? Hurry onward. And, Claire?"

"Yes?"

"Do be careful and watch out for Bishop; he was dangerous before, but I don't know what he is now, except much less stable. Also, I don't trust Gloriana. I don't know why on earth she's here in Morganville. Or why she's decided to come here *now*. As I said, she and Amelie never got along, despite their exquisitely polite manners toward each other. So I do believe we have to assume that there can't be a coincidence between Gloriana's arrival and Bishop's escape." He hesitated, then added, "Do be careful. I can't replace you as easily as all that."

That was Myrnin's idea of a compliment. Nice.

SHANE

☽

Claire went to school, and I had a day off, and I felt kind of . . . lost. I shouldn't have gone back to the gym, but I did. Don't know why, except that I was out and it seemed like the right thing to do. The jackass who manned the front desk gave me the same "you are a bug and I will crush you" look as before, but then he looked down at a list and nodded to me. "Go on in," he said. "You're taken care of."

"Taken care of how, exactly?"

"Paid for," he said. "No charge to use the gym."

Well, crap. Tough to justify walking out on that, so I went in the door and breathed in the scent of sweat, effort, old leather, metal, desperation. Gyms smelled like home to me, especially after my mom and Alyssa died; life with Dad had been boiled down to gyms, bars, cheap motel soap, and blood.

It smelled like . . . home? If that isn't too sick.

I tried the sauna, which was superhot and damp, and changed into an old pair of sweatpants. Bare feet, because I fear no athlete's foot fungus, and besides, I was planning on kicking the crap out of a heavy bag, anyway.

I didn't get the chance. I walked out, towel around my neck, hair damp and sticking to my face, and there, sitting on the railing on the second floor like a very beautiful bird on a wire was the girl I'd dreamed about.

The vampire I'd dreamed about.

I hadn't lied to Claire, not actually. I'd honestly figured that it had been a dream, because it hadn't seemed like me at all—what I'd been doing, saying, thinking. It's like that in dreams, right? You don't have to be yourself.

But there she was, just as curvy and fresh and gorgeous as she'd been last night, in the dream/not dream/maybe possibly dream.

And she was smiling down on me like we had a secret. I wanted to be angry, to feel that rush of adrenaline I almost always got in the presence of a vamp, but it seemed like whatever my brain thought, my body reacted to her like it did to a pretty girl.

A pretty girl smiling at me.

"Hey, Shane," she said. *She had a lovely voice, low and sweet, and it sounded like she was the only thing in the room when she spoke.* *"Nice to see you here. Did you think about my offer?"*

Oh, man. *It took me a minute to sort out what kind of offer she was talking about; that smile made a bunch of offers that had nothing to do with the gym.* *"The advanced sparring group,"* I said. *"Right?"*

"Yes." *Her smile took on a mischievous, knowing curl.* *"Whatever else could you possibly be thinking of?"*

Stop this. Stop it now. *Some part of me was angry, trying to shake me out of it, but it was a very small part, and the rest of me felt . . . calm. Right. Like all this was inevitable—fate, destiny, whatever you want to call it.*

But at the very least, I wasn't going to go chasing after some vamp girl, no matter how pretty she was. I couldn't do that to Claire, and deep down, there was always going to be a part of me that a vampire couldn't touch. I hoped. So I said, staring straight into her clear blue eyes, "I'm just here for the fighting, lady."

"Glory," she said. *"Gloriana. But you can call me Glory."*

Of course. I'd seen her before, and it came back to me clear as day this time; I'd seen her at her welcome-to-Morganville party, but not close up. She'd been trying to drag Michael off then, and she hadn't been focused on me at all. I'd thought she was pretty, but not, you know, pretty.

Not until she'd turned that smile and those eyes on me. Then I understood how swept away Michael had felt. It was like being hit with a tsunami of hormones, and, man, did it feel good.

"You came for the fighting," she said, and pushed off the railing. *She dropped twenty feet and landed like a cat, barely flexing her knees to absorb the impact. Her gaze never left mine, and her smile never faltered. "All right, then. You should get what you came for. Follow me."*

I expected her to take me to the mats in the center of the room; there were people working out there, doing throws, kicks, blocks, that kind of stuff. Your basic martial arts sort of activity.

But she took me another way, through an unmarked door at the back, down a plain hallway, and through another door marked PRI-VATE, *into a room with an actual boxing ring on a platform. Two guys stripped down to formfitting shorts were whaling on each other, and they were doing serious damage. I stopped and watched, analyzing speed, force, agility, endurance.*

"They're good," I said.

"They'd better be," Glory said. "Do you think you can hold your own?"

"Yeah." I said it without any particular sense of bragging; I just knew I could. These guys hadn't grown up with my dad. "Bring it."

"I need to match you up with a partner," she said. "Vassily? Who do you think Shane should spar with?" While she asked, Gloriana reached into a big, black refrigerator on the wall and pulled out a sports-drink bottle, which she held out to me. I frowned at it, but she raised her eyebrows and gave me a charming little smile. With dimples. "Trust me. It's good for you. Protein drink, special recipe. Free with your membership."

I took it and very cautiously sipped. I know, stupid, right? Who takes something from a frickin' vampire? But there was something so safe about her. It was like I couldn't distrust her, even though I wouldn't have ever taken any damn drink from another vampire, ever.

And it tasted good. Gritty, the way protein shakes do, but with a buzzing edge. Caffeine, maybe. It raced through me with a hot shiver. Made me feel amazing—alert, strong, pumped.

"Shane?" Vassily, the vamp who'd been teaching that first class, the one I'd put down, came over. He'd shed the gi and was wearing stan-

dard gym clothes, and he'd left his long, thick hair down to spill over his shoulders. "Ah yes. This one. Let's have him spar with Jester. That should be an interesting matchup."

"Are you sure?"

"Yes. Jester." Vassily smiled and beckoned someone over from the shadows, where he was leaning against the wall. As the man crossed into the light, I recognized the pale skin, the slightly too-bright eyes. Vampire. Unlike Gloriana, I didn't feel warm and fuzzy about him, not at all. "Jester, meet Shane. You'll be sparring."

Jester glanced at me, dismissed me, then stared at Vassily. "Hell no," he said. "I'm not fighting some punk human. They break."

"Suit yourself," I said. "Saves you a good ass kicking."

"What did you say?" Jester looked honestly surprised and puzzled, as if he couldn't believe I'd had anything to say, much less something that wasn't exactly complimentary. I shrugged.

"I can take you," I said. "Believe it."

"Prove it, Blood Bag," Jester said.

Gloriana laughed and waved. "Boys, boys, there's enough time for that. Today, you just . . . spar." She turned to Vassily. "I have places to be. But I believe that my work here is done for now."

"Yes," he agreed. "For now. Come back soon, lovely girl. I'm going to need your help with the old man. He's been getting a bit . . . impatient."

I watched her walk away, still feeling that subtle buzz of her presence, that seductive thrill . . . and it didn't go away when I looked at Jester and said, "Let's go, Fang Boy."

And that was the beginning.

Pain, yeah, there was a lot of that, but it seemed like the more time I spent in the ring, facing him, facing everything that I'd ever hated on such a primal level, the pain meant less and less. What mattered was *letting the monster out from inside me, the one I'd been starving for almost a year.*

I'd come to Morganville to take down vampires.

And Vassily and Gloriana were giving me the chance to do just that.

And oh, God, I loved it.

On the way to Common Grounds, Claire texted Shane—just a quick message to say she loved him. No immediate reply, but one buzzed through by the time she'd walked the distance to Common Grounds.

Shane's message said, *Be home late luv u.*

She was still smiling and feeling almost completely happy when she opened the front door of the coffee shop and heard the bell tinkle to announce her arrival. This time of day, it was full of students gathered together at tables, books and computers out. Study groups, mostly.

She spotted Gloriana right off, because she was at the traditionally vampire tables, in the deepest shadows at the back of the room . . . and she was surrounded by other vamps. All male. There must have been five or six of them at the table, more than she'd seen gathered together anywhere but in Founder's Square—old-looking, young-looking, all with identical expressions of rapt interest on their faces. All staring at Gloriana, who sat comfortably with one leg folded under her, sipping whatever was in her plain white mug, smiling, and talking. She really *was* pretty, and unlike a lot of pretty vampires, she came across as nice. Sweet, almost. Claire had good reason to think she wasn't, because Eve had taken an instant dislike to her, but still.

It was impossible to resist her charm.

The proof was that one of the guys sitting at the table was Oliver, still wearing his long, tie-dyed Common Grounds apron. He was staring at Glory with a small, bemused smile on his lips, as if he couldn't quite believe that she was here in front of him.

He glanced over and saw Claire standing there, and the smile disappeared. He stood up and came over to her. "What?" he asked. The warmer side he'd been showing to Glory was all gone in a flash.

"Uh, sorry to bother you, but could I get a mocha?" She was buying time, because looking at the situation in front of her, Claire honestly couldn't see how she was expected to get in close enough to talk to Gloriana, let alone gain her trust, or grill her discreetly about Bishop. Wasn't that Oliver's job, anyway?

But maybe Myrnin didn't trust Oliver with Glory. That would make some sense, given what she'd seen. She adjusted her earbuds. Nothing but a low hum of static on them so far, which was bugging her; she'd rather have her music on, but the idea of Frank interrupting it sounded worse than boredom.

Right on cue, there was Frank's voice, whispering to her through the magic of technology. That was creepy, with an extra-strength dose of frightening. She still had nightmares about Frank Collins sometimes. And she thought he'd probably be happy to know that. "Right. You should be able to see her now. According to the records, she looks harmless, but she ain't. Some female vampires have a thing called glamour, and she's got it more than most. She can make anybody like her, including other vampires."

Claire turned away a little, pretending to fiddle with her book bag. "Can you hear me?"

"Yeah, through the microphone on your cell."

"What about Amelie? Could she make Amelie like her?"

"Probably not. Amelie's got a thing vampires call compulsion; she can force people to do what she wants when she has to. Compulsion trumps glamour every time."

"Does anybody else have this compulsion thing?"

"Oliver," Frank said. "Not as strong, though. But Oliver's a lost cause, anyway. He's an old friend of Glory's, if you know what I mean by *friend*. Looks like he's given it up already."

Yeah, she knew about that. She could have guessed it just from seeing the smile on Oliver's face as he looked at Gloriana.

"Just be careful with her," Frank said. "If she tries to glamour you, pain may break you out of it—it sometimes works for girls. Not so much for boys, for some reason—probably because she's not as good at tapping into the girls, or they're wired up differently. But she probably won't glamour you, anyway. She doesn't think much of humans in general, and girls are definitely not her thing."

"Wait a minute. Back up. Your answer to how I'm supposed to resist is to *hurt* myself? How is that helpful? Do you think I want to be in pain?"

"Fine. Deal with it on your own, then. Enjoy the ride." And the hiss was back in her headphones, constant and featureless.

About that time, Oliver gestured impatiently at the counter and thumped a cup down for her. Her mocha, presumably, although she wasn't putting much faith in a decent brew, not with the scowl he was giving her. Her stalling tactic was pretty much dead in the water, and she couldn't think of a single reason to walk over there to join Gloriana's exclusively testosterone-filled—and pulse-lacking—admirers.

And then Gloriana looked up as Oliver slipped back in his chair, saw Claire watching her, and smiled. Their eyes met.

And Claire found herself walking toward the table. She wasn't afraid, and she wasn't thinking at all—she couldn't remember the last time when she'd felt this kind of *peace*. Freedom from *thinking* all the time.

Just *acting*.

"Claire, isn't it?" Gloriana said. She had a low, pleasant sort of voice, and her smile was bright. "Please have a seat. Oh, Jules, please bring another, would you? I don't want to leave little Claire standing! So rude."

Oliver wasn't scowling anymore, but he wasn't smiling, either; when he looked at Claire, it was an entirely neutral expression. Another vampire—Jules, presumably, although Claire didn't know him—brought her a chair and she sat down, sandwiched between two strangers who almost certainly would have been inclined to drink her dry under other circumstances.

And she didn't feel even a twitch of uneasiness.

I've been glamoured. That thought came from somewhere deep inside her, a kind of whispering doubt, but it wasn't strong enough to make any difference. Not when Gloriana was smiling at her, those wide blue eyes so warm and welcoming. "I've heard so much about you," she said. "So many people speak well of you. Even my old grouch Oliver, here." She laughed and put her hand on top of Oliver's in a gesture that was affectionate and, at the same time, a little bit patronizing, like an owner petting a dog. He gave her a quick look and a belated smile. "So, tell me, Claire, what do you think of Morganville?"

Normally, she would have been careful about what she said, but here, under the warm glow of Glory's eyes, she just . . . spilled.

"I love the people I've met here," she said. "But I hate how it all works. I hate how humans get treated. I hate that it's okay to hurt us. That has to change."

Gloriana raised one eyebrow. "I thought it already had," she said. "So Amelie tells me. No hunting without permission, and then only in restricted zones. It's all perfectly tiresome, but I do understand the need for conservation, of course. Or are you saying that we should *never* hunt?"

"Yes," Claire said. "Never." There was a low growl from around the table. And she *still* wasn't afraid. "Never," she repeated. "You get your blood from taxes. You don't need to do that to us. There's no reason."

Glory smiled. It was still a warm, charming smile, the kind that invited you to feel part of it. "Of course we have to do it," she said. "Ask anyone who works with predators; suppressing the instinct to hunt is very, very tricky, and some animals never quite manage it. You must provide a controlled outlet, or inevitably someone will run wild. That would be much worse. Don't you agree?"

"No," Claire said. "If somebody breaks the rules, then he's a criminal. And you ought to treat him like any other criminal."

"How amusing you are, little one," Glory said, and laughed just to prove it. "You're Michael's friend, aren't you? One of those who lives in his house?"

"Yes."

"And the other boy is called . . . ?"

"Shane," Claire said. She felt a pulse of dread, deep down inside, but it was just a twinge. "His name is Shane."

"I've seen him at the gym," she said. "He's got good instincts, I must say. A good fighter. He'd be very valuable, in the right situation." There was a glint in those lovely blue eyes, and Claire knew, in that same distant, unimportant way, that Gloriana was playing with her now, batting her around like a mouse. "Yes, I can see how he'd be *very* profitable to have in your corner."

Oliver leaned back. "Too bad you don't still own the boxing clubs that you were so fascinated by in Victoria's time. Those were very lucrative for you, weren't they?"

"Oh yes, quite profitable," she said. "Too bad. He'd be quite an asset, wouldn't he? And an orphan, too, I understand. So sad. Not having good influences makes one so . . . vulnerable." She leaned across the table, and the warm intensity of her gaze on Claire's cranked up so high that it felt like being bathed in pure, warm light, floating in it without a care in the world. "I understand you know my old friend Myrnin. How is he? I do so adore that mad old man. Is he working on anything . . . interesting?"

"Claire," said a voice in her ears, a metallic voice that took her a second to place. *Frank.* "Claire, you can't answer that. Snap out of it. Do it now."

But she couldn't. Even though Glory was talking about Shane as if he was a side of beef, even though she was asking questions about *Myrnin*, Claire still felt calm and entirely comfortable. She just couldn't bring herself to feel anything else. Frank sounded angry and upset, but she couldn't understand why. Glory was the best friend she could imagine having, better than Eve, because Glory would never judge her, never make her feel bad or guilty.

Claire said, "He's working on——"

"Claire, sorry, but you need to stop this before you get in over your head," Frank interrupted. And in the next second, she felt a burning, hissing pain that zipped through her body in a flash so fast, it was over before it registered. A shock coming from her headphones. Claire jerked a little, blinked, and her heart rate sped up with a jolt. She yanked out the earbuds, shuddering, and the calm fell away like a shed blanket.

Fear closed in, icy and sharp. Gloriana was still smiling at her, but it didn't look warm anymore. It looked...predatory. And cruel. Claire swallowed and stood up. Her chair scraped back loudly. All of them were staring at her now, and the only one who didn't seem to be on the verge of flashing fangs at her was Oliver. He was frowning, but now it was aimed at Gloriana.

"Glory," he said. "Were you glamouring the girl?"

"A little," she shrugged. "I just wanted to play."

"Oh, for pity's sake, play with someone else. She's Amelie's property. And she's hardly worth your efforts."

Glory laughed. "I know. But I didn't hurt her, did I?" She turned that smile back on Claire. "Leaving us so soon, little one?"

Claire took a giant step back. The smile didn't work now, probably because she had so much adrenaline racing through her body. "Stay away from us," she said. "Stay away from Shane."

Glory rolled her eyes. "I don't want your *boy*," she said. "Whatever would I do with him? He isn't good for very much except violence. So much of that inside him."

Claire left her mocha sitting on the table and moved for the door as fast as she could. She looked back over her shoulder as she left, but nobody had moved, not even Oliver, although he was watching her go. Glory was laughing and seemed to have forgotten all about her already.

Claire stepped out into the sunlight, ran half a block down, and leaned against the rough bricks between two storefronts. She closed her eyes and concentrated on breathing and controlling her shaking. Then, finally, she put her earbuds back in place. It took her two tries, thanks to her unsteady fingers.

"I didn't get anything," she said to Frank. "I didn't know she could do that, make me feel like that. I didn't know *anyone* could do that. Bishop couldn't."

"It's a pretty rare power, even among vampires," Frank said. "I only knew of three or four who had it. Killed two of them. Too bad I didn't make it a clean sweep."

"I didn't even know what she was doing. I had no way to fight it." Claire took a deep breath. "Thanks for snapping me out of it."

"She *wasn't* even trying," Frank said. "If she had been, you wouldn't have left that easily. Like she said, she was just playing."

That was awful. *Awful.* Claire felt ill and filthy, as if she'd drunk a gallon of sewer water. She wanted to throw up, thinking about how easily she'd been walked around like a puppet. About how she'd felt everything that Glory wanted her to feel. "It didn't do any good," she said. "We didn't find out anything."

"Maybe we did," Frank said. "She mentioned that she saw Shane at the gym, didn't she?"

"So? Even I've been to the gym. So has Eve. Lots of people go there. Including vampires."

"But why would Glory? She doesn't fight. She makes other people do her fighting for her." Frank's voice sounded oddly preoccupied. "I've been going over the rolls of vampires in Morganville. Looks like some haven't been surfacing in their usual routines recently."

"You mean . . . you mean they're missing?"

"I don't want to jump to that conclusion, but I found five—no, six—that aren't following their usual patterns."

"Well, some left, you know. With Morley. They're in Blacke, that little town outside of—"

"I know about Morley. I'm not talking about his people. These are other vampires that haven't surfaced in the past three weeks. No checkouts at the blood banks. They haven't shown up on surveillance. They're not communicating at all on the phones or computers."

"How can vampires go *missing*? Who are they?"

"Nobodies, in terms of the Morganville hierarchy. Just your regular vampire working class. And they haven't been missed all that much. Vampires may socialize, but not like humans do; they're used to not seeing each other for long stretches. Doesn't raise any questions."

"So where are they?" Claire asked. "Do they have any connection to Bishop?"

"Not that I can find. In fact, looks like they were on Amelie's side in the conflict with her father." Frank was silent for a moment, then said, "It bothers me that I don't have eyes inside the gym. I can't see or sense anything within those walls."

"What?"

"It's recent construction. No cameras. No portals. No way of observing what's going on there. It seems like a lot of this connects through there, some way. I wish I had some devices there."

"Inside the gym." She thought about it for a second. "You want me to . . . what? Put cameras in there?"

"What, you're scared to act as my spy?" Frank sounded amused now. "Knowing you, that doesn't stop you. Never seen a kid so fearless, deep down. Not even my son."

Shane. Claire remembered Glory talking about him, and felt a little sick—not because Gloriana was drooling over him, as Ysandre had, but because she *wasn't*. Because to her, Shane was just another piece of meat, something she might get some use out of. Or not.

Whatever was going on, Gloriana was in it up to her pretty little neck. Claire was sure of it.

"All right," she said. "If you want eyes in the gym, I'll make sure you get them. Somehow."

SHANE

☾

I felt like I was cheating on Claire, and I couldn't figure out why. All I did was fight . . . and I did damn good, too. Jester didn't totally wipe the mat with me, and I was able to keep on going. When I got tired, Vassily passed me more protein shakes. I didn't like the way he smiled or the way he watched me, like a proud owner of a pit bull in the ring . . . but that didn't mean I didn't like being in the ring, either.

So why, on breaks, did I go sit down with my phone and text Claire? It was like I'd been out kissing some other girl and felt like I had to tell her I did love her, no matter what I'd been doing that she wouldn't like.

Well, she wouldn't like this. I knew that without any doubt at all.

"Hey, meat! You done pushing buttons yet?" That was Jester, dancing around in the ring, looking lean and dead-fish pale, punching the air in a blur. "I'm ready to push yours!"

I shot him the finger and finished sending my message, took another drink of my protein shake, and felt the aches and pains magically recede. Not that they were healing, exactly . . . maybe they weren't as bad as they should have been, but I was going to have bruises tomorrow. Lots of them.

But you couldn't let pain stop you. I'd let it stop me once, when my house was on fire. I'd touched Alyssa's door handle and burned my hands and I hadn't kept on going, I hadn't saved her. I'd let them drag me out of the house, and she'd been lost in there.

I couldn't ever forget what it cost to fail. Dad hadn't let me forget, either.

Pain was good. Pain kept you sharp and kept you motivated. Pain made me feel alive.

Especially when I was facing a vamp who wanted to teach me a lesson.

The rest of the afternoon passed in a blur. I ended up on the mat a lot, and it was tough to get up and keep going. People gathered—humans, vamps—all watching as Jester and I toughed it out. He was faster than me and stronger, but I didn't give up.

Finally, Vassily made me stop. He clapped Jester on the shoulder and said something in his ear, and Jester smirked and ducked under the ropes and was gone, and all the motivation just . . . bled out of me. I dropped to my knees, gagging for breath. There was blood in my mouth and a weird buzzing in my ears, and I'd never felt quite that bad in my life, not even when I'd been in the hospital and circling the drain.

It was like I'd cannibalized parts of myself to stay on my feet, and now the pain and the emptiness flooded into me and swamped me, and I just wanted to lie down and die.

Vassily passed me another sports bottle. I didn't want it, but I couldn't help myself. I drank. I felt better, or at least not as prone to dying. He checked my eyes and nodded. "You'll be all right," he said, all business. "Dehydration and exhaustion. Four more of the drinks will put you right, but stay off your feet for two hours before you head home. There are bunks in the next room. Rest now."

"Thanks," I mumbled. I didn't feel grateful. I didn't feel much of anything except filthy and guilty inside. What the hell was I doing? Why was I doing it? I didn't even know, except that when I was fight-

ing, it seemed like I was fighting every bad thing in my life that had ever happened. I was fighting for my sister and my mother and even my dad. For Claire, trapped in this damned town. For Michael, turned vamp against his will. For Eve.

For me, for once.

I sacked out for the next two hours, sipping those drinks, and with every slow mouthful I felt better. More stable. Whatever was in them was great stuff, because the pain faded to twinges, and the guilt faded along with it. I was okay. No, I was better than okay.

I was strong and getting stronger, and that was what I'd always needed to survive here. I had people to protect. This was going to make all the difference.

I was emptying the last bottle when Vassily came in with Gloriana. Glory looked fantastic, and I felt sweaty and dirty and bruised, and I had to sit up. No lying down in her presence.

"Shane," she said, and gave me that smile. "I just met your little friend Claire. You should be proud; she's not afraid of much, you know. But so fragile. And I'm quite concerned about her relationship with Myrnin. He's so unstable, don't you think?"

I did think that, and had all along; she was just saying what was obvious to me and everybody else except Claire. "I don't like it," I said. "But she does what she wants."

"Yes, she does." Glory studied me for a few seconds, then glanced over at Vassily. "I think he's ready, don't you?"

"Ready for what?" I asked.

"Ready to hear the rest," Vassily said. "You showed tremendous courage today, Shane. And great talent. We have an opportunity for you, one that I believe would take advantage of your best qualities. You see, we can offer you the chance for two things you have always wanted."

"Money," Glory said. "Real money, enough to take care of yourself and Claire for the rest of your life."

Well, who didn't want money? I'd been scratching away at it, doing it the hard way like I was supposed to, but that sounded good. Really good. "What's the second thing?" I asked.

Vassily's turn. "A way out of Morganville," he said. "Before it's too late. Because this town is going to be destroyed, one way or the other, and if you're smart, you'll take the money and the chance to earn your free passage out while you still can."

Cash and a free pass? I blinked, because it sounded like they'd read my mind. I wasn't completely sure that wasn't the case. Glory was freaky good at guessing what I was thinking . . . or making me think that way. That should have alarmed me, but not coming from her. It just seemed . . . nice. Like I didn't have to fight to be understood anymore. Glory just got me.

"What about Claire?" I asked.

"Of course, Claire would be able to go with you," Vassily said. "And anyone else you'd like to see safely gone from Morganville. You can save them, Shane. All you have to do is what you do best."

"Fight," Gloriana said. Her eyes weren't blue anymore. They were a light, sparkling color, almost white, and it should have been terrifying, but it just looked beautiful. I felt warm and weightless and totally at peace. "All you have to do is fight on camera, for an audience. Do you think you can do that?"

I smiled and said, "Where do I sign?"

They had the papers right there, and I scribbled signatures in all the right places. Vassily gave me an envelope of cash, real money, more than I'd seen since my dad had been doing illegal arms deals out on the road.

Glory's eyes went back to blue, sweet, human blue, and she kissed me on my sweaty forehead and handed me another sports bottle. "Rest," *she said. Her fingers combed through my matted hair. "Don't you worry about a thing."*

I sank down on the bunk and closed my eyes, but I didn't go to sleep. Not quite. Not for a while.

Or maybe it was a dream. It felt like a dream, what they were saying when they thought I couldn't hear them.

"It's dangerous," Glory was saying. Her voice had gone flat now, not lyrical and lilting like it was when she talked to me. She didn't sound like the same person at all. "We have a limited time before Amelie discovers what we're doing. She's got spies everywhere, and I'm almost certain that there is surveillance, as well. Are you sure that the uplink is secure?"

"I'm sure," Vassily said. "The girl who gave us the encryption was one of the best. For months she had video streaming from Morganville without anyone suspecting it. She modified the code to ensure no one could detect this upgrade, in exchange for some favors. The money's already pouring in, my dear. The plan's going very well."

"And the old man? Is he pleased?"

Old man. That sounded ominous, and reminded me of things I'd hoped I'd never have to remember. Surely it wasn't the same old man. No, they had to be talking about some other vamp. They were all old, older than dirt, and black and rotting inside. I knew that.

"I wouldn't say pleased. He's . . . content to wait, for now. I've had to go to considerable trouble to lay false trails, since his disastrous intervention drew Amelie's attention. I believe I've convinced him to wait until we have adequate resources for the next steps."

"He's unpredictable. You need to watch him. He got away from me and tried to kill Myrnin, you know. If he'd succeeded . . ."

"I know. I've locked him up again. For his own protection."

Glory laughed. "Oh, he won't like that. Protect yourself, Vassily."

"I've been feeding him enemies," Vassily said. "I believe he's satisfied enough at the moment. How long until the boy's ready, do you think?"

"Oh, he'll fight, no question about it, but I don't like letting him leave us. Those friends of his, that girl, they could ruin everything."

"Or cement everything he's learned," Vassily said. "I believe in taking risks."

"Well, it's yours to take," Glory said. "I'll do what I can, of course."

"For a price."

"Nobody works for free, my darling."

When I opened my eyes, Glory was right there, bending over me. Her smile was like a drug, and the brush of her fingers on my forehead felt like the touch of an angel.

"Sleep," she whispered. "Dream of fire and strength, and remember how much this town has taken from you. Don't let it take the rest, Shane. Everything else is unimportant, except this: Michael doesn't mean you well. He's not your friend. And you can never fully trust him. Do you understand?"

"Yes," I said. It was something I knew already, something I should never have forgotten. You can't trust vampires.

Except Glory.

I was still smiling, drowning in the warmth of her touch, when I fell asleep.

NINE

Shane came home seeming just as normal as ever. He even brought brisket, and they ate, four friends together, like nothing had ever gone wrong. Even Michael's opaque "juice" bottle didn't set him off.

All Claire could think was that she needed to sit down and tell him about the call. But she didn't know what she was going to say, and she didn't want to say it in front of Eve and Michael. Not like that; it needed to be private.

But afterward, upstairs in his room, when Claire snuggled in next to him, talking didn't seem to be important. She kept thinking she'd bring it up, but after hours of slow, delicious kissing in his arms, she still hadn't managed to even start the conversation. Finally, she fell asleep. When she woke up, he was carrying her to her bed and tucking her in.

"Shane?" she murmured. He was leaning over her, close enough that his long, shaggy hair brushed her face.

"Still me," he murmured back. "Were you expecting someone else?"

She smiled. "Just you."

"Good girl." He gave her a slow, damp kiss, one that made her warm down to her toes.

"Shane, I was thinking . . ."

"About?"

"About . . ." She didn't want to do this—she really didn't. Not when it had been so nice. So perfect. But she tried. "About leaving Morganville."

To her surprise, he didn't pull back or act surprised or *anything*. He kissed her again, lightly, and said, "We will. I promise."

"I just— You know I want to go to MIT, right?"

"Of course. And you will."

Wow. Just like that . . . although she hadn't managed to work in the *January* part of the conversation. But it sounded good. Positive. They were on the same page, after all. One last, sleepy, damp kiss, and she slipped away into the best sleep she'd had in almost a week.

He was gone when she woke up, but he'd left a note. . . . He'd signed up for an extra, early-morning shift at the barbecue restaurant. He even signed it with *LY*, which she knew was Shane shorthand for *love you*.

That felt better. Lots better.

Claire was just coming down the stairs, humming and thinking about how nice it was to have things getting back to normal, and how she'd tell Shane about the January thing tonight, when Myrnin sent a message through the portal—well, more of a rock with a note tied to it, which rolled across the floor and scared Eve into a scream before the portal snapped shut. Eve kicked the rock resentfully with her thick black boots and glared at it, then at the wall. Claire, who was coming down the steps, gave her a "What the hell?" kind of look.

"Your boss," Eve said, and reached down to grab the rock, "needs to figure out texting. Seriously. Who does this? Is he *actually* from the Stone Age? And *you* need to figure out how to put something here that we can lock. What if this thing opens when I'm naked?"

"Why would you be naked down here?"

"Well—" Eve didn't have an answer for that one. She handed over the rock. "Okay, bad example. But I don't like it that he can just drop in any damn time he wants. Or throw rocks at us."

"I don't like it much, either," Claire admitted, as she untied the string and peeled the paper off the stone. She took a second to examine the rock. You never knew with Myrnin, but this looked just like what it appeared to be: plain granite. So the message was the paper, like if a normal person had thought of it . . . not that a normal person would have thrown a rock into their house in the first place.

The note said, *Stay away from the lab until further notice. I am fumigating. It might kill you. Also, it appears that Our Old Friend may have left town. Oliver is sending operatives after him, but the crisis may be over. For now.*

"Fumigating?" Eve said, reading over her shoulder. "What does that mean? And who's Our Old Friend?"

That was Bishop, of course, but Claire couldn't tell Eve any of that. "No idea. He probably thinks he's talking to someone else, anyway. Oh, and *fumigating* means that he's gassing the place. I guess he thinks there's some kind of bug problem."

"He usually just lets Bob loose on them."

"Maybe Bob's full. I hope he remembers to move him before—"

Maybe I'd better remind him." Claire pulled out her phone and texted Myrnin, who promptly texted back, *Of course i moved the spider. I am not an idiot.*

No, he was a very smart guy who responded to texts, but threw rocks with messages tied onto them.

Claire gave up.

"I got a message from Miranda," Eve said. "She didn't have your e-mail. You guys have a thing today?"

"Oh. Yeah, I'm taking her shopping."

"Shopping. Miranda. Really?" Eve looked confused, then a little bit fascinated. "Wow. Talk about the color-blind leading the blind."

"Hey!"

"Sorry, honey, but your amazing fashion sense is not the talk of anywhere. And Miranda doesn't go shopping. She's more of a Dumpster diver fashion victim."

"Well, she does with me," Claire said. She was stinging a little bit, because getting fashion dissed by a girl wearing red-and-black Halloween hose and a fake shrunken-head necklace was just too much. "Did she say where to meet her?"

"She said she'd be outside at ten."

Claire checked her watch. It was already ten after ten. "Guess I'm going, then. You heading out?"

"Some of us have work."

"Some of us have mad-scientist bosses who give them the day off for fumigation."

"Okay, you win." Eve winked and grabbed her stuff as Claire picked up hers. "Too bad I can't come with you two and give you decent makeovers. And *why* don't you ever wear that pink wig? That was the kick."

She wasn't wrong. The pink wig that Eve had practically made her buy in Dallas was, indeed, *the kick*, but away from Eve she always felt miserably self-conscious about wearing it. People looked at her. Claire was much more used to being invisible.

And right now, with all that was going on, seeming invisible sounded good.

Miranda was standing outside the fence, rocking a very unfashionable look—a plaid schoolgirl skirt that went past her knees and a wrinkled shirt in a color that might have been moss green in better light, but didn't match that skirt or her coloring at all. Her worried face actually lit up when she saw Eve and Claire. Eve waved and got into the big, black hearse, and Miranda waved back, as enthusiastic as a kid at her first parade. She sighed, watching the tail fins turn the corner. "She is so cool."

"She is," Claire agreed. "But so are you. Come on. Let's go shop."

Those looking for clothes in Morganville had two options: the resale stores, of which there were three, or the one off-brand department store that mostly had clearance items from the better places. After considering Miranda's budget, Claire steered her to the resale shops. College students often discarded their outfits here at the store next to the campus. Nobody was more fashion conscious than a TPU girl. It wasn't like most of them were on campus for the education.

To be fair, that applied to the guys just as well.

Miranda followed along happily enough to the first resale shop. She didn't say much, but there was a glow about her, something that made her seem much healthier and happier than Claire could remember. Just a little bit of attention, and the girl bloomed. That made Claire feel guilty and sad; she hadn't gone out of her way to make friends with Miranda, and she knew nobody else did, either. No doubt the girl could be weird and upsetting, but she was just like anybody else.

She needed to be *seen*.

"Here," Claire said, and held open the door of the shop for her. A tinny, cheerful bell rang overhead, and Miranda looked around as excitedly as if she'd never heard one before. That was impossible, wasn't it? That she wouldn't know what a shop bell sounded like?

Maybe not.

The woman at the back, dozing behind the counter, looked up and smiled sleepily. "You girls look around," she said. "Let me know when you're ready to try on."

"Okay," Miranda said, and stopped at the first rack of clothes. "Oh. Wow. There are a lot."

"Yeah, honey. Those aren't your size. Here. Look through these." Claire felt like she was unexpectedly channeling Eve as she pulled things out and held them up against Miranda's skinny frame, discarding some, keeping others. Strong colors didn't work on her, but earth tones did. Before too long, Miranda was pulling things on her own and holding them up, staring into the mirror as if she was seeing a future that, finally, didn't scare her at all.

"Can I try them on?" she asked. Claire waved at the shop owner, who unlocked the dressing rooms. Claire passed things over the top to Miranda, and leaned against the door.

"Nothing for you?" the woman asked, raising her eyebrows. Claire felt the look that swept over her outfit as if it had been an actual red-hot laser. She'd just been scanned, and found wanting.

"Well, maybe a top," she said. "Maybe."

"I have just what you need."

And she did, too. Claire ended up modeling it in front of the triple mirror, frowning at her reflection. With the khaki pants she'd picked today, the pink-and-white lace top looked weirdly appropriate—and kind of sexy. She'd come a long way in the last few months, but she wasn't sure she was ready for sexy in public. That just wasn't *her.*

The dressing room was too quiet. Claire knocked on the door. "Miranda? Hey, come out and take a look at this. Tell me if it's too much."

Miranda peeked around the edge, face gone ghost pale. Her eyes were dark, with that blank stare that people found so weird.

She was having one of her things. A vision.

"It has blood on it," she said. "You shouldn't buy it if it has blood on it."

Claire looked down. The top was perfectly clean. "Mir—"

Miranda suddenly opened the door. She had on one of the tops she'd been trying on, and Claire had a hurried impression that it looked totally good on her, but the girl was focused on something else entirely. She grabbed up all of the clothes, headed straight for the counter, and said, "I need this one, this one, and the one I have on." She put the *buy* pile down and then handed over the other one. "I just can't see myself in this, though."

Claire realized she meant that literally. As in, Miranda had looked into her future and couldn't see herself actually wearing that top. Bizarre. The shopkeeper didn't seem to get it, though—why would she?—and named her price. Miranda paid, and Claire barely had time to dig out five bucks for the pink-and-white top she had on before Miranda grabbed her arm and said, "We have to go. Hurry."

"But—"

"Now!"

Miranda hurried her outside, down the sidewalk, and then quickly turned her left, into an alley between two buildings. "Hide there," she said, and pointed. "Right there. Don't come out, Claire. Don't come out for anything. You understand? It's okay. It's going to be okay, but *not if you come out.*"

"Miranda, what in the hell—?"

Miranda's face was chalk white now, but very determined. She looked down at herself and said, in a sad sort of voice, "It's completely cute, isn't it? This shirt?"

"Yes, it's perfect. But what are you—?"

"Hush." Miranda turned toward the mouth of the alley and pointed again into the shadows behind some trash cans. "Don't come out!"

"Wait. What happens if I do?"

"I die," Miranda said very simply. "Hide."

Claire didn't like it, but there was something utterly sure about what Miranda had just said, and for all that Claire didn't believe in psychic predictions and that sort of stuff, she couldn't deny that there was something about Miranda. Something weird and powerful, at times.

So she pressed herself into the shadows.

For a long few seconds, nothing happened, and then she heard footsteps. Confident high-heel taps that echoed off the bricks, then slowed and came to a stop.

"I saw you come in here," said Gina's voice. "Freak. Hiding in dark alleys now? What's that about? You live in a Dumpster? Not that I'd be surprised."

Miranda didn't answer. Claire almost stepped out, because Gina was alone, and anyway, there was no way she was going to let Miranda face her down alone, no matter what Mir had said about it.

As if the girl knew what she was thinking, her hand moved behind her back and made a pushing motion. *Stay there.*

And Claire did. She didn't like it, but she did.

"You're going to hit me," Miranda said. "You're going to break my nose."

"Damn straight," Gina said. She sounded lazy and happy, as if she was enjoying all this. "You're lucky that's all I want to do. If you move, if you fight back, you're going to get it worse. Understand?"

"Yes," Miranda said. "I understand. If I don't let you hit me, you're going to kill me."

Claire actually felt a tremor of chill run through her, like a wave, because there was just *no doubt* in Miranda's voice at all. It wasn't scared. It was just . . . factual, as if she'd already seen it happen.

"You're smarter than you look, you spaced-out nutcase. So, yeah. Let me break your nose, and I'll let you walk away. You fight, and it gets worse and the knife comes out. We're clear?"

"Yes."

Claire tried to move again, because she knew with a nightmarish certainty what was going to happen and that she had to do something, *had to*, but again, Miranda made that *stay put* motion.

"It's okay," Miranda said in an eerily empty, remote voice. "It's not going to hurt that bad."

"Bullshit," Gina said, and she must have hit her, because Claire heard the wet crunch of the punch and Miranda's thin little cry, and then the sound of a body falling.

Gina laughed. Claire pushed off from the wall, but it was too late. Gina was walking off, humming to herself while she went. If she hadn't been wearing high heels, she'd have been *skipping*.

Miranda was getting up already, holding her broken, bleeding nose in one hand. Claire, angry and shocked, trembling with the sudden rush of frustrated adrenaline, started to go after Gina, but Mir grabbed her and shook her head furiously—and as she did, some of the blood gushing from her nose spattered Claire's new pink-and-white shirt. Claire didn't care at all. She crouched down next to the girl, helping her stand and holding her steady.

"That *bitch!*" Claire said. "You stay here. I'll—"

"No!" Miranda said. Her voice was muffled and small, but her eyes were wide and fierce. "It's the best thing. It's only my nose. She'd kill us."

"Then we're calling the cops. I am *not* letting her get away with this. . . ."

"Oh, don't worry. She won't," Miranda said. And beneath the blood, Claire was almost sure she smiled. "She's going to get in her car and drive real fast, and in two minutes she's going to run a red light. And then she's going to get hit by a big truck. My nose will set straight. *She's* going to the hospital, and she'll be there for a while."

Claire stared at her, this little, fragile girl with her bloody face and scary smile. Finally she said, slowly, "Mir, did you plan for that to happen?"

"No," Miranda said. "But sometimes it just happens the right way after all. It wouldn't have been right if you'd come to help me, though. She'd have stabbed me, right here, and then you, and she'd have died, too, but later and a lot worse. Amelie wouldn't have liked it."

It was fascinating and freaky, but Claire believed her. Every weird and scary word of it. She shook it off, with difficulty, and took Miranda back into the resale shop, where the clerk got her cleaned off, packed her nose with tissue, and even helped Claire sponge off the blood from her shirt.

As she did, Claire heard the distant sound of a car horn, then a crash, and then silence. She looked over at Miranda, who'd tilted her head back to slow the bleeding, and Miranda glanced back and shrugged.

"Karma," she said. "It's a bitch."

Miranda was dead right about Gina, not that Claire had any doubts; the accident was the talk of Morganville for days, and opinions were mostly on the "yay, finally" side of the scale. Gina had earned her suffering, not that Claire took much pleasure in it. She'd be weeks in the hospital and months in rehabilitation for the broken legs.

Miranda showed up the next morning for coffee, and the morning after, as if it had been planned that way. She probably saw it as inevitable, which it was, once she started showing up. A self-fulfilling prophecy. Eve thought it was weird, but she accepted it the way she accepted most things. It wasn't that she disliked Miranda; she just didn't know what to make of her, Claire thought. And she was fascinated by Miranda's psychic abilities.

Though she was just as shocked and fascinated by the spectacular bruises on Miranda's face and around her eyes. Double black eyes, and a swollen nose that had been reset at the hospital. "You look awful," Eve said on the second morning. "What color *is* that? Eggplant? You look like a special effect, Mir." She poured Miranda a cup of coffee and set out the milk and sugar.

"It's okay," Miranda said. Her voice sounded a little muffled and congested, but she was smiling. "It's just a bruise. Nothing much."

"It looks painful." Eve frowned at her over her own cup of coffee. "Seriously, if Gina wasn't already all busted up, I would be on her. I mean it."

"I know," Miranda said. "Thank you. But I'm okay. Really."

Michael came in through the swinging doors and smiled at Eve, and his smile turned brittle and strange when he saw Miranda sitting there. She didn't look at him. "Hey, Mir," he said, and it sounded casual, but Claire had seen that first, unguarded look. Michael got his sports bottle out of the refrigerator and warmed it up in the microwave, then left.

Claire got up and followed him into the living room. "Hey," she said. "Wait. What was that look?"

"What look?" Michael asked, trying to sound innocent. He took a drink from the sports bottle, and a little red flashed like sparks through his blue eyes. "I'm just wondering what she's doing here."

"Having coffee."

"Yeah, I can see that. Why?"

"Oh, come on, Michael—"

"I don't want to sound like a hard-ass, but Miranda's trouble," he interrupted. "Look, I feel for the kid—I do—but you have to understand, she's not . . . she's not safe to be around. Things happen. They always have."

"She's a *kid*. And it seems like nobody cares about her!"

"It's not that. It's just—" Michael gave up, sighed, and shook his head. "Not all strays are safe to bring inside, Claire. Trust me on that one."

Miranda was still sitting in exactly the same spot when Claire came back, still stirring her coffee with the same slow, dreamlike motions. Without looking up, she said, "He's right, you know."

"What?"

"Michael told you it wasn't safe to be around me. Well, he's right, mostly. Things do happen. Bad things, mostly."

Across the table, Eve looked up from her reading material, which looked like a celebrity gossip mag. She didn't say anything, but there was something weird about the way she looked at Miranda. Bad memories.

Miranda sipped her coffee. "I only came today because I needed to tell you something," she said. "They all think that the one they're looking for left town, but he hasn't. He's still here. He's got a plan; he's had one for months. And the pretty one, she's working for him. She's in charge of recruitment."

Eve's eyebrows were going up slowly but surely. "Hey, Claire? What's she talking about?"

"I don't know," Claire said, although she thought she did. She slid into the chair next to Miranda. "The pretty one. Do you mean Gloriana?"

Eve stiffened when she heard the name and rolled her eyes. "Oh, *God*, don't tell me that bitch is up to something after all. I *knew it*."

Miranda didn't seem to be listening to Eve; in fact, Claire wasn't sure she was hearing anything at all outside of her own head. "It's not totally his fault, you know, but you have to be careful now. He isn't in control anymore. All that anger . . ." She shook her head. "They're making him like this. They want to make you all like this."

It was impossible to follow what she was talking about. . . .

Was she still referring to Bishop? Or . . . God, was she talking about *Shane?* "Mir," Claire said. "Mir, are you talking about Shane?" Because Shane had a lot of anger; she'd always known that. He kept it locked down, mostly. But it was there.

Miranda, her bruised face distant and vague, sipped coffee and said, "Oh, I see. They want money first—money and soldiers. Then the rest of it. He won't make the same mistakes again. Tell Amelie. Tell her—"

She stopped talking, and her swollen, bruised eyes suddenly widened.

"Mir?" Eve must have felt the same thing Claire did, a powerful surge of dread, because they both got to their feet. "Mir, are you okay?"

"Oh," Miranda said. There were tears in her eyes now, and they flooded down her bruised cheeks. "Oh, that's bad. You have to stop it. You have to stop him."

"Stop *who?*"

"He's hiding in the dark. He's killing. He's killing all the time," Miranda said. And then her eyes rolled back in her head and she passed out in a dead faint, right at the breakfast table.

Bishop, Claire thought, frozen, as Eve cried out, ran to Miranda, and felt for a pulse. Claire couldn't seem to move. She felt icy and sick.

"Help me!" Eve yelled at her, and Claire blinked and jumped to it. Helping involved moving Miranda into the living room, where they propped up her feet higher than her head and covered her with a warm afghan until Miranda's frail eyelids fluttered and she woke up again.

"Oh," she said. "Did I fall down?"

"More like passed out," Eve said. "How do you feel?"

"Nauseous," Miranda said. Her voice sounded thin and a little feeble. "Too much coffee." She took a few deep breaths and smiled. "I don't eat enough."

Yeah, that much was obvious; Miranda was so thin, Claire could see the knobs of her bones at the joints. The girl needed sandwiches. "I'll make you something," she said.

"No, I have to go now."

"But, Mir—"

"I have to go," she said, and threw off the afghan and sat up, looking chalky and sick but very, very determined. "I can't answer your questions. It's too dangerous."

"For you?" Eve asked.

Miranda shook her head. "For you," she said. "You're in enough trouble already."

In the end, they couldn't stop her leaving; it was all Claire could do to delay her long enough to put together some peanut butter and jelly sandwiches and raid Eve's chocolate chip cookie stash. Miranda clutched the sack lunch and managed a smile as she walked, moving slowly and carefully, toward the door with them. Eve hovered near her elbow, but she seemed steady enough.

"I can't stay," Miranda said, and turned to meet Claire's eyes, then Eve's. "Michael's right. I'm trouble for you. I'm trouble for everyone, and it's better if I'm on my own. I'll be okay now."

"You're sure?"

Miranda nodded. She paused on the porch, looking like a sad little girl off to school, and said, "He's not going to stop this time. Claire, you need to understand, this isn't like it was before. This is war. Amelie's going to go to war."

Amelie went to war last time, Claire thought, but there was something sincere in Miranda's concern, something that made her feel anxious and breathless.

Shane. Shane was caught in the middle of all this. "Mir, is there anything else you can tell me . . . ?"

"No. Nothing that won't get you killed." Miranda lifted the sack of food. "Thank you for the sandwiches. And the cookies. I'm going to like the cookies a lot."

Then she walked away into the gray, chilly day, and they both watched until she was out of sight.

"Did we just do something bad?" Eve asked. "I mean, she's just a *kid.* We should have made her stay."

"I don't think we could," Claire said. "And she's probably right. It's safer for everybody if she goes."

Still, she couldn't forget about it . . . about Miranda, alone with all that going on in her head. As alone as Claire sometimes felt, she wasn't anything close to as isolated.

I wish I knew how to help her.

But the truth was, sometimes there wasn't anything that could be done.

SHANE

☽

Once I started fighting, it was all I could think about over the next few days. There was nothing like it, especially when Gloriana was there with Vassily, watching. . . . I felt invincible. Even the punishment was just another kind of approval; every time Jester hit me, it felt like a pat on the back, and an invitation to hit harder.

So I did.

Yeah, I wondered about the sports drinks, the ones Gloriana kept in the refrigerator. We all drank them, and it made it easier to keep up with the vamps. Some part of me wondered what was in it, but that part was small, and got crushed down by the part that was excited by all the freedom. It was freedom—freedom to be all those things I'd been holding back. Freedom to hate. Freedom to crush. No rules; no conscience. I was fighting like them now.

Because that was what it was going to take to beat them. Fighting like an animal, without any fear.

"You're fast," Jester said on the last day of the scheduled sparring. "Getting faster all the time." He sneered at me, and the sight of his fangs made my pulse jump—not with fear, but with aggression. Because I wanted to snap those fangs right off and wipe that sneer off his face. "You should take the bite," he said. "You'd be a good vampire."

"Shut up and fight."

"What's the matter? You afraid you'd bite your skinny little girlfriend?" Jester laughed. "She's already someone else's, you know. I can smell the bite on her. He's marked her."

Myrnin.

"Shut up," I said, and kicked him in the face. He wasn't expecting it, and he went down, but vampires were never that easy to put on the canvas for long. He bounced up, snarling now, and I danced back, watching his shifts of weight. He would come after me. Jester always came after me.

When he did, I hit fast, ducking under his rush, ramming my shoulder into his center mass and lifting him up off the canvas. Without leverage he wasn't much better than a regular human, but I had to be careful of his hands; they could crush bone, and his fingernails were as sharp as knives. I slammed him down on his head behind me and pinned his arms fast behind his back. It must have hurt, because for the first time, I heard something like a cry of pain.

From a vampire.

It made me feel great.

Someone clapped. It was Gloriana, watching me, leaning against the ropes with beautiful grace. "That was wonderful," she said. "Poor Jester. I think he may just be outclassed, Shane. You should let him up now. I think he's learned his lesson. Don't you?"

I twisted his arms tighter and felt something tear. This time, Jester screamed.

"Enough," Vassily barked, and ducked under the ropes. He grabbed hold of my shoulder to pull me off. "I need him more than I need you, boy."

I let go, because you didn't fight Vassily. You just didn't. It was the rule, one of the only rules left now. Glory and Vassily, they were off-limits.

Otherwise, though . . . it was just freedom. Fight until they said stop.

"Ah," Vassily said. "He's watching." He didn't sound especially happy about it. I looked up and I thought I saw a shadow upstairs, behind thick glass. A drawn, thin face, old and pale, that almost looked familiar, but it was gone in a blur of motion. Vassily sighed. "Did you see that, Shane?"

I nodded.

"I was afraid of that. Glory, if you would?"

It all blurred away, all the sharp edges and the surfacing memories. Gone. Whatever it was I was supposed to remember . . . Well, I didn't.

I looked up at the window reflexively, but I couldn't see anything. Probably just a reflection. I'd seen a reflection.

"This is too public," Glory said to Vassily. *"We need to move operations sooner than we'd planned—for the bout, at least."*

"Yes," he said. *"And we'd better have a third option, in case. I
don't want anyone crashing our party. You've got lists of people we can
trust to fill seats?"*

*"By the time I'm finished in this town, you'll be able to trust al-
most everyone."* She laughed. *"But yes. Reliable sources. We are very
close."*

"Good," Vassily said, and clapped me on the shoulder. *"Hit the
showers, Shane. You're ready."*

It was on Thursday when things started crashing down. To start
with, Shane was late, *really* late. When he finally got home, he
came bearing food—barbecue again, but with all the veggies and
everything. Which made him popular, of course.

But as she set the table, Claire watched him wandering around
the living room. He was pacing, and Shane usually didn't pace—
he was more inclined to drape himself over the couch and look like
he was asleep, even when he wasn't. Tonight, though, he was moving like he was pumped up and distracted, and when she touched
him on the shoulder, he spun around so fast, she took a step back.
It was easy to forget how big Shane was and how strong, until she
saw him in action. He was usually so gentle with her.

"What?" he snapped, and then some of the shadows left his
expression. "Oh. Sorry, Claire. Didn't mean that."

"Yeah, I know. What's up with you?"

He shrugged. "I don't know. Restless, I guess. Been like this all
day. I think after dinner I'll hit the gym, burn off some energy."
That was *not* like Shane. He was usually all about lazing around

on the couch, maybe putting some energy into a video game. He wasn't the nervous type.

"Okay," she said doubtfully. "Maybe play a game first? I've hardly seen you at all. We could spend some time together."

"Yeah, well, you're the one who runs off to High Wizard Crazy Pants every time he snaps his fingers. Don't blame me if you never see me. I've got a life, too. It sucks, but I've got one." Shane's words were blunt, and his tone—it was almost *mean*. Claire felt it like a slap, and it shocked her—why, she didn't know. He'd been angry enough over the Myrnin incident, but she'd thought . . . Well, she'd thought he'd gotten over it, that it was safe to talk to him again.

Clearly he hadn't moved past it. She decided not to say anything at all, which was probably wrong, but she didn't trust her voice. She didn't want him to hear how much he'd hurt her.

After another second of silence, he looked away. "Sorry. Game sounds good. I'm just in a mood, I guess. Maybe a little unnatural-creature killing is just what I need." Not *zombies. Unnatural creatures.* That might be nothing, but Claire's instincts told her it was a very bad sign.

Michael was putting out the food. Claire knew he was listening, but he didn't say anything, just shot her a glance. From that, she got that he was worried, too. Something was off. Definitely off.

"Hey, bro, you'd better play me first," Michael said. "Been a week since I got to beat your punk ass. Time for you to step up."

Shane bared his teeth. It wasn't a smile. "You want to play? Let's play. We'll see who gets bloody this time." That was Shane, but it *wasn't*. All the subtext was wrong—the body language, the tone, everything but the words.

Michael knew it, too. He locked eyes with Shane, frowned, and said, "Maybe you'd better lay off the caffeine."

"Maybe you'd better mind your own damn business." He said something under his breath. It sounded like *bloodsucker*.

"Hey," Claire said, and put her hand on his arm. "We're all friends here."

He flinched and shook her off. "Are we?" Shane asked. "You sure about that?"

"Hey!" Eve had come in, and now she thumped plates down on the table. She looked furious. Michael, on the other hand, was silent, watching Shane with a wariness that made Claire's skin prickle. "Hey, Van Helsing Junior, back off. How many times do we have to play this? What crawled up your ass *again*? Michael is one of us; you know that."

"He's one of them," Shane said. "Like my dad. Like Oliver and Amelie and all of those others. He *used* to be one of us. Now he just looks like us. You'd better stop drinking the suicide juice, Eve, before you wake up without a pulse, just like him."

"What are you *talking* about? What the hell happened? Michael? Did you say anything?" Eve looked to him, but Michael shook his head.

"Oh, come on. Stop pretending," Shane said, and took a step toward Michael. Michael tensed up. "I can feel it, man. I can feel you watching me. Watching *Claire*. Hell, Eve, too. We're all just walking snacks to you now. You think I don't know that?"

"Seriously," Michael said. "You need to check yourself. Whatever you're thinking, you're wrong. I wouldn't hurt you or Claire or Eve. Never."

"Never?" Shane laughed, high and tense. His eyes had a feverish kind of glitter. He crossed to Eve, and she shrank back, but too late. He grabbed her arm, and she dropped a handful of knives and forks with a clatter to the table.

She was wearing a black velvet choker with a skull and crossbones printed on it. He reached up and ripped it off her neck.

And on her throat were healing bite marks. Eve clapped a hand over them, eyes wide, but it was too late. They'd all seen it.

"You want to tell me that again?" Shane said. He was almost whispering now, face close to Eve's, but it wasn't kind. It was cruel. "You want to lie to me again about how you'd never hurt her, Mikey?"

Eve gave a little sound of distress and tried to pull free. His hand closed around her arm even tighter, holding her there.

"Shane, stop it. You're going to break my arm. . . ."

Maybe he would have let go—Claire didn't know—but Shane didn't get the chance.

Michael totally snapped, and sent Shane flying.

Shane hit the wall with a heavy thump, knocking over a table and sending a lamp crashing to the floor, which sizzled out with a frying sound as the bulb smashed. Claire was too shocked to move—it had happened too fast—but Shane rolled out of it and back to his feet in seconds. Michael was standing between him and Eve now, staring at Shane like he'd never seen him before. And Shane was glaring back, looking as angry and dangerous as Claire had ever seen him—chin down, head thrust forward.

Michael said, "Back off. You don't get to push Eve around. Or Claire, either. Not in my house. Are you drunk? Because you're damn sure channeling the ghost of Frank Collins."

That should have slapped Shane out of it; Claire winced, and it wasn't even directed at her. But Shane didn't react as if he'd heard at all. He took a step toward Michael, then another one, and then all of a sudden he rushed him.

Fast as he was, Michael missed the wind-up. Shane hit him and had him down on the floor in less than a second, kneeling on his chest to hold him down, fist pulled back for a second blow.

Claire ran forward and grabbed Shane's forearm, trying to hold him back, but he shook her off. She delayed him only by a second or two, but it was enough time for Eve to throw herself forward, over Michael, and look up at Shane with defiance and shock.

"No!" she yelled, right in his face. "Don't you dare start this, Shane!"

"I'm trying to *help* you, you crazy bitch! You can't trust him. Don't you understand? He's biting you! He's going to hurt you worse than—"

"We're getting married!"

Shane froze in place and his arm sagged. His fist opened and dropped to his side. He just stared at her for a couple of heartbeats, and then shook his head so violently, his shaggy dark hair lashed his face. "You're *what?*"

"We're getting married. And if I want to let him bite me, it's none of your damn business. And, anyway, you don't know what happened or why, so just shut your mouth, Shane." Her voice was trembling now, but she was trying to look sure of herself. "No, never mind. Open it and congratulate us. You owe us that."

"No."

"Why not? Because you don't *approve?* You *asshole!*" Eve shoved him, and Shane let her push him back, off Michael. He sat on the floor, suddenly limp, staring down at his open hands. His knuckles were bruised—they'd been bruised a lot lately, and cut and swollen. Claire had assumed at first that it had been martial arts practice, but now she was thinking . . . it was fights. Real fights.

Like this one.

Michael sat up, putting his arm around Eve. She touched his face where he'd been hit and said, "Does it hurt? Are you okay?"

"It stings," he said. "Shane packs a hell of a punch these days." He looked into her eyes for a long few seconds. "I didn't think you wanted to tell anybody yet."

"I didn't," Eve said. "But it just—it just kind of came out. Sorry. I wanted to have a big party for the announcement, you know, but . . . I had to say something to make him *stop*."

"He wasn't going to hurt me. Not much, anyway."

"Maybe not, but you were going to have to hurt *him* if he didn't back off. And I didn't want that."

Claire didn't know how she felt about all this. Sure, she loved Michael and Eve, and she knew they were together, but this . . . this seemed fast and final and odd. Like they were rushing into something.

She felt anxious about it, and she had no idea why.

Michael pulled Eve close again and kissed her with authority. Eve sighed and snuggled against his chest, and both of them looked at Shane and Claire, who was kneeling beside him. She wanted to ask Shane if he was all right, but it would sound stupid under the circumstances. Of *course* he wasn't all right. This was *so* not all right.

None of it was right.

She reached out, placed her fingers under his chin, and tipped his face up. His eyes were shimmering with tears, and he looked young and terribly frightened.

Lost.

"What's happening to me?" he asked. "God, Claire, why did I *do* that? I don't do that. I don't get angry for—for nothing. I didn't used to, anyway." He swallowed. "Do you think ... ? Is it ... ? Maybe it's because ... my dad ... He wasn't always an abusive asshole, you know; he just got that way. He'd get in these moods and he'd ... he'd ..." He gulped for air, as if he was drowning, and the misery and pain in his voice made her ache inside. She didn't think; she just put her arms around him and held him, fiercely loving him, afraid for him, afraid for *all* of them. "I shouldn't be doing this. It's wrong. It's all wrong. I don't want to be like him. I don't. I can't. Please help me."

"You're not," she whispered, lips close to his ear. "I swear you're not."

"Then why did I *do* that? I wanted to kill him, and it's like I couldn't stop myself."

She didn't know, either. She held him and they talked in soft, almost wordless murmurs, and his arms around her were strong but shaking, and she pretended not to feel it when his tears soaked through her shirt.

Michael and Eve left sometime during all that. The food sat cold on the table when Claire raised her head to check. Shane's skin felt cold and damp to the touch. "You should eat," she said. "You'll feel better if you eat."

He laughed wretchedly. "You think if I eat I'll stop being a complete dick?"

"You're not."

"Only because I'm not good at anything. Including that."

God, he was just falling apart, and she didn't know what to say. Claire got him to stand up and then sit down at the table.

She carried the food back into the kitchen to warm it in the microwave and found that Eve and Michael were in there, engaged in a quiet, intense discussion themselves. They stopped when they saw her.

"We should eat," she said, and pushed microwave buttons.

"Something's wrong with him," Eve said. "You saw. You know."

"Let's eat," Claire said. "We're all tired and hungry and nervous."

"Claire—"

"Please." Her voice broke when she said it, and she had to wipe her eyes to keep tears from falling. "Just sit down and *eat!*"

But when she carried the food out, Shane's seat at the table was empty. She checked his room, but he wasn't there, either.

He was gone.

And she didn't know where.

SHANE

I sat there alone at the table, looking at the house that had meant so much to me. My home. And it didn't feel like home anymore. Nothing felt right—least of all me. I didn't fit here anymore. I was dangerous. Something was wrong with me, and I couldn't take the risk I'd hurt Claire. I couldn't stop thinking about Eve's face as I'd been about to punch her, about the shocked, furious, haunted look she'd given me.

About how I'd seen my dad's face in that reflection.

I hated Michael now, hated him, and I didn't want to. He was my

*best friend, my buddy, my rock, but that didn't matter inside me now.
He was just one of them.*

It hurt. Bad.

*Hearing Eve say she was marrying him . . . It tore everything
apart. I hated him, and I couldn't hate him. I loved her, and I couldn't
not hate her, too, because she'd made that choice. None of it made any
sense anymore. I hated the people I was supposed to love. Not Claire—
that was pure; it was perfect. I couldn't hate her.*

*Not until I thought about Myrnin. Not until I remembered what
Jester had said . . .* She's marked. I can smell the bite on her. *Not
her fault, but I hated that Myrnin had that claim on her. That I
couldn't make it go away, no matter how much I tried.*

*Vassily had promised me money, and he'd delivered. He'd also
promised me and Claire a way out.*

*And I had to take it soon, because there wasn't going to be any-
thing left to save.*

*Claire was in the kitchen, talking to Michael and Eve, and a sen-
sation swept over me . . . paranoia, probably. I just knew that she was
trying to make it all okay, that we would all have to sit together and
pretend, just pretend that the cracks weren't big enough to fall through.*

And I couldn't do it. I just couldn't.

I got up and left, closing the door quietly behind me.

*Out in the dark, no Protection, no vampires who would snap
their fingers and make sure I could walk around in safety—not that
it worked that way, no matter what they promised. I had gotten a letter in today's mail; I was overdrawn at the blood bank again, and if
I didn't show up to pay my taxes soon, the Bloodmobile would come
calling. They weren't gentle when that happened. They came in, grabbed
you, strapped you down, and stuck a needle in your vein, whether you
liked it or not.*

Sometimes they forgot to take it out when you filled up your pint. Or two. Or three.

Sometimes people just didn't come out again.

No way I was going to do that anymore. I wasn't part of this. I was going to get out and take Claire with me.

I walked to the gym. If there were vampires out there in the dark, stalking me, they'd be sorry, and they must have sensed it, because I made it there without anybody touching me. I was sweating, even in the cold wind; there was steam coming off my skin. I felt shaky, though. Empty again. Not hungry, but thirsty.

When I got inside the gym and behind the PRIVATE *door, the first thing I did was pop open a sports bottle from the common fridge and down the protein drink. Then another one. Then another. By the third one I was feeling steady again. In control. Focused.*

Strong.

"Hey, man," said Greg, another human who was training. He was a juicer, bulked up with fake muscles, but he was cool, anyway. 'Roid rage was an advantage in the ring. We high-fived as I passed him, and then I went to sit on the bench with five others waiting for a chance at the ring. Shiemaa was the only girl—buzz cut, tougher than her weight in iron. She gave me a fist bump, and so did the others. All crazy together.

"I heard Stinky Doug got his ass killed," Shiemaa said over my head, talking to Keith, another juicer with arms as big around as Shiemaa's whole head. "Somebody said it was because he talked. True?"

"Guess so," Keith said. "Crazy little bastard. He wasn't going to last—didn't have the fire, anyway—but he could take a punch. I'll give him that."

"Yeah, you gave him plenty of those," Shiemaa said. She and Keith tapped fists in front of me. "Not like I miss him, but what did he say?"

"Don't know. Don't care."

"Doug," I repeated. Some of the fog cleared for me, even though I kept clenching my fists, burning off excess energy. "College guy? Got his throat cut?"

"Yeah, that's him. Stinky Doug. 'Cause, man, he had some hygiene issues."

"Which is a lot, coming from you," Shiemaa said. Keith threw a punch at her, behind my back. She blocked it without any effort. "Why? Did you know him?"

"My girl found the body," I said. "She knew him. I didn't know he was in this."

"Yeah, he was one of the first they asked in," Shiemaa said. "Probably because he was crazy and a loner and cracked out half the time. Wasn't even a Morganville kid. Guess they cut their losses."

Funny, but the idea that Vassily and Glory would kill one of us to protect their little messed-up fight club . . . that didn't surprise me. Didn't alarm me, either. Stinky Doug had brought it on himself.

Shiemaa tapped me on the back of the head, not gently. "Yo, pretty boy, you want to go a few?" The ring was empty now. The vamps were disappearing now, heading out to do whatever it was they did during the midnight hours.

"Nah," I said. I didn't feel like hitting anybody right now, not even Shiemaa, who could take it. "I'm going out to hit some bags."

"Suit yourself," she said, and tapped Keith. "Let's go, big guy."

I went outside, into the public area. Didn't matter at this time of the night, because there were few people who ventured in, and when the vamps cleared out—which they did nightly to go hit the blood bank or date or do whatever it was—we had the place mostly to ourselves. I waded into the heavy bag.

And pretty soon, the rest of them came out to join me.

Like a pack.

I hit the bag and felt better, because finally, I knew what I was doing.

I was leading the pack.

And that was okay.

TEN

He wasn't answering his cell, but it was a damn good bet that he had gone where he said he was going—to the gym.

In the end, they all went to find him, because Michael wasn't letting Claire go alone, and Eve wasn't letting Michael go without her. They took Eve's big, black hearse, which had a big enough front bench seat to hold three across. Claire ended up in the middle.

"Hey," she said as Eve navigated the giant Deathmobile down the dark streets of Morganville. "So . . . what is this about getting married? Did I even actually hear that? Because I'm pretty sure I would have been told about that by my *best friend*." She accompanied it with an elbow into Eve's side. Eve made a choked sound that wasn't quite a cry.

Claire was trying to keep it light, because she was feeling anxious now, not just about Shane, but about the two of them. It was tough being a vampire/human couple; there had been plenty of problems already. It would only get harder, and Eve—Eve was strong, but she was also fragile.

Michael was looking out the window at the passing houses, and he didn't turn his head. "It was kind of an impulse thing," he said. "Eve wanted to wait and have a big announcement and an engagement party. I just didn't expect her to blurt it out like that."

"Well, I had to stop Terminator Shane from punching your face off," Eve said. "I like your face. And it worked, didn't it?"

"Back on topic," Claire interrupted. "When exactly did this happen?"

"He asked me at the party. You know, Gloriana's big party." That had been one of those weird vampire welcome-to-town shindigs where they'd been basically the only people with pulses invited. Claire hadn't felt comfortable. She and Shane had ducked out as soon as they could, although later she wished she hadn't, because she'd heard that crazy things had happened, and the spectacle of *Eve* dancing with *Oliver* must have been, according to all the gossip, pretty compelling. Because Oliver apparently could *dance*.

That still seemed bizarre.

She hadn't known what happened after, because Eve hadn't said. Claire had assumed nothing had happened of any real notice. Obviously, she'd been way, way wrong.

"So where's the ring?" Claire asked. She was staring at Eve's left hand. Nothing shiny on the third finger.

"I didn't want to wear it until we told people," Eve said. "I guess I can now. Right?"

"Right," Michael said. He started to say something else, but fell silent.

It felt strangely awkward, suddenly. And Claire's mixed feelings got even more mixed. She *wanted* to believe this was the right thing, but why wasn't Michael more excited about it? Was that a guy thing? Or . . . God, was he having second thoughts?

Claire tried to fill the silence. "Any date yet or anything? And can I be a bridesmaid? Please let me be a bridesmaid! I've never been one."

"My bridesmaids are totally wearing black," Eve said. "Are you down with that? Because I'm wearing red."

"Yes!" Claire gave her an awkward, one-armed hug, and then did the same to Michael. "This is great. This is . . . Well, it's *great*. Isn't it?"

"Yes," Michael said. He was smiling again, but she saw his reflection in the glass, and what struck her, in a dreadful rush, was that it wasn't the right kind of smile. It was sad and brave, not happy and proud. Like he was doing what he thought he should do, but deep down he wasn't sure.

Oh, no. No.

Claire looked down at her lap. She said, "Well, let me know, okay? When you guys are ready. Because I'll be there, you know. All the way."

"I know you will," Eve said. She wasn't just smiling; she was glowing with delight. "Thanks, sweetie."

She turned the car again and pulled it into a parking space. The neon lights of the gym were on, and a sign glowing near the door said OPEN 24 HRS.

They sat in the car as the engine died. Michael and Eve exchanged glances over Claire's head. "So, we should do this," Eve said. "Right?"

"Right," Michael said. "We all go together. If he starts something, get out of the way, both of you. Let him take it out on me. I'm not as breakable."

Maybe not, but Shane had managed to land a punch on him, which had been unpleasantly surprising. Claire didn't want to see anybody get hit or hurt, not even a vampire who could bounce back. The sound of Miranda getting punched still haunted her, no matter how it had turned out later.

She'd always admired Shane's ability to defend himself—and her and his friends—but at the same time, she worried. Maybe there *was* something to his fear. Maybe his dad's legacy of abuse was tough to shake; she knew there was a dark core of anger inside of him, and guilt.

But she also knew that Gloriana was in it somehow. She had to be. No matter how much everybody swore she couldn't be interested in Shane, there was some reason this was happening, and Claire had seen firsthand how easy it was for Gloriana to twist people around.

Like Shane was being twisted.

I saw her, Claire thought. *Up in his room, that first night. That was her. It had to be Gloriana.*

That was when it had all started. When Shane's anger had started coming to the surface.

That bitch.

"We stay together," Claire said. "And I promise, I'll duck if anybody throws a punch."

The parking lot was—oddly, for Morganville—spacious and well lit. They didn't see anyone else on the way in. The same bouncer was at the desk. He looked the three of them over without saying anything. The lights buzzed softly, and Claire felt nerves start tingling right with them.

"We're looking for Shane Collins," Michael said. "Is he here?"

The counter guy checked a list, flipping pages. "Yeah, he signed in about half an hour ago. Hasn't left."

"We need to see him," Claire said.

"Ten bucks."

"We're not exercising," Eve said. "Really, you see these clothes? These are not made for sweating."

"Not my problem. It's ten bucks to go in that door, whether you exercise or not. Unless you want to buy a membership. Then it's five hundred."

"Are you *kidding?*"

"Do I look like I'm kidding?"

"No, you look like a dick who wants thirty dollars to let us talk to our friend," Michael said, and opened up his wallet. "Here's forty. The extra ten's not a tip, so give it back."

The guy counted out ten ones—even though there was a ten-dollar bill sitting right there in the cash drawer—and slid them over. "Knock yourselves out, kids," he said.

The buzzer went off, signaling that the door was open. Michael held it for the girls; Claire went first, heading past the busy weight- and exercise-machine area. Everything was full, which was shocking, considering the time of night. The weirdest thing was that Claire didn't see a single vampire here tonight . . . just humans. She'd have expected just the opposite.

Shane was in the corner, near the boxing stuff. That wasn't a surprise; Claire had known in her gut that he'd be here somewhere.

He was punching a heavy bag, which swung back and forth in slow, ponderous arcs as he danced around it, hitting with vicious intensity. He'd taken off his shirt, and he was sweating so much it looked like he'd just come out of the pool, his hair lank and plastered around his face. His skin shone and dripped.

And he was covered with bruises. *Covered.* She was shocked; she hadn't seen him like this, not ever. Some were just red spots—fresh ones—and others were old and blue and faded around the edges. The nastiest ones looked black and green. What the *hell* had he been doing?

Claire started to walk over to him, but Michael stopped her with a hand on her shoulder. "No," he said. "Let me, okay?"

"Okay." There was something very off about the way Shane was going after that bag, like it had personally tried to kill him. And she could tell that he'd been at it for a while now, ever since he'd walked in, probably.

As Michael came over, Shane grabbed the swinging bag in both gloved hands and stilled it. He was panting for breath, but his wide eyes were fixed on his friend.

Not in a friendly kind of way.

"Hey," Michael said. "We got worried when you blew out of the house. We wanted to be sure you were okay."

Shane didn't say anything. He clung to the bag and panted and watched Michael with that strangely blank stare.

"So," Michael continued, still moving toward him, more slowly now. More carefully, like he'd have approached a wild animal. "What do you say we blow this off and go get a pizza or something? You must be hungry."

He must have crossed some kind of invisible line, because Shane bared his teeth, and Michael stopped in his tracks. That was one crazy look, and Claire felt sick inside; it didn't look like Shane at all. He kept on grinning—if you could call it that—and reached down for a sports bottle sitting off to the side. He guzzled most of it in broad, thirsty gulps, but he still never took his eyes off Michael. Not for a second.

"I'm not hungry," Shane finally said. "Vassily's got me on a new diet. Protein shakes."

Michael tried again. "Bro, this is some unsettling crap going on. What the hell is up with you?"

"Can't you tell?" Shane asked. His voice sounded lower than normal—deeper in his throat. "Thought you knew everything, being part of the master race and all. Thought we mere mortals could never put anything over on you."

Claire had thought it was a private conversation, but behind her, she heard laughter—laughter in name only. It was bully laughter, meant to unsettle. There was no real amusement behind it, other than the anticipation of pulling some wings off particularly interesting flies. She risked a glance over her shoulder.

Shane had workout buddies all around them. She'd ignored them at first, thinking they were just people in proximity, but now they were all stopping what they were hitting or lifting or doing, and paying attention.

Big men. Tough. Sweating. A girl, too, but even she looked solid and muscular and ready to kick ass at a second's notice.

Claire realized that she was holding Eve's hand, and holding it tightly. She glanced over and saw that Eve, too, was riveted by Shane's behavior. She looked spooked and very worried.

Claire pulled her fingers free and walked over to stand next to Michael. "Shane, what are you doing here? Let's just go home, okay?"

Shane focused on her, but that didn't make it better. If anything, it made it worse, because there was none of the love and gentleness in him that she expected to see—that she'd seen only an hour ago. He stared at her, then at Michael.

She reached for Michael's arm for support. Something flared hot in Shane's eyes. "That how it is? You and Claire?" Shane asked. "Not surprised, man. Every girl I ever knew ended up liking you better than me. It's almost like you set out to make it happen."

"That's *so* not true!" Claire said, shocked—shocked he would even *think* it, much less *say* it—and stepped away from Michael. "You think— You think me and Michael . . . ?"

"Why not? He's cooler, right? He's rocking that whole guitar hero thing. Oh, and he's a vampire—I know how much all you chicks dig that. He could snap his fingers and pull any girl he wanted. Including you. Don't kid yourself thinking you've got a *choice*."

He didn't even say her name. Somehow, that hurt worse than anything else—and it made her angrier, too, which probably wasn't right, but she couldn't help it. "No, he couldn't get me, because I don't love him. I love *you*, Shane."

He gave her a cynical smile. "You don't have to love somebody to screw them."

"Shane!" Now she was embarrassed and horrified and sick, and she wished he would just *shut up.*

"I saw how he looked at you. C'mon, Michael, tell her. Tell her I'm wrong. Tell her you never think about it."

Michael didn't say anything. There was an odd light in his eyes, one Claire couldn't remember seeing before. She punched him in the arm. "Well?" she demanded. "Tell him!"

"Won't do any good," Michael said. "He's not listening to anything I have to say. Or you, for that matter. Come on, Claire. We should go."

"No! I'm not leaving him here like this, thinking that I'm—"

Shane lunged forward, grabbed her by the shoulders, and put his face very close to hers. Close enough to kiss, but that didn't seem to be on his mind at all. It was Shane, but . . . not. Not the Shane she'd always known. Even when he'd lost his memory, there'd been this core of gentleness, of control . . . and now that was gone.

It was like part of him had died. The best part.

"Let me make it *real* clear," he said. "I don't date fang-bangers. If it's not him, then it's that crazy-ass, bloodsucking boss of yours. So, go on. Do what you know you want to do. None of my business anymore. We're done."

And he pushed her away, hard. She banged against a steel post, which knocked the breath out of her and brought tears to her eyes from the instant, white-hot pain of bone ringing on metal.

Through the tears, she saw Michael grab Shane's arm and yank him away from her, unbelievably fast and strong. But Shane had strength and quickness of his own, more than he should have, more than she'd ever seen any human have, and he swung around inside Michael's defenses and slammed a fist into his stomach, then his chin, snapping Michael's head back. Then again and again and again, so fast it was a blur.

And Michael went down flat on his back. He rolled over, blinking, and got back to his feet, but his mouth was bleeding, and Eve was yelling and trying to get between him and Shane, and it was all just insane how this was happening. How could it possibly be—

Claire caught sight of a figure standing at a metal railing upstairs, looking down at them. A petite woman, masses of honey-colored wavy hair, a sweet face.

Gloriana. The vampire.

She was smiling—not an evil smile, which Claire could have understood, but a smile of childlike delight. A smile that should have been reserved for puppies and rainbows and true love.

Not for seeing Shane kick Michael in the side with enough force to shatter bone.

The onlookers watched with a kind of strange, hungry approval, and nobody moved in to stop it until a tattooed, muscled guy—Rad, from the car and motorcycle shops—grabbed Shane from behind, winding his arms through and locking his fingers together behind Shane's neck in a unbreakable restraining hold. He kicked the joints of Shane's legs and got him down on his knees.

Eve was down next to Michael, helping him sit up, wiping the slightly too-pale blood from his face with a lacy black handkerchief. "My God," she was saying numbly. "My God, my God... Oh, sweetie..."

Shane was trying to throw off Rad's hold, but his buddies were moving in now. As if he realized it was useless to try to break Rad's hold on him, Shane went still.

Eve must have decided Michael was okay, because she looked at Claire and asked her if she was hurt, at increasingly worried volumes. Claire shook off her daze and said, "No, I'm fine. Michael?"

He didn't answer. He was sitting up and all his attention was on Shane. Just Shane. "Let him go, Rad," he said.

"Dude," Rad said. "Don't think that's too good an idea. He ain't givin' up. He's just waiting. I can feel it."

"I said let him go."

"Your funeral." Rad released Shane, who turned and shoved him back. Rad held up his hands, signaling surrender.

And Shane turned back toward Michael, who wasn't showing anything like that. In fact, he was on his feet again, moving Eve—gently—and facing Shane squarely.

"This isn't you, man. What is causing this?" Michael asked.

"It's her," Claire said, and looked up at the railing above them. "She's screwing with him."

Only Gloriana was gone. No sign she'd ever been there. Claire looked around, but there were no vampires in view. Not one.

Just Michael.

Shane turned a scorching look on her. "*Her* who?"

"Gloriana," Claire said. "She's doing this to you."

He laughed. "I don't do vamps. You ought to remember that."

"It's a glamour."

"No, it's not," Michael said, very quietly. "Not exactly. Or not completely. Right, Shane? This is something else."

"Yeah," Shane said. "It's something else. Because there's a lot of us who are sick as hell of getting our asses kicked by vampires, sick of being your cheap wine bottles with legs, sick of letting you rule this town like lords. It's not going to happen anymore. Right, guys?"

The gym guys—and girl, too—had gathered around in a circle, and the rest had the same predatory glitter in their eyes, the same barely under-the-surface violence. Rad seemed to be the only muscled-up dude who was in the wrong place and had the wrong motives, and he was looking around now, frowning uneasily.

"Look, maybe you should go," he said to Michael, and then glanced at Eve and Claire. "All of you. Work this out later."

Her impulse was to say that she was staying, that no power on earth could make her leave Shane when he was like this, but if she did that, she knew that Michael and Eve would stick it out, too.

And that would be bad. Shane seemed especially angry about Michael being here—and, from the look he gave her now, Eve, too.

A big, overmuscled guy dressed in microfiber sweats and gold chains, like some cheesy reality-show reject, gave Eve a *really* nasty grin. It was mostly a snarl. "You always ran around town, dressing like a wannabe bloodsucker, and now you're banging one," he said. Well, he didn't actually say *banging*, but Claire's brain refused to completely translate it. It was too shocking when it was said with that much venom. "I hate fang-bangers worse than the vamps. At least the vamps are just doing what comes natural. *Your* kind, you're perverts."

Eve flinched a little, but then she lifted her chin. "Really? Considering what I hear from the girls you date, Sandro, maybe you ought to think twice about throwing that word around. 'Cause I had to look up half the things you wanted them to do on Urban Dictionary, and it was disgusting."

She was wearing the choker again, having tied it back on before they'd left the house, but now Sandro—like Shane had before—reached out and yanked on it. He didn't manage to pull it off, but he pulled it down far enough that Eve's fang marks were clearly visible. "Look at that. Walking blood bank. I heard you're a walking ATM, too. That stands for Any Time Michael wants it—"

Michael stepped in front of Eve, facing Sandro, and said, "You want to say it to me?"

Sandro laughed. "You didn't learn your lesson from your little friend there? Sure. 'Cause you ain't got no backup, Glass. Your whole family's been vamp pets from the Dark Ages, but we ain't having any more of that better-than-you crap. Not here. Here, you're all on your own, bitch."

Shane had gone very quiet behind them. Claire looked at him, at his set, unsmiling face, and felt panic ignite. This was real, and it was dangerous. Rad and the few others who didn't seem angry were backing off, edging out of the crowd. Maybe they'd send for some help, or maybe not. She certainly didn't trust that the dude taking their money at the door would bother to come charging to the rescue.

Michael was a vampire, but he was young, and he couldn't fight this crowd on his own. Plus, he'd be trying to protect Eve, and her, too.

And Shane didn't have his back. Or any of their backs. It was obvious and painful, and Eve gave him the worst, most heartbroken and betrayed look Claire could imagine. "You'd just stand there," she said. "You'd stand there and let this happen to us. *To us.* To your own girlfriend."

Shane turned away to start slugging the heavy bag again.

"Shane," Claire whispered. "Please. Please."

He faltered, and one of his punches landed light. He grabbed the bag and stopped its swing, and looked over his shoulder at her. For a long, awful second, she thought he'd just go back to what he was doing, but then he nodded sharply at Sandro. "Let them go," he said.

Sandro cracked his knuckles. "Gimme a reason."

"I owe her that much," Shane said. "Let them leave." He punched the bag again with stunning force. "But take my advice, *friends.* Don't come looking for me again. Any of you."

There was some grumbling, but the circle slowly parted. Eve grabbed Michael's hand and towed him off, heading for the exit. Claire hesitated, staring at Shane's back as he bobbed, weaved, and punched.

"Shane," she said. "I still love you."

He didn't answer. Sandro shoved her after her friends.

"You heard him," Sandro said. "Get the hell out and stay out. He ain't interested."

She looked back just once. There was pain—real pain—on Shane's face as he fought the training bag, and their eyes locked just for a second before he looked away.

His were red. It wasn't possible to tell tears from sweat, but she thought—no, she knew—how devastated he felt.

Because she felt exactly the same.

Tears welled up and spilled over, and she sucked in a trembling breath that smelled like sweat and metal and despair.

Eve took her hand. "Come on," she said. "Nothing you can do here."

That was true, and it hurt so, so badly.

SHANE

I wish I could say I don't know why I did it. That would make me feel better, cleaner, about what I said to her. But I knew. It was just like Claire figured: Glory had glamoured me. But I didn't care, because under the glamour there was a real bad streak of . . . me. I felt right. More than that, I felt righteous, like a knight in the old stories riding off to some God-justified war. I felt like I had when I'd had a purpose and my dad had been alive to tell me what it was.

I punched the heavy bag until my arms trembled and my legs felt like lead, and then collapsed on a metal bench. Somebody brought me another protein shake, and I downed the bottle in thick, thirsty gulps. My head was hurting, and I was having trouble catching my breath.

"Hey, man, you all right?" That was Sandro. I hated Sandro, I hated his greasy smile and his gold chains and his fake New Jersey cred. He was from Morganville, like the rest of us. Hell, his dad was a baker. You can't be a badass when your dad makes cakes.

Sandro squeezed my shoulder, tightly enough to bend tendons. I knocked his hand away. *"Fine,"* I said. *"Get lost."*

"Good job dumping that little Renfield. I don't know what you ever saw in her, anyway. She looks like half a boy. Me, I like my women with curves and bounce, if you know what I mean."

I drained the last of the shake and felt a fresh burst of anger and hunger. *"Maybe you need to look up what get lost means."* Michael wasn't here to take it out on, but Sandro would do just as well.

"Don't get attitude with me, Collins. You ain't that tough."

I knew better. Sandro was schoolyard tough. I was fight-for-your-life tough. But I wasn't going to teach him the difference, because for all his faults, for all he was a prime, grade-A jackass, he was breathing and his heart was beating, and that's all it took to put him on my side. Two kinds of fighters: us and them.

None of them were here right now. Glory and Vassily had separated us into humans and vamps, and it had worked. Now every time I saw a vamp it made me want to rip into it.

Including Michael.

That made me feel weird inside, but not weird enough to want to change it. This was where I belonged. This was what I was meant to do. Born and bred to it, honestly. My dad had taught me well.

In here, I didn't have to be Shane Collins, eternal slacker, orphan, lost boy. In here, with these guys, I was part of something. Part of the war.

Even if, right now, that war was fought one on one, in the ring, with people cheering.

Someday, it would be fought in the streets, and people would cheer there, too.

Even Claire.

Soon.

"It's Gloriana," Claire said once they were safely in the car. "I saw her, Michael. I saw her watching you and Shane fight. She was *smiling.*"

"I don't know how she could do it without affecting me or you or Eve," he said. "Glamour isn't that specific."

"Hers is," Eve said. He gave her an odd look as he drove down the street, heading for home. "What, you didn't know that? She can grab one guy out of a room if she wants to. I've seen her do it. I've seen her do it to *you.*"

Claire had seen it, too, at her welcome party—Gloriana had lured Michael away with just a smile and a wink, right out of Eve's arms. She hadn't been serious about it—at least, Claire didn't *think* she'd been serious—and Eve had gotten him back fast, but she'd felt Glory's influence now, and the worst thing about it was that it seemed like the most natural thing in the world. Frank had even warned her, and she *still* hadn't believed that there was anything wrong with what she was feeling or doing.

That was what had happened to Shane.

"Sure, she can draw men to like her," Michael said. "It's not that hard. But changing them, the way Shane's changed? That's a whole different kind of thing. I don't think even Glory can do that."

"Well, who'd know?" Claire asked. "Amelie?"

"Maybe. Or Oliver; he seems to know her better."

Claire remembered Oliver sitting with Gloriana at Common Grounds. Yeah, they had seemed cozy. Which made her stomach twist a little, because the last thing she wanted to think about was Oliver having any kind of love life, ever, with anyone. That was just disgusting. "Frank said something about—" She shut her mouth, suddenly flooded with alarm and adrenaline, with a snap, because she had *not* meant to mention Frank. Ever. "I mean, before he, you know—"

"Died?" Eve supplied. "Went to that big motorcycle rally in the sky? Took a dirt nap?" She sent Michael a warning glare as he winced. "*What?* Yes, I'm being insensitive, but Shane's not here, and besides, I am *pissed off* right now. Frank Collins was never Mr. Congeniality when he was alive, you know. I don't know why I have to give him any extra postlife respect."

That nicely distracted everybody from Claire's mistake, and she took the precious time to work out what she'd meant to say, leaving out Frank completely. "We need to find out what she's doing here," Claire said. "Something's turning the humans at that gym into a mob, and we all know that's what Amelie is most afraid of. Human mobs can take down vampires individually. She'll do anything to prevent that from starting. If it's Gloriana, then we need to prove it."

"What if it's Bishop?" Michael asked. Eve made a choked sound. "It's just the kind of thing Bishop would want—humans turning against vampires, creating chaos and death. He doesn't care who gets hurt."

"Nasty," Eve agreed. "If he's got Gloriana working for him . . ."

"Then this could be a whole lot bigger than anybody expected," Michael finished. He paused for a moment, and said, "I can find out."

"How?" Eve's voice had an edge, and Claire glanced over at her. She seemed tense, hands clenched where they rested on her thighs.

"By talking to Glory," he said. "Look, she likes me. She'll tell me things."

"Yeah, that in no way makes me want to barf acid," Eve said. "You getting cozy with *her*."

"Eve—"

"We agreed. You stay away from her."

"This is different. This isn't just— Look, it could be Shane's life we're talking about. And a lot of other people's. Innocent people. I can handle Glory."

"Can you?" Eve asked. "Because I notice you never call her Gloriana. Just *Glory*."

He shut up. *Which is probably about the only smart thing he can do,* Claire thought. Eve had a genuine point. There was something alarming about how fast Michael had jumped on the whole "let me talk to her" thing.

It was an uneasy silence all the way back home. As Michael parked the car and killed the engine, Claire said, "Do you think he'll come home?"

"You mean tonight? No," Michael said. "If you mean ever, I don't know. That wasn't Shane back there. I think you know that."

She did. It hurt like a huge ball of spikes inside her stomach, and she couldn't keep her eyes from clouding with tears every time she thought about him. It hurt—oh, God, it hurt. "Then I have to get him back," she said. "We just do. Whatever it takes."

Her cell phone rang, and she looked down at the screen, hoping wildly that it was Shane—but no. It had no picture and no number showing. Just blankness. She flipped it open and said, "Hello?"

"I didn't know your boyfriend was so *hot*," a girl's voice said. "So much hotter than you, you know. You're dating so far outside your league, you're making us all embarrassed." Giggles, and the voice took on a nasty edge. "He's a rock star now, and he doesn't need some flat-chested kid anymore. He's going to dump you faster than last week's Chinese food and date a real girl. A porn star."

"What— Who are you?"

"The future Mrs. Shane Collins." More giggles from other girls who must have been listening. "I'm watching it again. God, he is *smokin'* hot!"

A click, and Claire was left with nothing. Not even—when she checked—a call history. It was a blank number.

"What?" Eve asked, frowning. Claire shook her head.

"I have no idea," she said. "But . . . it probably isn't good."

"Well, there's a stunning surprise," Eve said. "Didn't see that coming. Was it Monica?"

It should have been, by all logic that Claire knew, but . . . it hadn't been Monica or Jennifer or any voice she knew. She'd made enemies in town, but not so many that she didn't know how to identify them.

So why was some random weird girl calling her about *Shane*?

What had she said . . . ? "I'm watching it again," Claire said out loud. Eve looked at her with a frown.

"Watching what?" Michael asked.

"Exactly," Claire said, and felt like she was falling off a cliff into the dark. "Exactly. Something's really, really wrong, Michael. I just know it!"

"Let's get inside," he said. "And we'll figure this out."

ELEVEN

A few months back, a girl named Kim had wormed her way into Eve's friendship, and she'd betrayed it. She'd recorded a lot of things all over Morganville, but her personal favorite had been sex tapes.

Claire, fingers trembling on the keyboard, did a search for *Shane Collins* on YouTube.

It came back empty, and she slumped back in her chair, so relieved she thought she might faint. If Kim had somehow gotten that on the Internet . . .

"Try Google," Michael said. He was crouched down next to her chair. Eve was hovering over her shoulder, all of them fixed on the glowing screen of her laptop. Claire bit her lip and tried that, and results scrolled down. Most of them weren't about *her* Shane, but one caught her eye. She clicked it, without even consciously realizing why she'd picked it.

A Web site came up, loud and red and edgy, all jagged type and torn-up graphics. The banner read IMMORTAL BATTLES. An animated thing underneath asked if she had the courage to enter the game.

There were lots of fragments of pictures making up the splash page—dark, gritty stuff, mostly guys looking intense and sweaty.

And immediately, one face jumped right out at her. She gasped at the same time Michael leaned forward and pointed. "That's Shane," he said. She nodded. "Click it."

"I—" *I don't want to,* she thought, but she squeezed her eyes shut for a second, then aimed the mouse at the glowing entry box.

She clicked. It exploded, and the sound rattled harshly out of the speakers. Michael didn't flinch, but she did.

When the screen cleared of the animated explosion, there was a sign-in box and a link to create an account. She clicked that. "It says I need a credit card," she said. "And that it's a hundred bucks to sign up."

Michael opened his wallet and handed over a card. He hadn't had it long, she guessed; it still looked shiny and new. It was black, with Amelie's logo in gray in the background and the bank's info at the bottom. "Do it," he said. She typed in the info and handed the card back, then clicked REGISTER. There was the usual wait, and then the screen cleared for a video.

"That's a vampire," Eve said, leaning forward. "What the *hell?*"

"His name is Vassily," Michael said. "I never liked him."

Vassily—whom Claire had never seen before, except maybe at a distance—was a long-haired guy only a little older in face-age than Michael. Kind of good-looking, if you went for lots of sharp angles and arrogant smiles. He was wearing period costume, which struck her as a little weird; some vampires did, but not many. They were anxious to fit in, not stand out. He looked like he'd ripped the clothes off Dracula in an old black-and-white movie.

"Welcome," Vassily said, and smiled. He showed teeth. "To Immortal Battles. We don't fight to the death—we fight *beyond* death, in the world's most dangerous sport. You'll never see ultimate fighting the same way again—I promise you. Ah, I see our betting windows are open. Choose to view previous matches, or place a bet on an upcoming one. And remember: we know who you are." Another flash of vampire teeth. It was all weirdly campy.

"What the *hell?*" Michael murmured, almost laughing. "Amelie's going to kill him."

The video went away, and Claire was left with choices. There were two previous-bout videos, and she clicked on the second one.

Michael sucked in a startled breath, and so did Eve.

Two half-naked guys in a wire cage, pounding the hell out of each other. Nothing you couldn't see on pay-per-view, except that one guy's skin was far too pale, and where he got cut and bled, the blood wasn't quite right. That was a human and a vampire, fighting each other.

Then one, the human, went down and was dragged out—Claire couldn't tell if it was theater or not, or if he'd been knocked out—and another guy entered the cage.

"No," she whispered. "Oh no."

It was Shane. He looked scared but determined, eyes dark and fixed on the vampire in the cage with him. The vampire hissed at him. Shane circled, looking for an opening.

"Is he insane?" Michael blurted, looking paler than ever. "He's not even armed!"

He also wasn't bruised, Claire realized. This had been shot before today, before she'd seen all the bruises on his body. Because of that—and only because of that—she was able to watch as Shane and the vampire bobbed, weaved, feinted . . . and attacked. The vampire looked weakened, thanks to the first bout, but Shane looked incredibly fast and strong.

Even so, he got pounded down, time after time. Claire found herself flinching every time a vampire fist landed. Shane kept himself alive, barely, and actually broke off one of the vampire's fangs with an unexpected kick. That earned him a slam into the wire mesh so forceful it cut the pattern into his skin.

"I can't watch this. I can't," Eve said, and put her hands over her face. "He's bleeding!"

It dawned on Claire that if the fight had been dangerous before, now it was incredibly risky—a bleeding human was like catnip to a vampire, and the one Shane faced seemed to get a second wind, so to speak, and come after him with a vengeance.

And Shane went down. The vampire pinned him, and Claire caught a glimpse of red, glowing eyes and one fang as it lunged for his throat.

Shane slammed a fist into the side of the vampire's head and snapped it sideways, and managed to use the momentum to roll him over. Once Shane was on top, he pounded the vampire with merciless punches, over and over again, and Claire could see the horror and anguish and rage that she knew was trapped deep inside him bubbling over, *taking* over. He wasn't just fighting for fun or money—he was fighting for his mother, his sister, even his father.

He was fighting his nightmares and his own hatred of Morganville.

A black-shirted referee jumped in and stopped the fight, and hefted Shane's sweating arm into the air to signal victory. Shane collapsed to his knees and had to be helped out of the cage.

But he'd won. His vampire opponent had to be carried out.

When the screen went dark, there was silence in the room, and then Michael said, very quietly, "Look at the hit counter."

Hundreds of thousands of views for this video, at a hundred dollars per account. Millions, for whoever was running Immortal Battles.

"That doesn't even count the betting, and you *know* there's betting. Shane's not just doing this for fun. He's getting paid," Michael said. "He's getting paid to fight vampires."

"Click the other one, the older one," Eve said. She sounded better now that she'd seen the ending of the first fight. Claire wasn't so sure she could handle another one; she never wanted to see Shane like that again, or be that afraid for him.

But she needn't have worried, because Shane wasn't in this one. *Stinky Doug* was.

Stripped down, with his hair tied back, Stinky Doug looked lanky, all muscle. His fight was over quicker than Shane's, although he displayed the same unnerving quickness and strength. It didn't go in his favor. Doug got his ass kicked by a slender young female vamp, and was dragged out unconscious. Not dead, Claire knew; from the date on the fight, this had been at least two weeks before he'd died.

So Stinky Doug had stolen blood from the lab experiment *after* this fight was filmed—why?

"He already knew about the vamps. He must have needed proof," she murmured. "Proof of the vampires. That's why he took the blood. He was going to go public, or he was blackmailing them."

"What?"

Claire pointed to Stinky Doug's slack face as he was dragged out of the cage. "He fought two weeks ago, right? Maybe he wasn't happy with what he got paid. He stole vamp blood from a college lab experiment. I think maybe he was going to use it for proof, or to get more money out of the Immortal Battles people. After all, they're playing the vampire part of it like theater. Like a joke."

She was right; the comments proved it. People were playing along with it, but clearly, nobody *believed* there were vampires fighting on screen. They were guys in makeup. But they liked it all the same.

Claire remembered the phone call she'd gotten that had tipped her off to the Web site. Somebody inside Morganville knew for sure, and they *would* take it seriously.

"There's something else," Michael said. "Shane's fast, yeah, sure, and he's always been strong. But he's not superhuman. Or he wasn't. But you saw him tonight. That was . . . different. He's gotten faster and stronger and able to take more punishment. They've done something to him."

And it all came together in Claire's head in a blinding flash. Doug . . . the lab experiment. Her discussion with Frank about why someone would want vampire blood in the first place. He'd told her it wouldn't make a decent drug, because there wasn't a high and it wore off too fast, but *it made you stronger and faster.*

"Vassily's giving them vampire blood," Claire said. "In the protein shakes, probably. It's a temporary boost, but it breaks down fast."

"Oh, God," Eve said. "That's bad. That's damn bad, isn't it?"

Michael didn't deny that at all. "Click on the link for upcoming bouts."

Claire did. In three days, Shane was scheduled to fight again, this time a vampire named . . .

"Jester," Michael murmured. "He's fighting Jester. And Jester will murder him." He didn't mean it figuratively. "We have to get to Shane and get him out of this. He can't survive that, not even with the help of whatever they're giving him. The human body's not made for it."

"We have to get him out of it before Amelie finds out," Claire said, "because she'll kill everybody involved, no questions asked. This is a high-security risk for the town. She won't hesitate."

Eve dropped down onto Claire's bed and buried her head in her hands. "And how are we supposed to do that, exactly? Shane's all *grrr* now. He's not going to listen to us. And he's got an entourage of his very own tough guys who'd gladly beat the crap out of us for breathing his air."

"What are we going to do, then? Just let him *die*? For *money*?" Claire stood up and glared at the Web site again in utter fury. Her hands ached, and she didn't know why until she realized she was clenching them into tight fists. That made her think about Shane fighting, and that made her even angrier. There was a red-hot pressure inside her head that felt like it might blow her apart. "We can't tell Amelie. We can't go to Shane. Then *what?*"

Her cell phone rang. She looked at the screen and it said nothing at all again. Her breath hissed out in a sound of pure, enraged frustration, and she answered it in a voice she hardly recognized as her own. "If you're calling to tell me how *hot* it is to see my boyfriend get beaten up, I'm going to come over there and—"

"It's Frank," said the weird mechanical voice on the other end. That hit her like a bucket of ice-cold water, making her flinch and shiver at the same time. *Oh, God, he could hear her.* Frank could hear any of them, anytime, if they had their cell phones on them and he cared to listen. The ultimate eavesdropper, and she'd forgotten all about it. "Get here. Now."

"The lab," she said.

"No, Candyland! Of course the lab! And you'd better come prepared to explain to me what the hell is happening to my son, Claire." He hung up on her. She'd just been hung up on by a disembodied brain in a jar. Fantastic. She hadn't even had time to say, *Don't tell Myrnin,* but she didn't think Frank would, anyway. He'd have picked up on how dangerous this was for Shane, and if Myrnin knew, well . . . Myrnin wasn't Shane's biggest fan at the best of times. Claire didn't think he'd rat Shane out just because of that, but he was, ultimately, Amelie's friend first. And Amelie would want to know.

This was so dangerous. *God,* everywhere she turned there was risk. To Shane and to Morganville. Even to the vampires, though she didn't care quite as much about that, because the vamps could always take care of themselves . . . and would.

"Who was it?" Michael's face was carefully blank, but she saw the glitter in his eyes. He was waiting to see how much she was going to lie.

She sighed and told the truth. "Frank Collins," she said.

"Frank's dead."

"Yes," she said. "And . . . I have some things you'd better know before we go any further."

"Oh, this should be good," Eve said, in a "not really" voice. "Somebody make popcorn."

✳   ✳   ✳

Claire told them about it on the drive to Myrnin's lab. It was darkest night now, and only vampires went out by choice; they took Michael's shiny, town-provided Vampmobile, with highly tinted windows, because Claire wasn't absolutely sure that they'd be back home before dawn, and, besides, it provided her and Eve with some extra protection from snack-inclined vampires. Just in case.

"So, wait," Michael said. "Back up. Myrnin chopped Frank's brain out and put it in a jar to hook up to his machine, after Amelie told him he was officially not supposed to be working on that machine. Is that about right?"

"Amelie was mad at him," Claire said. "But Myrnin was going to do it, anyway, and I think she knew it. It was just . . . timing. And whose brain he was going to get to use. Considering that he was thinking about using mine . . ."

"Yeah, I get it; it's a solid win." Michael shook his head, bemused. "Remind me to have myself cremated if I ever get killed around here. Can't trust anybody these days. But I have to say, if I had to pick somebody to trap in a jar for eternity, I'd vote Frank Collins every chance I got. He didn't deserve to live, but he did deserve to suffer. He's suffering, right?"

"Well . . . I guess." Claire hadn't seen much evidence of suffering, actually, but Michael seemed pretty happy about the whole idea. "The point is that Frank is connected to a lot of sensors, cameras, cell phone networks, Internet feeds. . . . I'm guessing that the site we looked at was encrypted, though, because he didn't start yelling about things until we started talking about them. He couldn't see it."

"Somebody knew enough to take precautions," Michael agreed. "Somebody on Team Vampire."

"Like Vassily," Eve said. "Or Gloriana, that bitch."

"She's not that bad."

"Michael, you're going to want to stop defending her now before I have to cut you somewhere you'll feel it."

"Ouch."

"Fiancée," Eve said, pointing one black fingernail at her chest. "Do *not* defend her to me. She tried to drag you off to her lair. I'll bet she has a lair. And a boudoir in her lair."

Michael gave up. Claire thought she saw him smiling, but if he did, he made it vanish pretty fast. "Who's Frank likely to tell? Myrnin?"

"Maybe," Claire said. "And Myrnin will blab to Amelie, and then—"

"And then the vampires involved get a slap on the wrist, and the humans involved get dead, and we redefine *snafu* in our time," Eve said. Michael made a left turn. Claire had no idea where they were; it was featureless blackness out the windows. Michael was the only one who had the super eyesight to make anything out. "We should have taken the portal."

"And what happens if Frank decides to lock down the portals to keep us from leaving?" Michael said. "I like having my own transportation."

He had a point. Claire didn't trust the portal system, which Amelie and Oliver—and sometimes Myrnin—used to skulk around the town. Sure, it was all magically amazing until it stopped working. She'd seen it stop working midtransit. The results hadn't been pretty.

Michael braked. "We're here."

"Maybe you guys should—"

"Go in with you," Eve said. "Because we're not dumping you

off on the curb like an abandoned puppy, Claire. You know that's not happening."

She did know, and she was grateful. Very grateful.

Michael, though, had one more question, as they were walking down the alley toward the lab, lit eerily by the bobbing flare of the little flashlight Eve kept in her bag for emergencies. "Does Shane know? About his dad being kind of alive?"

"No," Claire admitted. "I didn't want to tell him. I thought, *Maybe later.* It was too soon. He'd just come to terms with losing him. I couldn't stand to see him hurt all over again."

"I probably would have done the same thing," Michael said.

"Thanks."

"Don't thank me. Just because I'd have done it doesn't mean it was right."

That was not exactly comforting. Claire thought about it all the way inside the leaning, dry-rotted shack that stood at the end of the narrowing alley, and down the unlit steps that led to Myrnin's lab.

She was prepared for Myrnin to be there, but he wasn't. She found the light controls and brought up the glow on the wall sconces. The lab looked its usual disorderly self, half cool steampunk junk shop, half dump. She still hadn't broken him of the habit of leaving stacks of books everywhere, including blocking the paths between the lab tables. He'd just gotten in a new shipment, she saw. More alchemy books. The top one, designed in garish black and yellow and white, was titled *Alchemy for Idiots.* He'd probably picked that one out just for her.

"Myrnin?" She called out, but not very loudly. No sign of him. When she raised her eyebrows at Michael, he shook his head. Not here, then.

That was confirmed by the flickering black-and-white ghost dressed in motorcycle leathers that appeared at the far end of the lab and came toward them at a brisk walk, passing through everything in his way . . . stacks of books, lab tables, and Eve, who wasn't looking the right way at that moment. She squawked and jumped back as Frank Collins's arm thrust its way through her stomach. "Hey!"

He smiled. With Frank's craggy, scarred face, it was a gruesome sight, especially in horror-movie black-and-white. "Don't stand in the way if you don't want to get hurt," he said, and dropped his arm back to his side. "I see you brought your friends, Claire."

"I didn't have a choice. They needed to know about you."

"In your opinion."

"Yes. In my opinion." Claire stared at him, and he stared back, and finally Frank shrugged.

"Fine by me, but keep my son out of it. By the way, Myrnin's not home."

"Where is he?"

"Hunting," Frank said.

Claire stiffened. "Myrnin doesn't hunt. He has regular blood deliveries."

Frank just looked at her, then at Michael. "You. Best friend. What the hell's going on with my son?"

Michael exchanged a quick glance with the others, then said, "Probably easier if I show you. Got a computer? One with Internet?"

"Yeah, over there." Frank pointed, and Claire led the way to the laptop that she kept in the corner, the one that she'd set up for Myrnin but he never seemed to use. "I was monitoring your keystrokes, but I couldn't see the Web site. Somebody's gone to some trouble to blind me."

Claire pulled up the Immortal Battles site. "Can you see it now?"

"No." Frank's insubstantial, flickering ghost leaned forward, frowning. "Just a blank screen. White noise."

"Try this," Eve said. She took out her cell phone and turned on the camera, then focused it on the screen. "Can you see it now?"

He wasn't looking at her cell phone screen, but he grunted in acknowledgment. "That works," he said. "I can see your cell in real time, so I can watch it through your camera. Good thinking. All right. Show me."

He didn't have any comment until Claire loaded up the video of Shane's first fight. As he watched the boy get thrown into the fence and then turn it around on the vampire, he did the thing Claire most dreaded.

He smiled in genuine pride.

"Hey!" she said sharply. "Your son is being *hurt.* I know you're an abusive asshole, but could you maybe focus on the fact that he could have been *killed?* Maybe?"

Frank lost the smile, but the pride remained. "He won," he said. "My son won a bare-knuckles fight with a vampire. You, Glass. You want to tell me how unlikely that is?"

"Pretty damn unlikely," Michael said. "But Claire's got a point."

"I trained my son to survive in Morganville. I'm not apologizing for that."

"You beat the hell out of him," Michael said, and behind his soft tone there was steely anger. "I remember how many times he came to my house to stay the night because he couldn't face going home to you. How many times he had bruises from your *training.* My parents didn't do that to me to train me to survive."

"Yeah," Frank said. "And look how you turned out, Glass, with all the blood drinking. No offense."

"Lots taken," Michael said. "And by the way, you wound up with fangs, too. So screw you and your self-justification for being Worst Parent of Our Lifetime, Drunken Ass Division."

"I'd kick your disrespectful butt if I still had legs, but I'll let it go. For now," Frank said. "So my son's tangled up with this. I'll admit, it's risky, but it's right up his alley."

"He's doing it for money," Claire said.

"Good for him. I'd have done the same thing myself if it had been around in my day. Good training and cash, plus the chance to pound some bloodsucker in the face."

"It's illegal!"

Frank shrugged. "Maybe. But who cares?"

"Frank, it's run by *vampires*. They're getting rich off your son's blood!" Michael said. Frank raised his eyebrows.

"You think that's a news flash? That's how it's been from the beginning, Glass. Humans get boned; vampires get rich. It's their whole lifestyle."

Claire shook her head. "Maybe, but I guarantee you that Amelie *doesn't* know about this particular little project, and she's going to care big-time. Anything that puts Morganville on the radar is a bad thing, right?"

"Eh," Frank said. "They're playing it for the cheap seats, all opera capes and bad Transylvanian accents. Nobody out there's going to take it seriously. They're watching it for the fighting. They don't believe for a second there are actual vampires involved. Not much of a risk."

"Maybe not, but what happens when somebody takes it seriously and sends somebody to check it out? It would make a hell of a *60 Minutes* story," Michael said. "One guy already tried to extort them for money. He's dead."

"Wait," Claire said as Frank opened his mouth to reply. Not that he needed to have a mouth to talk; it was just theater. His voice was coming out of her phone. He waited while she thought for a second. "Michael. *Bishop* killed Stinky Doug. That's what Jason told me."

"And— Oh." Eve's eyes grew very wide. "Wait. You saw Jason? Where?"

Dammit, *again* she was saying things she shouldn't have been. Too late to call that back, anyway. "He's been arrested," Claire said. "Again. Sorry."

"And you were going to tell me that my brother was in jail *when*, exactly?"

"When they said I could. I'm sorry, Eve, but that's not the point. Jason accused Bishop."

"Wait, *the* Bishop? Evil old man who is supposed to be *dead*— that Bishop?"

This was a house of cards, and it was all crashing down around her. Claire decided she couldn't care about that, not now. Better to try to get it all out in the open. "Bishop broke out," she said. "And the next thing anybody knew, he grabbed Jason and had him take him to Stinky Doug. Then he killed him. Jason didn't know why."

"But we do now," Michael said. "Doug was trying to blackmail Immortal Battles. He lifted vampire blood and was probably planning to go to a reporter with it, along with his story and the Web site evidence. Proof."

"Proof nobody could afford, not even Bishop," Claire said. "So no more Doug. But the thing is, Bishop had to already know about the fighting. He was in on it. Or behind it. Amelie's got a full-scale search going for Bishop, and she's going to find out about this, probably soon."

Michael leaned against a lab table and crossed his arms. "That means Shane will be just as guilty as everybody else, for aiding and abetting," he said. "You know how she's going to feel about that. And if we knew and didn't tell her, we'll be there right along-side him."

"I know how *I'm* going to feel," Eve said. "I'm going to feel sorry, because I don't look good in prison clothes. Or I'll be dead, in which case I won't feel much. Claire, sweetie, I hate to say this, but I don't think we have a choice. We have to tell somebody. We *have* to."

"But Shane—"

"Shane needs to understand that this little sideshow is over, like it or not," Frank said. "And that he's falling with it if he stays. He'd better decide to end up on Amelie's side, not Bishop's, be-cause Claire is right: Bishop in the mix changes it from illegal fun to a serious threat."

"Shane doesn't know about Bishop's involvement. I'm sure. He'd never have anything to do with it if he had any clue," Claire said. "We just have to tell him, that's all. He'll break it off."

"That's *all*," Michael said. "You were there, right? The last time we tried to talk to him?"

Claire took a deep breath. "No offense, Michael, but I think—I think it was you who really caused the problem. Not what you said. What you *are*. Somehow he's gotten conditioned to be angry whenever it involves vampires. You saw how he treated Eve, and he *likes* Eve. I think I have to talk to him alone."

"No!" Eve blurted that out, but she didn't back down when

Claire turned to her. "No, seriously, just . . . no, honey. You can't, Claire. You saw how he was. If you go alone he might . . . he might hurt you. I know you don't think he will, but I saw him. I know he could. I hate it, and I wish it wasn't true, but . . . you can't take that risk."

"*You* take that risk all the time with Michael," Claire said, and stepped forward to touch Eve's choker, beneath which lay bite marks. "You trust he'll know how far to go. Right? I trust Shane. I have to trust him."

"Well . . . they'll never let you in," Eve said, but she sounded doubtful now rather than definite. "You'd never make it past the bouncer."

Claire locked eyes with her and held the stare, trying to put all her grief and passion into it. "I have to," she said. "Please understand. *Please.*"

Eve didn't want to, but she finally, unwillingly nodded. When Michael tried to interject, she shook her head firmly. "She's right, Mike. She's not a little kid; we can't always be there. And she's also right about how Shane feels about vampires. If either one of us shows up, it kicks it up to a whole new level. If she's alone, it's more personal. And no matter how wack Shane may be right now, I can't believe he would hurt her, not on purpose."

Michael clearly had his doubts, but he held up both hands to signal surrender. "First we wait to see if he comes home tomorrow," he said. "If he doesn't, then we'll drive you to the gym and wait for you—and Frank monitors your signal. Any sign of trouble, he pushes the alarm button, and all bets are off. Oh, and we tell Amelie. Immediately, regardless of how that conversation goes with Shane."

Claire didn't like it particularly, but she could see the wisdom of it, too. It hadn't occurred to her, but since she knew Frank could use the camera, too, she could be wearing her cell phone around her neck with the camera activated, and he could see and hear everything. He'd wanted eyes and ears inside the gym; this was the best she could do.

"I'll go there tomorrow," she said. "If he doesn't come home tonight."

"Hang on," Frank said. "What about this Web site?"

"Can you block access?"

"Only for people inside of town."

"How about, you know, launching some kind of attack? Like a virus or a denial of service?"

Frank blinked. "No idea what you're talking about. Look, I was never the Internet guy. And it's pretty freaking strange to be—this. I got no idea how to do that denial of whatever. And I don't have any viruses."

"What if I give you one?"

"Try it, and you won't need to be afraid of what my son does."

"Okay, right. Never mind," Claire said. "It was just an idea. Obviously not a very good one."

"Bad enough I'm stuck like this, without you getting any ideas about making me sick like the last occupant." Meaning Ada, Myrnin's old assistant. And girlfriend. Claire was suddenly glad she hadn't suggested the whole virus thing while Myrnin was around, because he would surely have been *very* unhappy with her.

And as if she'd conjured him up, thanks to even thinking his name, Frank suddenly turned to face the side of the lab where the portal door was located. "He's coming back," he said. "Nobody tells him nothing." And just like that, Frank vanished, leaving behind nothing but a trailing hiss of static in Claire's cell phone speaker, just as a pool of darkness formed inside an open doorway, then rippled into what looked like a dimly lit library.

Myrnin stepped through, and the portal collapsed behind him into darkness. He shut the wooden door and padlocked it, rolled the bookcase back in front of it as additional cover, and, without turning around, said, "To what do I owe the pleasure of your company, uninvited guests?" He didn't sound happy. Or even, as was more typical for Myrnin, wacky. Bad sign.

"I . . . needed to check on something," Claire said. "Sorry. We were just leaving."

"Were you?" He turned, clasping his hands behind him. He looked very old-school Myrnin, formally dressed, even down to shiny boots. Well, the shirt and vest *might* have clashed, but apart from that, he'd obviously been somewhere that didn't accept his usual wardrobe choices. Like, say, Amelie's office. "There are a number of odd things happening in this town, Claire. Most notably, the behavior of you and your friends. Including that boy most strangely absent from your little group. I don't often see him separated from you."

She felt a prickling of fear and tried not to let it show. "He's busy," she said. "So am I." She nodded to Michael and Eve and headed for the stairs.

Myrnin got there ahead of her. She came to a fast stop, wondering what the hell was up with him *this* time. She'd seen so much insanity from him that it was tough to work up real terror anymore. He'd wig out on her and grow fangs, or not. But she wasn't going to let him stop her.

"Wait," he said. Not angry after all, and not crazy. He looked worried and sad. "You know that you can trust me, don't you? You understand that I'm your friend. I am. I have always tried to be."

"I know," she said. It sounded hollow, because it wasn't true. She'd seen Myrnin be a whole lot of things, and she knew better than anyone how fragile he was. She couldn't depend on his current mood. She just *couldn't*. There was too much at stake.

"You'd tell me if there was anything wrong, wouldn't you? Something with which I might help?"

"It's—" She swallowed and studied her scuffed shoes. "Shane and I had a fight. That's all. It's—making me feel pretty awful. I'm sorry if I haven't been myself."

"Yes," Myrnin said a little helplessly. "Well. I see how that might—and I'm, of course, the last one to criticize anyone for not being themselves—but are you sure it's not . . . ? Perhaps it's for the best that you and the boy—"

She felt tears burning in her eyes, real and instant, and looked up to glare at him through them. "Just leave it alone, okay? It's personal!"

He was so surprised that he stepped aside, and she charged up the steps, panting with emotion that she couldn't control and didn't have the vaguest idea of what had brought it up. Everything, she guessed. Stress, worry, Shane, Morganville, Myrnin. Constantly being the one who had to be *okay*.

She was so tired of being *okay*.

Outside, in the alley, she realized that Eve was yelling her name, but she hit the pavement running. She had to run; she couldn't control it, even though it was dark and a dumb idea, and when she hit a trash can with a crash and went flying, she expected, with a kind of fatalistic satisfaction, to get hurt. Maybe badly.

Only she didn't, of course, because Michael had gotten ahead of her by doing that vampire jumping thing and was there to catch her, and she yanked free of his kindness, still furious. "Just leave me alone!" she shouted. It was shockingly loud. Lights went on after a few seconds in the Day House, next to the alley. She'd woken up old Gramma Day, another thing to feel bad about. "I don't need your help!"

Except she had, of course. She wasn't quite stupid enough to run the rest of the way; she walked, kicking bottles and trash out of her way with bitter anger, until she arrived back at Michael's car. She yanked at the handle, but it didn't open. Locked, of course. It beeped at her softly as Michael remotely unlocked it, but he didn't come closer as she pulled it open and got in and slumped in the backseat, feeling blackly miserably. She probably should apologize, she realized. But she didn't care.

Michael got in the driver's side, and Eve, after bending over to look at her over the seat, got into the shotgun position. Nobody said a word. The engine started and the car pulled away with a crunch of tires, and Michael said, "I think Gramma Day thinks I've just abducted you."

"Why?" Claire snapped.

"Because she's out on her porch, loading up a shotgun." He hit the gas. "Good thing she doesn't keep it ready and waiting, or we'd be in a little bit of trouble."

"Oh." Some of her anger managed to fade away as she considered what could have happened. What if Eve had gotten caught in the crossfire? Michael wouldn't have been hurt, but Eve . . . "I didn't mean for that to happen."

Eve cupped her ear at Claire. "I'm sorry—was that an apology? Because it didn't sound like one."

"Don't push it."

"I'm not, but you're acting like a drama princess."

"Drama queen."

"Hello, no. You need a *lot* more practice at door slamming, flouncing, and pouting before you can even *pretend* to deserve my throne, bitch. But you're coming along." Eve paused and fixed her with a long, serious look. "That wasn't a compliment, by the way. In case you're wondering."

"I wasn't."

"Good." Eve faced forward. "I get it, though. It's all coming down around you, you don't know what to do, it's all too big and too scary to face, much less fight, so the first person who shows you compassion gets slapped. Been there so often, I pay rent."

"I—" Claire intended to defend herself, but after running it through her head, that was a pretty accurate assessment, all things considered. She finally shrugged. "I guess."

"Progress." Eve laughed. "I love you, CB, but let's face it: we can all be tools. It's in our DNA. Yeah, even yours, Michael." She punched his arm. He pretended to feel it. "So. Next step. We go home, get a good night's rest, hope Shane slinks back with his tail between his legs and realizes what a douche he's been. Right?"

"That's the plan," Michael said. He didn't sound optimistic. "Give him some time. But one way or another, tomorrow we go to Amelie and tell her everything we know. Including about Shane."

Claire raised her chin and stared at the back of his curly blond head, because that hadn't sounded quite right, either. Not the words; the tone. Something just a shade off. "Michael? You're not going to run off and do anything dumb *tonight*, are you?"

"Last time I checked, I wasn't the one running full speed in the dark in Vampireville."

That checked her for long enough until they pulled up at the curb at their house on Lot Street, and by the time Eve and Michael were out of the car, Claire had forgotten the original question.

It was only later, when she woke up in the middle of the night, wondering if she'd heard Shane's door open and close, that she realized that Michael hadn't actually answered her at all.

TWELVE

Claire got up early, mostly because she just couldn't sleep, and checked Shane's room. Empty, and just as messy as it had been the last time she'd seen it. The pillow was even in the exact same position, half off the bed, with the sheets twisted over the side next to it. She noticed things like where his head had been the last time he'd slept there. She walked over, like a sleepwalker, and in the gray predawn light put her hand in the hollow where his hair had been pressed not so long ago. It was cold, of course.

She picked up the pillow and hugged it, burying her face in it, and the smell of him flooded into her, overwhelmed her, and she sank down on the narrow bed and just . . . collapsed. Her eyelids felt raw from lack of sleep and crying, and she felt empty. Exhausted. When her eyes were closed, all she could see was that cold, set expression on Shane's face as he'd punched that vampire over and over. It wasn't the same Shane who'd been here with her, who'd been right here in this bed, holding her, who'd critiqued new songs with her until she'd lost her breath laughing, and tickled her and kissed her and whispered how much he loved her. That Shane wasn't here, and she didn't know if he was anywhere or if he was coming back.

No. He's coming back. I'm going to get him back.

Somehow.

She wasn't thinking of anything specific, nothing on the order of a plan, but all of a sudden she had a vision of the Web site. Immortal Battles. *Someone* knew something, and it wasn't just Vassily and Bishop and Gloriana. Vampires weren't generally computer savvy. A few, maybe, but it was much more likely that a human was doing their Web work for them.

Maybe even someone inside Morganville, since they'd specially coded it to be invisible to Morganville's monitoring sensors.

She sat straight up in Shane's cold bed, pillow still held in her arms, and stared at the mirror on the wall. She looked awful— dark circles around her eyes, hair a mess, skin sallow. But she *felt* better.

Because she had a good idea of what to do next.

Was it safe? No, definitely not. But waiting to see if Shane might change his mind was worse than torture. It was like being eaten an atom at a time.

Claire raced back to her room, grabbed clothes, showered in record time, tied her shoulder-length hair back in a sloppy knot, and was down the stairs and out the back door without even stopping for coffee, although she did take her book bag, mainly because it contained her wallet and some potentially useful vampire-repelling equipment.

Because she was going to see the wizard. Not Myrnin . . . the *real* wizard.

*   *   *

"Excuse me?" Amelie said. "You barge in on me without an appointment, *in my office*, and you expect me to grant your request without an adequate explanation? Not like you, Claire. Not like you at all."

Amelie, regardless of the hour, looked cool and fresh and unnaturally beautiful. She was wearing pale blue today, in a straight, subdued style, although she'd condescended to put on pants. She even had on *pearls.* At six in the morning.

Claire stood, because she hadn't been invited to take one of the thick leather armchairs next to the desk, and, besides, she wasn't in a sitting kind of mood. Amelie's office in Founder's Square had been a little tricky to access; she didn't want to use portals, and popping in uninvited on the Big Vampire Boss (much less popping in with a bag full of antivampire equipment) probably wasn't a fabulous survival tactic, anyway. But getting through the levels of guards and social secretaries also hadn't been easy. Amelie had hired someone to sit at a desk in front of her office, and that vampire—the nameplate on her desk said her name was Bizzie O'Meara, and she'd looked deadly serious about her job—hadn't been at all understanding about the concept of emergencies.

Amelie herself had opened the door, looking cross at all the noise, and waved Claire inside. That didn't mean, however, that Claire was welcome. Just stuck.

"Well?" Amelie said. That tone was about as close as the Founder of Morganville ever came to showing temper, at least with humans. There was an icy, cutting edge to it that left the unmistakable impression of a threat, even if the details weren't exactly specified. "Explain yourself."

"I can't," Claire said, and readjusted the book bag on her shoulder. "Not yet, anyway. I'm investigating. When I'm sure about what I know, I'll tell you. But in order to get proof, I need access to someone who's being held for crimes against Morganville."

Amelie raised her eyebrows about a millimeter. "Really. Of course, the answer to that would be no."

"But I need—"

"Prisoners who are held on that particular charge don't get visitors, Claire. Nor do they get furloughs. They are mine, for life, to do with as I wish. And this . . . individual . . . may not even be alive, for all you know."

That was scarily true. Claire hesitated, then said, "Kim."

"Kim," Amelie repeated, as if she had no idea who Claire was talking about. "Oh. *Her.* Well, yes, she is alive—I'd hardly execute someone so young, even if she is unpleasant and unmanageable. She remains in custody, as she will at my pleasure until she proves to me that she deserves to see daylight once again."

"She's good at doing things online that even you and Myrnin couldn't find, and that's pretty rare. I need her expertise." Claire was in danger of giving things away and she knew it; she had no idea if Frank would lie to the Founder, or even if he *could.* Part of what drove him was machinery and programming; his human brain might want to lie for his son, but what about the rest of him? She couldn't be sure about anything. "I need her help to find someone."

"Does this have to do with my father?"

That was an extremely dangerous question, because it did, in a small and indirect way, but to answer *yes* meant spilling everything. It was ninety percent *no,* anyway. "Not directly," Claire said. "But it might help."

"Hmmm. And do you think she'd actually help you?" Amelie sat down at her desk, looking every inch the woman in charge. "I think you don't know this Kim very well. She loathes you, in particular, more than anyone else. Even more than me, I believe."

"Because of Shane. Yeah, I know. She likes him."

Amelie just shrugged, completely uninterested in mere mortal feelings.

"I think she'll help me on this. Please. Just let me talk to her. I do need her help."

Amelie drummed her pale-pink-painted fingernails on the desk in a slow rhythm, staring at Claire with those unsettling gray eyes. Her phone gave a low buzz for attention. She ignored it. "I don't like you assuming that you have the run of my office, Claire. Are we understood?"

"Yes."

More drumming. Claire couldn't stop glancing at those long, shapely, pale fingers, with their razor-sharp (and perfectly manicured) nails. As Amelie probably intended.

"All right," Amelie said. "I'll give you access for five minutes. If you can get that person to agree, I will let her help you on this . . . project. But she cannot leave her confinement. Are we understood?"

"Yes. Thank you."

"Don't thank me," Amelie said. "You're not going alone." She pressed a button on the phone, which had stopped buzzing, and said, "Bizzie. Please get Michael Glass to my office immediately."

"Ma'am," Bizzie's disembodied voice said. "Oliver is calling for you."

"Oliver can wait. I want Michael here. Send a car."

"Yes, Madam Founder."

"You, Claire," Amelie said, lifting her finger from the phone button, "will sit and be quiet. I am greatly annoyed with your behavior. I realize that it is all the rage among young people to defy authority, but I do not tolerate it. Not in my presence."

"It's not—" Oh, what was the use? Claire dropped her book bag to the floor and sat, folding her arms. She knew that looked defensive. She didn't care. "I'm not defying you. It's just that I want to be sure of things before I tell you about them."

"That's quite an interesting assumption to make, as I may not require the gift of your expertise," Amelie said. "For instance, I am well aware that my father, Bishop, is missing. I am also aware that several vampires once loyal to him have been acting oddly, and several who were not are now missing. I am aware that Gloriana's presence in this town is somewhat . . . unsettling for many, although perhaps not for Oliver." She sounded just a shade sharp on that last part. About *Oliver?* Weird. "Has Gloriana, perhaps, decided to practice her wiles on your Shane, then?"

That was *way* too close to the truth. "Oliver says she's not interested in human boys that way." That was true. It just didn't quite answer the question. "She went after Michael; that's what Eve said."

"Yes, I'm aware of that. But it seems to have passed without any significant bloodshed." More fingernail drumming. When Claire glanced at Amelie's face, she saw the vampire was staring out her tinted windows, which minimized the rising sun. There was a distant expression on her face. Amelie could look almost as young as Claire herself sometimes; she'd probably been only about twenty when she'd become what she was now. But just now, she looked her actual age, with all the weight of centuries on that smooth, unlined face. "You're well aware how dangerous this town is, Claire. But what you may not understand, not fully, is that it is held together by will. My will. Without my influence, vampires would fight for control, and humans would be slaughtered in the streets. Not all my kind have the vision to understand that such behavior is . . . counterproductive to the long-term survival of my species. Like some of your own contemporaries, younger vampires want what they want, when they want it, regardless of consequences." She paused for a moment. Claire didn't know if she was supposed to say anything, so she kept quiet. "I've been struggling to educate them for many years. And, in truth, I'm growing tired of the struggle. I remember what it was like when I had no responsibilities, no worries. And that is beginning to seem quite good to me."

That seemed ominous. "What . . . what do you mean?"

Amelie's gray gaze came back to her, but the expression didn't change. "Morganville is an experiment," she said. "One I've fostered and encouraged for a long time, in human terms, and even for a significant period in vampire measures. But it doesn't seem to me that my kind have learned much about living among humans productively. Or that humans have learned how to tolerate our differences. Oliver thinks it's a fool's errand, you know. And he may be right about that."

"It's not," Claire said. "I know there are problems; there are always problems. People—people can't even live with each other without violence and problems, much less with you. But somehow we manage. We *can* manage."

"I've always thought so," Amelie said softly. "And I've fought for that principle. I've bled for it. I've buried loved ones for it. But what if I'm wrong, Claire? What if Morganville is a folly of arrogance? You know as well as I that there are humans who will never accept living with us. And vampires who will never accept living with humans. What are we fighting so hard to prove?"

Claire didn't know how they'd gotten to this; it felt completely wrong to be having this conversation. She wasn't old enough; she didn't understand where it was coming from. And hearing that *Amelie* had doubts . . . that hurt. And it scared her. *So many things crashing down.* Maybe she wasn't the only one with that feeling, she realized with a start. That was a new and entirely unpleasant sort of thought.

It actually made her blink.

She fell back on something her parents had taught her. "Anything worthwhile is worth fighting for," Claire said. "Not always with guns and stuff. But with . . . taking a stand. Right?"

Amelie seemed to focus on her again. For a few seconds she regarded her, frowning, and then smiled just a little. "So I recall," she said. "Not all wars are waged with bullets and swords, indeed. Some are wars of wills and ideas. It's good we both remember that." The smile faded. "But not all ideas win the war, and not all wills are strong enough. Darkness can descend so easily."

"It won't here," Claire said. "We just have to be stronger."

Amelie inclined her head, but Claire couldn't tell if it was agreement. She frowned again, this time at the phone, and after a hesitation, pushed the intercom button. "Bizzie?" she asked. "Have you confirmation that Michael is in the car?"

The answer came back immediately. "No, Founder. The car is there, but the others in the house report that Michael Glass is *not* there."

"Not there," Amelie repeated. "Very well. Call his cell phone. I believe he has one of those. I will wait."

Bizzie left the speaker on as she dialed. It rang and rang on the other end, and then Michael's recorded voice said, "Michael Glass's phone. Leave a message," over the sound of his guitar. It cut off. Bizzie said, "Madam? No answer."

"I can hear that," Amelie said. She looked at Claire. "Do you know where he is?"

"No," Claire said. She felt her stomach tightening unpleasantly. "He— We all went home last night. I don't know why he's not there." But she did. Deep down, she did. Michael had tried something, something that had got him in trouble—and, worse, he hadn't even told anyone.

Eve was going to kill him. And if Eve didn't, Claire decided she'd be next in line. The idea of Michael going missing *now* made her feel as shaky as if the earth under her feet had moved. Michael was a rock; even the first time she'd met him, as a half ghost, he'd been the calmest and most capable one of the group.

But this time, if he'd gone off on his own, he'd made a mistake. A big one.

Amelie must have read something on her face, because she said, "Have my car brought around, Bizzie. The usual complement of guards."

"Yes, Founder."

Amelie rose to her feet. Claire just stared at her in confusion, until she said, "I am, of course, going with you. And you will tell me where you believe Michael might have gone, because I am not losing yet another of my people to this mystery."

Claire resisted the urge to say, *Yes, Founder*, and silently—in defeat—followed her to the limousine.

By *usual complement*, Amelie must have meant "more vampires than a Dracula convention" because besides Amelie and her driver, there were two silent, suit-wearing guards in sunglasses, and a heavily tinted town car carrying four more that followed along. Amelie ignored their presence—but then, she'd grown up in an age when servants were no more than moving furniture—and leaned forward, hands clasped. She still sat like a lady, knees together and demurely angled, even though she was wearing pants. "Now," she said. "You will tell me everything you declined to tell me earlier. We are past the amusingly amateur portion of this problem. If you know where my father is, or even suspect you have a clue, no matter how small, you *will tell me.*"

Claire felt sick, hot, and trapped—mostly because she *was* trapped, no doubt about it. She squeezed her eyes shut and said, "If I tell you everything, you have to make me a promise."

Ominous silence, broken only by the faint hiss of the road noise beneath the car. Claire had no idea where they were heading, and realized that she'd just done the same thing Michael had: she'd taken off without letting anyone know where she was going. She could disappear just as quickly. She risked a look at Amelie, and saw the same expectant, waiting expression. No anger yet.

Amelie smiled, very slightly—in fact, if Claire hadn't known her as well as she did, she'd never have seen it at all. "You're always asking for promises, Claire. Sometimes that seems charming, as if you simply expect me to be honorable enough to keep them."

"How about today?" Amelie inclined her head. That wasn't a yes, though; Claire could see it in the cold glitter of her eyes. "It's just that if Shane . . . if Shane's got anything to do with this, it's because he's been glamoured. By Gloriana. It's not his choice. And he'd never, ever help Bishop. You know that." It came out in a rush, and even to her ears, it sounded incoherent.

Amelie straightened, settled back in her seat, and said, "From the beginning."

Claire tried. She thought about holding some things back, but the truth was that it was all going to come out sooner rather than later, and lying to Amelie's face . . . well, that wasn't a good strategy. Amelie was understanding sometimes. Still, Claire cringed when she had to mention Shane. All she could think about was how bad it had been when he'd been accused of the murder of one of Amelie's own, when he'd been trapped and condemned and she'd felt so useless to save him.

Here it was again—that black, swelling, suffocating sense of utter helplessness.

Amelie made no comments and had no physical reactions to what Claire said. She looked not at Claire, but at the scenery beyond the tinted window—visible to her eyes, presumably, though Claire felt like she was confined in a crowded black box—while she listened. When Claire finally paused, feeling short of breath, Amelie inclined her head slightly.

"Thank you," she said. "A very honest accounting. I had wondered how much you'd try to conceal from me. I'm pleased you didn't attempt it."

Claire squeezed her eyes shut for a few seconds. "You knew."

"Of course I knew," Amelie said. "Most things, at least. The Web site is new, and therefore of great interest; I have operatives tracing its origins now, though you are entirely correct that a more expert approach will be needed. But the role of Gloriana and Vassily—these things were already known to me and to Oliver."

Oliver. Of course. "He was keeping an eye on her for you," Claire realized. "That's why he was hanging around her."

"Gloriana believes it is due to her own charm, of course, but Oliver is not so easily manipulated as that. He knows her too well, and has good reason to be wary of her and her motives." Amelie finally looked at her, unsmiling. "How my father is involved in all this is somewhat of a mystery, but it will be solved."

"Do you know where he is? Bishop?"

"No." Amelie looked away again. "One thing he's very good at is hiding when he feels threatened. He's within the town's borders. Alerts would have gone off if he'd crossed the boundaries. We'll find him, even should he be buried in the dirt like some hunting spider." She sounded bitter and cold at the end, and Claire shivered a little. "When he's found, I will ensure that this particular danger to us doesn't return. You have my word on that."

The car slowed, and Amelie nodded to one of her guards, the one sitting on her left side. He nodded back, and as the limousine drifted to a smooth stop, he immediately opened the door and exited. Claire couldn't have tried to get out even if she'd wanted to; there were two guards between her and the outside.

And Amelie didn't move. She sat, composed and erect, until the first man looked back into the car and said, "Clear, Founder." Then there was a sudden scramble from the guards on both sides, and Claire and Amelie were left sitting across from each other, temporarily alone. Amelie began to slide toward the exit.

"Wait," Claire said. "Shane."

Apart from a very small hesitation, Amelie didn't respond to that at all. She simply continued on her way. A guard offered her a hand, and she left the car in a graceful stride.

Claire gulped air and scrambled out to follow.

There was a moving wall of black-suited vampires around Amelie, escorting her away from the idling limousine and up a covered walkway leading to . . .

Claire blinked. She knew this building. She'd been in it at least five or six times, mostly to add or drop classes, pay fees—

that kind of thing. It was the Admin Building of Texas Prairie University—closed, of course. Nobody around.

Amelie's guards had keys.

Inside, they didn't proceed the way Claire had always been, toward the main processing area; instead, Amelie turned left, down a paneled hallway filled with the fading photographs of university presidents, donors, and not-very-famous alumni. It ended in what looked like a blank wall, except for an ornate brass lock plate.

This one Amelie herself unlocked, with a key she kept in the small clutch purse she carried. She didn't bother to open it; she had people to do that for her. She merely handed it over. Claire trailed her into the next room and was surprised when only two of the guards came in behind her. One of them shut the door, which sounded like it locked with a snap.

They were in a plain concrete room with a white table that was, as far as Claire could tell, bolted to the floor, as were the two chairs on either side of it. There was a big steel ring locked onto the table on one side. Apart from that, it couldn't have been more blank and boring.

Only two chairs. Claire wondered if she was supposed to sit across from Amelie, but no, that didn't make any sense unless *she* was the one being questioned. Unfortunately, that wasn't beyond the realm of possibility.

It was a guilty relief to hear the sound of metal grinding and doors opening and closing somewhere else. Finally, a thick silver door on the far wall slid open and a guard came in, wearing not a black suit, but a black knit sports shirt and blue jeans. There was a hard-to-see emblem embroidered in the same color on the shirt. Amelie's Founder symbol.

He was a vampire—that much was obvious from the unnatural shade of his skin—but other than that, he looked boringly mundane. An all-American kind of guy, no different from half the boys Claire went to college with daily. Neatly cut brown hair, a friendly and professional smile, a confident set to his expression. He looked more like a personal trainer than a prison guard.

He stepped aside, and Kim shuffled in.

Claire drew in a sharp breath. She remembered Kim way too well; she'd been a lying, traitorous bitch, but she'd started out okay enough. She'd always had a kind of bizarre charm, but there was no trace of that now. Her face was pale, set, and expression-less; Claire saw faces like that in the hospital when she'd visited her dad after his last heart attack. People who looked like that were focused on just getting through the minute, the hour, the day. They had no future and no hope of one.

Kim's hair had grown out long around her shoulders, and part of it was still dyed Goth black, but the rest was dirty blond. Her visible piercings were no longer so visible, even in her ears, because she wore no jewelry at all. She was wearing a knit shirt like Mr. All-American, only hers was in bright yellow. The embroidery on the front read PRISONER in giant black letters, with Amelie's symbol up in the corner. Claire guessed it was the same on the back. She wore stretchy, yoga-style pants and sandals.

Her fingernails were short, and two were bleeding from where she'd bitten too deep. No funky nail polish now. Kim looked sad and alone and more than a little frightened, especially when she saw Claire and Amelie.

She fixed on Claire, though, and took a step forward. Her guard tapped her on the shoulder gently, and Kim looked away and went still. He guided her to the chair. Without a word, she sat and put her hands on the table.

He pulled out a set of handcuffs and hooked one to her right wrist and one to the steel ring on the table. Then he stepped back and turned into a parade-rest statue near the metal door.

Kim kept staring down. Where was all that bad attitude she'd displayed from the beginning? Or the bitterness? Or the crazy— that was what Claire remembered her best for at the end. Now she was just . . . empty.

Amelie said, "Claire, sit down. You wanted five minutes. You have them. I suggest you use them well."

She hadn't wanted it like this, with the two of them surrounded by staring, listening witnesses. Claire was suddenly very glad she'd spilled the beans to Amelie in the limo, because having this conversation while trying to hold all that inside would have been very difficult. Probably impossible.

Kim didn't look up even when Claire sat down. She looked cold. "Kim?" No response. "Kim, you remember me, right?"

Kim looked up then, and her eyes were hot and angry. "Of course I do. Who forgets *you*? How's Shane, by the way? Getting tired of schoolyard crushes yet?"

The sudden flare of rage made Claire flinch, but after a glance at the man standing behind Kim's chair, she wet her lips and continued. "Shane's in trouble," Claire said.

"Good." Kim sat back in her chair, as far as the cuffs would allow. "Hope it's fatal for both of you this time."

That was harsh, even for Kim. Claire was surprised. She could understand Kim's anger toward her, but why Shane? He'd always been the focus of her stalkerish obsession. "You don't mean that," Claire said.

"Oh, I completely do. I've had therapy, you know. I'm in touch with my feelings and crap." Kim raked untidy hair back from her face with her left hand and laughed. It sounded raw and aggressive. "He never cared about me; I know that now. So screw him. And you. Thanks for dropping in." She glanced backward, at her guard. "I'm ready to go back now, sir."

"Kim," he said, still smiling. He had dimples, even. "Her five minutes aren't up yet. Be nice."

Kim faced Claire again, once again back to that thousand-yard stare and closed-down expression.

"There's a Web site that's operating," Claire said. "Running encrypted video. Do you know anything about it?"

"Because I did the whole encryption thing first?" Kim shrugged. "Why would I? They haven't given me a computer to play with, you know. Said I had to earn one. Screw that. I'm not playing the games to get what I want."

"You were working with someone outside Morganville, though. You were planning to make a deal for a TV show. That was what all the streaming video was for. I think whoever it was found another . . . source. And another program."

"Good for them." Dismissive words, but Kim was eyeing her with a little more interest. "What kind of show are they running?"

"Pay-per-view," Claire said. "Extreme fighting."

"With *vampires?*" Kim actually laughed. "Dude, that's brilliant. I should have thought of that. Would have been a lots-better show than you sickeningly cute couples playing house and getting your wild thing on."

Claire wanted to smack her—badly. But she took a deep breath and said, with unnatural calm, "I need to know how to break the encryption and figure out how to trace it to the source. I figured you'd know."

"Sure, I know, if it's the same encryption I put together," Kim said, and leaned back in her chair. "But why should I tell you?"

"Because it's the right thing to do?"

Kim rolled her eyes. "Wow, you actually *are* an idiot. Do you think the vamps are going to do the right thing once you point the finger at whoever's behind it? You think this is all going to end with somebody getting a slap on the wrist and a fine? I was lucky, you know. Lucky to still be breathing. *People are going to die.* You need to get that through your head. It isn't about the *right* thing. It's about the thing that gets you something. If you think the world works any other way, you're just as stupid as you look."

Claire said, "You know, you've got something wrong."

"What is that? I swear, you're more clueless than a Care Bear."

"You think that because I want to do what's right, because I want to make things better, I'm weak," Claire said. "Or that I'm stupid. But I'm not. It takes a lot more strength to know how bad the world is and not want to be part of that, give in to it. And I *do* know, Kim. Believe me."

Kim's sneer faded as Claire stared at her very steadily. Then she looked away. "You should say that after you spend a few months in this hellhole."

For the first time, Amelie stirred from where she stood at the back of the room. She advanced to the table, leaned forward, and rested her palms on the flat surface. Her gray eyes were intent and level on Kim, and again Kim couldn't hold her stare.

"You might bear in mind that in earlier times, young lady, your crimes would have meant you died in a particularly horrible way, with your screams ringing in the ears of decent folk," Amelie said. "You're kept in a clean cell, with decent if unremarkable food. You receive reading material and have television. In what way is that a *hellhole?* What can someone of your age possibly know of surviving *hell?*" There was a keen edge to her voice that Claire had rarely heard. "The man guarding you today knows of hell, very well. He can tell you what it was like to survive in a prison camp with nothing to eat but crawling insects and rotten bread, for *years,* until one night his life was taken—"

"Saved," the guard in the knit shirt said.

"Saved, by one of us," Amelie finished softly. "Ask *him* about the kindness of your treatment, and then speak to me or him of *hellholes.*" She let that sink in for a moment before she said, in a brisk and businesslike tone, "Now, you wanted to know what helping us means for you. That entirely depends on what you can do for *us.* Can you reverse the encryption and tell us the location where these . . . people are staging and broadcasting their fights?"

"Yeah," Kim said. She picked at a rough spot on the table with a short, well-chewed fingernail. "I could do that. But not for free."

Amelie didn't seem too surprised. "Your price?"

"I want out of here."

"That will not happen. And you know it will not happen."

Kim smiled down at her lap—a secret, cynical kind of expression that made Claire feel a little tingle of alarm. "Oh, I don't know. You want to keep Morganville's big secret, right? How are you going to do that with millions of people watching vampires flashing fangs at each other on pay-per-view? Maybe most don't believe it, but maybe some do; maybe somebody decides to come check it out, like a news crew. Then where do you run?"

"Farther and faster than you can, Kim. You'd do well to remember that."

Kim said nothing. Amelie, after exchanging a look with Claire, shook her head. "Take her back to her cell, please. We're getting nowhere."

"Wait!" Kim said as the vampire behind her stepped forward. "Wait. You want these people, right? I can find them. I'm probably the only one in Morganville who has the skills!"

"I doubt that, but you are the one I have readily available."

"Then come on. What do I get for it?"

Amelie's eyes turned red—a muddy, rippling crimson that sent prickles of warning across Claire's skin, like the feeling before lightning strikes. "You get to survive this meeting with me, little girl. And I warn you, that possibility is fading with every unpleasant word you utter. Be careful."

"You wouldn't do it. You're like *her*." A flick of Kim's eyes included Claire in her scorn. "Full of talk, short on action."

Amelie smiled, very slowly. It was one of the most unsettling things Claire had ever seen her do . . . as if a mask had been pulled away and something *terrible* looked out of her eyes. Kim saw it, too. Her handcuffs clicked as she tried instinctively to draw away. "Oh, child," Amelie said. "I have worked very diligently to achieve that image, because a ruler should be seen as just and fair and merciful. But you would *not* like to see me take action. I am, after all, my father's daughter. Now. You will give me the help I require to trace this signal that Claire has found, and you will be grateful that I choose to allow you to continue in your presently comfortable state. Once you have demonstrated *results*, we may discuss an improvement in your conditions."

Amelie rarely exerted the power that Claire knew she had, but she felt it now—heavy, suffocating, full of dread. It pressed down on everyone in the room; she even saw the other vampires shift uncomfortably.

But mostly it was directed at Kim, who crumbled like a sugar cookie. "Okay," she said, after about a second's delay of false bravado. "But I can't do it in here. I need access to the Internet."

"We can arrange that."

"And I need to get out of here. Just for a little while." Kim looked up, and Claire saw that, incredibly, she was *still* trying to bargain. Maybe she wasn't quite the sugar cookie, after all. "A day. Just a day. I need—I need to see the sun."

Amelie didn't move, and the dark atmosphere didn't let up, but finally she gave a regal nod and stepped back. It felt like a storm had passed without breaking, and Claire instinctively took in a deep breath, and heard Kim do the same. "A day," Amelie said. "First, you locate the source of this transmission for us. Then you will be supervised *closely* on your furlough. Mr. Martin will go with you—" Mr. Martin, the vampire standing behind Kim, inclined his head. "And Claire."

"Wait," Claire said, at the same time as Kim. They both had identical tones of alarm. Claire kept talking. "You're making me stay with *her?*"

"You don't like her," Amelie said. "And therefore you won't give her any . . . breaks, I think you call them. At the first sign that Kim is misbehaving, tell Mr. Martin, if he doesn't know already, and she will be immediately returned to custody."

"But I—"

"No arguments," Amelie said. "The deal is done. Mr. Martin, arrange for the girl to have her Internet access, but I want it to be closely monitored. You are not to leave her for a moment. Do you understand?"

"Yes, Founder." Mr. Martin inclined his head. "What if she's unable to complete the task?"

"She has an hour," Amelie said. "If she can't solve the problem within that time frame, I no longer need her."

Kim, tough-chick 'tude or not, flinched at that pronouncement. There was no mistaking what it meant. "An hour's not enough time!"

"I sincerely hope you're wrong," Amelie said. "Let's call it . . . motivation."

Claire felt an unexpected sense of sympathy for Kim's stricken expression. . . . She'd been there not long ago. She'd been under threat of death, or having her friends and family suffer, if she wasn't able to live up to Amelie's expectations. It wasn't a comfortable place, especially if you weren't sure you could get it done.

But she just couldn't sympathize much in the end. Kim was a cold-blooded sociopath, at least as far as Claire was concerned, and she'd never shown any sign of remorse. No point in empathizing with someone who'd turn around and stick a knife in your back, with a smile.

Claire felt the minutes ticking away as the details were dealt with . . . the computer located, the Internet access enabled and hooked up, the security protocols negotiated. Then, finally, Mr. Martin moved out of the way and Kim sat down in front of the keyboard.

She drew in a breath, put her fingers on the keys, and said, "Okay, what's the URL?"

"ImmortalBattles-dot-com."

Kim typed it in, then flipped to a view of the code, then started up a new coding window.

"What are you doing?" Amelie asked.

"Running a trace route."

"And that is how you will find them."

Kim laughed. "No way in hell. A six-year-old could figure out a way around that. But it'll give me a starting point, and I can work from that."

Amelie settled back in her chair. Mr. Martin leaned over Kim's shoulder, watching the screen intently. If he didn't know what he was looking at, he gave a good imitation of it. Kim cast him doubting looks from time to time, and once he asked her to stop and explain what she was doing. She did it in quiet, calm tones, apparently creeped out by having him hovering so closely.

Claire sipped a cold drink that had been delivered by one of Amelie's guards and waited. She checked her watch from time to time, feeling useless and increasingly worried; every minute they sat here was another minute that something bad might be happening to Shane or to Michael.

She was also aware, though she didn't particularly want to be, that the minutes were counting down for Kim, who was looking paler with every tick of the second hand. Her fingers worked fast, blurring motion, then stopped and hovered indecisively as she leaned closer to the screen.

Thirty minutes. Forty. Forty-five. Claire drained her glass and felt the tension growing in the room. Mr. Martin, hanging over Kim's shoulder, glanced up at Amelie, who gave him some imperceptible signal Claire couldn't read. It probably wasn't good, at least for Kim.

Although Amelie never so much as glanced at a watch, it was exactly sixty minutes by Claire's timepiece when the Founder said, in precise and soft tones, "Your time is up, Kim."

Kim froze, then looked up with glittering eyes through the tangled hair that had fallen over her face. She shoved it back, and for the moment, at least, she looked defiant and unafraid. "Yeah? Well, good thing I'm done, then."

"Get up."

Kim did, and Mr. Martin moved her away from the computer and fastened handcuffs on her again, looping them through a solid ring set in the concrete wall. He studied the screen of the computer and said, "I have an address here. And a map."

"It had better be accurate," Amelie said. "I won't look kindly on misdirection."

"Do I get my day outside?" Kim said.

"Indeed, though you may not enjoy it," Amelie said. "You're coming with us. Mr. Martin, you're in charge of her. Claire, you also have responsibility. Are we clear on this?"

"Yes," Claire said. Mr. Martin nodded.

"Then put her in less . . . attention-getting clothing," Amelie said. "I have calls to make."

"Now, this is more like it," Kim said, once they were all inside the limousine again. It was a tight fit, with Mr. Martin and Kim added to Amelie, Claire, and the two other guards, but Amelie managed to arrange for her own personal space. It was the rest of them who were crowded. Kim was in the middle, but she didn't seem to care; she was busy running her hands over the plain black hoodie she'd been given to put on and the blue jeans. The Skechers had to be hers, from before; they looked ragged, well-worn, and had tribal patterns of black thorns and roses all over them, hand-painted. She'd tied her hair back in a ponytail and secured it with a rubber band. No fancy hair things available, Claire guessed, or at least none Kim wanted to wear. All in all, she made it look reasonably her again. "I wish we could see out."

"Nothing much to see," Claire said. "It's Morganville. Rusty buildings, flat desert, dusty, tumbleweeds. You know the drill."

"You'd be surprised how good that sounds when all you've seen for months are gray walls. So, how's Eve?"

"She's fine." Oh, she *so* didn't want to talk about her friends with Kim, of all people. "And she doesn't want to see you."

"Call her and see."

"No." The last thing Claire wanted was for Eve to get sucked back into the black hole of Kim. That hadn't turned out well for anyone last time.

Kim laughed dryly. "She still dating that vamp hottie Michael?"

"Would you please, please, *please* shut up now?"

"I guess that's a yes. He's going to dump her, you know. Sooner or later."

Claire felt stung, mostly because she'd wondered about that herself, guiltily, from time to time. "No, he's not! They're—they're getting married." She blurted it out, and Amelie's head turned toward her with eerie, machinelike precision.

"Are they." It didn't sound like a question. It also didn't sound like Amelie was pleased with that particular news. "I'll have to have a chat with Michael. He's failed to inform me of his plans."

Kim smirked. Claire fought the urge to hurt her, but mainly because there wasn't any room to get in a good punch. *Maybe,* she thought, *Shane is rubbing off on me with this prone-to-violence thing. Dammit!* She should have thought before she said anything about that; she should have known better. Michael and Eve weren't exactly the most popular couple among the vampire side of town, much less the human side; it made sense that Amelie wouldn't be completely happy about the idea—and that Michael wouldn't have come right out with it to the head vampire, either.

Kim had goaded her into saying it, just as Kim manipulated everyone around her and always had. Claire made herself breathe slowly, through her nose, trying to calm down. She had to think clearly and go slowly. Otherwise, Kim would drive her into saying other things, worse things. There were all kinds of secrets Kim didn't need to be part of, starting with . . . well, everything.

Amelie ignored the two of them and held out her hand to the guard seated next to her. Without a word, he took a cell phone out of his pocket and handed it over. She dialed, waited, and said, "We are on our way. You have the address, yes? I will expect you there. And, Oliver? Come prepared for a fight. We're going to wipe out this nest of vipers. There can be no delay. Things have gone far enough."

But what about Shane? Claire reached out toward Amelie but didn't touch her; she didn't dare try. As it was, a guard grabbed her wrist and held it there in midair, frozen. He didn't hurt her, but there was no doubt that he could have. "Stop," he told her. "Think what you're doing."

"Amelie," Claire said. "I told you, Shane's not part of this. Please don't—"

She didn't take the phone away from her mouth. She looked directly at Claire with no expression in her iron gray eyes and said, "Detain everyone. We will determine guilt or innocence on-site." She handed the phone back to her flunky, who turned it off and put it away. "Why do you have your hand out toward me, Claire? Do you believe that I would harm your . . . friend, without proof?"

Actually, Claire *did* believe that. She'd seen Amelie go full contact before, and she knew that she wouldn't hesitate to sentence Shane if there was even a suspicion that he was willingly part of all this stuff.

Not reassuring.

And right on cue, Kim was there to articulate all that terror in her head. "She's going to kill them all," Kim said. "And you and me, we're the ones to blame for that. If Shane's still there, she'll go all Red Queen on him, too. Off with his head. Talk about poetic justice."

That was exactly what Claire was afraid of, and what she was afraid to put into words. Trust Kim to blurt it out, make her worst fears real. Amelie didn't confirm or deny any of it. She looked toward Mr. Martin, who took Kim's hand in his and said, "Enough." He sounded quiet and not especially threatening, but Kim shivered. Claire felt it. "Be quiet, now. Enjoy your hours of freedom."

"You call this freedom? I'm trapped in a town car with a bunch of fanged prison guards. Oh, and *her*." Kim bumped shoulders with Claire, not too gently. "The Team Vampire mascot."

"I actually am going to punch you," Claire said.

"Yeah, I am absolutely terrified, Danvers. Without Shane around to fight your battles, do you think you can take me?"

Claire turned and stared Kim full in the face. "Yes," she said. "I'm pretty sure I can."

She meant every word of it, and Kim must have decided to back off—or Mr. Martin's presence decided it for her. They lapsed into a heavy silence as the limousine drove and drove and drove . . . and, finally, to Claire's simultaneous relief and terror, began to slow down.

Claire took out her phone. Amelie gave her a sharp look. "I'm only calling Eve. I want her to know I didn't just disappear. Like Michael and Shane. You know how she is."

Amelie looked bemused and nodded. "Do not tell her where we are."

"I don't actually *know* where we are." Claire dialed. Eve picked up on the first ring.

"Hello?" Her voice was tense and madly uncontrolled. "Michael?"

"No, it's Claire—"

The yell blasted out of the cell phone loud enough to echo around the inside of the car. Claire yanked it away from her ear, and she could still hear very clearly what Eve was shouting. "What the hell are you doing? Where are you? You can't just run off and leave me and not even leave a *note*. My God, you're as bad as the boys. How do I know the vamps haven't dragged you off and snacked on your—?"

"Eve," Claire said, yelling into the phone. "Eve! *Shut up!* I'm with Amelie!"

Silence, and then much lower in volume, "Oh. Sorry."

Claire put the phone back to her ear. Next to her, Kim was smirking again. Claire sincerely wanted to put her shoe through that smile, but again didn't. She took a deep breath. "We may have found out where the fights are being held. I'll call you if Michael's here, okay?"

"Okay," Eve said. "Uh, you're being careful, right?"

"Sure." She glanced around at the heavily fanged contingent. "Safe as houses."

"I've been in some pretty shaky houses."

"I'll be fine. Call you later."

The car had come to a complete stop now. Amelie looked out

through the heavily tinted windows. "There's very little cover out there," she said. "Move quickly. When we stop, get out and go directly to the shade. We may not have time for protective clothing. I assume all of you can handle the sun for a limited period."

Her guards murmured affirmations; then sunlight lanced in, bright and harsh, as the vampire guard threw open the door. He was out and moving fast, followed by the second guard. Mr. Martin practically yanked Kim's arm out of its socket dragging her from the car, and somehow, although she started moving as quickly as she could, Claire was the last one out of the limousine. Amelie was just ahead of her, though.

It was a good thing they were toward the back.

Claire was never sure exactly how it happened until much later. Right then, it was impressions: a big, empty desert area. A flapping, rusting tin barn, apparently abandoned, with a thick area of shade under a leaning awning that probably was used to park cars or something. The vampire guards in their black suits heading for it at top speed, with Mr. Martin slowed down by a foot-dragging Kim, and Amelie holding back, probably to stay closer to Claire.

And then the explosion.

It hit her as a hard, hot shove, and then she was down and rolling across the sand, and then the massive roar rattled in her ears and she saw the plume of fire and smoke, and finally, *finally* she realized that the building they'd been headed toward, the one Kim had led them to, had just *blown up*.

Claire sat up, staring. The tin building was collapsing in on itself, burning, sagging—a wreck. The awning, the one where the guards had been headed, was utterly gone, destroyed. Flames and smoke hissed straight up in a black-and-red column, and the wind caught it and blew it out in a plume that drifted west. There were pieces of wrecked metal and junk everywhere, still falling like flaming rain, and Claire covered her head as a thick piece of sharp-edged siding slammed down into the ground a few feet away.

Amelie lay on her side about ten feet closer to the explosion site. Claire got to her feet, weaved around a little, and shook off the lingering dizziness.

Amelie moved before she reached her—a twitch at first, and then she rose to a standing position in one unnaturally fast, smooth motion. There was blood running down her face. More cars were pulling up now, black and heavily tinted. Oliver got out of the first one, dressed in a heavy coat and hat, took one look at the burning building, and then moved in a blur. He reached Amelie, and when he paused, his hands were on her shoulders. He took a handkerchief out of his pocket and mopped up the blood; the cut had already closed. Claire saw the look on his face for a few seconds, and then it smoothed out into a cynical neutrality.

"Functional?" he asked her. She nodded. He let go, then stripped off his coat and hat and put them on her. "Get to the car. You should not be here."

"You think I will run from cowards who try to kill me from a distance?" Amelie laughed, and it sounded wild and strange to Claire's blast-deadened ears. "You are my second in command, not my bodyguard."

"Your bodyguards are indisposed," he said. "And at least one is not coming back. I can see parts of him in several places. Don't be foolish. Be safe."

Kim and Mr. Martin were getting up now. Kim was holding her arm like it hurt, and she was covered in ashes.

Amelie focused in on her with narrowing eyes. Oliver's head turned, too. Claire couldn't see his expression, but she saw the tension gathering in his shoulders.

"How very odd," Amelie said. "She begs for a day off and leads us here. To our deaths, presumably." She gestured to Mr. Martin. "Bring her here. Now."

Kim clearly didn't want to come; she was staggering all over the place, but Claire didn't think she was dazed. Just worried about her chances. "Wow," Kim said. "That was intense." Her lips curled into a vicious little smile. "Guess we got the right address after all."

Amelie didn't seem to move quickly, but suddenly she had hold of Kim and was pulling her very, very close. Amelie's eyes had gone an intense, scary white that Claire had seen only once or twice. Kim stopped smiling and began to look very worried.

"Someone tipped them off," Amelie almost whispered. "And you, my dear Kim, are the most likely suspect. Convince me you didn't do this."

"Why would I?" Kim shot back. "I've got everything to lose. You'd kill me if I did that!"

"Yes. I would. I still might. Explain how this could have happened, if you didn't betray me."

Kim hesitated, licked her pale lips, and then said, "They could have been watching for any trace activity. Didn't even have to be a live person; it could have been a program. A trip wire. Once it knew I'd found the address, it could have sounded an alert. They'd clear out once they knew they'd been found."

"And the bombs? Surely that is not now a common home-defense mechanism."

"I have no idea, except maybe they planned it in case you showed up looking. Would I have been heading for the building if I'd known they were there? My arm is practically broken! It *hurts!*"

"Yet you still breathe," Amelie said. "For now." Her white eyes were fading back to gray, though, and Claire knew Kim's moment of fatal danger was passing. That was almost too bad. "Very well. I will accept that this is not due to your will, except that you were negligent. Negligence is enough." She looked at Mr. Martin, standing with his arms folded behind Kim. "Take her back. Now."

"No!" Kim blurted, but Amelie pushed her roughly toward the other vampire. "No, *please!* I didn't do anything, I didn't! *You need me!*"

"Why?" Amelie shot back. "You've performed the only task for which you were fit. You've proven yourself unworthy by your conduct and your words and your callous behavior. I am returning you to your cell, where you will live out your days in silence and solitude. No more films, Kim. No more books. No more soft living. You will be fed, but no one will speak to you, no one will acknowledge your existence. You will live as a ghost until you are one. Because in the end, I do not believe that you are innocent. I think you knew about the trip wire, as you call it; I believe you triggered it, knowing that they would run. I believe you didn't know about the bombs; you are far too fixed on your own self-preservation to be that daring. But I saw your smile. We all did. You knew."

Kim's face lost color, so much so that she almost looked like that ghost Amelie was talking about. "No," she said. "You can't do this. You can't prove anything."

"I am the Founder," Amelie said. "And I don't need to prove anything." She nodded to Mr. Martin. "Take her. I don't wish to look on her face again."

Kim's eyes met Claire's stare. "Help me!" she shouted. "Don't just stand there, bitch! I'm human! I'm one of *you!*"

Claire shrugged. "You're not anything of mine. You knew," she said, "and you didn't care."

Kim looked shocked for a flash of a second, and then she bared her teeth in a white, feral grin. "Yeah? Well, you know what else I don't care about? Whether Shane was in that building or not. I hope he's dead. I hope he died thinking about you and wondering why you *didn't find him.*"

Shane.

She hadn't thought about it at all; she'd just assumed . . . but he could be in there.

He could be burning.

Claire didn't even think about it. She started to run for the building, which was still belching red flame and black smoke high into the air.

"No," Oliver said, and caught her around the waist, swinging her off the ground. "Not the time for your gallant suicide attempt, Claire."

"He could be in there!"

"Yes," Oliver agreed. "And if he is, you can't help him. Now just—"

That was when someone shot Mr. Martin in the back.

Claire didn't know what had happened; she heard a crack and saw him lose his grip on Kim and pitch forward. Kim didn't hesitate. She broke and ran.

Oliver dropped Claire and jumped for Amelie, taking her

down flat. Claire staggered, off balance, and went down, too, which probably saved her life. She heard the crackle of guns— more than one—being fired, and staying down seemed like a good idea all of a sudden. Mr. Martin was lying near her, but he wasn't moving. His eyes were open, and as she looked at him, she saw him blinking.

"Are you all right?" she asked.

"Bullet in the spine. It will take a few moments," he said. "Where is she?"

Claire carefully raised her head. "Escaping."

Kim was running for the cover of the wreckage—not away from the guns firing at them, but *toward* them. And they seemed to be deliberately missing her, too. Claire finally spotted a dusty, tan-camouflage jeep parked between two sand dunes. There were two men with rifles using it as a firing platform, and Kim was heading for it, fast. One of Oliver's men went dashing after her and almost made it before a bullet sent him spinning and crashing to the dust.

Kim jumped in the jeep, and it revved its engine and spewed up sand as it raced away. One last shot echoed in the dry air, and then they were gone.

"Get off!" Amelie barked, and Oliver rolled away from her and smoothly to his feet. He offered his hand, but she got up without needing it, looking bone-sharp and very, very angry. She glanced at Claire and Mr. Martin, then out toward where Kim and her rescuers had disappeared. "I misjudged," she said. "Kim didn't make a mistake. She's part of this. Somehow, she is part of it. I should have snapped the little animal's neck long before this, but I was too merciful. Too conscious of responsibility." She glanced down at Claire, but there was no sense of recognition in her eyes; she was too angry. "Get up, unless you're too badly injured to stand."

Oliver didn't even *bother* to look down at Claire. Or Mr. Martin, for that matter. It was like they no longer even existed. "They're bold," he said. "And daring. That could have gone very badly for them."

"Yet it didn't," Amelie said. "It appears we have a war on our hands, Oliver."

He smiled. It was a lovely, almost charming smile, and that made Claire feel a little sick. "Finally," he said. "No more diplomacy, my lady. No more half measures. Give me rein and I'll bring you your enemies with their heads decorating my pikes. *All* your enemies. Humans and vampires."

This was out of control, going too fast. Kim gone, Shane, Michael . . . Bishop and Gloriana, the fights, Vassily . . . it was all a big, messy, bloody ball of confusion, and now Oliver was going to wade in and devastate *everything*.

Amelie should have said no. Instead, she looked levelly at Oliver, folded her hands in front of her in a formal kind of way, and said, "So be it. War. Bring me their heads."

"Wait," Claire said, and scrambled to her feet. "Wait, you *can't*. You can't kill everybody. I told you, Gloriana was using some kind of—"

"Glamour, yes, so you said," Amelie interrupted. "But you see, I no longer care. They've tried to assassinate me, and attacked and killed my own. There are times when mercy and measured justice is not appropriate. And this is one of those times."

Oliver inclined his head, turned on his heel, and stalked away, moving quickly in the sun. He was starting to turn a bright, sunburned red, but he was grinning viciously.

Mr. Martin. Claire looked down and saw that he, too, was burning, turning an alarming lobster shade. She found a piece of tin that was still mostly intact and dragged it over to shade him. He smiled at her gratefully and a little painfully. "I'll be on my feet in another minute," he said. "Amelie, I'm sorry. I should have stopped her."

Amelie gave him a distant look. "Yes," she said. "But I will overlook it. You are a valuable asset." She walked away, Oliver's black coat rippling in the wind, looking like a child dressing up as an old movie detective, but there was nothing soft about her. Small, but very deadly, like a snake. She called back, "Come away, Claire. There's nothing more for you to do here. I will require you elsewhere."

Claire looked down at Mr. Martin. He returned the look and shrugged a little. "She's very angry," he said. "You'd do well to obey promptly."

"Will you be okay if I leave?"

His smile faded. He seemed honestly puzzled. "Why do you care?"

"I don't know," she said. "I just do, I guess." Claire ignored Amelie and turned slowly toward the burning wreckage of the building and started to move. She was far enough from Oliver and Amelie at the moment, and their attention wasn't on her.

Shane.

Claire started to run. She heard someone shouting behind her, but she didn't stop. She sped up, leaping over a bent piece of metal, then dodging a piece of burning timber.

"Oh, just let her go," Oliver said. Claire was afraid he'd be after her, but, in fact, he hadn't left Amelie's side. "She has a right to see for herself."

She arrived alone at a ruin of metal. The building had collapsed in on itself where it hadn't blown out in shreds. One part was sticking up at a strange, awkward angle where the supports were still standing. Claire ran for that, hearing the wreckage creak and shudder under the whipping wind.

She didn't think about the danger until she was inside, hearing the deep groans of metal shifting overhead. This place was going to come down, all the way down.

But first, she had to find out. She had to find *him.*

"Shane!" She screamed it, but her ears were still ringing from the blast, and it came out oddly muffled. Maybe he couldn't hear her, either. Maybe that was why she didn't hear anything back. "Shane, *answer me!*"

She almost tripped over the stairway that led down from the cracked concrete floor. It had probably been covered up before, or had some kind of railing around it, but now it was just a dark, open space in the floor. A ray of sunshine pierced the shattered roof and shone down the steps, all the way to the bottom.

She followed.

Down there, the light didn't go far, but enough that she could make out a few things. The steel bars of a giant cage, for one thing. And the bleacher seats. She'd seen this room before, on the video. Shane had been here, fighting.

Claire edged forward, trying to see if there was anyone here, anyone at all. It looked empty.

She tripped over a piece of fallen metal and went down. She caught herself on the palms of her hands, but they skidded damply over the concrete, and she had to fight not to do a face-plant.

"Shane!" Her voice echoed back wildly from metal and concrete, and she could hear the grief and fear in it. "Shane, please answer me!"

No sound at all, except for the continued crashes and groans of the wreckage overhead. She edged back into the sunlight.

There was blood on her hands, bright and red. And on her pants where she'd fallen on her knees.

Fresh blood.

Claire screamed.

THIRTEEN

It was like *CSI: Vampire*, only without sunglasses.

The vampires brought lights, although they probably could have gotten along without them. It didn't take long for them to clear the potentially dangerous wreckage from overhead and get down into the basement, where Claire sat huddled at the foot of the steps. She was still staring at the drying blood on her hands when Oliver stepped down carefully, watching her as he did so.

"It's blood," she said, feeling tired and oddly calm now. "Is it going to make you go all crazy and bite me?"

"Do you go insane with hunger when you see an old, decaying hamburger on the ground next to a trash can?" he asked.

"No," she said. Then, belatedly, "That's disgusting."

"Then let me assure you, the idea of ingesting that filthy, contaminated blood has no appeal to me whatsoever." His voice was oddly quiet, and he looked from her to the pool of blood near the cage. "You're afraid it's Shane's."

She swallowed and managed to whisper, "Is it?"

"No," Oliver said. He crouched down and touched the blood, rubbed it between his fingers, and cautiously sniffed it. "Doesn't smell like his. It's human, but not of the Collins bloodline." He lifted his head again and surveyed the room. More of his people came down the steps, bringing portable lights with them that they set up and turned on, bathing the room in merciless white light. The blood looked almost insanely red, drying to brown patches at the edges. Oliver stood up and stalked over to another spot, then another. "It's also not alone. There are many bloodstains here. Some older; some only a few days old." He walked to the cage and swung open the unlocked door, which creaked like a haunted house. Claire shivered. It felt like that high-pitched squeal had gone straight through her head.

It isn't Shane's blood. She felt an immense, late-breaking wave of relief, and her hands, the hands she'd been holding so rigidly out from her, fell back to her sides. She wanted to cry, but she wasn't sure she had it in her.

"More in here," Oliver said. "A lot more. Many different donors, and vampire blood, as well, as you'd expect from the fight recordings we saw."

"It's barbaric," Amelie said. Claire hadn't heard her arrive, but suddenly she was there, like a white and tattered ghost, glowing in the brilliant lights. If the sun hurt here, why didn't those bright lights? Maybe not the right spectrum. Claire's brain felt sluggish and too tired to work it all out. "Pitting men against each other like fighting dogs in a pit. I can smell the stink of fear and violence here."

Oliver nodded slowly and got to his feet from where he'd been kneeling, examining something Claire couldn't see. "They've been here very recently," he said. "Recently enough to kill someone and set the traps outside. Pressure mines, presumably, triggered when your guards advanced into the shadows. Someone knew precisely what you'd do when you arrived."

"They only misjudged how many I'd bring with me," she said. She seemed all bone and muscle now, and her eyes glittered like ice. "They've made a fatal error. They should have made sure to kill me."

"I'm sure they'll take that to heart," Oliver said. "They knew we were coming. That much is quite obvious."

Amelie turned. Claire thought at first that she was getting her attention, but no, the gray eyes were staring out at something else.

"They've moved operations," she said. "And we have no way of knowing where that is at present. But we will find them, and when we do . . . when we do, no one will be exempt. No one."

"But—"

"No one," Amelie said. Oliver nodded. "They've allowed humans to fight on equal terms, and humans have the advantage of numbers. They will destroy us with this, even without the danger of exposure. It must stop. Dead."

That, Claire thought with a sick feeling, *wasn't a metaphor.*

She had to find them first and get Shane out.

Eve was waiting on the street next to her car when the limousine dropped Claire off at home. Amelie hadn't said a word to her, although Claire had tried to talk. It was like she no longer acknowledged Claire existed at all.

"What the *hell* is going on?" Eve demanded as the limo sped away, gliding like a sleek, black shark. She was dressed in a black corset dress with purple net underneath it, and her lipstick was a shocking magenta. When Eve got distressed, she sometimes channeled it into her wardrobe. And from how she looked today, she was *screaming* on the inside. "Claire? First Shane going over the edge, and you said you'd call! You didn't call! Was Michael there?" That was a sudden flare of hope that glowed inside her like a spotlight, but it dimmed suddenly at the look on Claire's face. "He wasn't. He's not with Amelie, either."

"No," Claire said very reluctantly. She took a step toward her friend. "I don't know where he is, but I think Michael went to go talk to Shane without us, to try to get him to snap out of it."

"And that didn't go well," Eve finished. Her eyes were dark and bleak. "Guys. Why do they *never* listen? Even the cute, hot, smart ones? Didn't we agree *you'd* talk to Shane?"

"I think Michael was trying to protect me," Claire said. She felt miserable, and she ached all over. "In case Shane got violent. I'm sorry, Eve. I'm so sorry." She wanted to cry. Everything had gone so wrong, and unlike most times, she felt like she couldn't control *any* of it. Everybody was lying or sneaking around or under someone else's control. Amelie had gone all Warrior Princess on her, and Oliver—well, he was being Oliver, but squared. Even Kim had boned her, and she'd *expected* that one. But it still hurt, at least physically.

"Oh, honey, it's all right," Eve said. She blinked and looked closer. "What the hell happened to you?"

"Kim lured us into a trap. A building blew up."

"A building blew—" Eve edited herself, backed up, and said, "Wait, did you just say *Kim*? *My* Kim? I mean, the Kim we all hate now who's in *prison*? That one? Were you locked up? When were you locked up? *Why* were you—"

"They let her out," Claire interrupted, and squeezed her eyes shut. "And it was my idea. I thought she could help us trace the signal to where they were holding the fights."

"Oh? Oh. Well, that was a pretty good idea, actually."

"It was a terrible idea. She alerted them somehow. They almost killed us. And they royally pissed Amelie off." Claire's tears were really threatening now, triggered by the warm, concerned look Eve was giving her. "It's all coming apart. I don't know . . . I think they know we're looking for them. I think—oh, God, Eve—I think Amelie's going to kill everybody now and I don't know what to do!" It came out as a plaintive little wail, and Claire instantly felt ashamed of herself. She was falling apart, and it wasn't like her. She'd stood up to Oliver. To Bishop. To Amelie. Even to Bad Crazy Myrnin.

The problem was that this time, the enemy, though known, was for all intents and purposes invisible. Faceless. Worse, the enemy she'd seen, faced, was *Shane.* And that hurt; it had cracked some fundamental, unshakeable strength in her that she needed right now. Desperately. There wasn't anyone or anything she could stand up to, because they were shadows, smoke, invisible or untouchable, like Bishop and Gloriana and Vassily.

Or like Kim. The thought hit her and vanished. God, she hated her. She hated her most, truthfully, for saying that she hoped Shane died.

That, Claire couldn't forgive. It burned in her guts like a beaker full of acid.

"I'm sorry," she said, and caught her breath. Her voice sounded ragged. "I'm sorry. It's been a very bad morning."

"You look like somebody dragged you by the hair through an ash factory," Eve said. "Come in. You need a shower."

"No. We need to find Michael and Shane!"

"And we're not going to do it without getting a plan together, right? Because I'm pretty sure that wherever they are, they're not wandering the town looking for *us*." Eve, suddenly, was all business. Usually Claire was (or, at least, thought she was) the logical, planning part of the team, while Eve provided the passion and intuition. But today, Eve was in charge, and she took Claire firmly by the shoulders and steered her up the walk, toward the steps. "I called the police and talked to Hannah. No sign of the boys, or this messed-up fight club they've gotten themselves mixed up with. It's quiet out there. They've searched the gym, too. No sign of them there."

"Eve, we have to *do something*."

"I know," Eve said. "And the first thing you're going to do is take a shower, wash off the— Oh, my God, is that *blood*?"

"It's not his," Claire said. "It's not Shane's, I mean."

"Or Michael's?"

She hadn't even *asked*. That made her want to beat her head against the wall . . . but then she remembered Oliver had been specific. "No, it was human blood, but it wasn't Shane's. So not Michael's, either."

"Thank God." Eve rested her shoulder against the wall of the house for a second, next to the door, and squeezed her eyes shut. She looked almost dizzy with relief. "Okay, inside. I don't know whose blood it is, but it doesn't need to be all over you."

No arguing with that, really.

Cleaning up had a definite stabilizing effect, to Claire's surprise; she got her emotional bearings again, dressed, and found Eve pacing downstairs in the living room, talking on the phone. When she saw Claire descending the stairs, she hung up and dropped her cell back in her pocket. "Listen, I was thinking. What if we go talk to Frank again? Now that Kim busted open the encryption on that Web site, maybe he can tell us more. What do you think?"

"I think I should have thought of it," Claire said, and managed a smile. "I'll call Myrnin. We can use the portal."

"Ugh. I *hate* that thing," Eve said. "But yeah, okay, I'm up for scrambled molecules today. But if that thing ruins my dress, I am hurting somebody. Probably your boss." She reached down and grabbed a black canvas bag, which she slid across to Claire as she lifted another, identical one.

"What's this?"

"Picnic lunch. What do you think it is?"

"Antivampire kit?"

"Yes. *And* lunch. I made us sandwiches. I even cut off the crusts." Eve grinned fiercely. "You and me, girlfriend. Let's go rescue the menfolk for a change." She held up her hand, and Claire high-fived it and returned the grin just as fiercely. Suddenly, she felt like herself again: in control, with a plan, armed. No Shane at her back, but that was okay. She and Eve would do it. Together.

She faced the wall, did the mental calculations, and created the portal that led through to Myrnin's lab. It was dark on the other end, and she sensed the presence of the locked door. "Dammit." She pulled out her phone and dialed. "Myrnin? Open the portal. I need to get through."

"It's not a good time," Myrnin said. He sounded distracted.

"That's too bad. I'm coming through. If you don't want to see me get splattered and killed, open the door."

He sighed in exasperation and dropped the phone, which might have been read as *whatever*, but in the next moment, she sensed the door unlocking and opening, and beyond, a slice of light widened and became the lab. Myrnin was standing there, holding open the door, looking just as harassed as he'd sounded.

"Well?" he demanded. "Are you coming through or creating a breeze?"

Claire gestured for Eve to go ahead of her, which she did, moving fast, dancing around Myrnin on the other end. Claire followed and let the portal snap shut behind her. Myrnin slammed and padlocked the door, then rolled the bookcase in front of it before he whirled around, clasped his hands behind his back, and said, "I have gotten a series of calls from Amelie. You've been keeping secrets, Claire. From *me*. And I do not appreciate it."

"Normally, I'd care about that," Claire said. "But right now, you're going to have to get over your hurt feelings, because we've got things to do. A lot of things, probably. And you're going to help us."

"No, I'm not."

"Yes, you are," Claire said. "You owe me, Myrnin." She pulled the neck of her shirt down to show the silvery bite scars that never quite seemed to go away. "You're going to help. That's all there is to it."

He looked . . . completely puzzled. "You can't talk to me this way, Claire."

"I can and I am and I will," she said. "And you're going to help us find Shane and Michael before Amelie and Oliver do."

"I'm *definitely* not. I'm on thin enough ground with Amelie at the moment. I won't cross her just for the sake of your wandering boyfriend."

"Myrnin, this is *serious*. Amelie could kill him, if she gets her

hands on him first, and it's *not his fault.* It's Gloriana. Shane wouldn't
do these things, say the things he's said . . . not unless someone was
manipulating him. I know him."

"And Michael's just trying to help him," Eve put in. "You can't
let Michael get hurt, can you?"

"Dear girls, I can let anyone get hurt, because in my world, my
safety and well-being come first," he said. "I thought you knew
that by now."

"I was hoping that I was wrong," Claire said. Her mind was
racing, and all of a sudden, she knew *just* how to get Myrnin to
help, after all. She made sure her voice sounded uncaring as she
continued, "But, anyway, we don't need you, Myrnin. We need
Frank."

"Frank," Myrnin repeated, frowning. Over his shoulder,
Claire saw Frank's image flicker into black and white. He didn't
smile, and there was something in his computer-generated expression that made her nervous. "No, I shall not allow Frank to help
you, either. This is very dangerous territory. Amelie and Oliver
have their plans, and you shouldn't get in the way. Not for your
lives' sake."

"Look, I don't *care* about the risk," Claire said. "We're finding
Shane and Michael, and we're going to get them out of there before they get hurt worse than they already have been. We have to
do this *now.*"

"It's too late." Frank's voice came from the speakers of her
phone, Eve's phone, the radios positioned around the room. It was
toneless and dark, and Claire felt all her resolve and energy go
cold in its wake. "I'm sorry, kids, but when that first Web site got
hacked, they moved to a secondary location. I can see it, but I can't
track it. I don't think they had time to do the full encryption, but

they did enough. I do have one piece of information that could help, though. . . ."

"Frank, be quiet," Myrnin said. "I didn't give you permission to—"

"Don't make me say nasty things in front of the juveniles," Frank said, "because I'm not your dog, crazy man. You plugged me in, Myrnin. You don't get to shut me up now."

"We'll see about that. I can very easily shut you *down*, you know."

"And sacrifice all the security protocols around the town, *now*? How do you think Amelie would feel about that? I'm guessing she wouldn't be too thrilled, what with the risk of Bishop getting away undetected." Frank's image drifted closer to Myrnin and flickered unsteadily, as if he was having trouble keeping control of it. "He's my *son*, Myrnin. Maybe that doesn't mean anything to you, but it does to me. And I'm going to help, no matter what you say. If you want to pull my plug, go for it. I always said I'd be better off dead."

Myrnin's lips parted, then closed. He made a frustrated gesture and stalked away, arms folded, back stiff. "Do what you wish," he said. "My hands are clean."

"Yeah? How long did it take you to wash off a thousand years of blood?" Frank returned his focus to Claire. "I got an open IP address during the switch over, just for a second, and it routed through a private computer right here in Morganville. Happens to be a guy I know. It was one of the names I gave Myrnin when we first started talking about this."

"Who is it?"

"Harry Anderson, small-time thief and hacker, big-time idiot. If Harry had a motto, it would be 'Anything for a buck.' He's good with computers, but bad with staying out of trouble. I pulled him out of the fire a couple of times when he almost got his head taken off. Literally. The good news is that Harry's got the backbone of a bacteria. Go get him."

"Awesome," Eve said. "Lock and load. What's the address?"

Myrnin sighed and buried his hands in his hair, tugging at it like a crazy man. "You're actually going to do this foolish thing. Why can't you just stay out of it? Amelie said—"

"Do you always do what Amelie says?" Claire asked, and grabbed her black canvas bag.

"Yes." He thought about it. "Almost always. Or, well, occasionally, when it suits me. But the point is that it suits me this time."

"I try to do what people say, if they have good reasons, but Amelie doesn't have a good reason. I don't intend to let her kill Shane just because she's in a bad mood and has some ancient feud going with a bunch of other vampires."

Myrnin shrugged. "All right. But don't ask me for any help."

Claire smiled. She knew what she was doing now; Myrnin was actually pretty easy, once you figured out how competitive he was with Frank. "I won't. I don't need it. Frank's already given us what we want."

That made him give her a strangely hurt look. "I *would* be useful, you know. I can scare people quite easily when I want to. It's a valuable skill. Frank can't do *that*."

"We're going to get what we need," Eve said. "And we don't need a vampire to make it happen, either."

"But it would, in fact, make things easier."

"I said we didn't need you," Claire said. "And you said you didn't want to help. So you don't have to come with us now."

He pulled himself up with great dignity. "I never said I wanted to!"

"Doesn't matter what you say. You're not coming."

"Why not? Provided I had any desire, which I don't."

Eve shook her head. "Where do you want me to start? You're nuts, and you just told us you're not interested in saving Shane and Michael. So why should we bother with you? What's the point?"

Myrnin turned his back on her and looked at Claire. "And you don't think you need me?"

Claire looked him over. He was reasonably action hero today, with a long, black velvet coat and a turquoise vest and some kind of dark red shirt beneath that. If you liked your action heroes from the late 1800s, at least. "If you go, you do exactly what we say. And no running off to tell Amelie."

"I don't like that last bit."

"You don't have to. Take it or leave it."

He shrugged. "I'll take it, then. Stay here. I will get my things."

He left, heading for the room at the rear of the lab that doubled as his bedroom, supposing that Myrnin ever actually slept. "Things?" Eve said. "He has *things*?"

"Probably lots of them," Claire said. "He invents them in his spare time."

Sure enough, when Myrnin came back, he was carrying a bag just a little bit bigger than the ones Eve and Claire carried. His was also black, with a popular swoosh-y logo on the side. *Just do it,* Claire thought. Well, that made sense for Myrnin, mostly because he rarely thought things through, anyway, unless they were mechanical and mathematical.

"What's in the bag?" Eve asked. "Your bunny slippers?"

Myrnin hefted it to his shoulder and said, "A projectile weapon that fires silver aero-dispersant cartridges, among other things."

"I don't understand what you just said."

"Like tear gas, but with powdered silver," Claire said. "Airborne. Right?"

"Exactly so. I have several things I'd like to try." He seemed gruesomely enthusiastic about that, actually. "I so rarely have the chance to field-test anything. Amelie is so conservative about these things."

"No kidding," Eve said. "Holla."

Myrnin's eyes widened. He looked at Claire, who shrugged. "She agrees," she said. Eve started for the stairs, and Myrnin moved to follow, but Claire held him back. "Wait. You'd better not be following us and reporting back to anybody else."

"I wouldn't do that. I am not a—what do you call it? Snark?"

"Narc. Or snitch."

"I would tell you quite honestly if I intended to betray you to Amelie," he said, and his luminous black eyes locked onto hers. "I'm not as fond of your friend Shane, but I will help you. For one thing, I don't like it that Gloriana has such a hold on this town, or that Bishop is at large. These things can't end well for anyone. I'd rather take them on now than risk Amelie coming to harm."

It was the first time she'd heard Myrnin say anything about Amelie that she could interpret as *friendship*. Claire said, frowning, "Because you care about her?"

"Well, that, of course, but I can't see Oliver supporting my research nearly as thoroughly. Can you? He doesn't have much respect for the scientific or alchemical arts." He swept his hand in the direction of the stairs in an elegant gesture, and bowed from the waist. "After you, my dear."

"You're going to need a hat and coat. It's sunny."

"Bother." He grabbed up a ratty-looking old trench coat with a torn sleeve, and a floppy hat that looked like something a little old lady might have worn to work in the garden, if she'd been color-blind. "Is that sufficient?"

"Brilliant," Claire said. "Let's get this circus on the road."

FOURTEEN

Myrnin had a car. Somehow, this surprised Claire; she hadn't thought he had any use for one, but Amelie would have undoubtedly thought about emergencies, which was why there was a conservative, dark-toned town car sitting in a dilapidated shack behind Gramma Day's home. It wasn't locked up, and it had a coating of dust that made Claire wonder if it had ever been moved at all. Myrnin had no idea where the keys were. Claire found them on a nail, hanging behind the shack's sagging door.

They were loading the black bags into the trunk of the car when the door slid back and a squat, round, stooped shape was silhouetted by the sunlight at its back. It took a second for Claire's eyes to adjust, but when she did, she recognized the lined, hard-set face of Gramma Day under that soft cloud of gray hair. Gramma was wearing a flowered dress and house shoes, and she was carrying a shotgun that Claire would have sworn was too big for her to lift.

She sure looked like she knew what she was doing with it. The sound of her racking a round into the chamber, that heavy metallic *chuk-chuk*, made all three of them freeze. Even Myrnin.

Gramma leveled the shotgun at them, squinted, and then started to lower it. "Is that Claire?"

"Gramma, it's me. And my friend Eve. Oh, and you probably know Myrnin."

Gramma clearly did, because the gun came right back to her shoulder. "I know who all my neighbors are. Don't much care for *that* one."

Myrnin raised his chin. "Dear lady, I've *never*—"

"Only 'cause I don't allow you anywhere near my property. You know what I call you? Trapdoor Spider."

Myrnin blinked. "That is . . . surprisingly accurate, actually. Well, feel free to drop in on me any time you wish. Oh, of course, I promise not to hurt you."

"Don't think I'll be relying on your *promises.* What are you doing in here?"

"Driving my car."

"Oh." She did lower the gun now and staggered a little. If she'd actually fired it, she'd probably have broken her shoulder, as thin and fragile as she was. "Didn't know it was *yours.* Knew it belonged to some vampire or other, but I never asked any questions. Never saw anybody driving it."

"Well, you have now," Claire said. "Providing it starts." She pitched the keys to Eve, who managed to field them while Myrnin was distracted with Gramma Day. "And before you ask, no, you're not driving, Myrnin. I remember the last time."

"That accident was not my fault."

"You were the only one on the road, and the mailbox actually didn't leap out in front of you. No arguments. You sit in the back, too."

"You've turned into quite a bossy little thing," Myrnin said. "I think I might like it." He opened the back door and slid inside. Eve shrugged, got in the driver's seat, and cranked the engine. It wheezed and coughed, but it did start. Gramma Day shook her head and hobbled out of the way, holding the door back.

"Claire," she said. "You want to watch yourself. That man ain't right. You keep a good watch on him. You hear me?"

"I know. I will."

"You want my shotgun?"

"No," Claire said very politely. "But thank you."

Gramma waved at them as Eve piloted the car out of the garage and then applied the brakes sharply and said, "Um . . . problem?"

"What?" Claire looked up from fastening her seat belt. Eve was staring at the front window with a horrified, mortified expression on her face.

The *black* front window. "It's a *vampire* car," she said. "And I can't believe neither of us thought about that."

"I can," Myrnin said from the backseat. "Now. Could I please drive my own car, seeing as how I am the only one who is actually qualified to do so?"

He's been just waiting *for that,* Claire thought. She sighed and rubbed her forehead. It was going to be a long, long day.

"Switch," she said. "Myrnin, drive *carefully.* Understand?"

"Of course."

He didn't.

*   *   *

Afterward, Claire tried not to think how hair-raising the ride was; Myrnin was the only one who could actually *see* the danger, but she could *hear* it, and it was horrifying. Squealing brakes at virtually every intersection as other drivers put all their skills to use in avoiding the moving target of their car. Yells. Honking horns. A siren that Myrnin blissfully ignored, and that finally turned off without him ever pulling the vehicle to the curb.

At least he didn't hit anything that she could tell. She was almost sure about that. Almost.

Myrnin finally hit the brakes way, way too firmly, sending her and Eve hurtling against their seat belts, and put the car in park. "See?" he said, with an unholy amount of glee. "I hardly broke any laws at all. I should drive more often."

"No. Trust me, you shouldn't," Eve said. "Think of the little old people and the children. Please tell me we're there."

"Of course."

Eve opened her door and peered out cautiously. She shut it again. "By *there* I mean *parked*, Myrnin."

"We're not moving."

"Against the curb."

He started the car and drove another two feet at an angle. Claire felt the bump as he ran over the curb. So much for not hitting anything. He left it there, with the car's right wheels up off the street.

"Not exactly what I meant," Eve said.

"Do you imagine they're going to issue me a citation . . . what was your name again?"

"Still Eve."

"No, I'm sure it's something else. That doesn't seem right." Myrnin got out and opened the trunk of the car. They all loaded up on bags, and Claire took her first real look around. It was a decrepit old neighborhood; most of the houses looked deserted. The one where they were parked had sheets tacked up as curtains in the windows—those that weren't covered up with peeling, rain-warped plywood. Trash had blown up against the walls, and from the look of it, some of it was older than Claire was.

"This is it," Eve said. "You're sure."

"This is his address."

"Good. You go first."

Myrnin gave her a wicked smile. "Whatever happened to *we don't need you?*"

"We don't," Eve said. "But while he's busy staking you, we can get the drop on him."

Myrnin didn't seem to see the humor in that, but he shrugged and hurried to the door, looking ridiculous in his flapping trench coat and old-lady hat, right up until he kicked in the door with one casual blow, leaned in, and said, "Please don't run. I'm not in a good mood. Better if you just sit still."

He cocked his head and listened, then smiled. What was it with vampires and chilling smiles? His made Claire grip her anti-vampire bag tighter and wish she hadn't stood quite so close. "Ah," he said. "And there he goes. You two wait here."

He dashed off, moving like a flicker of light. Claire looked at Eve, who shook her head and stepped over the threshold into the house. Claire stayed with her. There was some kind of commotion at the back of the house, where she presumed a rear door was located, and as the two girls walked through the deserted, messy living room (what was it with guys and old pizza boxes? Could they not throw them away?) Myrnin reappeared from the back, shoving a pale, skinny man ahead of him. The guy they were looking for, Claire supposed. He looked terrified.

"Sit," Myrnin said, and shoved the guy onto the threadbare couch. He looked around, sighed, and pushed some old pizza boxes and fast-food bags off an end table, then sat down. "You really should look into a maid. Just a thought."

"Are you Harry?" Claire asked. "Harry Anderson?"

The man was not only pale and unshaven; he was also shifty-eyed. He looked like he was lying even when he wasn't talking. When he did finally answer, it looked even worse. "No," he said. "I'm, uh, watching the place for a friend. Harry's my friend, I mean."

Eve reached into her bag and pulled out a crossbow. She stuck a lethal-looking metal bolt on it and cranked back the string. The man watched with increasing worry. "Uh, I'm not a vampire," he said.

"Yeah, I can see that, since you're wearing Oliver's Protection bracelet," Eve agreed. "That's not the only thing this is good for. You'd be surprised how effective it is on liars, too, Harry."

He licked his lips, staring at her, and then shifted his gaze to Claire. He must have decided she was nicer, because he said, "You're not going to let her do this, are you? What are you girls, anyway, twelve? Do your parents know you're hanging around with vampires old enough to be your—"

Eve snapped the trigger, and the bolt whizzed past Harry's head and buried itself in the wall next to him. He yelped and almost jumped off the sofa, but Myrnin put a hand on his shoulder and held him down as Eve reloaded.

"Now," Eve said. "We've got some questions, Harry, and I'm going to suggest, *strongly*, that you just go ahead and answer them. If you think Claire is going to be any kinder to you than I am, you're very mistaken. My boyfriend's only missing. Hers is in your little fight club."

"Oh," Harry said, and then, in an entirely different and much more worried tone, "*Oh.* This is about—"

"ImmortalBattles-dot-com," Claire said. "You helped set it up, so you know these people. You know where they were."

"Uh, sure, but they're not there now."

"Nobody's there, idiot. They blew it up," Eve said. "You see the bruises and cuts on my friend there? That's what your friends did. They tried to blow up the *Founder.* How do you think that's going to go over, Harry? Because I'm thinking that you should just take this crossbow bolt straight in the heart and get it over with. She's not the forgiving type."

Harry closed his eyes and sweated, a lot. Claire waited, content to just stand there and look—well, not menacing, but maybe impatient. Myrnin, on the other hand, looked menacing. He'd shed the hat and coat, and now was perched with inhuman grace on the arm of the couch, staring down at Harry with those glowing, scary red eyes.

"Harry," he said quietly. "Do decide what you want to do. I'm hungry, and if you're going to cooperate, please indicate it immediately, before I assume you're not. I'd hate for you to be trying to utter a dying declaration and be unable to do so."

Harry's eyes snapped open again, full of panic, and he scooted as far away from Myrnin as was possible. That wasn't very far, because the other half of his couch was a rat's nest of piled-up papers, mail, boxes, and wadded-up old clothes. The place was a pit. Claire shuddered and decided not to sit down *anywhere.*

"Wait," Harry blurted. "Just wait, okay? Uh, right, the fight people. Yeah, they paid me to move everything. You know, the cameras, the equipment, the server, the whole setup. And to run the re-encryption, not that it's going to do any good; somebody cracked it pretty good the first time. . . ."

"Where?" Claire asked. When Harry didn't answer immediately, she opened up her bag and rooted through it. She came up with one of Eve's silver-coated stakes, decorated with shiny crystals in the shape of a Gothic cross. She showed it to Eve. "Pretty," she said.

Eve smiled. "I like things to be nice," she said. "But you can never get the blood out from between those—"

"Okay!" Harry interrupted. "Jeez, you're just *kids!* All right, fine. I moved it all to a place near the edge of town. I can give you the address, and then I'm done, okay? Done. I pull the phone, grab my stuff, and I move the hell out of here. You won't have any trouble from me—no, sir."

"I can think of an easier way to ensure that," Myrnin said. "Girls? What do you think?"

Eve stared at Claire, who stared back, twirling the silver stake in her fingers. It was all theater. She wasn't going to kill anybody, and neither was Eve. Myrnin might have, but Claire thought they could hold him back. Maybe.

"I think we should give him a chance," Claire said. "Mr. Anderson, you understand that if you give us the wrong information, or if you do *anything* to warn them we're coming . . . well, it won't be nice. Will it?"

"I knew it: you're the nice one," he said. "You called me Mr. Anderson."

Claire stabbed the stake in the coffee table, point down, with all her strength. It sank in, not as deeply as she wished, but enough to hold it upright on its own, with its red Gothic cross shining in the dim light. "Harry," she said. "I'm really not that nice."

He swallowed and nodded and reached for a piece of paper and a pencil. He scribbled down an address and sketched out a map. He even noted on there which doors were safe to go into. He looked at her, then Myrnin, then Eve, and finally handed the paper to Myrnin.

Who smiled. "Why thank you, Harry. What a good decision you've made." He jumped down with a loud thump, pulled on his trench coat, and slapped the hat on his head. "I think we can go now."

"No," Eve said. She held out her hand. "Cell phone."

Harry dug in his pockets and came up with one, which she dropped to the floor and stepped on, a lot, until it was just pieces of glittering junk.

"Your computer?"

"Back there." He pointed.

"Myrnin, would you mind?"

"Of course not. I told you I was useful."

"Then go rip it up. Claire, find his landlines."

In the end, they left Harry sitting miserably in his filthy living room, with a pile of broken phones and shattered computer equipment, and instructions to stay out of things, *or else.* Claire was pretty sure he'd gotten the message. Loudly. But just to make sure, Eve had tied him up with duct tape. He looked like a silver mummy.

"Don't worry," Eve said. "I'm going to call the cops and ask them to look in on you in about, oh, three hours. None of those cockroaches look hungry—that's the good news. They're all about the pizza, not the human flesh. So you'll be just fine, Harry." She patted his head and smiled so brightly that Harry looked momentarily dazzled. Eve was pretty, and she could be totally stunning when she smiled like that.

"Bye," she said. He mumbled something around the duct tape, and that was that.

Eve did do what she'd promised; as Myrnin drove (another terrifying, in-the-dark experiment), she called Hannah Moses's office and reported the whole thing.

"Wait," Hannah said. Claire could see why, as head of the Morganville police department, she was a little puzzled about this whole thing. "You're telling me you just assaulted and terrorized a Protected citizen of Morganville and left him tied up, and you want *me* to check on him for you? Did I get that right?"

"Yeah," Eve said. "Well, it sounds bad when you say it like that, but that's pretty much it. Just so he doesn't choke or have a heart attack or something. Also, there are a lot of cockroaches. I worried about that."

"You realize that you're admitting to crimes, Eve."

"No," she said. "Because we're sort of doing stuff for Amelie. Following up a lead. She'll, ah, back us up." She raised her eyebrows at Claire, a clear *Right?* in her expression. Claire shrugged. "Besides, Oliver's his Protector, and Oliver won't care what we did. If he'd gotten to him first, I'm pretty sure you'd be doing a whole lot more cleanup."

Hannah was quiet for a few seconds and then said, "I remember when this was a quiet little town. That was nice."

"It was never quiet, Hannah. You just went off to Afghanistan."

"And it was quieter there, too. All right. I'll check in on your prisoner. What are you girls up to?"

"Do you want to know?"

"Shouldn't I?"

"Uh . . . I don't think you should," Claire said. "Seeing as how you'd think you needed to do something about it, and staying out of the way is probably a whole lot safer right now."

"Are you going to take your own advice?"

"We can't," Claire said. "Shane and Michael are in trouble. We're going to get them out."

"You're sure I can't help with that?"

"Yeah," Eve said. "I'm sure. We've got all the help we can handle already."

Myrnin whipped the wheel in a sharp movement that made tires squeal, and threw the girls around in the backseat of the car. Eve almost dropped her phone.

"Are you in the car that's almost caused three accidents on North Vance?" Hannah asked. "Because I'm following you with my lights flashing, and whoever's driving isn't pulling over."

"Let him go," Claire said. "Trust me. You aren't going to get him to stop."

"Oh, God. It's Myrnin, isn't it?"

"Tell that police lady to stop chasing me," Myrnin said, annoyed, from the front seat. "Really, I'm not *that* bad at this."

All evidence to the contrary. But Hannah hung up on her end, and the wail of her siren died away. Claire supposed that at the moment, that was as much of a win as they might reasonably hope for. So here they were, hurtling into the dark on the tip of a terrified thief who might or might not be screwing with them, and they'd just refused police assistance.

This was turning out *so well*. But Claire had to admit, Eve was all kinds of awesome, when she had the chance to shine. She glittered and flared and was sharp enough to cut, just like a diamond.

All Claire had to do was look reasonably intense, which right now wasn't a problem. She *felt* intense, because she couldn't stop thinking about Shane. Where he was. What he was doing. What was being done to him.

Gloriana.

Claire's cell phone rang, and she jumped and looked at the screen.

Mr. Radamon, MIT.

Oh, God.

She took a deep breath, squeezed her eyes shut, and answered. "Hello?"

"Ms. Danvers, hello. This is Mr. Radamon from MIT. I'm very sorry to bother you, but I need to check in and see how things are going. With your arrangements. As you can imagine, these places are very difficult to hold, and I do need your answer fairly soon to—"

"I know," Claire said, and tried not to let her voice shake. She felt like she was being squeezed in a vise now, and her head was about to explode. "I'm sorry, I'm kind of in the middle of something. I promise, I'll call you as soon as I can, sir. Thanks."

"All right, thank you—"

She hung up. Fast. Silence in the car. Eve gave her a curious look.

"Well," Myrnin said quietly from the front seat. "I would suggest we focus on the problem at hand. The fewer distractions, the better, I believe."

His tone of voice was entirely different than it had been before, and Claire realized that he'd heard the conversation. Heard every word on the other end of the line, too. No secrets from someone like Myrnin.

She couldn't tell what he was thinking, but he was unnaturally still.

"Myrnin—" she began. He held up one stiffened hand in a sharp gesture.

"No," he said. "We don't discuss this now. Later, perhaps." He glanced at her in the rearview mirror, and his eyes were dark and very troubled. "We should be at the address Mr. Anderson gave us in just a moment. You should be ready."

"About that . . ." Claire forced herself to stop marveling at the incredibly bad timing, and remembered just what it was they were doing. "We know the safe entrances, but how are we going to do this? Go in together? Separately?"

"I assume the priority is to find your friends and remove them from the premises first, before calling in Amelie and Oliver—that being equivalent to summoning a nuclear strike. Is that correct?"

"Yes," Eve said. "Shane and Michael, first priority. Oh, and not getting killed. That one's big, too." She frowned and grabbed Claire's cell phone back. "Hey, is this thing Internet ready?"

"Yeah, it's a smartphone," Claire said. "Why?"

"I think we should see what's going on at the Web site," Eve said. She worked with the phone for a minute or so, then held it out so Claire could also see the small but clear screen. The Immortal Battles site loaded slowly, but it loaded, and Eve expanded the part that talked about upcoming bouts.

There was a countdown counter going, and it was winding down fast. The banner read LIVE EVENT. There was a video embedded next to it that started playing when Claire clicked it.

Vassily again, dressed in his dumb Halloween interpretation of a vampire (although, truthfully, Myrnin wasn't costumed so differently right now). Vassily looked excited and a bit nervous as he leaned toward the camera, enough that it caught glimpses of his long, white teeth. "Hello, members," he said. "We have a very special treat for you, so get ready to place those bets. On one side, we have our reigning champion, Shane 'The Hammer' Collins." And Vassily drew back to show Shane sitting there in a chair, stripped to the waist, all those awful bruises showing. He wasn't tied up or anything. He seemed fine, but very focused.

Vassily moved on, and the camera moved with him. They went through some kind of a door, very walk-and-talk, and all of a sudden the camera fumbled and focused on another familiar face. *Michael.* He seemed okay, but unlike Shane, he was tied up—no, chained. Chained to a wall. He lunged for Vassily, but he came up short. Vassily flashed fangs at him. Michael flashed them right back.

"And this, my friends, is our newest warm-up contender for our champion . . . Michael! These two have been building a grudge match for more than a year, and it's all the more violent because they were once best friends. So, who do you think will come out on top: the current victor, or the vampire? Place your bets! The match starts in just a few minutes, with the winner meeting our special benefactor . . ."

Vassily was walking and talking again, leaving Michael's frustrated, anguished face behind. The camera jostled after him, through tunnels and darkness, and quite suddenly, apparently to Vassily's surprise, there was a man standing in his way. His patter faltered and stopped.

It was Mr. Bishop. Not the skeletal, desperate thing that Claire had seen before . . . no, Bishop had showered, found fresh clothes, and, clearly, fed until he was completely recovered. He looked *younger* than before. And very, very strong. The menace came off him like black light.

"Well," Vassily said awkwardly. "Uh, sir, I don't think you should be—"

"Shut up, Vassily. I make the decisions here," Bishop said. "And I have decided that today—I will fight the winner of today's match. I feel the need for a bit of exercise before we move on to bigger prey."

"Sir, this isn't . . . this isn't what we agreed—"

Bishop's eyes went red and his fangs came down, and Claire almost dropped the phone. Even whoever was running the camera was moving backward. "I'm changing our agreement, *minion*. Tonight I'm changing all the agreements. Tonight we will take the fight out of the cage. Into the streets. To the Founder."

"Sir—"

Bishop hit Vassily hard enough to knock him into the wall, and stood there staring down at him. "I've waited long enough," he said. "I don't need your filthy money. What I *need* is to feel her blood in my mouth. Are we understood?"

Vassily got up, cringing, and bowed his head. "Yes, sir. Understood. Uh, but first, we bring you the fighting . . . ?"

"By all means," Bishop said, and smiled. "I want to see these two do damage to each other. It would please me a great deal."

The video ended. Claire fumbled with the phone and, hands shaking, pulled up the counter again. Next to it were odds. Shane was favored over Michael two to one. Bishop was heavily favored to beat either one of them.

And the counter . . .

The counter for the fight had run out.

"No," Claire whispered. "No . . ." Bishop didn't intend for this to go on much longer; he'd gone on camera in open defiance of Amelie. He was serious; this would end in slaughter, whatever happened in the cage match.

They were out of time.

FIFTEEN

SHANE

He'd been crazy to try it.

When I saw Michael show up at the barn, Vassily and Gloriana had been loading us up in the van to take us to the new place. I don't know how he found me; I could have sworn nobody at the gym knew anything about where we were, but there he was, Michael effing Glass, walking up in his stupid black vampire coat and hat and gloves, trying to talk to me like we knew each other.

Like he hadn't stabbed me in the back the second he'd agreed to stop being human.

He'd joined them, the vampires. Our masters, who'd made my dad a loser and let Monica Morrell run wild, doing whatever, which turned out to be fatal for my sister. They'd sent killers after my mom. Michael should have known better. He should have known that no matter what, I couldn't forgive him, not deep down. They'd taken my family away.

Vassily and Glory had had him grabbed, of course, and stuffed in the other van, the one that held the vamps. They didn't try to transport us together, not anymore. Too many fights. He kept yelling at me, but I just watched until they had him locked down and then I walked away.

He used to be my friend, and, damn, it still hurt to know he'd done this to us, to me. He'd changed everything. About time he knew how that felt.

Maybe it was the shock of seeing him—I don't know—but I found I wasn't feeling quite as pumped up about the upcoming bout as before. My head was hurting and I was tired; sleep hadn't come easy lately because of all the bruises and cracked bones. When Glory was around, it was better. I didn't think so much. But now, in the van, I noticed how there was a thick wire mesh between us human fighters and the driver's seat, like we were vicious dogs or something. When I looked around at the others, I thought maybe that was true. There were four of us in here, and, to be honest, I was probably the toughest. I didn't look it, though. They looked like my dad's biker buddies, all sweat and muscles and tats, with shaved heads and goatees. They were ready to tear it up. I guess I was, too, or at least I would be once we got where we were going.

Once Glory smiled at me again.

I leaned my head back and closed my eyes, and instead of seeing Glory's wicked, cool smile, I saw Claire's sweet one, the one she gave only me, the one that had made me forget all about being angry or tough or hurt. With her, things were good. I was good. Because of her. It was the exact opposite of what Glory's presence did; hers made me remember all the bad stuff, boil it up and over, and want to take it out on anybody who was in the way. Claire made me forget all that and realize that I didn't have to be angry.

No, I was doing this for her. For her. I needed to earn my passage out of town, before it was too late. She'd even said that the other night, before that awful moment at the gym when she'd been so close to Michael, and I'd—I'd thought . . .

I knew it wasn't true. I knew Claire wouldn't hurt me like that.

I opened my eyes and took in a quick breath. I needed Glory. I couldn't stay tough if I thought about Claire; I missed her, and I hated that it made me feel weak and sick. She'd left me first, hanging out with that bastard Myrnin, sneaking out to be with him. No matter what she said, that was the truth.

But I couldn't help it. I wanted her. I wanted her with me, and the only way it could be right was away from here. Out of Morganville.

"Hey, Collins, don't fall asleep on us!" yelled Brett, who had his first match coming up later, after mine. "Gotta get hot, my man!" He punched me in the shoulder, right where I had a big, spreading bruise and swelling. I didn't wince, but the pain that shot through me made me see waves of red, and it was suddenly tough to breathe. I rode it out and forced myself to grin back at him.

"I get any hotter, I'll burn you alive," I said. He howled like a wolf. Some guys didn't need Glory's influence to go nuts; Brett was like that. "Hit me again, and I'll bust you up, man."

He flexed his fists and grinned, but he took me seriously and sat down against the wall of the van. "You thinking about that girl again?"

"No," I lied. I was trying not to, because it hurt. It hurt thinking that somewhere out there she might be looking for me. All I could think about was that somewhere she could be alone, afraid, maybe crying. Because of me.

I shut my eyes again and banged my head on the wall of the van, enough to hurt and leave a dent. I wished Glory had ridden with us.

I really, really did.

*   *   *

*When I got out of the van, we were at some falling-down old ware-
house, another crappy piece of Morganville ancient history that nobody
cared about. I saw fading letters on the outside. It must have been some
kind of carpet mill. Big brick building, not many windows, and what
windows had been there were broken out three stories up by some local
kids with good arms. Not a lot of time for sightseeing, but I recognized
the area; you don't grow up in this stupid town without prowling
around the places your parents don't want you to go. Me and Lyss had
poked through some of these abandoned warehouses when she was about
twelve and I was stupider than usual. We'd gotten away with it, but
looking back on it now, I couldn't believe we'd ever taken that chance.*

*Now that she was gone, it made me cold to think all the risks I'd let
her take. If I could make things right again, make that fire stop, get her
out of the house before all the smoke and the flames . . . then I'd never
let her take another risk again. I'd protect her. That's what a big brother
is supposed to do: protect.*

*But no, I'd been a jackass to her, and I'd fallen asleep on the
couch, and by the time I woke up, the house was burning and I couldn't
get her out. I don't know if she woke up. I hoped not. I hoped she never
knew, never felt the kind of screaming fear that I did while trying to
get to her.*

Shake it off, Collins. *Lyss was gone. My mom and dad were
gone. I had to focus on getting myself through the next two hours or
so without joining them. If I did this right, I'd make a lot of money:
enough to buy my way out of town, get lost, make a new life. Forget Claire.*

That was what I had to do. Forget. Forget everything.

It was easier when Gloriana prowled over and took my arm. She was a vamp, yeah, but she didn't feel like one; I didn't hate her and I didn't want to hurt her. I wanted to please her, in all kinds of ways—not that she wanted anything from me except to put up a good fight. She went for the fanged boys. Like Michael.

Just another reason to hate him. Like I needed more.

"Are you ready?" she asked me. "Are you going to be my knight in shining armor, Shane, protecting me from all the big, bad men?" She said it with a smile, but I had the feeling she didn't mean it. She seemed to be making fun of me, but I couldn't get too upset about it. There was something about her . . . something that deep down I knew I hated but still couldn't resist. "Because we have a lot riding on you tonight. We need you to make us a lot of money, very quickly, and we're going to take that money and pay off some debts. Old debts, to someone we'd rather not owe, if you know what I mean. Then there will be new owners for Immortal Battles, and Vassily and I will be safe. And we can all be out of Morganville forever."

She was telling me things that I knew she didn't intend for me to understand, and on some level I did understand . . . and I knew that something was very wrong. But it was too late for any of that, for caution or thinking or resistance.

I hated her kind, but I'd do anything for Gloriana, and she knew it.

"Now," she said, and patted my hand the same way she would have patted a dog on the head. "You're not going to have a problem with your warm-up match, are you?"

"Who am I fighting?"

"Your old friend. Michael."

Michael. I turned that over in my sluggishly working brain, and I wanted to say no, but I couldn't quite get it to come out of my mouth. Instead, I said, and I meant it, "Sure, no problem." Michael and I had *fought before. Hell, I'd put him down on the ground a couple of times, even though he was vamp-fast. I could take him.*

"I only ask because it would be inconvenient if you had . . . second thoughts. We're going to do this live, not on tape, you see. More excitement that way. More money. There will be a live audience as well as one online."

Didn't matter to me who was watching or why. "I fight vampires," I said. "That's what I'm supposed to do. Doesn't matter who they are or who they used to be. Right?"

"Right," she said, and laughed. *I tried not to notice the flash of fangs in her mouth.* "I love a man who knows what he wants, Shane. Oh, and remember . . . this fight doesn't stop until one of you gets carried out. No mercy."

"No mercy," I said. *I felt weirdly hollow inside, empty where I'd been full of all kinds of stuff before. There was only the hate now, glowing and radiating inside of me, and it was starting to feel like something toxic. Something that was eating me up inside, spawning cancers like black clouds.*

But it didn't matter. None of that mattered when she opened the door and I saw the cage in the middle of the bleachers, and the people getting in their seats.

"That's yours," Glory whispered to me. "That's all yours, Shane. Because you're going to win tonight, and we're all going to be free."

I looked at her, suddenly sure she was lying . . . but there was something oddly open and honest in her blue eyes.

"You mean it?" I asked. "Free?"

"Free," she repeated. "I promise you. After tonight, you'll never have to fight again."

Then she led me down a hall and sat me in a chair, and Vassily showed up doing his stupid Dracula impression, with cameras that

leered at me with empty eyes. And then it was all over and the count-
down was up.

Time to fight.

"Paying customers," Myrnin said. He nodded to the people getting out of cars and walking toward the far door, the safe door,
of the warehouse. There were all types—what passed for white-
collar in Morganville, moms, college kids, tough guys. A cross
section of crazy. There were vampires, too, working the door . . .
Claire recognized one of them, and said so. "Yes," Myrnin
agreed. "He was with Bishop before. One of those Amelie said
has been missing. Now we know where he's been. No doubt
Vassily hired many of Bishop's former employees to staff his little venture."

"But what does he *want?*" Eve asked. She was watching the parade of people forking over cash with a baffled and faintly sick-
ened expression. "All this for money?"

"Millions of dollars, which to a vampire means safety and sta-
bility," Myrnin said. "And independence. Our friends who broke
away from Amelie to form their little colony in Blacke aren't the
only ones who want out of Morganville; Bishop's friends and sym-
pathizers fear Amelie. Outside of this town, they could be their
own little petty kings and queens." The way he said it, he seemed
bitter and distant, as if he'd considered it before. Or done it before. "In any case, never think money is any less a good motive
than passion. You'd be surprised what people will do for money
that they wouldn't do for love."

"We have to get in," Eve said.

"No doubt," Myrnin agreed. "But they will know you immediately. Claire is less recognizable, and hardly anyone knows my face. I suggest you stay here and—"

Eve gave him a withering look and said, "Pass me your hat."

"Pardon?"

"Your *hat*. And your coat."

Myrnin gave her a doubtful look and handed them over. She shook them out, sniffed them, made a face, and then put it on. On Eve, the coat looked even bigger and more ill-fitting than it had on Myrnin, and the hat practically swallowed her head. All that Claire could see of her was a white flash of face.

Just like a vamp.

"Huh," Myrnin said, and cocked his head with great interest. "For someone so singular, you can disappear quite effectively."

"Shut up and get ready," Eve said. "You're going to need to move your butt if you don't want it lightly fried."

He looked down at himself and frowned. "Won't do, won't do. Far too individual. No . . ." And before Claire could stop him, he stripped off his coat and dumped it on the floor, along with his brocade vest. He left on the crimson shirt and black pants—very piratical. "Better?"

"Sure," she said. She couldn't imagine it was. "Ready?"

"Ready."

Eve got out first and hurried toward the door, head down. The vampires got one look at her face and waved her in without a word. Claire followed her, carrying both black bags. They stopped her and asked for admission money, which Myrnin dug out of a pocket and handed over . . . in gold coins. Probably not all that unusual for the fanged bunch, Claire guessed, because they just shrugged and pocketed the money and gave her and Myrnin plastic strips to wear around their wrists. "You can't bring blood in," one of them said as he sealed the wristband. "Concession's at the back of the room. Ten bucks for a pint."

"That's ridiculous!" Myrnin said. "The prices—"

Claire nudged him along. He looked outraged. "Well, it *is* very high," he muttered. "Oh. There's your friend, Even. Ever?"

"Eve," Claire said. "Here, take your bag. I've got mine and Eve's. I'm going to go find Shane. You and Eve—"

"No need for that," Myrnin said as the lights dimmed and the door boomed shut at the back of the room. Claire had the distinct impression that it was being locked up, and anyone who arrived after was going to be standing outside enjoying the day, human *or* vampire. "Here he comes."

Claire turned around. They were standing on the concrete floor, and the cheap aluminum bleachers extended up for ten rows or so on all four sides of the big, open room. In the center was a platform, and on the platform was an iron cage with an open door. It was about the size of a boxing ring, and there were bright, white-hot lights pointed down into it from all angles to turn it into a blank white canvas.

Vassily walked out into the middle of it, fangs flashing as he smiled and waved at the crowd. The stands were about half full, Claire realized; maybe they hadn't been able to get the word out quickly enough. Didn't matter. Their real money came from the Internet betting and memberships.

Vassily was wearing just about the exact same outfit as Myrnin, only on him it looked cheap and stupid. He had a wireless microphone, and now he raised it to his mouth and said, "Welcome, friends, to Immortal Battles, where those with eternal lives gamble to lose them, and those with merely human strength learn what it is to be heroes!" He got some yells and applause. Next to her, Myrnin was standing very still, watching. Claire realized he was gripping her arm, holding her still. She didn't know why until Vassily said, "And now, meet our mortal hero of the night: Shane 'The Hammer' Collins, winner of two previous bouts, survivor, and hunter! Give him a warm, Immortal welcome!"

The crowd cheered. Claire stood there feeling fragile and hot, like she'd been turned to ashes that might be blown away at any second, and watched as Shane, *her* Shane, walked into the steel cage, arms held high.

He was smiling, but his eyes were dead and haunted by the ghost of the man he'd been. Claire wanted to fall down. Myrnin's hand was crushingly tight around her arm, but she didn't feel like doing anything stupid; she wasn't sure she could move on her own. It felt like a nightmare.

And then, of course, it got worse.

"And the challenger," Vassily shouted. "Vampire novice, musician, aspiring champion, *Michael Glass!* This is a grudge match, ladies and gentlemen, years in the making! Now watch as—"

Vassily had miscalculated, Claire saw; he'd thought he could keep on vamping (pun intended) to drive up the betting, but Shane had other ideas. He did a long circle of the cage, and then, with unnatural quickness, he turned around and slammed into Vassily, who was still talking into his microphone. Vassily dropped the mike, but Shane had him by the collar of his fancy coat and threw him in a rolling, flapping heap on the floor. Before Vassily could get up, Shane was on him.

Michael pulled him off and held his arms behind him. "Stop," he said. Claire could hear him, but she wasn't sure the crowd could; they were all stomping and yelling, setting up a metal-crashing racket that drowned out most things. Michael wasn't playing to the crowd. He was talking urgently to Shane. "Bro, stop this. This isn't you."

Shane did stop. He went still in Michael's hold and his eyes closed. But when Michael let go, thinking he'd gotten through, Claire saw the smile twist Shane's lips, and tried to yell a warning.

She heard Shane clearly when he said, "You're wrong about that. *Bro.*"

SHANE
☽

I'd been wanting to take a bite out of Vassily for a while, and hearing him go on and on about Michael, well, that was it. Michael frickin' Glass. Mr. Perfect. He wasn't just any vampire, now, was he? No, he came from a long line of human Renfields, all bending over for the vamps. Hell, Sam had even . . .

No. Something in me shut down when I tried to free-associate Michael's granddad Sam into that mental rant; Sam, I knew, didn't deserve it. I'd liked Sam. Hell, everybody had loved Sam.

Like everybody loved Michael. Mr. Perfect.

I jumped Vassily, and that felt good. It felt good to think with my body instead of the confusing tangle of hate and guilt and fear that was inside of me—to just be something, do something, without the higher brain getting in the way. I kicked him, but with the hardest angle of my foot. You don't kick with the toes, not with bare feet; you use the side or the heel. I chose the heel, and put some momentum behind it, and felt Vassily's ribs creak when the blow landed.

Nice.

Then Michael was pulling me off, and, dammit, he had me from behind. He had leverage and strength. Vassily got up and retrieved his microphone and scrambled out of the cage, slamming it shut behind him.

Michael said urgently, "Stop. Bro, stop this. This isn't you."

I closed my eyes and let my tense muscles go loose in his hold. Only an idiot would fall for that, but Michael liked to believe he could do anything. And he didn't think I was very smart, anyway.

When I felt him release me, I was smiling so much it hurt. "You're wrong about that. Bro."

He probably had warning, hearing that, but I didn't dive forward to get away from him. Oh no. I launched myself backward, piledriving into him, and slammed us both down on the springy, booming canvas floor. The crowd was screaming; it sounded like thunder in my ears. The lights pounded down on my skin, and I could feel Glory in my head like a searchlight.

She wanted me to win. Win at all costs.

I twisted around. Michael was pinned under me and he was fighting to get up. This time I had the weight and leverage, and as long as I stopped him from getting organized, I could hurt him.

I wanted to hurt him.

"Shane!" he was yelling. I saw him but I didn't see him, not clearly; he was a shape, a voice, an opponent, and who he was didn't matter. He wasn't a person; he was a thing, and I hit him full force in the face. Again and again. Every time, pain jolted up my arm and nausea followed with it, like I was drunk and tipping over into the throwing-up stage, but then it would recede and I'd hit him again.

I hit him with special force, and I felt a bone snap in my hand. One of the little ones—no big deal—but the high, bright snap felt like a flash of red strobe light going through me, and for a second or two after, my head was crystal clear.

And I saw a girl yanking on the cage door, trying to get it open. A tall girl in a ratty, torn raincoat and a stupid, giant hat that fell off as she fought with the door's padlock, revealing shiny, close-bobbed black hair and a face as pale as any vamp's.

"God, Shane, stop!" *Eve was screaming, and pounding on the bars hard enough to make them ring.* "Stop it! What are you doing?"

It was shocking, like seeing Alyssa standing there, and for a second I thought I did see Lyss, the way I'd last seen her, looking so pretty and smart and ready for anything, ready to die, and I couldn't save her because I was a loser and I'd been weak, so weak. I should have opened the door *even though it was hot, so hot, and I'd been passing out from the smoke.*

I looked down.

I'd done some damage to Michael's face, but it was healing. There was blood on the canvas and on my hands and dripping down his cheeks. Any human dude would have been ready for the hospital.

I realized that he wasn't fighting back.

Easy money.

I pulled back my fist for another punch, and he didn't flinch. He didn't look away, either. He just said, "It's not your fault, man. I don't blame you."

For some reason, that was the first thing he'd said that I really heard. *It was almost like I was hearing my father's voice again, saying something that I'd needed to hear every day since Lyss disappeared from our lives.*

That it wasn't my fault.

That I couldn't have stopped it.

The truth was, the fire hadn't been my fault. Nobody could have gotten to my sister to save her.

But this—this was my fault.

I sat back, staring down at him. His blue eyes were bloodshot, flickering with red, but he wasn't going vamp on me even though I'd hurt him badly. He was just going to take it.

"It's Glory," he said. "You know that, right? Not your fault."

Glory. I looked around but I didn't see her. It was just a sea of faces now, screaming faces that didn't care about me or Michael or anything but their own entertainment. Except for Eve, looking so stricken and horrified on the other side of the bars. She cared. Too much, probably.

"Bishop's here," Michael said. "They're going to put him in here with you once I wear you down. I can't let that happen. I have to stay in here with you. It's going to take us both to get him. You understand? We have to stand up together, Shane."

I did. I'd been right before; this was some kind of nightmare, some weird spell that was going to snap any moment now, and things would be okay, all okay. None of this was . . . real. . . .

Then I saw Claire.

She was standing outside the cage by the bleachers, and Myrnin was holding her arm like he was trying to keep her from going full-out Eve and running for the cage, but I didn't think she was trying. Like me, she was paralyzed, trapped in her nightmare, and those dark eyes were looking at me, seeing me, and I saw myself, too. Sweating, bruised, feral, angry, cruel.

It made me sick.

I rolled away from Michael and curled into a ball, facing Claire, staring back. Maybe it was the pain from my hand still tearing through me; maybe it was, finally, my own brain waking up and screaming.

Maybe it was seeing that horrified look on her face. I didn't even care that she was with Myrnin; I was glad she had someone to protect her here. And I knew he would. He'd better. Him, I would kill if he let anything happen to her, and he knew it.

I saw her lips shape my name. Shane. *I couldn't hear her, but I knew how it would sound, how heartbroken and disappointed and scared. I'd let all this get away from me. I'd hurt her and she'd hurt me, and we had to fix it. We had to. Because I couldn't let this destroy the people I loved.*

That included Michael, the jackass. I flopped over on my back, breathing fast, and saw him sitting up. Too-pale-to-be-normal blood ran down his chin and dripped on his bare chest. Without a shirt he looked buff but very, very pale, almost ghostly. Still Michael, though.

Still my friend.

Always my friend, even when I was the biggest dick on the planet.

He was looking at me with a frown, checking out whether I was still in that other, scary place, and I nodded to him and wiped sweat off my face. I felt cold now, not burning hot like I'd been. When I flexed my hand, the pain from the broken bone sliced through me like a clean red knife, driving away all the lingering ghosts of anger.

"You didn't fight," I said. "Jesus, man, I could have killed you."

"Don't think you could have, not for a long time," he said. "Anyway, you didn't." He looked around and saw Eve. His smile was real and full of delight, but there was something else mixed up in there, too. Something almost scared. "I'm okay, Eve. No permanent damage."

She was clinging to the bars like she intended to force her way inside with sheer fury. "Shane, if you hurt him, I'll kill you!"

I waved at her wearily. "Yeah, thanks. I'm the one with a broken bone."

I exchanged a quick look with Michael, who was making plans. "Get away from the door," he said.

"Why?"

Michael stood up. "Because I'm kicking it open."

It took seven sustained, vampire-strength kicks to snap the lock and send the thing flying back; Eve moved off, but not far. I was watching the outside, the crowd. Vassily had, no surprise, disappeared. He'd never intended to be around for long, just long enough to grab the betting receipts and catch his ride. But I wasn't worried about him. He was a greedy ass hat; no big deal.

I was worried about Gloriana, because I could still feel that subtle gray tension inside me that meant she was around. Not focused on me, not right now, but definitely . . .

I saw her a second before she grabbed Eve by the throat and yanked her backward, holding her tight like a Gothic human shield. Eve's weird hat got crushed in the chaos—and now it was chaos, because the people in the stands were figuring out that things weren't going according to the standard fight-club plan, and they wanted out. Only there wasn't any way out of here. The doors were locked. Most of the vamps had already bolted, leaving Myrnin and Michael and Gloriana behind.

Glory's blue eyes met mine over Eve's shoulder, and I froze in the act of getting up. My mind clicked over and blanked into a perfect, smooth whiteness, and I felt that fury boiling up again, hot and crazy and perfect. *She knew me. She knew just where to push, and what would cause me the most pain. I didn't even have to think about it consciously anymore for it to hurt.*

Hurt. *Of course . . .*

I slammed my right fist down into the floor and sent another jolt of agony through my body. The fury shattered and melted away, and I gave Gloriana a smile. A nice, big one. "Guess not," I said. "You wanted to make me kill Michael, didn't you? Kind of an if-I-can't-have-him-nobody-can stalker thing, right? I'm just your weapon. Man, girl, get therapy."

She smirked at me. "That's all you're good for, Collins—being a weapon," she said. "That's all you'll ever be good for. Taking out enemies."

"Good enough for me," I said. "But you just made the top slot on my enemies list. Too bad for you. Don't you think?"

She squeezed. Eve's eyes got huge and she gave me a pleading look, then cut it toward Michael, who was coming down the stairs out of the cage, heading for her and Glory.

I felt Glory's power, her glamour, slam into him like a freight train, and he slowed down . . . and stopped. He reached out for Eve, moving like he was underwater . . . and Gloriana laughed a little, one of those sweet, innocent little laughs that had seemed so pretty before, and said, "I hate it when you look at her that way, you know. Such a waste. She doesn't deserve you, Michael." And I knew right then that she was going to kill Eve in front of him.

And there was no way Michael would be able to stop her.

He didn't have to. Eve was fumbling at the pocket on the side of her über-Goth dress, and I saw a flash of silver a second before she plunged it under her arm, across her own body, and into Gloriana's chest.

"Damn," I said. Because she must have gotten it right, first try—no easy thing, even when you're facing a vampire and able to see your target.

Gloriana went down, dragging Eve with her. Her mouth was open in a silent scream, and her eyes were bright and red and running over with fury. She was still trying to close her hand and crush Eve's windpipe.

Michael lunged forward and slammed the silver stake down harder into Glory's chest, all the way in, for all I know, all the way into the cement floor beneath her. Then he dragged Eve away and put his arms around her and held on like the world might be coming apart, but the two of them never would.

It was kind of beautiful.

And I watched Gloriana—the prettiest vampire I'd ever seen,

*and the most dangerous—go still and quiet as the silver began to burn
and discolor her body, killing her from the inside out.*

She was all done.

*I let just a little bit of the rage back out. Just a little, and felt it
evaporate into a warm, scary satisfaction.*

And God, it felt good.

"Shane?"

Claire hadn't seen what had happened for the past few
seconds—too many running, screaming people, and she'd lost
sight of Eve. When the chaos thinned a little she saw Eve sitting on Michael's lap on the concrete. And Gloriana lying next to
them, staked half into the floor. Silver, Claire realized. She was
well on her way to totally deceased.

And Claire decided she couldn't care too much about that.
What she did care about was that Michael and Eve were okay,
and that Shane was still standing inside the cage, staring out
at Glory's dying body. He looked . . . blank, except for his eyes.
They were full of something hot and wild and strange, and
then . . . peaceful.

Myrnin was still hanging on to her. "Hey!" she said, and shook
her arm to try to throw him off. "Let go already! I'm fine!"

He was frowning and trying to look everywhere at once. "I
think we should leave," he said. "I can easily break a hole in the
bricks over there. Yes, we should go now. See, your boy is fine.
Everything's fine. Except Glory, obviously—that's definitely *not*
fine—but honestly, do any of us care? I certainly don't."

"Let *go!*"

"No," Myrnin said. "You're my responsibility. And this is

dangerous. I don't know where Bishop is, and until we find him, I don't want you on your own."

Claire threw down the black bag she was holding, reached in, and came out with a thin, silver-plated knife. "You know what's dangerous?" she asked. "Me. If you don't *let go*."

He sighed, rolled his eyes, and released her. She snatched up the bag and ran for the cage, bouncing off panicking strangers and a few people she actually knew who'd come to bet on her boyfriend *dying in a cage*—God, she wanted to hit them—and then made it to the steps that led up to the big, square cage. The fight cage.

With Shane.

Shane looked over as she pounded up the risers and flew like a bird into his arms. It felt like the best thing she'd ever done, putting her arms around him, feeling his warm, damp skin pressed against her.

He let out a long, wordless breath and collapsed against her, hugging her like the world was ending, like he never wanted to let her go again. "I'm a fool," he said. "And an asshole. You ought to run as far away from me as you can. I am so sorry."

"If I run, you run with me," she said. "Are you all right?"

He held up his right hand. It looked red and a little swollen. "Broken bone," he said. "Nothing I can't handle."

She took his hand in both of hers, cradling it, and put it gently to her cheek. He was staring at her with a hungry expression, one that seemed to her to be more about hope than anything else.

"Just like that," he said. "Just like that, you're going to let it go. All the things I did. What I said. God, Claire . . ."

"Uh, no, idiot," Claire said. "You're going to have to work for forgiveness. But this . . . this you get for free. Because I love you."

He smiled a little and then he kissed her, and for a few long, sweet, breathless seconds, it was all okay again.

And then Claire heard the sirens.

"The hell?" Shane said, because it wasn't just *a* siren. It was a chorus of them, wailing over each other in waves. Every siren in town, it sounded like, all heading toward them.

Claire felt a sick surge of understanding, which became even more clear when Myrnin came up the stairs to join them inside the cage, took her by the upper arm, and said, "And *now* we are going. No arguments. Amelie and Oliver are coming, and they're bringing as much overwhelming force as is available to them. If you want to maintain your body, soul, and freedom, stop dwithering and *come*. No one in this room will be safe once they arrive. They're very much in a shoot-first, ask-questions-never mood."

"Dwithering?" Claire repeated blankly. "What is——?"

"Must we argue word choice? Now?"

"Nope," Shane said. "We're with you. And we're going."

And they would have been, except that as Myrnin turned and headed for the open iron gate, someone else came up the steps and blocked the opening.

Bishop. Impossibly, he looked even *younger* than he had on the video, like he was aging in reverse. There was fresh blood on his mouth and smeared on the collar of his shirt. His eyes were ancient and vicious and pretty much crazy, Claire thought, as he smiled with his fangs out and said, "Let them come. My daughter thought she could starve me, wall me up, make an example of me. I'll make such an example of this roomful of people—no, this entire *town*—that no one will ever say its name again without shuddering. The nightmare is coming now. Wake up and enjoy it."

Myrnin stared at Bishop in outright horror and backed up fast. He let go of Claire. In fact, he put her and Shane in the way.

"What's the matter, my old friend?" Bishop asked. He calmly reached back, grabbed the door, and slammed it closed behind him with a rattle and boom of metal. Then he bent the frame so that it wouldn't open—more effective than a lock. "No clever plans? No silly games? Because you know I haven't forgotten what you did when you betrayed me. You know I'll take you apart one piece at a time . . . fingers and toes first, then working my way in. And your little humans here, they're only a moment's work. By the time Amelie and her court reach us, I'll be drinking their blood out of your skull."

"You could still run," Claire said. She couldn't believe she had enough strength to talk, but she did. She was scared, but not *that* scared. Somehow, after everything she'd seen, Bishop wasn't the worst anymore. "You could break out of a wall and disappear in the confusion. You know if Amelie catches you, she'll kill you."

"Indeed, I think Oliver's quite convinced her that making an example of me is bad strategy," Bishop said. He paced side to side, but every turn closed the distance between them. "I expect she'll execute me instantly. Or try. But I'm better at this than they are, either of them or all of them. I am the best killer who ever lived."

"Yeah, you don't seem too worried," Shane said.

"I had a great deal of time to consider my place in this world, while she had me sealed up in that tiny, airless hell. Nothing to eat. Nothing to hear or feel or touch. Just endless, dark eternity. Do you know what I decided?"

Shane shook his head. Claire realized she was still holding the small, silver-coated knife, and now she nudged the black bag closer to Shane, who glanced down at it.

"I realized that if I can survive that, survive being starved down to bones, I can survive Amelie's worst," Bishop said. "I don't need Vassily and Gloriana. I thought I needed an army to take this town, and they were making me one—humans like you, Shane, who'd take out vampires without flinching. But I don't need them. Or you. Any of you." His eyes flared blood red. "Except as fuel."

Shane crouched down and reached inside the bag, pulling out a crossbow, but it wasn't set. It would take seconds to cock and load, and Bishop wasn't going to give it to them.

Bishop smashed the crossbow into splinters with one blow, and threw Shane headfirst into the bars.

Claire screamed, because it should have killed him . . . and probably would have, if he hadn't been dosed up with that drugged sports drink Vassily had given the fighters. Instead, it only stunned him. Shane collapsed to the floor, moaning, and tried to get up. Bishop kicked him twice: once in the stomach, once in the head.

Claire didn't think. She threw herself at him, and when his strong, pale hands reached for her to rip her open, she slashed with the silver knife she held. She didn't know what she cut off, but Bishop howled and backed away from her. Then he came for her.

Shane couldn't get up, but he *could* roll, and he did, right in front of Bishop's feet as he moved. Bishop fell, twisted, and grabbed Shane's head in his mangled hands.

Claire tried to stop him, but couldn't get close enough. She slashed with the knife and delayed him from snapping Shane's neck, but it was useless; she couldn't get to him, not without getting killed, too.

That was what Bishop wanted. To kill one of them while the other watched.

"Hey!" Eve shouted, just on the other side of the bars. She

had something in her hand, something long and thin and sharp. "Heads up, CB!" It came flying at her, and Claire grabbed it.

It was a sword. One of those things Eve had used against Oliver. She'd gotten a touch on him with it.

This one had a point, not a button, and the edges were sharp on all three sides of the triangular blade.

Claire grabbed the handle and threw herself into a lunge. It probably wasn't a good lunge, probably wasn't steady, but it was *fast*.

And she stuck the point straight into Bishop's throat.

He let go of Shane and clawed at the sword. Claire dropped it and grabbed Shane's ankle, and dragged him back to the other side of the cage. She raced forward, but Bishop got the blade before she did. Shane tried to get up, but failed.

Claire was the only one still standing up.

Myrnin. What the hell was he doing? He was down on the floor, rummaging around in his bag, ignoring her, ignoring their mortal danger. *Stupid*, cowardly idiot . . .

Claire couldn't even look at him—she didn't have time, because Bishop swished the blade through the air with a noise like tearing silk, and he gave Claire a long, slow smile.

"This will take approximately ten seconds," he said. "I'd like to make it last, but, alas, my daughter awaits. I have a whole town to destroy. I can't take as much time with you as I'd prefer."

He took a step toward her.

"Claire," Myrnin said from behind her. He sounded preoccupied and actually quite calm. "Please fall down now, if you don't mind."

She had absolutely no reason to trust him, but she did. She just . . . did.

She hit the canvas and looked up. Myrnin stood over both her and Shane, straight and tall, and there was a wild-looking shotgun kind of thing in his hands, and his Nike bag lay on its side at his feet. He was pointing the gun directly at Bishop.

"Now," he said, "you appear to have brought the wrong weapon, Bishop. Surrender?"

Bishop buried the sword in Myrnin's chest in a move so incredibly fast, Claire didn't even see it happen.

Myrnin didn't flinch. He pulled both triggers.

The heavy *boom* rattled the bars of the cage around them, and for a second Claire thought that something had gone wrong, very wrong, because the air was thick with smoke and glitter and Bishop was still there.

He fell, clawed fingers tearing long furrows in the canvas only an inch or so from Shane's face. He was burning, burning fast, all over. It looked like he'd been hit with napalm, and he screamed and rolled and kept on burning while Myrnin calmly reached down, pulled the sword out of his chest, and reloaded the shotgun.

"That hurt," he said. "But not, I imagine, as much as this will." He aimed and then stopped himself. He looked at Claire. "Perhaps it would be best if you took your boyfriend outside for this."

Claire swallowed. "It's locked."

Myrnin walked over and slammed his booted foot into the cage door. The hinges bent and cracked. His second kick sent it flying off the hinges to crash down five feet away, with a sound like tin cans dropping off a roof.

"Out," he said, and stepped aside as Claire grabbed Shane and the two of them jumped over Bishop's convulsing body.

Outside, Claire turned to look. Myrnin went back to Bishop and aimed at the center of the downed vampire's chest.

Bishop bared his bloody teeth. He was disintegrating, pieces of him melting off in a horrible mess. The pain must have been extreme.

"You don't have the courage," he spat, and then coughed up rivers of too-pale blood. "You never have, shadow hugger. Get the little girl to do your work for you. She's braver than you ever were."

Myrnin raised his eyebrows and stared down at him, then flipped the shotgun up and rested it against his shoulder. "Oh, I think that's probably true," he said. "And I think I'd like to tell Amelie you went slowly and in pain. Die on your own, you evil old animal."

It took a long, agonizing minute. Bishop never screamed. He left behind a skeleton that slowly collapsed into ash in the middle of the cage.

Myrnin sagged and leaned against the bars, head down. Claire came back up the steps and reached through to touch his shoulder. "Why didn't you?" she asked.

For answer, Myrnin aimed the gun at Bishop's disintegrating bones and fired both barrels.

Nothing happened. Just a dry, empty click.

"I realized that I never loaded the pellets into the cartridges," he said. "Those should have been round, silver buckshot."

"But you knew that *first* thing would work."

"Actually," Myrnin said in a low, confidential voice, "I thought I'd forgotten to load those shells, too. See how it all worked out?"

There was a massive banging on the outer doors, sending the people running around into a freak-out panic. Myrnin sighed, pushed away from the bars, and followed Claire down the stairs. She grabbed hold of Shane's unbroken hand and held tight, and the three of them found Eve and Michael, still sitting next to Glory's badly burned body. Only her golden hair was left, and even that was flecked with ash and slowly crisping.

"Follow me," Myrnin said. "And do stay together. And by the way, this is the *last* time I go anywhere with you people. You are all insane."

He picked up an iron bar and slammed it into the wall about half a dozen times in the space of seconds, and the bricks flew out in a haze of dust and splinters.

Claire and Shane stepped through the hole together, and froze as guns turned toward them. A whole lot of cops were yelling for them to freeze, and they did, putting up their hands and leaning up against the wall to be searched and handcuffed.

Claire looked back. Amelie and Oliver were in the next row, behind the cops, along with ranks and ranks of vampires. Amelie was staring straight ahead with a blank, empty expression; Oliver, on the other hand, was *smiling.* He was giving orders, sending one set of vamps that way, one up top, one around the side . . . the general deploying his troops, while the queen waited in icy isolation for victory.

Myrnin stepped out of the hole in the wall, glared balefully at the police, and waved to Amelie with demented excitement. "Hello! Your dear father is unfortunately very dead," he called. "And you said my dispersal system would never work!"

Amelie blinked and focused on him. "What did you say?" she called.

"Dead," he said, clearly and distinctly. "Your esteemed forebear is no more. He is dust and angel tears, though I shouldn't think any of us will be mourning him for long. You may see for yourself, but I will swear to you that it is, indeed, your unlamented

Mr. Bishop. Now could you please ask these idiots to stop pointing their bullets at me? It's terribly wasteful."

Claire tried to keep from laughing, but it turned into a choking cough, and then Shane started laughing, too, and suddenly it was all right.

Amelie swept past them, making for the hole they'd come out of; Oliver hurried to dart in front of her, holding what looked like an actual old-fashioned *broadsword*. Claire supposed that in the world of vampire wars, a sword could be pretty useful, especially with a silver edge. Beheading always worked.

Michael and Eve came out after a few more seconds, and Eve looked around and saw Shane and Claire in their almost-arrested poses. She snorted. "Leave it to you two," she said. "What is it with you and cages, Shane?" It must have occurred to Eve a second later that maybe that might not have been cool to say at the moment. But Shane just shrugged.

"If Amelie wants to throw me back in jail, it's okay. I did sign on for the fighting. I did beat a couple of vamps pretty bad. And I could have hurt Michael."

Michael leaned against the wall next to him, arms folded. He was wearing the stupid hat—now at least fifty percent stupider, thanks to being crushed by running feet— and the ratty trench coat, but under the shade, his smile was full-on smug. "Sorry. What did you say? You could have *hurt* me?"

"Dude, I was kicking your ass." It occurred to Shane, Claire guessed, that maybe he shouldn't have been quite so proud of it. "Which is why I'm sorry."

"I wasn't even trying, Shane."

"Yeah, I know. But . . ." Shane fell silent.

Now Michael stopped smiling and looked at him for a long

few seconds. He nodded and stepped away. "We'll talk about it later," he said. "And, yeah, you *will* be sorry. You know that."

"Oh, I know," Shane said. "You have no idea how sorry I already am."

But Claire did. She saw the look in his eyes and the shine of tears.

And the shame.

She hugged him and whispered, "We'll get through this. We will."

He took in a deep, shaking breath, and relaxed against her.

SIXTEEN

In the end, the score was seventeen vampires captured; Vassily was one of them, which surprised Claire, until she heard that Frank had locked down his funds transfers, and Vassily had spent way too much time trying to get his money. He'd always been about the profits. By the time he'd finally given up, it had been too late for him to avoid the roadblocks set up at the exits out of Morganville. He ended up on his knees in front of Amelie, while Oliver stood there with the sword in his hands. Vassily begged and generally excused himself, but Amelie wasn't amused. At all.

Claire got to leave before any actual beheadings started. Later, she heard that of the seventeen, four were judged most guilty, including Vassily. Nobody said what had been done to them, but really, nobody had to. She just assumed.

Shane got a special hearing in front of Amelie and Oliver in closed session, with Mayor Richard Morrell as an official council member. Claire wasn't allowed in. Neither was Myrnin, not that

Myrnin would have bothered to show up, anyway. Claire sat in the waiting room with Eve and Michael and Amelie's assistant, Bizzie O'Meara, waiting for some word.

The doors finally opened, and Amelie and Oliver came out and walked straight past them, ignoring the waiting trio. Richard followed, looking like he had a headache and the town had just run out of aspirin, but he didn't look angry or upset. That was good.

Shane followed him. He wasn't in handcuffs, at least, and when he spotted Claire, he said, "Don't look so worried. I'm on probation."

"What kind of probation?" She held out her hand, and he took it with his left; his right was still bandaged tightly, and it must have hurt, because he didn't move it much.

"The kind where you don't do anything stupid or bad things happen," Shane said. "Everybody agrees that Glory screwed with my head. Not everybody agrees that it's all better now. So I have to prove that I'm not going to go pick fights with vampires anymore."

"Jeez, Shane. You've done that since you were twelve," Eve said. "That's going to be a tough habit to break."

"You know what I mean." Shane's dark eyes met Claire's for a second. "They're right about it. I still feel . . . you know, angry. Uncomfortable. I guess it'll take some time."

Michael stood up. "You're okay with me?"

"As okay as I ever am. I wish you weren't . . . what you are. But you're always my bro." He took a deep, unsteady breath. "Gloriana couldn't have made me do what I did, you know. Not without it being part of me, all twisted up with who I am, how I was raised, what my dad was like. I've always hated vampires. Blamed them.

It's hard for me to look at you and not think about all that. I'm trying. That's all I can do."

Michael held out his hand, his left, and Shane took it, then hugged him.

"That's all you can do," Michael agreed. "You're my brother."

"Some brother."

"Brothers fight." Michael shrugged and let go. "Just remember, I could have taken you if I'd wanted to."

"Dream on, fang boy. Dream on."

While they were talking—if taunting was a conversation—Claire spotted Amelie loitering in the hallway, speaking with Oliver in low tones. She headed that way. "Ma'am?" she said. "Could I ask you something?"

"I trust it's not a favor. I am not feeling very generous just now." Amelie looked tired and peeved and—like Richard—in need of a very big aspirin. "Well? Declare it."

"I . . . got a call from a recruiter. At MIT."

"MIT," Amelie repeated. "What is this MIT?"

"Massachusetts Institute of Technology. It's . . . the fantastic school I wanted to attend. They've accepted me. It's very important, and they . . . said they'd take me."

Amelie's eyebrows rose ever so slightly. "When?"

"At the beginning of next year."

Silence. Claire held her tongue, waiting; Amelie was thinking, but she was also testing her. Wanting her to babble nervously. Well, she wasn't going to. She wasn't going to show any weakness. Instead, she mimicked Amelie's stillness, her direct stare.

Amelie smiled. It happened slowly, almost imperceptibly, but it definitely happened. She nodded slightly and said, "And the question is, do *you* want to go to this MIT?"

"It's what I've wanted my whole life," Claire said. "It's always been my dream."

Amelie didn't fail to notice the past tense in her verbs. "Wanted," she repeated. "Been."

"I *should* go. It's a once-in-a-lifetime opportunity. And if I don't go now, they won't take me; they've got way too many people, good people, trying to get in."

"So," Amelie said. "What do you think you should do?"

"Ask you for permission to leave Morganville," Claire said. "Permanently, maybe."

Amelie considered that for a few seconds. "And do you believe that you, of all people, need my permission to leave? You know Morganville's secrets. You can leave more easily than anyone, except possibly Myrnin. I'm quite sure you've identified many ways to slip away undetected."

She had, of course, and Amelie knew it; Claire didn't confirm or deny any of that. She just waited. *Funny*, she thought. *A year ago, I would have been shaking.* Now she didn't feel afraid at all. Amelie could kill her if she wanted. She'd always had that power. There was no point in fearing it.

Claire suddenly remembered Miranda facing Gina, knowing she was going to get hit, but also knowing that sometimes a little pain and blood was better than the alternative.

"I won't order you to do anything, Claire," Amelie said then. "It would be a useless exercise. You will do as you wish, and I will do as I must. Let's hope that our wishes don't conflict too badly. Shall we?"

She walked away. She didn't even ask the question.

What are you going to do?

But Claire already knew. She turned back to her friends, and

Shane gravitated toward her without even consciously heading in her direction.

"Can we go home?" she asked.

"Seems like a decent plan," Shane said. "I'm on community service four nights a week. But not tonight. I guess she wanted to give me a break." He held up his right hand. "Already got one, though."

Eve groaned and kicked him. "You are *so* lucky I'm too tired to murder you right now. I am *not* putting up with your humor."

"I am," Claire said. She smiled. It felt like something had actually been lifted right off her shoulders. She was going to go home and make a call that was going to change her life, maybe forever. But not for the worse.

"What are you smiling about?" he asked her.

"I'm not going to MIT," she said, and kissed him. He was surprised, but he kissed her back sweetly, then warmly.

"Of course you are," he told her. "As soon as Amelie lets you, you're going. You promised me you would."

She looked up at him and her euphoria faded a little. She *had* promised him that. But now the moment was here, and she didn't want it.

Her cell phone rang, shattering the moment, and Claire gritted her teeth and looked at the caller ID. Of course it was Myrnin, at exactly the wrong time.

She hit the button and said, "Hello, Myrnin." Shane took a step back and looked away. So that hadn't gone away, either, that feeling of jealousy. Of betrayal, even though she hadn't betrayed him at all. This was going to take time. Could she pick a worse time to run off to MIT? No. No, she couldn't do it—that was final.

Myrnin sounded agitated. Not a real surprise. "They've forgotten my delivery again," he said. "I'm completely out of O positive. Stop in and get my cooler, please."

"Now? I'm on my way—"

"Now, or I won't answer for my unpleasant behavior later." Myrnin hung up on her without waiting for a reply. Not that there was anything she could say other than *Yes, of course I'll pick up your blood before you go eat someone.*

"Side trip?" Shane asked.

"I can go on my own. You guys go home."

"Nope. I'm going with you," Shane said, and hesitated. "I ought to apologize to him, too. I mean, what I said—"

"You didn't say it to him."

"Kind of still need to tell him I'm sorry. He did save our lives."

She wasn't happy with that; Myrnin didn't like Shane dropping in, and then there was the Frank problem. But Frank would have to be crazy to manifest himself with Shane there. Right?

So Shane walked with her to the blood bank, picked up the cooler, and carried it all the way back to the alley and down the steps, into Myrnin's lab.

Same old crazy place. Myrnin was standing stiffly in one place, hands behind him, just behind one of the lab tables. He was wearing that white coat over his Hawaiian shirt, looking like the world's least reliable scientist ever.

"Hey," Claire said. "We brought it." Myrnin didn't move and didn't speak. She frowned. "Are you feeling all right?"

He twitched slightly, blinked, and said, in a flat voice, "Hungry. Just leave it there."

"Here?" Shane asked, and when Myrnin didn't reply, shrugged and dropped it. "Okay. There's your fast-food delivery. We're going now."

"I thought you wanted to apologize," Claire whispered. Shane's jaw looked tight and set, and he sent her a quick, unreadable look.

"I did," he said. "But now I don't. It's just about maxed me out, not punching him. So let's go, okay? I don't want to feel like this. Not anymore."

"Wait," said a new voice. Female. Myrnin snapped his head around toward it, and Claire blinked as she saw Kim—*Kim?*— step out of the shadows and walk toward them. "I knew you'd come with her. Hi, Shane."

Shane blinked, clearly as confused as Claire felt. "Uh, hi?" He looked at Claire. "Where did she come from?"

Oh. She hadn't had a chance to explain—Kim, the escape, all that. She'd figured Kim would have run for the borders of town, not come *here*. Why would she?

"Myrnin, what's she doing here?" Claire asked. She knew she sounded a little on edge, but it was very weird of him to have guests. Especially guests that Amelie wanted to arrest.

"She's doing exactly as she pleases," Myrnin said, and turned slightly so they could see the silver chains wrapped around his arms, from elbows down to wrists. Some of it was covered up by cloth, but not all. Where it touched his flesh, it was burning him. "I'd very much prefer it if you'd take these off."

"How did she—?"

"She posed as my delivery person," he said. "I was focused on signing for the blood. Really not my fault, Claire."

Kim was still coming toward them—no, toward Shane. Her eyes were focused on him with weird fascination. "You don't look so good," she said. "I heard Bishop almost killed you."

"One of us is still standing," Shane said, and held out a hand to fend her off when she got too close. "Hang on. We are not hugging."

"Oh, we will," Kim said. "You and me, Shane. It's always been the two of us. All we need to do is get rid of the interference."

Shane's eyes widened, and he looked from Kim to Claire. "No—"

An *arrow* hissed across the room, a blur of wood and metal, and Shane shoved Claire out of the way. The arrow plunged into his shoulder, and she felt the warm spatter of Shane's blood across her face.

He spun away from her and fell.

Who was *shooting*? Claire tried to get to shelter, but another shot came her way, ricocheting off the wall, and brought her to a quick, skidding halt.

Kim was smiling, and now it had turned bitter and cruel. "I don't come without friends," she said. "Boys?"

There had been two men in the jeep that had rescued her in the desert, Claire realized, and now she saw them, dressed in camouflage, blending into the shadows. Both had crossbows.

"Friends," Claire said. "You don't have friends, Kim. You stab your friends in the back—"

"Just *shoot her*," Kim said. One of the men aimed and fired again, but Claire managed to duck. The arrow tugged at her hair. She hid behind one of the lab tables.

Kim rolled her eyes. "Wow, you guys are terrible. You can't shoot *her*?"

They had all pretty much forgotten about Myrnin, but suddenly, there was a sound of metal snapping. Kim looked over at him, startled. "Weak link," he said. "How appropriate." He ignored Kim and flashed across the lab in a zigzag pattern, then veered into one corner. The camouflaged man there cried out, then went quiet. The other one tried to shoot at Myrnin, but it didn't go so well, either.

Myrnin was heading for Kim when she picked up a crossbow lying on a table nearby and shot him point-blank in the chest.

He staggered backward, muttered, "Not *again*," and then went down, wood through his heart. Not enough to kill him. Just enough to immobilize him.

Kim dropped the crossbow.

"Stop," Shane said. His voice sounded ragged and anguished, and as Claire looked, she saw him getting to his feet. "Just *stop*. What are you *doing*?"

"I'm sorry you got hurt. They weren't aiming for you," Kim said. "I don't want to kill you, Shane. I spent a lot of time thinking about this. How to get it right."

Kim sounded earnest and very crazy. Claire didn't know who she was more afraid for—Shane, wounded, with blood running down his fingers to pool around his feet, or the vampire lying completely still nearby.

"You *are* crazy," Shane said, and meant it. "If you're expecting me to love you—"

"You do love me." Kim sounded utterly sure of it. "It's just that she's in the way."

"Trust me, that's not it."

"So you're saying you don't want me?"

"Pretty much."

Kim pulled a *gun* out of her pants pocket, and she aimed it right at Shane. He didn't flinch. Maybe he was just too tired.

"How about now?" she asked. "Do you want me now?"

Shane sighed. "About as much as cancer. So shoot me already."

She was going to—Claire could see it in her eyes—but then Frank Collins flickered into view just a foot away from Kim's face.

She shrieked in terror. Even crazy people could do that when a ghost with the vicious face of Shane's father showed up in their moment of triumph.

"Not my son," Frank said. "You're not hurting my son."

Shane's eyes snapped open. "Dad?" He sounded dazed and disbelieving, but he could see it, too—the flat, black-and-white image of his father, translucent and standing between Shane and his would-be killer.

Kim fired, but the shot went wild, missing Shane by at least a foot. Claire gasped and ran as fast as she could through the maze of books, discarded clothing, and glass beakers. She vaulted over a chair and landed next to an open cabinet where Myrnin kept all kinds of things that were too dangerous to handle.

Including a set of silver stakes that Eve had made for Claire, and that Myrnin had confiscated and put in the cabinet for safekeeping.

Claire grabbed one and threw it desperately, just as Kim tried to aim again. It didn't kill her, but it did hit her solidly in the head, snapping her skull sideways, and she staggered and went down to one knee.

Frank Collins turned to Claire and yelled, "Handcuffs, second shelf! Hurry up, dammit!"

She found them. They were silver, but they'd work just fine. She got to Kim just as the girl was climbing to her knees, and knocked her down to put the restraints on her. Kim yelled and kicked and cursed, but Claire held her down. She wanted to bang

Kim's stupid head into the floor, but didn't dare, because she knew she wouldn't be able to stop. She was shaking all over with rage.

She looked up and saw Shane staring at them with an empty, horrified expression on his face. She couldn't think why for a second—it couldn't be Myrnin; he didn't care about that. He wasn't worried about *Kim*, surely . . .

And then the adrenaline haze faded, and it hit Claire with a sickening thud what he *was* looking at.

His father.

Frank Collins.

The black-and-white ghost of a man he thought was safely, and even heroically, dead.

"Hello, son," Frank said. His voice sounded gentle but inhuman as it whispered out of the radio and phone speakers all over the lab. "Sorry you have to learn about it like this. I never meant it to be this way. I never wanted you to know."

Shane had an arrow in his shoulder, but it seemed like he'd forgotten all about it, because this hurt so, so much worse. He took a step forward, then another, then seemed to just . . . collapse. Claire *did* bang Kim's head into the floor then, just once, enough to make her stop struggling for a minute, and then she went to her boyfriend's side.

Frank Collins stayed where he was, a safe distance away. "Don't take the bolt out," he said. "Best to do that at the hospital. Could have nicked an artery."

"You're dead," Shane said. "You're *dead*."

"I still am," Frank agreed. "It's just a picture, son. I'm not really here."

"Yes, you are." Shane's throat worked as if he was trying to swallow a huge, unchewable chunk of shock and sorrow. "He did this. Myrnin brought you back. For his *machine*."

"Don't blame Myrnin. It was either me or Claire. I'd rather it was me."

Shane shook his head. He wasn't looking at his dad anymore, or at Claire, or at anything but the bloodstained fabric of his blue jeans. His face was pale from shock, his eyes very wide.

"Shane . . . I'm calling the ambulance," she said. "You're going to be okay. It's all—"

"It's not," he said, and met her eyes. She flinched. "You knew. You *knew*. And you didn't tell me."

"I told her not to," Frank said.

Shane ignored him. "You knew," he said as if his heart was breaking. He pitched over on his side and closed his eyes. "You knew, Claire."

She felt breathless and terrified. Was he dying? No, the bleeding wasn't that bad; surely he'd be okay. . . . Surely *they'd* be okay. . . .

"Claire." Myrnin's voice, just a bare whisper. "Claire, help. Help."

She looked over. His eyes were open, dark, and suffering . . . just like Shane's. It was the arrow. It hadn't hit him completely through the heart, but it was close enough that it was hurting him.

But that meant leaving Shane.

"Go," Frank said. "Shane's stable enough. See to Myrnin."

She didn't have a choice, but she knew that Shane didn't see it that way.

She went to her vampire boss and took hold of the bolt and yanked it free in three awful tugs.

Shane was curled up now, looking awful and beaten and defeated, and the second the bolt was free of Myrnin's chest, she left him and ran, *ran* back to Shane. She took him in her arms and said, "I'm sorry. I'm so sorry. I'll never leave you again. They called me to go to MIT, but I won't go now, not in January, not ever. I won't. I love you. . . ."

Shane's dark eyes opened and fixed on her, and she felt the whole world crumble into darkness underneath her.

"You *knew*," he said, and then a spark of understanding flared in his expression. "January. You were going in January."

"No, I—"

"You didn't tell me that, either."

"Shane, I—"

"I can't do this. Just leave me alone."

Claire scrambled backward, through Frank's flickering image, back until she was pressed against the cold, heavy bulk of one of the lab tables.

Then she used her cell phone to call for help.

Shane didn't say another word to her. Not another word to anyone.

Not for days.

It had been almost a week, and Claire still felt frozen, stuck in a horrible, empty place that was full of darkness and loneliness. Eve tried to cheer her up. So did Michael. But it was the specter of Shane, who never left his room except to get food or visit the bathroom, that haunted their house now.

Shane, who hated her.

The doctors had given him good scores on his wound; with a little time and rehab, he'd be fine. Kim was going back to prison for good. Myrnin had recovered in less than two hours, drained half the cooler of blood, and looked suspiciously interested in the bloody floor where Shane had been standing. But Claire didn't want to think about that. She hadn't talked to him, and he hadn't pressed.

Frank kept trying to talk to her on her phone, so she finally turned it off. Today was the first day she'd switched it back on.

There were three messages from MIT.

Claire lay on her bed, staring at the ceiling, playing them one after another on the speaker. *Ms. Danvers, just calling you to see if you've reached a decision. . . . Ms. Danvers, I urgently need to hear from you by the end of the weekend if we're to hold your place for the next term. . . . Ms. Danvers, I'm concerned that you haven't returned our calls. . . .*

She started to dial the phone. Her fingers felt numb and thick, and she wasn't sure she wasn't going to burst into tears, but she dialed.

He answered on the second ring. "Sir?" She'd been right; the tears threatened immediately. Claire cleared her throat. "Sir, this is Claire Danvers. I'm sorry it's taken me so long to get back to you."

"Oh, excellent. I've been waiting to hear from you," Mr. Rada-mon said. "Have you worked out all your arrangements? Can we confirm you for the records? Because I have to tell you, Ms. Danvers, it's a little puzzling that it's taken so long to hear from you. We normally have no hesitation at all."

Claire heard a sound at the door. Shane was standing there, looking at her. He had on a ratty old T-shirt and sweatpants, and his shoulder was still bulky with bandages. His hair looked like he'd combed it with an eggbeater . . . and still, she felt her heart skip and then race.

Claire sat up slowly, phone at her ear.

"About the January start," she said, and wet her lips. "I know you need my final decision." She was staring right into Shane's dark eyes, waiting for a sign. Waiting for *something*.

He didn't give her anything at all. But he was *there*. For the first time, he was *there*.

Claire drew in a sharp, hurting breath, and said, "I'm sorry, but I won't be available. Thank you for considering me. If it's possible to put my application in again next year, I will."

"Ms. Danvers, I hope you realize that this is a very momentous decision," Mr. Radamon said. "MIT would be very happy to have you as a student."

"Yes, sir. Thank you." She hesitated, and tried to put all her love into the stare she was holding with Shane. "But I need to stay here for now. I absolutely can't leave. Not now."

She hung up and dropped the phone on the bed.

Shane said, very quietly, "Did you do that for me?"

"Yes. And no. Because I can't leave when you're hurting, but I also can't leave because there's so much I can learn." She took in a quick breath. "MIT can teach me amazing things, but it'll always be there, and science isn't a dying field. Myrnin knows things nobody else in the whole world can teach me, things that have been forgotten and need to be remembered. I know you don't like him, but learning from him is . . . unique."

"Well, that's a point." He didn't have any expression yet, and his body language was guarded at best. "What else?"

"I can't leave before Eve and Michael work out this marriage thing."

"That could take a while."

"And I'm not even eighteen yet. I think my parents were right all along. I don't think I'm ready to move that far away."

He almost smiled. "Not ready to leave Nowhere, Texas, to go off to *Boston*. You think that through?"

"Oh yes," she said. "I've been thinking about it for days."

"You ever think about the other answer?"

"Yes," she said. "But not for a while now. Because there's one more reason: I don't want to leave you."

Shane took a step inside her room. Just a single step. She slid off the bed and took two toward him.

And they met in the middle, not touching, just looking. Trying to find something in each other's faces. Hungry and scared to hope.

Claire said, "I need to make this right with you, Shane. Because I love you." She'd promised herself she wouldn't cry, *promised*, but now her eyes were burning and full of tears. She didn't let them fall as she twisted the claddagh ring from her finger and held it out to him. "But I understand if you want this back. I understand if you don't think you can trust me. You think I betrayed you, but I didn't. I really tried—"

"God," Shane said. "You don't understand me at all."

And then he leaned forward and, with his good hand, slid the ring back on her finger. He put his forehead against hers for a moment, then kissed her. It was the sweetest, most tentative kiss he'd ever given her, and it made the tears break free, and all she could taste was salt and desperation and the silence between them. . . . And then his arms went around her.

"I wasn't mad at you, and I didn't think you betrayed me," he said. "Not after the first few minutes. I know why you did it, why you kept it secret. You had to. You didn't want to hurt me. I get it."

She shuddered in relief and relaxed against him. His hand stroked her hair.

"I wish you'd told me," he said, "but Frank was right. I'd rather it was him living in that machine, if it had to be somebody. And maybe it's okay this way. He's not exactly gone, but he can't hurt me anymore. He's just a voice. A ghost. A memory. Maybe all the best parts of my dad, and none of the worst."

"Then why didn't you *talk* to me about this?" She tried to say it reasonably, but it came out in a wail, full of pain.

"Because I wanted you to decide on your own. And I knew that if I said anything at all, you'd know how much I need you right now."

"You need me?" She looked up at him and felt her heart speed faster.

"It's been the toughest week of my life, not touching you. Not talking to you. Waiting to see what you were going to do." He kissed her again, a warm, damp touch of lips, exquisitely controlled. "But it doesn't matter whether you stay or go. I'll still need you. So if you want to go off to Boston, I'll wait. Right here, whenever you need me."

Claire smiled against the press of his lips and felt him smiling, too. It was like the sun coming out after all the long, cold days.

"You know what?" she murmured. "I need you right now."

His voice dropped lower. "Now?"

"Right now."

"Oh," Shane said, and backed her slowly toward the bed. "That's so exactly what I was going to say."

"Jinxies," she whispered, but the word was lost between them when he kissed her, so hot and sweet.

And once again . . . she liked his version better.

TRACK LIST

In case you want to listen along to the songs I used to help me write this book, here they are! Buy the tracks, please. Don't be a vampire preying on the artists.

"Game On"	The Guild, feat. Sandeep Parikh & Felicia Day
"La Villa Strangiato"	Rush
"Land of the Living"	The Stone Coyotes
"My First Kiss (Gucci Mane Remix)"	3OH!3, feat. Ke$ha
"I Just Wanna Run"	The Downtown Fiction
"Drumming Song"	Florence + The Machine
"Gold Guns Girls"	Metric
"Ride to California"	Paper Tongues
"Cooler Than Me (Single Mix)"	Mike Posner
"If I Die Young"	The Band Perry
"October"	Broken Bells
"Something More"	Secondhand Serenade

"Catch My Fall"   The Elliots
"The Silence"   Deepfield
"How You Like Me Now"   The Heavy
"Hit 'Em Up Style"   Carolina Chocolate
                                           Drops

"Pump It Up"   Elvis Costello
"Here Comes the Hotstepper"   Ini Kamoze
"So Obvious"   Runner Runner
"Crash into the Sun"   Jim White
"Islands"   The xx
"Los Angeles"   Sugarcult
"Been a Long Time"   Gary Jules & The Group
                                           Rules, feat. Jim Bianco

"Letters from the Sky"   Civil Twilight
"The Good Life"   Three Days Grace
"Heart of Steel"   Galactic, feat. Irma
                                           Thomas

"Baby Boy . . . Baby Girl"   The Dark Romantics
"Tell Us"   The Elliots
"I'll Be Thinking of You"   Jamie McDonald
"Sleepwalking"   Fear Blind
"Stomp"   Boomkat
"I Want You To . . ."   Jem
"Emergency 911"   Sloan
"Supernatural Supergirl"   Josh Kramon
"Between the Devil and the
  Deep Blue Sea"   Black Mustang
"Shades Off (Dirty Radio Edit)"   X & Hell
"Please Don't Stop"   Carina Round
"Outsider"   Jessie Malakouti

"Lone Wolf"	Eels
"She's Got to Be"	Amy Ray
"Fever's Burning Up"	Alyx
"Song of Yesterday"	Black Country Communion
"The Way I Feel"	Alyx
"Dirt Room"	Blue October
"Sleepless Nights"	Mia Doi Todd
"Me and the Devil"	Ferocious Few
"In Between the Lines"	The Feud

Read on for an exciting excerpt from the next
Morganville Vampires novel by Rachel Caine,

Last Breath

Coming in November 2011 from NAL

Shane's lips felt like velvet against the nape of her neck, and Claire shivered with delight as his breath warmed the skin there. She leaned back against him with a sigh. Her boyfriend's body felt solid and safe, and his arms went around her, wrapping her in comfort. He was taller than she was, so he had to bend to rest his chin on her shoulder and whisper, "You sure about this?"

Claire nodded. "You got the overdue notice, didn't you? It's this or they come and collect. You don't want that."

"Well, you don't have to be here," he pointed out—not for the first time today. "Don't you have classes?"

"Not today," she said. "I had an oh-my-God a.m. lab, but now I'm all done."

"Okay—then, you don't have to do this because you're tax exempt."

By *tax exempt*, he meant that she didn't have to pay . . . in blood. Taxes in Morganville were collected three ways. The first was the polite way, via the collection center downtown. Another was the not-so-polite way, when the Bloodmobile showed up like a sleek black shark at your front door, with Men in Black–style "technicians" to ensure you did your civic duty.

The third way was by force, in the dark, when you ventured out un-Protected and got bitten.

Vampires. A total pain in the neck—literally.

Shane was entirely right: Claire had a written, legal document that said she was free from the responsibility of donations. The popular wisdom—and it wasn't wrong—was that she'd already given enough blood to Morganville.

Of course, so had Shane . . . but he hadn't always been on the vampires' side at the time.

"I know I don't *have* to do it," she said. "I want to. I'll go with."

"In case you're worried, I'm not girly-scared or anything."

"Hey!" She smacked at his arm. "*I'm* a girl. What exactly are you saying? That I'm not brave or something?"

"Eeek," Shane said. "Nothing. Right, Amazon princess. I got the point."

Claire turned in his arms and kissed him, a sweet burst of heat as their lips met. The lovely joy of that released a burst of bubbles inside her, bubbles full of happiness. *God*, she loved this. Loved him. It had been a rough year, and he'd . . . stumbled, was the best way she could think of it. Shane had dark streaks, and he'd struggled with them.

But he'd worked so hard to make it up—not just to her, but to everyone he felt he'd let down. Michael, his (vampire) best friend. Eve, his other (nonvampire) best friend (and Claire's best friend, too). Even Claire's parents had gotten genuine attention: he'd gone with her to see them twice, with permission from the vampires to exit Morganville, and he'd been earnest and steady even under her father's stern cross-examination.

He wanted to be different. She knew that.

When the kiss finally ended, Shane had a drugged, vague look in his eyes, and he seemed to have trouble letting go of her. "You know," he said, moving her hair back from her cheek with one big, warm hand, "we could just blow this off and go home instead of letting them suck our blood. Try it tomorrow."

"Bloodmobile," she reminded him. "People holding you down. You really want that?"

He shuddered. "Hell, no. Okay, right—after you." They were standing on the sidewalk of Morganville's blood bank, with its big cheerful blood-drop sign and meticulously clean public entrance. Claire pecked him lightly on the cheek, escaped before he could pull her close again, and pushed the door open.

Inside, the place looked like they'd given it a makeover—more brightly, warmly lit than the last time she'd been in, and the new furniture looked comfortable and homey. They'd even installed a tank full of colorful tropical fish flitting around living coral. Nice. Clearly the vampires were trying to put forth their best efforts to reassure the human community, for a change.

The lady sitting behind the counter looked up and smiled. She was human and sort of motherly, and she pulled Claire's records and raised her thin graying eyebrows. "Oh," she said. "You know, you're entirely paid up for the year. There's no need—"

"It's voluntary," Claire said. "Is that okay?"

"*Voluntary?*" The woman repeated the word as if it were something from a foreign language. "Well, I suppose . . ." She shook her head, clearly thinking Claire was mental, and turned her smile on Shane. "And you, honey?"

"Collins," he said. "Shane Collins."

She pulled out his card, and up went the eyebrows again. "You are definitely *not* paid up, Mr. Collins. In fact, you're sixty days behind. Again."

"I've been busy." He didn't crack a smile. Neither did she.

She stamped his card, wrote something on it, and returned it to the file, then handed them both slips of paper. "Through the door," she said. "Do you want to be in the room together or separately?"

"Together," they chorused, and looked at each other. Claire couldn't help a bit of a smirk, and Shane rolled his eyes. "She's kind of a scaredy-cat," he said. "Faints at the sight of blood."

"Oh, *please*," Claire said with a sigh. "That does describe one of us, though."

The receptionist, for all her motherly looks, clearly wasn't sympathetic. "Fine," she said briskly. "Second door on the right. There are two chairs inside. I'll get an attendant for you."

"Yeah, about that . . . Could you get us a human?" Shane asked. "It creeps me out when a guy's draining my blood and I hear his stomach rumble."

Claire punched him in the arm this time, an unmistakable *shut up*, and gave the receptionist a sunny smile as she dragged him toward the door that had been indicated. "Really," she said to him, "would it be that hard to just not say anything?"

"Kinda." He shrugged, then opened the door and held it for her. "Ladies first."

"I'm really starting to think you *are* a scaredy-cat."

"No, I'm just flawlessly polite." He gave her a sideways glance and said, with a curious seriousness, "I'd go first in any fight, for you.

Shane had always been someone who best expressed love by being protective, but now it was deliberate, a way for him to make up for how he'd let his anger and aggression get the best of him. Even at his worst, he hadn't hurt her, but he'd come close, frighteningly close, and that lingered between them like a shadow.

"Shane," she said, and paused to look him full in the face. "If it comes to that, I'd fight beside you. Not behind you."

He smiled a little, and nodded as they started moving again. "I'd still jump on the first bullet. Hope you're okay with that."

She shouldn't have been, really, but the thought, and the emotion behind it, gave her another little flush of warmth as she walked down the carpeted hallway and into the second room on the right. Like the rest of the human side of the collection center, the space felt warm and comfortable. The reclining chairs were leather, or some vinyl approximation. The speakers overhead were playing something acoustic and soft, and Claire relaxed in the chair as Shane wriggled around in his.

He went very still as the door opened and their attendant stepped inside.

"No way," Claire said. First, their attendant was a vampire. Second, it was *Oliver*. He was wearing a white lab coat and carrying a clipboard and looked vaguely official, but it was *Oliver*. "What exactly is the second in command of vampire affairs doing drawing blood?"

"Yeah, and aren't you needed pulling espresso at the coffee shop?" Shane added, with a totally unnecessary edge of snark. Oliver was often found behind the counter at the coffee shop, but he wasn't *needed* there. He just liked doing it, and Shane knew that. When you were as (presumably) rich and (absolutely) powerful a vampire as Oliver, you could do whatever you damn well wanted.

"There's been flu going around," Oliver said, ignoring Shane's tone as he took out the supplies and laid them out on trays. "I understand they're short staffed today. Occasionally, I do pitch in."

Somehow that didn't quite feel like the whole story, even if it was true. Claire eyed him mistrustfully as he scooted a rolling stool up beside her and tied the tourniquet in place on her upper arm, then handed her a red rubber ball to squeeze as he prepared the needle. "I assume you're going first," he said, "given Shane's usual attitude." That was delivered with every bit as dry an edge as Shane's sarcasm, and Shane opened his mouth, then stopped himself, his lips thinning into a stubborn line. *Good*, she thought. He was trying, at least.

"Sure," she said. She managed not to wince as his cold fingers palpated her arm to feel for veins, and she focused on his face. Oliver always seemed to be older than many of the other vamps, though she couldn't quite pin down why; his hair, maybe, which was threaded with gray streaks and tied back in a hippie-style ponytail just now. There weren't many lines on his face, really, but she always just pegged him as *middle-aged*, and when she really stared, she couldn't say why he gave her that impression.

Mostly he just seemed more cynical than the others.

He was wearing a black tee under a gray sweater today, and blue jeans, very relaxed; it wasn't too different from what Shane was wearing, actually, except Shane managed to make his look edgy and fashionable.

The needle slid in with a short, hot burst, and then the pain subsided to a thin ache as Oliver taped it down and attached the tubing. He released the tourniquet and clamps, and Claire watched the dark red line of blood race down the plastic and out sight, into a collection bag below. "Good," he said. "You have excellent flow."

"I'm . . . not sure how I feel about that, actually."

He shrugged. "It's got fine color and pressure, and the scent is quite crisp. Very nice."

Claire felt even less good once he'd said that; he described it like a wine enthusiast talking about his favorite vintage. In fact, she felt just faintly sick, and rested her head against the soft cushions while she stared at a cheerful poster tacked up on the back of the door.

Oliver moved on from her to Shane, and once she'd taken a couple of deep, calming breaths, she stopped studying the kitten picture and looked over at her boyfriend. He was tense, but trying not to seem it; she could read that in the slightly pale, set face and the way his shoulders had tightened, emphasizing the muscles under his sweater. He rolled up his sleeve without a word, and Oliver—likewise silent—put the tourniquet in place and handed him another ball to squeeze. Unlike Claire, who was barely able to dent the thing, Shane almost flattened it when he pressed. His veins were visible to her even across the room, and Oliver barely skimmed fingertips over them, not meeting Shane's eyes at all, then slipped the needle in so quickly and smoothly that Claire almost missed it. "Two pints," he told Shane. "You'll still be behind on your schedule, but I suppose we shouldn't drain you much more at once."

"You sound disappointed." Shane's voice came out faint and thready, and he put his head back against the cushions as he squeezed his eyes shut. "Damn, I hate this. I really do."

"I know," Oliver said. "Your blood reeks of it."

"If you keep that up, I'm going to punch you." Shane said it softly, but he meant it. There was a muscle as tight as a steel cable in his jaw, and his hand pumped the rubber ball in convulsive squeezes. Oliver released the tourniquet and clamps, and Shane's blood moved down the tube.

"Can I specify a user for my donation?" Claire asked. That drew Oliver's attention, and even Shane cracked an eyelid to glance at her. "Since mine's voluntary anyway."

"Yes, I suppose," Oliver said, and took out a black marker. "Name?"

"The hospital," she said. "For emergencies."

He gave her a long, measured stare, and then shrugged and put a simple cross symbol on the bag—already a quarter full—before returning it to the holder beside her chair.

Shane opened his mouth, but Oliver said, "Don't even consider saying it. Yours is already spoken for."

Shane responded to that with a gagging sound.

"Precisely why it's not earmarked for *my* account," Oliver said. "I do have standards. Now, if either of you feel any nausea or weakness, press the button. Otherwise, I'll be back in a few minutes."

He rose and walked toward the door, but hesitated with his hand on the knob. He turned back to them and said, "I received the invitation."

For a moment, Claire didn't know what he was talking about, but then she said, "Oh. The party."

"The engagement party," he said. "You should speak with your friends about the . . . political situation."

"I— What? What are you talking about?"

Oliver's eyes held hers, and she was wary of some kind of vamp compulsion, but he didn't seem to be trying at all. "I've already tried to warn Michael," he said. "This is unwise. Very unwise. The vampire community in Morganville is already . . . restless; they feel humans have been given too much freedom, too much license in their activities of late. There was always a clearly drawn relationship of—"

"Serial killers and victims," Shane put in.

"Protector and those Protected," Oliver said, flashing a scowl at her boyfriend. "One that is of necessity free of too much emotional complication. It's an obligation that vampires can understand. This . . . connection between Michael and your human friend Eve is . . . raw and messy. Now that they threaten to sanction it with legal status . . . there is resistance. On both sides, from vampires and humans alike."

"Wait," Shane said. "Are you *seriously* telling us that people don't want them to get married?"

"There is a certain sense that it is not appropriate, or wise, to allow vampire-human intermarriage."

"That's racist!"

"It has nothing to do with race," Oliver said. "It has everything to do with species. Vampires and humans have a set relationship, and from the vampire standpoint, it's one of predator and prey."

"I think you mean parasite and host."

Oliver's temper flared, which was dangerous; his face changed, literally *shifted*, as if the monster underneath was trying to get out. Then it faded, but it left a feeling in the room, a tingling shock that made even Shane shut up, at least for now. "Some don't want Michael and Eve to marry," he said. "You may take it from me that even those who are indifferent believe that it will go badly for all involved. It's unwise. I've told him this, and I've tried to tell her. Now I'm telling you to stop them."

"We can't!" Claire said, appalled. "They love each other!"

"That has exactly *nothing* to do with what I am saying," the vampire told her, and opened the door to the room. "I care nothing about their feelings. I am talking about the reality of the situation. A marriage is politically disastrous, and will ignite issues that are best left smoldering. Tell them that. Tell them it will be stopped, one way or another. Best if they stop it themselves."

Photo by Sharon Sams-Adams

Rachel Caine is the *New York Times* bestselling author of more than thirty novels, including the Weather Warden series, the Outcast Season series, the Revivalist series, and the Morganville Vampires series. She was born at White Sands Missile Range, which people who know her say explains a lot. She has been an accountant, a professional musician, and an insurance investigator, and, until recently, still carried on a secret identity in the corporate world. She and her husband, fantasy artist R. Cat Conrad, live in Texas with their iguanas, Popeye and Darwin. Visit her Web site at www.rachelcaine.com, and look for her on Twitter, Livejournal, MySpace, and Facebook.